Where
Water
Lies

ALSO BY HILARY TAILOR

The Vanishing Tide

Where Water *Lies*

HILARY TAILOR

LAKE UNION
PUBLISHING

Text copyright © 2024 by Hilary Tailor
All rights reserved.

Published by Lake Union Publishing, Seattle

www.apub.com

Amazon, the Amazon logo, and Lake Union Publishing are trademarks of Amazon.com, Inc., or its affiliates.

ISBN-13: 9781542036597
eISBN: 9781542036603

Cover design by Emma Rogers
Cover image: © Ildiko Neer / ArcAngel; © Anna Nahabed © Iuliia Klepikova © J.D.S © RachenStocker / Shutterstock

Printed in the United States of America

For Satish

It is said we are drawn to water because water is where we begin. We are aquatic creatures when we start out, and our body never forgets. I don't know if any of that is true, but I do know that ever since I was a child, I have had a peculiar relationship with water. It has always been something I could not resist, a friend I couldn't keep away from. But friendships can turn. When your head is above water, it's easy to forget what lurks beneath: that the lower you sink, the colder and more dangerous it gets.

Chapter One

WINTER, 2015

It is not yet light, and it's so cold the mist that hung low on the ground last night has turned to a hard, stubborn frost. I pass the sign that says: *WOMEN ONLY. MEN NOT ALLOWED BEYOND THIS POINT* and I walk down the narrow path between oak and willow. The little blackboard sign that hangs outside the changing room tells me the temperature of the water is two degrees. If it gets any colder, the ice must be split. Yet still I return like a spawning salmon, unable to resist a ten-year habit scored into the surface of my life.

I stand on the platform, absorbing the peace, my bare feet used to the cold. The water stretches like a long shadow in front of me, and I step towards the railings where the ladder reaches down into the dark. Tied to the railings by a narrow red ribbon is a heart made of willow branches, arched and fastened with twine. My own heart sinks. I had forgotten the date. When I go to work today, the school will be filled with giddy teenagers exchanging Valentine's cards. No matter how hard I try, I still can't conjure up my own, youthful optimism. It remains in 1995 on a hot summer's day, crushed under the weight of a single sentence.

I touch the willow branches, bent into submission. The days here are marked by things like this. A basket of rose petals on midsummer's morning, a chalked message encouraging us to make a wish as we take a handful and throw them into the water. On All Hallows' Eve, strings of ghosts and rubber spiders are tied up around the lifeguards' hut to twist in the chilly air. Some women come in fancy dress, shrieking in pointy hats and wigs. These are the days I find difficult. It is the everyday, the average, I crave, the days without decoration and seasonal greetings.

I climb down the ladder and lower myself in, my limbs becoming ghostly as they fade into the gloom. The breath that leaves me returns in a hard, raw gasp. I push my body through the water, slow and thick with cold, urging myself to breathe. Something within me appreciates the brutality of it all. I can feel it stirring my thoughts, a creature waking after a deep sleep. As I swim, it talks to me, driving me on to the farthest reach of the Ladies' Pond.

The pond is an open secret, a sacred space for some, tucked away behind the ancient greenery of the Heath. Any woman can come here to swim, but, during the winter months, few do. Especially at this hour. In the summer I've seen kingfishers and dragonflies here, skimming the water so near to me I could close my fist around them if I was quick enough. But now is the time I like best. The insects are gone, and the trees are stripped to their bones. The population of swimmers dwindles to a hard core of fanatics. There's something about this colourless state of affairs that appeals to the voice in my head because it's always more vocal when the mornings are dark, and the nights darker still. I can hear it now as I move through the black of the water, urging me to duck under the boundary rope and swim to the murkiest corner, where we are not allowed to go. It tells me it wouldn't matter if I didn't turn back, that nobody would miss me. When I go home, at the end of the day, there will be no cards on the doormat, no messages on the phone. It will be a day like any other.

I swim behind a curtain of willow branches, reaching through the skin of the pond. There, I tread water, my breath caught in clouds, feeling the sly creep of cold move through my limbs. There are two worlds here: the one above and the one below. The world above is for the living. Below the surface, it's not the same. This is a place for the things we don't like to think about: the shadows that slide beneath our feet, the tangle of weeds we try to avoid. It is a quiet, dark place, secretive and slow. When the water closes over me and my ears fill with silence, the voice in my head becomes muffled and I am, finally, left with my own thoughts. If I'm patient, if I hold my breath for long enough, I can see what I came here for. Sometimes they are memories, circling like fish, half-remembered images, hard to reach. But every now and again, I see his face.

A hand, hard on my shoulder, fingers digging into my flesh, pulls me roughly out of the water, back to daybreak.

'Hey!' A woman's voice cuts through my sluggish thoughts. 'You've been in too long.'

She shakes me out of myself, her voice an insistent, buzzing insect.

'You need to turn back right now,' she scolds, 'and . . . as if you didn't know already . . . you're on the wrong side of the rope.'

I squeeze my eyes shut and ignore her, willing her to leave me alone.

'What you're doing is incredibly stupid.'

I open my eyes, orientate myself, then duck under the rope and swim hard and fast back to the ladder, leaving the woman behind me, riddled with indignation. When I get out, Carole the lifeguard is waiting and gives me a telling-off, threatening me with a ban. It's not the first time. I apologise and try to look contrite. My lips are blue, and I'm sent to the changing room to get dry.

It is still early, and the room is empty. I ignore the showers, preferring to strip off and dry myself as quickly as I can, my fingers stiff and non-compliant. When I'm slowly folding my towel into my backpack, she comes in.

'What was that all about?' The indignation has gone. She's curious.

I recognise her as one of the regulars. She could be in her fifties or her seventies, it's hard to tell. Her hair is grey and her body lean and strong, the softening of age kept at bay with a swim routine as punishing as my own.

'Nothing,' I say. 'I lost track of time.'

'Not the first time though, is it? I've seen you do that before. Cross the rope. It's there for a reason.'

'I know.' I pull the contents of my bag out onto a wooden slatted bench, blackened with damp, to find my hat. She looks at me carefully and, for a moment, I stop what I'm doing, feeling exposed.

'That's what worries me. The fact that you know.' She turns away and begins to towel herself. 'The boundary rope across the pond,' she continues, 'I know it's tempting to swim beyond it, but it's dangerous in these temperatures. A few minutes more out there and you might not have had time to get back. It's very easy for the lifeguard to miss you in that spot. You were lucky I saw you.'

I pull the hat low, scooping up the contents of my bag and stuffing them quickly back in. She notices my book, which has landed on the wet floor. 'You enjoying that?'

I nod, stooping to retrieve it, wiping the cover on the front of my coat.

'Then we have something in common. I don't know anyone else who could finish it.'

6

I know what she means, and a smile escapes me before I can squash it down.

'I set up a small library in the lifeguards' room. It's for the regulars. You can borrow any of the books there. Do you know about it?'

'No.'

'All the books I bring in never get taken away. Maybe that'll change if you go and have a look. You can take as many books as you donate.'

I hesitate, suddenly shy.

'Iris.' She extends her hand towards mine and our fingers find each other in an icy embrace. 'And you?'

'Eliza,' I reply, not quite meeting her gaze. Her hair is short, like mine. My body is thin and muscular, like hers. We could pass for sisters, or mother and daughter.

'Nice to finally meet you.'

I know what she's implying. Mine must be the only name of the winter cohort Iris doesn't know. It's different in the summer when the fair-weather swimmers come; the changing room fills with noisy chatter and the water churns with women. The year-round swimmers look forward to autumn when the tourists leave, and the pond thickens with leaf mould. They relish the early morning, the dead flat of the black water shrouded in a dank mist. They are bound together by it all. It's a bond I have never understood. They swim because it makes them feel good, they are energised by the cold. I swim because it blunts the sting of life. It is the only thing that makes me numb.

Chapter Two

Iris follows Eliza out of the changing room. She stops after a few steps, watching Eliza make her way down the path, her footsteps fast and full of purpose.

'Thanks for doing that,' says a voice behind her. 'I was just about to get in there and haul her out.' Carole is dressed in the red and yellow of the lifeguard's uniform. Her hair is stuffed into a fleecy hat, a scarf knotted around her neck.

'That's the first time she's ever spoken,' says Iris, frowning. 'I was beginning to think she was mute.'

'Tea?' asks Carole. 'I've just boiled the kettle. Do you have time?'

'Yeah, my shift isn't until this afternoon.'

'You're up early.'

'You know me.'

'Somebody told me magnesium makes you sleepy. Have you tried that?'

'I have no problem getting to sleep. I just can't seem to go back once I wake up.'

'Here.' Carole offers her a mug. 'Be careful.'

'Yes.' Iris takes the cup, resisting the urge to take her gloves off. She has made that mistake before, trying to warm up too quickly.

'What did she say?' Carole nods towards the path. Eliza has now gone, and the pond is quiet apart from the sounds of two squabbling ducks who are fussing over a life ring, floating in the water.

'Not much. She's a funny one. Said she lost track of time.'

'I could understand that if it were summer. But the water's slushy like a margarita today. I don't know anybody who stays in as long as her when it's like this.'

Iris looks out over the pond. By the ladder, the water is black, still rippling from the memory of the ducks. But beyond the winter boundary rope, towards the undisturbed edges, the surface is life-less and beginning to turn white, where the ice is taking hold. It is beautiful and sinister at the same time. Iris shudders. She only followed Eliza on impulse. Eliza could have brought them both down if she'd struggled. But she hadn't. She'd been dead calm.

'I think you're going to have to watch her,' Iris says, frowning. 'Something isn't right.'

'She's always been like that. Spends more time under the water than above it, even on days like this.'

'How long has she been coming here?'

'Years. Always early. I've never seen her come for an afternoon swim and a sunbathe when it's warm. She's straight in, straight out again. Doesn't seem to enjoy it the way everyone else does.'

'Does she know anyone else? Does she talk to anyone?'

'Are you kidding? She doesn't even make eye contact. I wasn't sure she could speak English when I first started working here. You know, that being the reason she didn't talk. But then someone told me she lives in the farmhand's cottage on the West Heath. She's Val's niece, would you believe it?'

'Val!' exclaims Iris. 'I remember her. Shame about what happened. She died a while back now, didn't she?'

'At least ten years. Eliza came to look after her. Inherited the cottage.'

'The little one that backs onto the woods?'

'Yeah.'

'Lucky.'

Carole shrugs. 'Depends how you look at it. I heard she nursed Val through the worst of it. Can't have been easy. It must be lonely in that house. No neighbours to speak of. It's pretty cut off.'

'She must have been young when she was looking after Val. She doesn't look more than thirty.'

'I think she came here as a teenager, yeah. I'd say she was closer to forty now, though. She's just small, like a kid with those big eyes and that short hair.'

'Spring chicken in any case,' says Iris, draining her tea. 'Not like us old birds.'

'Speak for yourself,' sniffs Carole. 'I'm not sixty yet.'

'Not far off though,' counters Iris, with a sly grin. 'You'll be getting your bus pass soon. Just like me. Best birthday present I could have asked for. Free travel into London. Saves me a fortune getting to work.'

'Don't wish old age on me, Iris,' chides Carole, taking her cup.

'It's not a curse, you know,' Iris replies.

A group of women come down the path. They can be heard before they can be seen, but their voices are hushed. They emerge from the shadows, bags swaying slowly on their shoulders, their words low and sparse.

'I'd better look as if I mean business,' says Carole, waving at the women as they disappear into the changing room.

'Keep an eye on Eliza,' Iris calls over her shoulder as she leaves.

Carole gives her a thumbs up as she goes into the lifeguards' room with the mugs.

Iris walks down the narrow path. When she gets to the end, she should turn right to reach the road where her car is parked, but something stops her. Instead, she looks to her left, where the lane stretches down towards the west. She knows the cottage Carole was talking about. She has often walked past it, obscured by trees and thick shrubbery, and wondered who lived there, now Val is dead. There aren't many houses that back onto the Heath and certainly none she knows of that stand, tiny and alone, as if they were in a Brontë novel, a stone's throw from the centre of London.

It's an anomaly, that little house, Iris thinks. And so is Eliza. There is something odd about her. Iris remembers the expression on her face when she grabbed her shoulder and Eliza's head came out of the water. For a second, she had looked right at Iris with unseeing eyes. In fact, she had looked right *through* her, with the gaze of a sleepwalker.

Iris recalls what Carole said about her spending more time below the water than above. It's true. While most of the women put on a hat in the cold weather to protect themselves while they swim, Eliza was bareheaded, below the surface like a diver.

What are you doing under there? Iris wonders as she stares down the lane, thinking about that absent expression on Eliza's face. Iris is familiar with that expression. She has seen it on the families she works with. She has seen it on her own face, many years ago. There had been times when Iris had simply walked all day. She did that a lot, in the beginning. She used to think she'd lost her centre of gravity. She felt weightless, as if she might float away, high above the roofs of London's townhouses, above its glassy skyscrapers, into the ether. So, her instinct was to walk, to try and find some way of anchoring herself to her new life. Sometimes she turned and saw her reflection walking next to her in a window, or in the mirror shine of an office block. She would stop and stare at the woman beside her and not know who she was.

11

Chapter Three

I arrive at work, still annoyed. It only takes twenty minutes to walk here from the pond and the journey hasn't been long enough to soften my anger. That interfering woman, Iris. I'm familiar with the type. Sharp-elbowed-do-gooders. The pond is full of them, setting the world to rights as they swim around in their bubble of privilege. A couple of them are probably parents of the students here, the same ones who fire off emails asking why their child isn't being pushed enough. *Stretched.* That's the word they use now. It has always puzzled me, that parental desire to change the shape of a perfectly good child.

The school is in its lull before the storm of pupils arrive. I see some of my colleagues heading towards the staffroom. I look at my watch, the sting of being told off by Iris still smarting. My own classroom is on the first floor, where I have a kettle and coffee stashed away in a cupboard full of old poetry books that won't ever make it back onto the curriculum. I go there now, anticipating a full hour before the silence will be shattered by the first bell.

There is something church-like about a school anticipating its pupils. The whole building seems to hold its breath, waiting for the congregation to arrive. Some of my colleagues choose to spend the time chatting in the staffroom. For me, the mornings are sacrosanct, a moment to spend in quiet contemplation, when I can gather my thoughts and prepare for the day ahead. Someone told me once that the building used to be a Victorian orphanage, and I swear I can still sense the children who lived and died here, their bare feet running up and down the corridors, their laughter and sorrow echoing in and out of the classrooms. They have tried to modernise the building, but budgets are always tight. The electrical circuits are temperamental. I imagine little ghostly fingers breaking currents and flicking switches. I'm told it's just bad wiring.

I pass the science labs on the ground floor, their familiar chemical scent bleeding into the air. My shoes squeak on the linoleum and the echo races ahead of me down the corridor, vanishing quickly in the shadows. The lights haven't come on yet. They've recently been put onto some kind of automated system that often doesn't work. The long passageway ahead of me stretches into gloom.

And then I hear it: piano music, quietly making its way through the fabric of the school. At first I don't register the tumble of notes, they are lost in the other noises of the building gearing up for the day: the soft whirr of the floor polisher being pushed around the assembly hall, the noise of the traffic outside, building towards a bad-tempered rush hour. But I hear several notes, clearly, in swift succession and I become sensitised, piecing the sounds together in my mind until I am sure what it is: the falling and rising of a melody that I know by heart, so intimately painful I cannot go on. I stand, rooted to the floor, listening to the undulating tune of 'Für Elise'. There's the playful opening that I tried to learn myself once when my life was different. It's not a recording. I can tell it is coming from the music department and my mind turns to my first day in a new school, a shy seventeen-year-old, watching a boy I would fall in love with play the notes with such assurance he didn't even have to open his eyes.

My feet find themselves once more and I walk, a woman in a trance, following the music as it gets louder and louder. The door to

Practise Room B is open, allowing the melody to roam the corridor like a lost soul. I know it is not him playing that tune. It can't be. But I will him to be there, all the same, and I slow my footsteps, not wanting to break the spell, wanting to believe that it is Eric sitting at that stool, conjuring up the magic I can hear. I lean against the wall outside the practise room, and, when the weight of my body becomes too much, I let my legs lower me to the floor. I sit there, knees bent, my head tilting back in the dim winter light, letting the music fill me up. Finally, when the notes are spent, I hear the lid of the piano shut softly, and a woman I have not seen before walks out of the room, away from me. She doesn't notice me, down here on the floor, she doesn't look back. I wait until the sound of her footsteps smudge into silence, and then I get up.

For a moment I am motionless in the doorway, holding my breath. The piano is new. Its burnished wood glows in the morning light in a way that is so familiar I cover my mouth with my fingers and press them there as if some noise might spill out and break the spell. I collect myself and walk over to it, knowing it is a Yamaha before the golden letters resolve themselves before my eyes. I reach out tentatively and, as I trace the name with my fingers, I'm transported back to the Bellingham house, sitting on an identical stool, learning how to play 'Für Elise' on a piano just like this one. I can feel my arm touching Eric's, hear the notes slipping through the air like confetti. I can taste the happiness I'd found in such a short space of time. A happiness made perfect by him. My mind spools further back, into the practise room at Ivydale, on the first day we met; the smell of loose music scores stacked in the corner, the dust motes falling through the syrupy autumn air. I can smell the warm, cracked leather of the armchair, my legs thrown over one arm, my head resting on the other, listening to him play. I know this piano couldn't possibly be the same one. But there is the familiar strip of red cloth astride the keys. So, for a moment, I pretend it is.

14

I lower myself onto the worn velvet stool and slowly remove the cloth like a doctor undressing a wound. The keys are cool and smooth, they yield easily under my fingers. A low, mournful note slips out into the air and, as it fades away, I feel history closing in. Several minutes tick by as I sit there, head bowed, listening to the faint whimpers of the voice in my head. When I finally look up, I catch the scent of citrus. I see myself reflected, darkly, in the polished wood. And there, standing right behind me, in the grey and burgundy of Ivydale Grammar, is Eric.

Chapter Four

Autumn, 1994

I arrived at Ivydale as I had arrived at all the other schools: with a second-hand uniform and no one to talk to. My parents never saw the point in buying one new. The longest I had stayed in the same school was two years. The average was one. I had more experience of student hierarchy than most. Even after a day, I knew who was at the bottom of the social pile, who was at the top, just by casting my eye over the classroom. But when I met Eric, in the headmistress' office at Ivydale Grammar, there was something about him that I couldn't put my finger on. He should have been one of those boys who filled the room with their sense of entitlement, but he wasn't. His presence felt soothing, benign.

'Eric.' The headmistress smiled. 'This is Eliza. She's joining us in the upper sixth and I would like you to be responsible for her, just for a few days. Make sure she knows where everything is, that sort of thing.'

He looked at me, unable to hide his curiosity, and when he moved through the room to open the door, I caught the smell of citrus on his skin.

I expected him to march ahead of me down the corridor, dropping the charade of friendship he had put on for the headmistress' benefit, but his step fell in with mine and he began quizzing me in earnest. There was something unselfconscious about him, something uncomplicated. It was hard not to like him, but I tried my best, because I knew he wouldn't be in my company for long.

'Where have you come from, then?' he persisted.

'Everywhere. My parents renovate houses for a living. When they finish, we move on.'

'To a different area? How many schools have you been to?'

'It's really none of your business,' I replied, as neutrally as possible.

He held his hands up. 'I'm just asking. It seems a bit weird.'

'Yeah, well,' I responded. 'Like I said, it's none of your business.'

He laughed. He had a generous laugh that showed large, even teeth. It was all I could do, not to warm to that laugh.

'OK,' he said. 'Keep your hair on. Not that you have much. I've never seen hair as short as that on a girl.'

Reflexively, I touched my head.

'Can I?' he asked, suddenly serious.

'What?'

'Can I touch your hair, please?'

That word, *please*, it melted something inside me. I bent my head towards him, and he stroked it with his fingertips. I felt as if I were being blessed. For a moment, I wanted to stay there for eternity, his warm hands stroking my head, soothing my troubles.

'It's soft. Like a rabbit,' he murmured to himself. 'Why d'you have it so short?'

'I don't like the feel of long hair. It makes my neck itch.'

'So you don't want to be a boy then?'

I turned away from him, shaking my head, embarrassed at his touch and my response to it.

17

'Come on, there's no point going back to lessons, we may as well have a bit of fun together before lunch.' He led me through the school and out onto an expanse of perfect, clipped green. A solitary low building lay to the side of it, with narrow, horizontal windows.

'What's that?' I asked.

'Nothing,' he said, veering away from it.

The interior seemed illuminated from within by a light in perpetual movement. I was drawn to that light like a moth in darkness. 'What's inside?' I persisted.

'It belongs to the caretaker. Let's go to the music block. I need to pick up my stuff.'

But I had already left his side, striding over to the low building that had piqued my interest, wanting to see the source of the light.

I cupped my hands to my face and leaned into the glass, misting the surface with my breath and I saw, to my great surprise, a half-length swimming pool. Even though there was nobody in it, the pool moved slowly, deliberately, like the ripple of muscle, keeping to a rhythm of its own making. The water seemed to have a skin on it, something that stopped the energy below from spilling out. The low autumn sunshine licked the surface, and it was fractured and reflected back in sparks and flashes. I wanted nothing more than to enter that room filled with light, submerge my body, and experience a feeling of weightlessness.

I swam in the sea whenever we had lived close enough to walk there. When we moved inland, my parents never took me to the local pool. They didn't have the time and I didn't have the friends to go with. On the few occasions I had managed to take myself, the pool had been noisy and full. In contrast, this body of water was gloriously empty and silent.

'No one said anything about a pool,' I said, thrilled. 'When do we get to go in?'

'We don't,' said Eric, wrinkling his nose and looking over the playing field towards the music block. 'There's some kind of problem with the insurance.'

'You mean nobody's allowed to use it?' I gazed at the water, hypnotised. It had a surface that demanded to be broken. I wanted to be enveloped by it, to have a few moments where the world was obliterated in favour of a muffled, wordless nothing.

He shrugged. 'That's what I heard. Until they sort it out. But it's been off limits for months. I reckon the caretaker uses it. And the staff. Once we're out of the way. Otherwise, they'd drain it, wouldn't they?'

I looked back through the window at a prize I wanted to claim, and my hand strayed down to the door handle.

'You can't go in there,' he said.

'Where's the key?' I asked. 'I only want to look.' I imagined I could smell a waft of chlorine escaping through the empty keyhole and it made me ache with longing.

'Dunno. It's usually in the door.' He looked at his watch. 'Come on, it's nearly lunchtime. I need to pick up my stuff.'

Reluctantly, I followed him back to where the music block lay, and Eric took me into a little practise room to collect his books. There was a sagging leather armchair in the corner of the room. I flung myself into it, still thinking about the swimming pool. Eric sat at the piano, polished to a lacquered shine, and began to play. He didn't read the music. His hands moved with an assurance beyond his years. I'd never seen anyone play a musical instrument in front of me like this and it seemed he had mastered some kind of obscure language. His face changed, his eyes glazed over, as if he'd been transported out of my reach. I felt the melody fill the room, amazed that somebody my age could produce such a sound. The notes wrapped themselves around me, charging the atmosphere. For the length of that score, it felt as if we were somewhere far removed from others. The room was warm and dark, the sound of the outside world muted and meaningless. Shafts of sunlight played across the air, thick with dust motes that hung, suspended, moving to their own, invisible current.

'What was that?' I asked him when he finished.

'You've not heard it before?'

'No.' I wanted to tell him it was one of the most beautiful things I had ever heard, but I was embarrassed to admit it.

'It's called "Für Elise".'

'"Fur Elise"?'

'Not fur. Für,' he said kindly. 'It's German. It means "For Elise". Beethoven composed it.'

'Who was Elise?'

'I dunno. I think it's a bit of a mystery, actually. Nobody really knows who she was.'

To have a whole piece of music as beautiful as that dedicated to you seemed to be the most wonderful thing. And for the muse to remain in the shadows, it made the tune mysterious and romantic.

'You really liked it, didn't you?' he asked, his head tilted slightly, an amused expression on his face.

I blushed and tried to look nonchalant, but that tune got under my skin somehow and the notes of it stayed with me like a perfume that doesn't quite fade.

Whenever I recall the day I first met Eric, I feel as if something meaningful should have happened, some kind of portent: a clap of thunder or a cloud passing over the low September sun. But he walked into my life like an ordinary boy, and the drama that would envelop us both lay hidden, in the future.

Chapter Five

I blink and breathe deeply, pulling myself back into the present. I close the lid of the piano, blind to the minutes that have ticked by, the scent of citrus still in my nose. It is like this, always, when I think of him. Time becomes irrelevant, noises recede to nothing. I sometimes wonder what I must look like, submerged in another place, my face slack as my eyes see beyond what is in front of me. I glance at the clock on the wall and make myself get up, reluctant to tear myself away from him.

'Are you OK?' A voice cuts through the quiet. A kind voice, rich with warmth.

I turn, and see it is the woman who was playing 'Für Elise'.

'Sorry,' I say. I feel caught out, the beginning of a blush creeps up my neck. 'I haven't seen this piano before. I was just . . .'

'It's new. Someone donated it to the school. I'm new too. We haven't met before, have we? I'm Rosa.' She gives me a little wave, like a child, that instantly endears her to me.

'I heard you playing,' I say, shyly. 'You're really good.'

'I've been playing since I was a kid,' she smiles. 'My parents made me, and I hated them for it. Then the resentment turned to appreciation when I finally started getting pleasure from it. It's turned me into an evangelist, actually. I think everybody should be given the opportunity to play a musical instrument. Do you play?' she asks.

'No. I tried once. But it didn't work out.' I try to make my voice sound light, like it doesn't really matter.

'This is a great piano,' she sighs, stroking it appreciatively. 'We were lucky to get it. Good ones like these aren't cheap to buy and it's been well maintained.'

I look at the piano, not needing to be converted. 'Yeah, it's beautiful,' I agree.

'You have a wistful look in your eye. I can give you a few lessons if you like?' Rosa says, tilting her head to one side. 'It would be nice to teach an adult, and a good way to make a new friend.'

I feel my ears heat up. 'Oh . . . I don't think so. I'm not . . . I'm not a good student.'

'There's no such thing as a bad student. Just bad teaching. It would be my pleasure.' She laughs at the panic on my face. 'Think about it. It's an open offer.'

I get up awkwardly, embarrassed and eager to leave. 'I better get back.'

'You haven't told me your name.'

My face heats up. 'Eliza. I teach English. First floor.' I point my finger to the ceiling.

'Nice to meet you, Eliza. Come back any time. I mean it about the lessons.'

'Thanks,' I mumble, scrambling to get out of the door.

When I finally enter my own classroom, Noah, one of my favourite students, is sitting at his desk, head bent. He glances at me and gives me a look that says *don't ask*.

'I was about to make a coffee. Do you want some?' I say, sounding as if I am used to this, careful not to communicate my concern.

'Do you have any tea?'

'Do I look like I run a cafe?' I reply. 'Actually yes, I think I do have some, but if you want Earl Grey, or milk, you're out of luck.'

Noah screws up his nose. 'Earl Grey tastes like dishwater.'

'True.'

'I can drink it black. As long as you have sugar.'

'Don't want much, do you?'

I boil the kettle and hunt around the classroom for a second mug, wondering why he has come to school so early when most teenagers are clinging to the warmth of their beds. I find a mug that I use to water the plants and decide it will do.

'I have a pack of biscuits somewhere. Have you eaten this morning?' I ask.

'Not yet,' Noah replies.

'Well, this is hardly breakfast, but you're welcome. Take the pack.'

'Thanks.'

'Is that homework? If you're running late, you just need to tell me, and I can—'

'If I don't finish it on time, it makes everything else late.'

I nod, familiar with the horrible juggling act of revision and homework.

And then, under his breath, 'Home's manic at the moment.'

'You know you can always come here.'

'Thanks.'

'I'd like some reassurance you're getting enough sleep though.'

Noah rolls his eyes. 'With a new baby? You must be kidding.'

'So, what have you got? A brother or a sister?'

'Sister.' He tries to look world-weary, but he can't keep the smile out of his voice.

'Congratulations.'

'I won't really be here, though, will I? To see her grow up.'

I think about the implication of this softly spoken statement.

'Noah, have you had an offer?'

'Yeah. From Bristol. But they want three As. I dunno.'

I put my mug down, very carefully. 'They wouldn't have made you an offer if they didn't think you could get in. That course is so oversubscribed, they only pick the brightest.'

'Yeah, but—'

'Just a few more months. Weeks, really. Then this will all be over. No more exams, no more school. You can begin the rest of your life.'

He throws his pen down. 'How can I, with a baby in the house? I have to look after my brothers now because my mum's so knackered. She needs help. And I'm the eldest.'

'And your dad?'

'He has to work more, now Mum's on leave. I don't know how I can do all of this . . .' He gestures to his schoolwork, laid out in front of him, a hastily scribbled essay he should be handing in, in less than an hour.

'Is there anyone else who can help, just for the next few months? While you get through your exams?'

'My auntie was here for a bit, but she went last week. That's why it's been difficult.'

'Can your brothers go to a neighbour? Just for an hour or two? You could stay behind after school, get some work done in peace.'

'I dunno,' Noah says, doubtfully. 'Mum said she needed me to step up. She thinks I can do my homework with my brothers killing each other over the TV remote. She doesn't see what the problem is. I've tried talking to her.'

'If it came from the school, she might listen. I could get Mr Brooker to call, just to explain you need an hour or two of peace and quiet before and after school to get everything done.'

'I dunno.'

'It's worth a try though, right?'

I leave my classroom and hurry down the corridor to find Lucas Brooker, wondering, not for the first time, why I can talk to my students with certainty and confidence, but I'm completely unable to string a sentence together in the company of adults.

Chapter Six

Teaching in a school like this can be stressful and frustrating. Lucas Brooker, the deputy head, breezes through his days with a wellspring of humour and patience that never seems to run dry. Although he is only a couple of years older than me, I admire him, because he is the only adult I can be myself with. I cannot remember how this happened, only that Lucas hired me, a rookie teacher, still grieving for my Aunt Val, and I have never left the space he made for me under his wing.

He will be in one of two places. I want to go straight to his office, but the staffroom is nearer, and I am running out of time before lessons begin. As I approach, I can hear the chatter of my colleagues, a crescendo of noise, as they discuss the week ahead. The school is admired for its team spirit, Lucas takes time to foster the right mix of people, and, as a result, the staffroom is a raucous place. I am the anomaly. Maybe he needed somebody quieter, a listener more than a talker. Maybe he thought I would eventually come out of my shell. The fact I didn't is a source of puzzlement for him, a source of guilt for me. I screw up my courage and open the door as quietly as possible, but when I enter, the noise level drops as everyone stares at me and stalls their conversation. I feel my face heat up as I scan the room and try and look as if I'm too busy to talk. Lucas isn't there. I duck back behind the door and walk briskly away, willing my heart to behave.

I finally find Lucas, sitting in his office, squinting at an ancient computer screen. A familiar smell of coffee fills the room as his pride and joy, an expensive-looking Gaggia, dribbles out a tiny cup of the black stuff.

'Are you busy?' I ask, knocking quietly at the doorframe as I walk in anyway.

'Always,' he replies, not looking at me. He taps the keyboard and swears. 'I can never get these forms to work.'

'I need a favour,' I say, an urgency to make something good happen overtaking my manners. 'Can you give Noah Linzee's family a call?'

Lucas looks up from whatever is frustrating him on the screen. 'You have something in your hair.' He gestures vaguely, looking amused. 'A twig or a leaf, I can't be sure.'

I reach my fingers to my short hair and pull whatever it is out without looking at it, hoping it isn't duck poo.

He looks at me more closely. 'Don't tell me you've been to the pond this morning.'

I shrug.

'Seriously? What's the water temperature?'

'Two degrees,' I say, knowing I need to go through the usual pantomime before I can get what I want.

'One day they'll drag you out of there in a giant ice cube, like a woolly mammoth.'

I fight a smile. 'I'm only in there for a few minutes.'

'Then what's the point, I have to ask?' He leans back in his chair, bending a plastic ruler until I'm sure it will snap.

I shrug again, waiting for him to move on.

'No wonder the students like you. You're a water witch. They probably think you'll cast a spell on them if they misbehave.'

I seize my opening. 'Talking of students. Noah Linzee.' I explain the situation to Lucas, Noah's need for some study time away from his home. 'He's just got an offer from Bristol. It's where he wants to go. He's worked so hard.'

'They all work hard, Eliza. Well, most of them. But yes, I can give his family a call.' He makes a note on a bright-pink square of paper. 'It's such a shame you don't expend this amount of energy on your colleagues,' he says, sticking the note to the edge of his computer screen.

'What's that supposed to mean?'

'You were missed at the staff social. Again.'

I sigh. 'Seriously?'

'There was talk.' He gives me a look, half serious. 'Why don't you come out with everyone next month? We have some new recruits.'

My mind turns to Rosa. How hard it was to have a conversation with her. 'I dunno,' I say, suddenly inhabiting the language of a teenager. I think about how easy it is to enter a room full of children, how hard it is to do the same when there are adults in the room. 'I'm not great with socials. I have tried.'

'Once. I think you came once, about three years ago. The point of being sociable is that you come back, so people can get to know you. You have to keep at it.'

'It's so awkward. I can never think of anything to say. Everyone stares at me.'

'They probably stare because they're trying to place you. They're probably wondering who you are, the woman with twigs in her hair.'

'Talking of twigs. I think that Ficus is dead.' I point to the sorry-looking ornamental fig on his windowsill. 'You should give it a decent burial. That's the last time I give you a living thing to look after.'

He looks sheepish. 'You told me they like to dry out in between waterings.'

'You actually have to water it more than once for there to *be* an in between. I should have given you a cactus.'

'Is this an attempt to divert the conversation away from your lack of social interaction with your colleagues?'

'No,' I say with a sulk in my voice. 'I'm concerned for the plant life I put into your care.'

Lucas continues, 'It's a shame, that's all. For me and for you. I would have put you forward for this pastoral role if you were a bit more amenable to being a team-player. Now I have to fill out this stupid form and advertise.'

'What pastoral role?'

'In the sixth form. The students need someone on their side, and I need someone to flag up any issues early. They have a lot on their plates and they're better at hiding their misery than the lower years. I don't want a repeat of what happened with Amanda Stokes. We should have picked up on her mood earlier.' He puts the ruler down onto the desk and his fingertips tap lightly on the surface of the plastic, making minor adjustments, until it is dead level with the edge.

'How is she doing?' I ask.

'Well enough to retake her exams this year, thankfully. But we need to keep tabs on people like her, we need someone they can check in with for a chat. Someone who'll look out for them.'

I feel something I haven't felt for a very long time. The flutter of hope. 'But that's . . . I could do that.'

'I know, but it's senior leadership level. I need someone to be across all departments, have a good relationship with everyone so the communication is seamless. This is mental health were talking about, it's not just about hanging out with the students.'

I feel my face heat up with the betrayal. 'I can't believe you didn't think to put me forward for that. I could do it with my eyes closed. It was me who saw what was going on with Amanda in the first place. Lucas . . .'

Lucas holds up his hands in defence. 'I did think about it. And then I remembered how you never contribute to meetings if you can help it and you don't like staff socials. It's a big part of the job, networking with your colleagues, seeing what the temperature of the water is, so to speak.'

I feel a squeeze of disappointment.

'Look,' Lucas says, gently. 'I don't mean to hurt your feelings. But it frustrates me that we get along like a house on fire, yet when you're in a group situation, you clam up.'

'I'm used to you. We've known each other for years.'

'How are you supposed to get used to anyone else if you won't mingle?'

'I hate that word.'

'Then pick another.'

'Put me forward for the job.'

Lucas sniffs. 'I'm the deputy head. I have my good reputation to protect. I can't recommend someone who might not be up to it, no matter how much I like them. It makes me look bad.'

'Please.'

'If I do, you have to make an effort. It's my fortieth birthday party in three weeks and you haven't replied to my invitation yet.'

I picture Lucas's birthday party; a louder, more chaotic version of the staffroom. 'I told you I'd take you out for dinner or something,' I mumble.

'If you want that job, you have to put on your sunniest smile and make some conversation with adults above the age of eighteen. No party, no job.'

A noise of fury leaves my throat as I stamp out of his office. 'Fine!' I shout over my shoulder.

Chapter Seven

Iris is used to not being able to get back to sleep, but this is ridiculous. Defeated, she gets up in the darkness, her house cold, the heating not timed to kick in for another hour. She lights a fire in the wood-burning stove while she waits for the kettle to boil. It doesn't throw out much warmth for a while, but the sight of orange flames snaking their way through paper and kindling cheers her up.

Iris shuffles into the kitchen, pours the tea and makes herself a bowl of porridge. She pulls the milk from the fridge, thumbs the silver foil from the rim of the bottle, empties it into an ancient pan. She could buy her milk from the local supermarket, but she likes getting a bottle delivered by the milkman every day, something that never happened in her house when she was a child. In her day, the milk came into the kitchen, straight from the milking parlour, unpasteurised and animal warm, in a jug.

Iris finds the electric whine of the milk float soothing, up and about even earlier than she is, the clink of glass against the stone of her doorstep, a sign of life in an otherwise sleeping world. The wooden spoon scrapes against the pan as it stirs the oats into the milk. It is these old-fashioned noises that bring her comfort. She has been thinking about the past a lot, these last few days. More than she usually does. Something's rattling her cage, and it has everything to do with talking to that woman, Eliza.

Eliza has been on Iris's radar for a long time. Not many women have their hair as short as they both do, but it's not that, not really. Iris has a sixth sense for these things. There is something about Eliza, something hidden and closed off. Iris assumed they would talk, eventually, but Eliza is good at avoiding eye contact. So Iris left her alone. You can't make people want a conversation. She knows that, with time, things change. Hard edges soften in the water. Women cleave to one another like the willow branches Carole shapes with twine. But Eliza is stubborn. She cleaves away from others, not towards them. There is no softening with her. Whatever has shaped Eliza's life, it has left her brittle and hard.

Iris turns the issue over in her mind as she stirs the swelling oats. She remembers perfecting the art of avoidance herself, the technique of developing a brusque manner that discouraged further questions and a practised resistance to eye contact. The porridge thickens as Iris remembers.

Your eyes are a window into your soul, her mother used to say. That phrase always struck a chord. When she arrived in London all those years ago, lost, and rudderless, she felt exposed. She wondered if people would see her for what she really was. She wondered if what she had done would leak out somehow, if she let someone look into her eyes. Maybe that's why she changed her name to Iris. Funny, she hadn't thought about that until now.

When she started work at the charity, it had taken her a long time to snap out of it. She had to learn to meet the eyes of others and hold their gaze. And now she is sensitised. She sees it all the time, in the families she works with. She doesn't force anyone to look at her when she talks to them. But when they do, when they raise their heads and look right at her, asking for her help, it feels as if a milestone has been reached.

Iris switches off the heat and tips the porridge into a bowl. She picks up her tray and shuffles back to the fire. The wall in the

32

hallway is long, and the antique wallpaper has been obliterated by scores of framed photographs. Identical in size, they are all portraits. The photographs are of varying quality, some are grainy and hard to read, some are crisp with the eye of a professional. One head, two shoulders, cropped close, so there is no doubt what the focus is. Some are snapshots of happiness: a mouth open, midlaugh, some are solemn, wistful, a taste of things to come. Most of them look directly at the lens, square on; a few shy away, their eyes elsewhere. None of them resemble one another, though Iris considers them her family. Her families.

These are her successes, her moments of joy. She can name every person in each picture frame. She remembers all of their stories. And what stories they had to tell her! Terrible dramas of suffering. Well-trodden tales of ordinary distress. Misunderstandings, impulsive mistakes, unaffordable debt, bottomless regret. The depth of tragedy, or the age of the subject in the photograph doesn't make one person more or less important than the next. They are all equal in Iris's eyes. They matter to her as much as the breath that enters and leaves her body. She talks to them sometimes, out loud. Takes a moment to remember them and their path to her. Many of the faces that look out have passed away, and all of the children have grown up. She bends down to look at one of the youngest, a twelve-year-old called Sophia. Sophia still writes a Christmas card to Iris every year. She's a midwife in Sunderland, now, bringing new life into the world. Iris looks at the faces. There is not much space left on her wall. When the wallpaper is covered it will be time to stop.

Iris settles herself down in front of the fire and eats her porridge, staring into the jumping flames. She thinks back to the darkest time in her own life. The worst thing about it wasn't being hungry, or finding somewhere safe to sleep, it was being cold. Funny how she ended up, jumping into an icy pool every day. She wouldn't have believed it, if someone had told her twenty-something self she would develop a liking for cold water swimming, and she would continue to swim well into her sixties. Iris sometimes thinks she does it to remind herself that being afraid is really nothing to fear at all. She wonders if Eliza feels this too, if she and Eliza share some kind of kinship.

Iris stopped running away years ago. It was working at the charity that stilled her feet. But Eliza is different. There is nothing about her that is settled. The way Eliza didn't look at her, the way her gaze rested on a point beyond the present. It seemed to Iris, when she pulled Eliza out of the water that morning, that Eliza was desperate to be somewhere else. If Iris hadn't grabbed her shoulder like that, she thinks they could have gone on for years without talking. But since she touched her, things have changed. A connection has been made, and it's opened a door. Iris turns the issue over in her mind as she washes up her empty bowl. It might be that they look a bit similar. Same colouring, whatever. It's not that though, not really. It's something about her attitude, that look on her face. A mirror held up to Iris's past.

Everybody makes mistakes, but Iris has made more than most, and she believes that each mistake leaves an indelible mark. She sees them in herself, and she saw them in Eliza.

Iris sighs, heavily. She doesn't like thinking about the past. She doesn't like waking up in the early hours dwelling on things she can't change. She begins to wish she had never spoken to Eliza. She hopes that her impulse to help won't turn to regret.

Chapter Eight

When I turn down the path to reach the pond, the rain starts to fall. It strikes the bare branches and drums at my feet, in steady applause. The rain puts people off coming here, even though it is a Saturday. If a bit of drizzle stops even a few women from showing up and disturbing my peace, then all the better. But my good mood is thwarted by the sound of singing coming from the changing room. I am surprised and dismayed to see Iris is already there.

'Morning,' she trills. 'I just missed the rain.' She nods towards the blackboard outside the changing area, where Carole has chalked up the temperature. 'The water's a bit warmer today. The ice is melting.'

Iris, naked, is standing in a pink plastic washing-up bowl filled with lukewarm water as she gets dressed. The only thing she is wearing is a bright-yellow bobble hat that looks like it might be home-made. Plenty of the women wear woolly hats to swim in during the winter. Some do it to keep warm and some do it so the lifeguard can keep tabs on them. I've seen women bring newspapers to stand on when they get dressed, to warm their feet. Others, like Iris, fill up a bowl and use that instead. I don't do any of these things. It feels like cheating.

'I suppose you've heard all the hoo-ha about the pond closing?' Iris puts her clothes on in a business-like manner and opens a Thermos flask when she is done.

'Closing? This pond?' I say, unable to grasp what she means.

'Some drainage scheme to stop flooding. The dam walls aren't high enough around the reservoirs. They want to dig up some of the Heath to do it and the Ladies' Pond is part of the plan. Apparently if the work isn't done, then Camden's going to be flooded in the next big storm.' She raises her eyebrows at me as she takes a sip from her flask.

'Hang on,' I say. 'They can't just close this pond. It's been here for over a hundred years.'

Iris removes her towel from the hook screwed into the wall and wraps her swimsuit in it. 'It won't be for ever,' she remarks. 'But the way some people are going on about it, you'd think they were proposing it be filled in with concrete and turned into a skate park for delinquents.'

'I don't understand. I didn't know anything about this,' I say, feeling helpless and ignorant.

'That's because you don't talk to anybody,' Iris replies, briskly.

I ignore the jibe. 'Is there anything that can be done?'

'You're too late for that.' She stuffs the towel into her bag. 'There was a legal challenge, last year. It failed at the end of November. They got planning permission last month.'

'You don't seem very bothered.' I am incredulous she isn't more emotional about it.

'I'm bothered about climate change and people losing their homes to flooding if the Heath dams fail. I'm not too bothered about losing the pond for a few months. Besides, we'll get a new changing room and platform. I've put in a request for a diving board. I don't see why they should have all the fun in the Men's Pond.'

'A few months?' A panicky feeling envelops me, and I sit down on the slatted bench.

'Well, three months,' she qualifies. 'We can use the Mixed Pond when it's shut, though, I assume. Have you ever been over there?'

I know the Mixed Pond. It is exposed. Members of the public can stop and watch the swimmers on the footpath that crosses the end. 'No,' I reply, horrified at the idea. 'I don't swim in the Mixed Pond. This is where I swim. This is . . .' I struggle to find the word. 'This is . . . barbaric.'

Iris rearranges her bobble hat and ties a scarf around her neck. 'It's a pity really,' she mutters, 'they probably could have done with someone as articulate as you on the action committee. Too late now though. Earthworks start in April,' she says cheerfully, emptying out the washing-up bowl into the sink and stacking it with the others. 'The pond will close next February so we have a year.'

Iris shoulders her bag and leaves the changing area. For a few moments, I am too stunned to move.

Behind the drumbeat of rain, I hear another noise: the sound of a saw, eating its way through wood. I leave the changing room and peer into the thinning gloom. Carole is knee-deep in a sloped area of the meadow, wild with last year's spent grasses, hacking a branch from a willow. She's not in uniform, she's in civvies, an over-sized man's raincoat making her look like a wet boulder amongst the scrub. I watch her put the saw down and reach for a pair of long-handled loppers to cut back the thinner branches. The sight of her brings back memories of my Aunt Val, out in all weathers, tending to the landscape.

Carole can't reach the branch. She climbs onto a little step stool to gain the extra couple of feet she needs, and it topples over, sending her backwards into the tall grass below. I wait for her to right herself and when there is no sign of her, I look around, hoping someone will go over to help. When it becomes clear it's not going to happen, I reluctantly march out of the changing room and find her, face to the sky, her tongue out, catching raindrops.

'What are you doing?' I call through the rain as I run over to help her up.

'A moment of appreciation and understanding, that's all. I think I'm being told not to do this today. I didn't realise it was going to rain so soon.' She struggles to right herself and I give her a hand as she heaves herself up off the wet grass.

'Aren't you supposed to be watching the water?' I say.

Carole shakes herself off. 'Is that what you think I do? Spend all my days sitting in that little room, making sure nobody dies?'

'Well . . .'

'This is my day off. The pond is being watched by others today.'

'Oh,' I say, aware of saying something wrong.

Carole regards me with a hard stare. 'We're invisible to you, aren't we?'

'No,' I say, defensive.

Carole folds her arms. 'Then tell me who's on duty this morning. Or if you don't know her name, tell me what she looks like.'

I remember passing someone sitting at the entrance of the lifeguards' hut. I had assumed it was Carole.

'I know you didn't like Iris pulling you out yesterday, even though it was for your own good. And I could see by your face I annoyed you for ticking you off. But sometimes I feel people like me are taken for granted. A *hello* and a *thank you* every now and then wouldn't go amiss.'

'What are you doing here on your day off, then?' I ask, hoping to avoid further scrutiny.

'Maintenance. I'm the one who keeps all of this ticking over.' She gestures to the meadow, which I had always assumed looked after itself. 'And I needed some more willow for the spring equinox next month.'

I think of the hearts, which have only just been removed from the railings.

Carole mutters as she gathers her tools and I can't work out if she is talking to herself, or to me. 'Spring equinox is the time of year when there is a balance between the darkness and the light. It's a time for new beginnings.'

'Right,' I say. 'Well, I should get in the water.'

But Carole ignores me. 'At dawn, on the morning of the equinox, we gather here to celebrate the coming of the light. Someone usually brings breakfast. You should come.'

I have a vague memory of seeing this ceremony taking place with candles and singing, and making a U-turn on the path when it happens. 'So that's what it is,' I say.

'Yes. That's what it is. It's important to acknowledge and feel grateful, otherwise where would we be?'

'Are you grateful that the pond will close next year?' I ask, unable to keep the sarcasm from my voice.

Carole doesn't seem to notice. 'I sometimes wonder if the pond could do with a break from us all, to be honest. Whatever happens, this place will recover, because it has no option. And I will come back and care for whatever the builders leave behind. When you force nature into a corner, it's frightening what she's capable of.'

I leave Carole in the meadow, content to be soaked by the rain, trying to curb my irritation. I want her to be as angry as I am about the building work. I want this place to myself, whatever she says about the pond needing a break from us all. The weekend stretches out in front of me. I know I will spend the time thinking about the closure. I will worry it like a knot in a rope, turning it this way and that until the shape of it becomes ugly and frayed. Her talk of new beginnings doesn't sit well with me. I don't want new beginnings. I want things to stay as they were, before everything stopped.

By the time I enter the water, the rain has turned into a torrent and the surface of the pond is boiling with movement. When I begin to swim, the raindrops shoot up past my face in a surreal reversal of gravity as they violently bounce off the water and claw their way back up to the sky. As soon as the downpour has wrung itself out, I am left with the mineral smell of stirred-up silt. A silence slowly swells over the water, eventually giving way to the babble of the ducks, who get back to courting. I swim towards the boundary rope, looking beyond it to the wall of mature trees at the end of the pond. They tower over the water, several stories high, and I can see the rookery exposed in the bare branches of the horse chestnuts, like ink blots on a line drawing. Above them, the dawn skies announce a new day.

It is time. I lower my face into the water, hold my breath, and wait.

There is a moment between sleeping and waking, a slip of twilight, when things are neither real nor imagined. The pond has its own kind of twilight, a dusk that never brightens, a life suspended in eternal gloom. But occasionally, there is a flash of colour and I see the shape of him moving through the water, unaware that I am here, always swimming out of reach.

Eric! Wait for me!

I don't say his name out loud. My mouth is closed against the water. But I think it. I shout it, over and over again.

Chapter Nine

After one week at Ivydale, I felt as if I'd known Eric for most of my life. Starting over in a new school, year after year, had taken its toll on me. The relentless cycle of making new friends, only to lose them again, had closed me off. It was different with Eric. It was as if he knew the code that would crack me in two, and he used the most powerful tool in his armoury: music. Oasis has just released their debut album, *Definitely Maybe*, and Eric and I were both obsessed with it. We listened to the third track, 'Live Forever', on a loop. He brought the CD into school, and we often spent our lunch hour in the music block, Eric on piano, learning the lyrics, so we could belt it out, word perfect, when we walked home from school. We never felt self-conscious about aping our idols. Some kind of familiarity existed between us from the very first day we met, some sense of an understanding we shared. Our initials were the same. We even looked similar. Our friendship felt preordained. But slowly, desperately, I began to realise I wanted more than friendship when my thoughts were filled with him, that citrus scent of him, whenever we were apart.

I never asked him if he had a best friend before I came along, and he didn't tell me. Maybe he, too, had not needed one, until now. Perhaps he'd been treading water, practising the piano at break-time, the chair in the corner of the room waiting to be filled.

Then, one afternoon, a few weeks after we met, things changed. When we approached the corner of the road, by the cemetery gates, he turned to me casually, as if he had just thought of something, and asked me if I wanted to come home with him. I felt the gear change of our relationship and a small thrill of satisfaction unfurled in my stomach.

'I want you to meet someone,' he said.

'Who?' I asked, confused. He had never mentioned any other friends. I wondered if he was going to introduce me to his parents.

'It's a surprise. Can you come? Now?'

I thought about the state of my own house. The first few months were always the worst. It was dusty and noisy. That morning I'd had to tiptoe across a plank to get to the toilet because the floor in the hall had been pulled up. There were bare pipes and several desiccated mice in the exposed cavity.

'Yeah. Sure.' I tried to sound casual, but it was hard to keep the eagerness out of my voice.

This was the first time we walked in the same direction all the way from school. I glanced down the road to the cut-through I normally took home, each new step a novelty as I walked in a different direction, synchronising my footsteps with Eric's.

'Who do you want me to meet?' I asked once more.

'Someone special,' he replied.

I pictured a granny or a great-aunt, waiting for him at home, proffering buttered crumpets. Then I wondered if he meant a girlfriend, and my stomach knotted in disappointment.

'My twin,' he said, saving me from agonies.

I stopped walking, floored at the answer. 'You have a twin? How come I didn't know anything about this before? Why didn't you say anything?' The idea of there being two of him was intriguing. I couldn't imagine another Eric. He seemed so unique.

'Because I wasn't sure I wanted you to meet each other. I have to be sure.'

'Sure about what?'

'About new people. We have a close relationship. We both have to agree if we want to introduce someone new to one another.'

'Seriously?'

'Yeah. Some people don't like it. Our relationship. We do a lot of stuff together. So if we bring another person into the mix, they have to be the right type.'

I glowed with the implication that I was considered *the right type.* 'How come you don't go to the same school?'

'My parents thought it would be better to spend some of our time apart when we went to secondary school. Anyhow, Lakeside is a better fit.'

'Lakeside?' I echoed.

'It's a sports school. Everyone round here dreads playing them at anything because it spells humiliating defeat. They're top of all the league tables. By miles.'

'Was that . . . difficult being split up?'

'At first, yes. But now we're actually closer because we live more separate lives, if that makes sense?'

Suddenly, things became clear to me. The quietness Eric had. It was confidence, not shyness. He had somebody exactly like him who always had his back, a brother in his corner, no matter what. I had always wanted a sibling, someone to anchor the transient nature of my life. For years, I had conjured up the company of an imaginary friend. Someone to talk to when my parents were busy. Tabitha was the polar opposite of me. Long, shiny hair and beautifully-pressed dresses. It hadn't occurred to me to construct a version of myself. Now I thought about it, to have someone who was your mirror image, someone more similar to you than anyone else in the world – there was a kind of power in that, something mysterious and hard to penetrate.

I was desperate to ask how identical they were, but something stopped me. I figured it was a question twins get asked a lot. And I didn't want to be the same as other people. I had been singled out by Eric and his brother. I had been approved of. I wasn't going to blow it by asking the same questions everybody else did. I spent the rest of the journey talking about something else. I wanted to show him it wasn't a big deal, but it was. I couldn't wait to see him replicated. And I couldn't wait to become part of their inner circle.

Eric's house was everything mine was not. It was old, in a gracious kind of way, and lovingly maintained. The garden, which wrapped around the building, was properly looked after, unlike the gardens I had experienced in the houses I had lived in. My parents viewed outside space as a depository for tools, cement mixers, and supplies. When they finished a house, the garden was the last thing they focused on, and it often showed. Even now, in the autumn, Eric's garden was a blaze of colour, the house covered in Virginia creeper, turning a fiery red, heavy with black berries. We approached a brick and stone porch with attractive twisted pillars, like barley sugar. It was the kind of architectural detail my parents would view as unnecessary and expensive. I loved it. There was a sense of permanence in the Bellingham house, a feeling that when you left in the morning, things would remain exactly as they were, until you returned. Here, change was a slow-moving animal, surprises were few, and always pleasant.

I looked around. Wellington boots lined the floor of the porch to the right of the door, four pairs arranged in size, upside down on a wrought-iron rack. A large planter, glazed in a deep emerald green, contained umbrellas. The number of the house announced itself on a metal plate with a fancy curlicue screwed into the brickwork. There was a weight to the building, something steadfast and durable. Eric turned his key in the lock and the door opened wide into a generous hallway. Before me, I saw a wooden staircase, the surface polished to a warm shine; the oak panelling burnished by the low autumn light coming in through the windows. I half expected to see Labradors skittering across the large grey flagstones in welcome.

We hung up our coats, took off our shoes and walked through to the kitchen, which was at the back of the house. Eric turned to me before he opened the door.

'Ready?' he asked, his eyebrows raised, looking amused.

I nodded in reply, fizzing with anticipation.

Eric opened the door and I looked for his double. But all I saw, leaning against the marble countertop, eating a bowl of cereal, was a girl. Her unbrushed dark hair fell around her shoulders and obscured her face in disobedient curls. She stood on one leg like a flamingo, her knee bent, her bare foot flat against the side of her thigh. Her school tie was pulled loose, and her skirt rolled up as short as it could go, exposing long legs that were covered in bruises. Her shirt was untucked and there was an ink stain on the pocket. She was as unruly as Eric was neat.

'Eliza,' said Eric, his voice full of affection. 'Meet my other half.'

The girl grinned at me, and a small thread of milk escaped down the centre of her bottom lip. She quickly used the end of her tie to wipe it off. She put down the bowl, swallowed her cornflakes and looked at me as if she were deciding my value. Her eyes flicked from her brother to me, and back again. I caught that same, citrus scent that Eric wore, but it smelled different on her. It was greener, grassier, with a hint of earth.

'I'm Maggie,' she said, eventually. 'Eric's told me *everything* about you.' Her voice was rich and husky, as if she had just woken up after a long and satisfying sleep.

The words were friendly, and her smile was wide, but it wasn't like Eric's. There was something guarded about the way she looked at me, as if she was holding back.

'My god, Eric,' she said, turning to him. 'She looks more like you than I do.'

Although she said this in a jokey way, there was a shadow behind the words that stopped me from laughing. Later, I wondered if I'd imagined it, but when I replayed that sentence in my head, I was sure there was a note of heartbreak in her voice.

Chapter Ten

By the time I return to the cottage, the rain clouds have cleared, and my body is beginning to warm up. The school is on half-term holiday and the long week ahead, without the comfort of the classroom, feels like a black hole in front of me. I need something to fill the time. I hang out my swimsuit and towel in the bathroom, toast the crusts from last week's loaf, and make my way out into the garden, a cup of coffee in my hands. Val used to tell me that being outside was nature's antidepressant. Her habits have rubbed off on me. I haven't forgotten the little surge of hope I felt when Lucas mentioned that job. I haven't forgotten his lack of faith in me, either. I walk around the side of the cottage and into the back garden. The key to the greenhouse turns stiffly in its lock. As the door swings open, I inhale the scent of possibility, and for the first time in a long time, the sun shows itself, and the glass panes catch the light briefly, beautifully, before it disappears.

The greenhouse is old. It leans up against the cottage like an affectionate friend. I remember coming here as a child, on the rare occasions we visited. I remember Aunt Val letting me help her move seedlings out from its quiet protection and into the garden. I loved the damp warmth of it, the sweet smell of new life. Sometimes, if I waited for long enough, held my breath and didn't blink, I thought I could see the seedlings move, pushing themselves out of the earth and into the light, opening themselves up, spreading their little leaves wide to soak up the sunshine.

'That's why they call it a nursery, see?' Val said to me once, as she pricked out and potted on seedlings from their trays into their own, individual containers. 'It's a bit like having rows and rows of babies that need to be kept warm and fed, until they're old enough to go out into the world and fend for themselves.'

There was always a haphazard feeling to the place: tall, staggering columns of plant pots shoved in corners, lengths of string and wire hanging from rusted hooks. Val never threw anything away, everything had a use, eventually, but she was careful to keep the place clean. Every autumn, at the end of the growing season, she cleared out the greenhouse, washed the surfaces and cleaned every pane of glass until it shone before moving everything back in again, ready for spring. This became my job when she was too weak to do it herself. She taught me about caring for things that couldn't care for themselves, and sometimes I wondered if she was talking about me, not her precious seedlings.

We never discussed the reason I had landed on her doorstep. Val and I had only met on a handful of occasions. She never left her beloved Heath. She was the aunt who sent generic cards with flowers and ferns on them. The birthday greeting or Christmas wish was always in her own, illegible hand. I didn't admire her economy then, but I came to respect it later. She never asked me for the details of what had happened to me, and the gratitude I felt for her discretion turned into love. When she died, I wanted nothing more than to curl up under the duvet and never come out, but I couldn't let the life she had nurtured in the greenhouse die, too. I completed the cycle she had begun, surprised at the knowledge I had absorbed over the years, moving young plants out into the vegetable patch and watching them thrive. There was something deeply satisfying about walking into the garden on a warm summer's evening, a pair of secateurs in my hand, nurturing myself with the food that Val had brought to life.

Even though it is still cold, I am impatient to make a start in here. My fingers itch to begin planting and fill the deep, empty shelves with greenery. I have cleaned off the flat plastic labels that stick out of the seed trays. They languish in an old tin, waiting for their time. I survey the blank canvas in front of me, wondering what to change this year, what to try. For the first couple of years, I sowed the same seeds that Val always did. She was a vegetable grower, always preferring practicality over decoration. But I have found my own way, and as I become older, I find the same comfort in growing flowers as I do in growing food. I open the seed drawer and pull out packets of lobelia, snapdragons, and geraniums. I have early potatoes ready for chitting and tomato seeds I may as well start off. I turn to the place where I have carefully dried and stored my dahlia tubers over the winter, inspecting each one before I lay them out, ready to go into pots once more.

I spend a happy morning, submerged in my own microclimate, and I forget about the pond closure, but I don't forget about the job that Lucas doesn't think I can do. I admire Lucas because he is rarely wrong. I believe I can do that job, but there is a seed of truth buried in his doubt that I know I will have to overcome. Introverts aren't as valued as extroverts, and that makes me angry.

As I sink my fingers into the soil, inhaling it's earthy, sweet scent, I leave my anger there, in the darkness, to be broken down into something less toxic. I drop seeds into holes and grooves I have carefully made with a pencil in the potting compost. I use that pencil to label my handiwork. When I am finished and the floor is swept clean, I plug in the heated propagators and switch on the thermostatic fan heater to keep the frost away. It is only when I consider sitting out in the garden for the afternoon, weighing up if it is too damp to build a fire, that the memory of Maggie surfaces, and for the millionth time, I wonder where she is and what she is doing right at this moment.

I ball up some newspaper and throw it into an old metal drum, feeding the fire with wood that's been drying under cover over the year. The smoke, thick at first, gradually thins out as the heat gathers momentum and I drag up an old deckchair and watch the flames leap up, throwing out sparks into the sky. I sit there for a long time, brooding on the conversation I had with Lucas, the commitment I have made to become more involved with the school. But all the time I think about my future, the job I know I would be good at, it is the past that drags me back. It is Maggie's face I see.

I always associate Maggie with fire. There was a preoccupation in the Bellingham household that involved setting light to things: candles were always lit for dinner. Fires were built in the garden for birthdays; barbecues were made if the weather permitted. Maggie incinerated her school exercise books at the end of the summer term. But as 1994 turned to 1995, she introduced me to a Bellingham tradition that captured my imagination.

'Every New Year's Eve,' Maggie said, 'we make a paper lotus flower for each member of the family. 'At the end of the meal, at the stroke of midnight, we unfold the flower, write a secret wish on it, fold it up again and then set light to it so our wish comes true.'

The Bellinghams were a family that clung to routine, something I had no experience of. When I returned to my own home at the end of the day, I wasn't sure what to expect. The front door might be a different colour, or the stairs might have been knocked out and a sofa bed made up on the ground floor for me to sleep on. It could be exciting, to see all these changes, but it was destabilising, too. I never knew where I stood, sometimes quite literally. To be with a family that had touchstones in their lives, fixed points in the year when they all knew exactly what would happen, it was something I yearned for.

'Why don't you join us this year?' said Eric, perhaps reading my face.

I looked at Eric, gratefully. *This is why I love you.* The words popped into my head without any thought, as clear and as simple as water in a glass. I had tried not to think of Eric in any other way than that of a friend, but as autumn turned to winter, it had become impossible. A door had opened in front of me, and I had fallen, headlong, through it.

Maggie wasn't happy, I could tell by her face. 'You can't just invite someone without consulting me,' she growled. 'This is our family tradition.' It took a week of favours for me and Eric to earn her approval. Eventually, she allowed me to come.

On New Year's Eve, Eric and I set about looking for the origami paper that supplied the lotus flowers. I already knew what I wanted to write in mine, I had thought about nothing else.

'Here!' Eric shouted, at last, after we had emptied several cupboards. He showed me the square sheets of paper. 'Choose a colour, it doesn't matter which, but they should all be different. I always use this colour because it's my favourite.' He pulled out a sheet of brilliant blue.

'Aqua,' I said.

'Not aqua. Electric. Electric blue.'

'Whatever,' I laughed. I pulled out a sheet and followed the movements of his fingers, which had a dexterity I could have watched all afternoon. They slid over the paper and manipulated the folds as gracefully as they manipulated piano keys. I noticed his tongue poke out in concentration, I analysed the way he nibbled his lip when he wasn't quite satisfied with his handiwork. Finally, he held up the finished article and his trademark grin lit up his face. His flower was perfect. *He* was perfect.

That evening, replete with steak and mash, and a little merry on champagne, at the stroke of midnight, I wrote my secret wish inside the folds of the lotus flower and set fire to it, just like everyone else around me. Eric had appropriated the large emerald glazed pot that usually housed the umbrellas in the porch and placed it in the centre of the table. I waited until everybody had thrown their flower into it and the fire was burning bright, worried Maggie might snatch my flower from the flames and read out my wish to the whole table. But she didn't. There was a moment when we all sat together, quiet for once, even Maggie, and we contemplated what we had written. Nobody shared what they had wished for, it was a rule of the evening that everybody respected. I would have given anything to know what Eric had written, and I would have died a thousand deaths if he had read my words:

Love me back.

I glanced at Maggie as we watched the fire die down, and she gave me a wistful grin. It must have been difficult for her, to share her family like this, to share her twin. I wondered if she put up with me because she knew Eric wanted her to. I wonder, now, if we both did a lot of things because we knew it would please Eric. We were both in love with him, in our own way.

People say there are five stages to the grieving process. If that's true, I am still to reach the final stage with Maggie. Acceptance. She is out there, somewhere, I know it. Living a life I am not allowed to share. I wonder if she thinks of me as much as I think of her. From the moment I met her, I sensed she was the dominant twin, that I had to impress her to keep my friendship with Eric. What I didn't anticipate was how addictive the feeling of her attention would become, how it felt to be the focus of her fierce energy. She was a source of heat for everyone around her, the sun in our solar system. When she disappeared on the day she turned eighteen, a light went out for all of us.

Chapter Eleven

The afternoon sky begins to dim, and the air takes on a purplish hue. I make sure the fire is out, I gather my tools and put them back into the greenhouse. The smell of woodsmoke clings to my hair, my clothes. I should have a bath, but my mind cannot let go of Maggie. It's the silence I can't deal with. The possibility she might be dead.

Maggie was a risk-taker with a high pain threshold. When she decided to do something, she committed herself, absolutely. She came home from the playing field covered with scratches, her skin mottled with green and blue. She relished the fight because she knew she would win. These were the reasons she captained every team she played on. These are the reasons I worry she may be dead.

Over the past twenty years, I have come to know seventy-six Margaret Bellinghams. Of that number, only a handful call themselves Maggie. There is a Maggie Bellingham in Edinburgh who likes rock climbing. She split up from her husband a couple of years ago and tried it on a whim when she was feeling low. Now she can't imagine her life without it. My favourite Maggie runs her own business in Liverpool crocheting miniature versions of people's pets. You have to send her pictures from different angles, and she'll create a doppelgänger in three weeks for thirty-five pounds.

None of these women are the Maggie I once knew. She remains stubbornly out of sight. But I check regularly all the same.

Sometimes I wonder if I'm missing her in a corner of the internet, some other, younger, channel of social media, but she is the same age as me and I bank on the fact she is not as invested in chasing every new trend as the kids I teach are.

Every time I open my laptop and type in her name, I still don't know what I'm really looking for. I just want to see from a distance, a safe distance, that her life turned out well, that she has moved on. It would make me feel better, I suppose. But it's been twenty years and I still haven't found her. Unless she changed her name, which is unlikely. It's her last connection to Eric. Sometimes, I imagine scrolling through Facebook and seeing her face, finding out where she lives, what her hobbies are, who she loves. I imagine myself messaging her. But that's a line I was told not to cross.

I used to get letters from Mrs Bellingham. She asked me to call her Lorella so many times. But the habit I'd formed was hard to break. I wrote back, but I found it difficult. If she had known the truth, she wouldn't have been so nice to me, and that made me feel like a hypocrite. So I kept it factual. Always a postcard, where there's less room to write.

I'm fine thanks. No, I haven't heard from Maggie, I'll let you know when I do.

Now Lorella is dead, it is Maxwell Bellingham who writes, a man who never invited me to call him by his first name. This afternoon, as I locked the greenhouse door, the postman handed me a large, padded envelope, the return address as familiar as my own. Max's writing is shaky and childlike. I put the envelope on the kitchen table and look at it. It isn't my birthday, and Christmas has passed. The card he sent is still in the house. I am suddenly filled with unease. I open the envelope and pull out a file of papers, the name *Maggie* written across the cover with care. There is a note attached by a paperclip, and although I am tempted to open the file, I resist, and open the note instead.

Eliza,

Lorella created this file when Maggie disappeared. She passed it on to me, hoping I would continue her work. Now, I am giving it to you. I am unable to go any further. I regret the tone of the card I sent you at Christmas. It was unfortunate. But I still believe you know more than you told us, though I do not expect you to help me now. If you are in contact with Maggie, she should know that we thought about her every day. You may think I left the grieving to Lorella, but I assure you, I felt the pain of loss as acutely as she did.

You won't be hearing from me anymore. I am too ill to write letters and cards.

Good luck,
Maxwell Bellingham

The dry formality of Maxwell Bellingham reminds me of the man I once knew. I imagine him, frail and alone, with nobody left to care for him. Customs become meaningless when there is nobody to share them with. He must have found the past year hard, even though he would never admit it.

This is killing him, hisses the voice in my head. *You are killing him.*

I open the folder he has sent me, and it is then that I see handwriting I am more familiar with. The papers have been bound together and put in a cheap plastic sleeve, but the contents are precious. This sheaf of papers documents hours of labour, years of research, into the whereabouts of Maggie. I sift through the file and amongst the newspaper clippings, and Lorella's written notes and observations, I see a typed report from a private detective they must have hired when the police stopped looking. The conclusion that she has gone abroad is stated in a single sentence that must have crushed Lorella. The more I read, the more guilty I feel. It is my fault that family fell apart, and now Maxwell will die not knowing where she is.

Twenty years. I wonder what the passage of time has done to Maggie. What she looks like now. I remember the moments before I met her, picturing a boy as handsome as Eric, as neatly turned out. Not the mess of a girl I grew to love.

Lorella died suddenly. I had no time to stew in guilt. But this is different. Max isn't dead yet, but he will be soon, judging by his letter. I stare out of the window, past my garden and on to the Heath beyond, remembering what Carole had said about forcing nature into a corner. Maggie was a force of nature and look what she did. She disappeared, like a storm that had blown itself out, a trail of destruction in her wake. I was always a little bit afraid of Maggie, but the guilt that Maxwell's letter has provoked begins to make me wonder if I should stop looking for her behind the safety of a screen and start looking for her in real life.

After an evening of trawling through Australia (there are nine Margaret Bellinghams there) I decide to write to Eric.

> *Dear Eric,*
>
> *Sorry I haven't written for a while. I only ever seem to write to you when I'm unhappy. Things have been wrong somehow. Life is interfering with my routine, and I don't like it. There is some upset at the pond. Some building works. I don't know what I'll do if I can't swim there. It's the only place I can find any peace.*
>
> *Work is no better. There is a job. Something I think I could be good at, but I'm not trusted. Those kids – my kids – they are the same age I was when I first met you. So full of bravado, especially the boys.*

But sometimes, I notice their vulnerability escape them, like steam off a racehorse. I was one of them, once, and a part of me is one of them still. I feel it. I was unable to process everything that happened, and when I catch a glimpse of myself in these kids, I can see inside them with a clarity of understanding that hurts. And it terrifies me, to be in that place, but it is a place I cannot leave.

I got a letter from your father and now I'm not sure what to do. I might have a chance to prove I can be good again. Maggie told me never to contact her, but that was so long ago. What if I could find her, Eric? What if I could bring her home before it was too late, for Max? If I could set up a reunion between them, it would be the only positive thing to come out of the mess I created. Tell me what to do.

Love, forever,
Eliza

Chapter Twelve

It is Monday, the first day back after the half-term break, and already, I can feel the restless boredom of my students. I have abandoned the lesson I originally planned because this particular class is a tricky one. We are supposed to be studying poetry and form, but I could tell that it was going to be an uphill struggle with the text I have chosen. I look at it, old and irrelevant, seeing it through their eyes.

'OK,' I say, defeated, putting the photocopy down on my desk. 'Let's look at the kind of poetry *you* like. We'll take a verse and break it down. Who wants to choose a poem? It can be anything.'

My class looks at one another, sceptical expressions on their faces. I love this moment, when they have no idea that much of their spare time is taken up by poetry, and I am about to enlighten them.

'Right,' I continue, 'who knows this? Don't shout the answer, it might take some of you a while to recognise what it is. Let everyone else figure it out in their own time.' By pitting the class against itself, an agreeable silence fills the room while I write down the song lyrics on the whiteboard.

After the first line, there are several noises of astonished recognition. Dizzee Rascal, beloved in this school because he was born and raised only a few miles from here, has dropped out of favour because of some stylistic transgression I could never fathom. His latest offering, 'Pagans', was released a couple of months ago, and it is seen as a jubilant return to form. The words have been shouted in the playground, whispered in the corridors, chanted in classrooms. The song, a rap, really, is a little risqué – it generates a frisson of delight – but I am only writing down one verse and it is clean. When I have finished, I turn to the class, loving the mix of emotions on the thirty faces squinting at the board. Some of them have recognised the song right away, others know the words, but can't recognise where they know them from. It's an interesting process, watching memory convert text into sound.

When most of them have it, we spend a productive afternoon together deconstructing the rhythm, rhyme, and meter of the verse, figuring out why it works and what has made it popular. By the time the kids file out of the room and go home, I am left in a pleasant silence and decide to do some marking at my desk before I go home. I take out a stack of year 7 workbooks. These students have only been with us for six months and their enthusiasm is beginning to wane. The beautiful handwriting I saw in September is falling apart in a haste that wasn't there before. They are losing interest and I don't blame them. The way the curriculum has been butchered recently is enough to turn anyone off the English language. I make my way through the pile on my desk, picking out mistakes and trying to give helpful feedback.

Then I hear 'Für Elise' in a jumble of notes, making their way through the floor and into my classroom. I sit and listen to it for a while, knowing it isn't Eric, that it must be Rosa, the new music teacher. Over the half term week, I have thought about socialising with my colleagues to please Lucas, and I have come to the conclusion that Rosa might be the key. She needs a friend and so do I. The fact she can play that particular tune seems like a sign.

I get up, leaving the workbooks in a pile, and follow the music down the stairs. The light has already leached out of the afternoon, and a sombre grey fills the sky. The fluorescent bulbs in the long corridor light my way, clicking on as I pass, marking my progress, until I stop outside Practise Room B. The door is open, an invitation I cannot refuse.

Rosa slowly turns round, still playing, and smiles when she sees it is me. 'You came back,' she says.

'I think my classroom is directly above you.'

She stops playing. 'My bad. I should have closed the door. Sorry.'

'No, it's nice.'

'You seemed a bit freaked out last time you saw this beauty.' She touches the wood appreciatively, as if she is stroking the pelt of an animal.

'I was introduced to that tune when I was a teenager. It really captured something in me. I guess I never shook it off.' The familiar heat rises in my cheeks.

'If it means so much to you, imagine if you could play it?' Rosa has a gleam in her eye.

'I told you, I tried to learn once. I'm not a great student.'

'Well, you're a completely different person now, I imagine. I won't judge, I promise. What was your teacher like?'

'Oh, they were . . .' I don't even know how to finish that sentence. I don't even know where to begin.

Rosa looks at her watch. 'Dammit. I have to run. I'm living with my parents until my tenancy starts. There'll be hell to pay if I'm late for dinner. You wouldn't think I'm a grown woman.' She rolls her eyes and reaches for the red cloth to cover the keys.

'Leave it, I'll do that for you,' I say, feeling absurdly proprietorial.

'Here, have a little go, by yourself.' She plays the first, the most well-known, nine notes that open the tune. She winks at me and swings her backpack onto her back, pulls her coat off the stool, leaving me once more alone with the piano. I wait for her footsteps to fade away and I reach for the keys, tracing the movement of her hands. As I play the notes, they transport me back to the Bellingham house on a winter's afternoon.

Eric's piano lived in the dining room. It was the most formal room in the house, with grainy sepia photographs of ancestors gathered on the walls. Silver cutlery, nestled in velvet cases, delicate china tea sets and dinner services that had been handed down through the generations were displayed in a huge Welsh dresser that dominated the room. Some of the china was ancient and chipped. I thought about all the Bellingham fingers that had passed these items to one another, how many meals had been served on these plates, how much gravy, custard and bread sauce had been spooned from the jugs. I thought about the Ikea plates and glasses that were stacked in a cupboard in our kitchen. In the houses I lived in, there was nothing old or interesting enough to put on display. If anything broke, my parents didn't repair it, it was thrown away. Or sent away.

The piano had its own space against a wall at the far end of the room. Above it, a huge framed cross stitch made by somebody's great-great-grandmother hung above the lid. When Eric played certain notes, the music made the glass vibrate against the frame. I often made Eric play 'Für Elise' when we were alone together. I treasured the thin slices of time when I had him all to myself, observing him at close quarters without being observed myself. Maggie had caught me a couple of times, looking at him a second too long, and the expression on her face told me it was something I should stop.

'If you love this tune so much, you should learn how to play it,' he said to me on that particular day, warming up with a few scales. I looked up at the cross stitch, the letters of the alphabet picked out carefully in different shades of silk, a simple wreath of ivy winding its way around the edge. I wondered about the relative who had sat in this very room, perhaps, patiently stitching those ivy leaves, how many long winter evenings it had taken to complete.

'I can't read music,' I replied, thinking what it must be like to live with such a deep sense of your own bloodline.

'You don't have to. I could teach you. You just have to follow my hands. Do you want to try?'

I nodded and tried to look casual, when really, all I could think about was sitting next to him and receiving his undivided attention.

He began to play the first few notes and showed me how to position my fingers on the keys. The warmth of his arm against mine felt like fire. The citrus scent I had become so familiar with had changed to something more heady. It clouded my brain.

'Yeah, maybe the piano's not your instrument,' he concluded after twenty minutes of very slow progress.

Too late, I realised my mistake, that the lessons probably wouldn't continue.

'Look,' he said, thinking my disappointment stemmed from not being able to learn. He shooed me off the music stool and lifted the lid. A pile of music scores lay in the space of the seat with a couple of pencils in need of sharpening. He drew out a book, folded backwards on the page of 'Für Elise', and altered the letters with one of the pencils.

'See?' he said, showing me his handiwork. 'You might be a terrible pianist, but it can still be your tune. I will think of you every time I play it.'

A clumsy *For Eliza* in misshapen lettering replaced the original title. I was so touched, I couldn't speak.

'You like it?' he asked, softly.

I nodded, looking at the letters he had crafted, a lump in my throat, wondering how to declare my feelings for him without ruining everything. I knew our friendship was too new, too fragile, for a confession like this, but when these moments happened between us, I felt like gambling all of that away and telling him how I felt. When some of the right words began to surface, and I began to stammer them out, I heard the key in the door and Maggie, throwing her bag down in the hallway, grumbling about some temporary traffic lights making her bus late.

The moment was immediately broken by her distinctive voice, and my words died in my throat. I gave a little laugh instead, reversing the gravity into something lighter, funnier, and he laughed, too, in reply. I noticed him slip the music score back into the storage space in the piano stool, though, away from Maggie's curious gaze.

I look at the clock on the wall of Practise Room B. It is getting late. I replace the red cloth on the piano keys and close the lid. I walk back to my classroom to pick up my bag. It is dark, but the lights have gone off, refusing to light my way. My classroom door is open, the streetlights beyond my windows provide enough light for me to gather up my things. I walk towards the huge pane of glass and see my dim reflection looking back at me, superimposed on the street below. I watch the slow crawl of traffic queuing down the hill, a row of brake lights flashing on and off like fairy lights. Then, amongst the shadows, I become aware there is a shape behind me, in the classroom. It moves, as slowly as the traffic, the head and shoulders of a person, silently leaving the room. I turn around, disorientated, trying to make sense of it.

'Hello?' I call, thinking I imagined it, wondering if it is a student, playing a trick. But the students went home long ago. I hesitate, not knowing if I can trust my senses, and walk back to the door. I look along the corridor, but there is nobody there in the shadows. The only sign of life is the sound of footsteps, disappearing down the stairwell.

I turn back to my classroom, unsure of what I have just seen, unable to trust my own judgement. As I look down to my desk to gather my things, I see, carefully placed on the corner, an origami lotus flower, neatly folded, the creases sharp and crisp. The blue is bright and vivid. Electric.

Chapter Thirteen

Iris should be responding to emails but instead, she makes a trip to the kitchen and toasts a fat slice of bread. The charity has recently moved premises and Iris is still not sure she likes the new office. The old building was a dirty, dusty, old-fashioned place with draughty Crittall windows, but it had an integrity to it that she rather admired. It didn't pretend to be anything it wasn't. This, on the other hand . . . Iris sighs as she looks around the self-conscious interior.

The whole office is covered in rubber floor tiles, divided into zones. The zones are coded by a change in colour. The work zone has a blue floor. The cook zone has a yellow floor. The relaxation zone is picked out in a very strident acid green. An earnest young man with overly large glasses and a twirly moustache came into the old office to explain to them all what a glorious place the new office would be. He was especially pleased with the colour-coded zoning.

'Green is halfway between yellow and blue on the colour wheel. So we have positioned the relaxation zone halfway between the cook zone and the work zone.' Iris could tell he was pleased with that idea. During the Q and A session, she had to stop herself asking him how much of the charity's money he'd taken to come up with that one.

When the new premises opened, her younger colleagues had embraced the hot-pink bean bag chairs, the orange ping pong table. Iris wasn't so sure. The colours gave her a headache. To her mind, the workplace was exactly that. A place to work. Weren't you supposed to lounge around and play ping pong in your spare time? She could see she was out of step with everybody else, and it made her consider retiring before the move. But when she mentioned it, the chorus of dismay amongst her colleagues touched her. She might be the oldest one in the building, but she's a walking encyclopaedia when it comes to all the missing people they have dealt with over the years.

Iris pulls the toast out of the toaster with her fingernails and considers how the year has progressed so far. January has been a busy month. Christmas is a tipping point for many families, and the charity often gets called in the new year when things are out of hand. Valentine's doesn't help, either. People expecting a level of affection and commitment that cannot be reciprocated. Iris smears a generous dollop of butter on her toast and eats it before she gets back to her desk. When she sinks into her chair, her phone rings. There is a tell-tale silence at the other end when she answers, so Iris listens, and waits, aware that her heart is beating in quiet anticipation.

'I, uh . . . my name is Jason.'

'Hello, Jason, I'm Iris.'

'I think someone is looking for me.' The man sounds middle-aged. His voice wavers. She can feel the emotion in it, hear the effort he is going to, to stop himself from crying. Iris glances up, and not for the first time, cannot believe the discord between the pathos in life and her perky office decor.

'You think someone is looking for you?'

Iris repeats back what she is being told almost verbatim, something she has learned is a useful thing to do. It makes the person at the other end feel heard, and it embeds the information into Iris's brain. She reaches for a pad and pen, writes down his name.

'I saw myself. On a poster.'

'Are you a missing person, Jason?'

'Yes. Yes I am.' He sniffles and sighs, a big, juddering sigh.

Iris wonders how long it has taken him to decide to pick up the phone and call. She can feel the relief and panic filling the silence.

'How long have you been missing for, Jason?' She asks this question as if she is asking him about the weather, as if it is not a big deal, that she is not surprised he has called.

'Um. More than a year. A year and a half.'

'OK,' she says lightly, gently. 'So you've been missing for a year and a half.'

'Yes. Am I in trouble? I saw myself.'

'No,' says Iris. 'You aren't in trouble. If you see one of our posters, it means someone has reported you as a missing person.'

'Who? Who's reported me?'

'I'll need to look on our system. Can you tell me your second name, Jason?'

'Um, it's Riley. Jason Riley.'

Iris looks at her computer screen and taps in the name. She asks him for his date of birth. 'Can you tell me who you think might have reported you missing, Jason?'

'My wife?' He phrases it as a question, as if he's not sure.

'And what's her name, Jason?'

'Nicky. Nicola Riley.'

'Yes,' Iris confirms. 'Your wife Nicola reported you missing in August 2013.'

She hears him let out another long, noisy breath, as if he has been holding it in for a very long time. And then he sobs.

Iris waits until she feels he has regained some control. 'You sound upset. Do you want to tell me what happened?'

He tells her, skittering back and forth in detail, a story she has heard before, but it is new for him. Raw and painful. He tells her about his teenage children, the fact he cannot believe his family wants to find him, has gone to the trouble of having posters made.

'It sounds to me that you'd like to be in touch with them. Is that right?' Iris asks.

'I don't know.' His voice is full of anguish. 'I don't know what to say. I walked out on them. I didn't even leave a note. I thought they must hate me.'

'Well. I can pass a message on. I can call Nicola and see if she's happy to receive a message from you. If Nicola agrees and wants to send a message back to you, I can pass it on to you.'

'What will you say to her? Will you tell her where I'm calling from?'

'I don't know where you're calling from. Anything you say to me is confidential unless you agree that I can share it. I'm a sort of middleman, if that makes sense?'

'OK. I just want to know how they are.'

'How are you? Have you found somewhere safe to stay?'

'I'm fine. How does it work? The message?'

'Well, I can discuss with you what you want to say to Nicola, and when you're happy with the message, I'll call her, and I'll explain you've been in touch with us. I'll ask if she wants to hear a message from you. If she says yes, I'll repeat it, exactly. Then I'll ask her if she wants to respond to you with a message of her own.'

'Tell her . . . tell her I'm sorry. And tell her I hope she and the kids are OK. And tell her . . . tell her that I love them, that none of this was their fault.' His voice wavers with the effort of stopping the tears. He sounds exhausted.

Iris repeats the words back to him, writes them down in capitals on her pad. She tells him she will call his wife now, that they have her number, and she will ask if she is happy to receive the message. Then she tells him to call her back in half an hour.

'What if she doesn't want to talk to me?' he asks, a note of desperation in his voice.

Iris pauses. 'I can't promise that she will want to pass a message back, or that she will want to hear yours. All I can do is try. Will you call me back?'

'Yes. Yes, I'll call.'

'OK. I'll speak to you in half an hour.'

Iris puts the phone down. A familiar paradox of feelings rises up in her, like a wellspring: hope that she can fix things, fear that she cannot. And something else. Something personal that she doesn't really want to confront. She takes a deep breath, copies out the number for Nicola onto her pad and stares at it. A year and a half is a long time to do without your husband. She has seen many different reactions to phone calls like these over the years. Some wives are still waiting for their men to come back, for it is usually men that walk out of a house in the way Jason has described. Some women, though, find the kind of strength they never thought they had, and they reinvent themselves. Sometimes the wife has found a new partner. There are no guaranteed happy endings. Iris picks up the phone on her desk and dials the number, wondering what kind of a conclusion she is about to set into motion.

Chapter Fourteen

Friday afternoons are always infused with a feverish anticipation for the weekend, no more so than in the school playground. I have asked Lucas to put Rosa on duty with me, and he has complied. She was due to be on duty with the head of Computer Science, possibly the most boring man in North London. But really, this act of charity is more self-serving than anything else. I need to socialise with my colleagues more, so Lucas considers me for the pastoral job. Besides, since Monday, when I saw the lotus flower on my desk, I don't feel like being by myself.

I look at my feet, stretched out in front of me, as I sit on a cold metal bench which is bolted to the floor. There is an amiable cacophony of screams and shouts swirling around us. The students gather and part like birds, a murmuration of noise and movement. There is a group of year nine students kicking a football up against a wall. They jostle for a turn and when one of them kicks the ball against a metal grille high above their heads, it makes a clanging sound and this signifies some kind of ritual where they all pile onto one another, bellowing.

'Is that OK?' Rosa asks, looking concerned. 'Do you think we should do something? Someone might get hurt.'

The ball is jettisoned out of the crowd and sails towards me. I stop it with my leg, dribble it over to the wall and kick it, bullseye, onto the grille. The bellowing becomes hysterical and a smattering of applause echoes around the playground from the few that noticed. I stand over the pile of kids and encourage them to celebrate in a way that doesn't involve suffocating the child at the bottom of the heap.

'How did you learn to do that?' Rosa asks in admiration.

I grin, absurdly pleased she is impressed. 'Honestly? I'm not sure. Maybe something to do with moving around a lot when I was young. Being able to kick a ball is good currency in a new playground.'

'I'm terrible at sport,' Rosa confesses.

'I imagine most people would rather be able to play a musical instrument than run around after a football.'

'Let me give you a lesson after school today. To thank you for switching the playground rota. Lucas tells me you saved me from a fate worse than death. I'll make it fun, I promise.'

Her offer catches me off kilter and I find myself agreeing, without really knowing why. I don't want to play that tune with someone else sitting beside me. I worry how I might feel when those notes come from my own fingertips, on a piano that looks like Eric's. It's hard keeping my memories at bay when I'm in that room. But a part of me does want to be able to finish a job I started so many years ago. I imagine myself, at night, or early in the morning, when the school is quiet, sitting in Practise Room B, playing that piano, summoning the reflections I see in the lacquered wood. Then the voice in my head decides everything for me.

It's better than going home, it says, *where you'll be alone.*

I meet Rosa, as agreed, after the last bell has rung and most of the children have raced out of the building. There is a netball match going on outside the window of Practise Room B. The noisy shouts and the constant peal of the whistle makes what I am about to learn seem less significant than it is. I breathe in, inhaling the scent of recently departed sweaty teenagers and open myself up to the lesson.

Like Eric, Rosa doesn't bother with the music, 'I just want to get you playing,' she explains, and she makes me mimic her hands, one octave above her, so we play 'Für Elise' together, with the right hand at first, then the left, echoing one another. Her notes are perfect, mine hesitant and slow. But I'm not as bad as I thought I would be, and after an hour together, I look up and realise the netball match finished long ago, that I have forgotten my disquiet over the lotus flower. That things look different now.

I leave the school feeling happier than I have been for days, the notes of 'Für Elise' undulating in my head pleasantly as I march home. I look up to the sky, feeling sure it is lighter than this time last week, sensing the warmth that is to come. I have left lamps on timers in the house, and the sitting room looks cosy as I walk down the driveway and let myself in. I pull an easy meal out of the freezer and drop it in the oven, then I decide to treat myself to a glass of wine, a reward for tackling 'Für Elise' and a celebration of the weekend to come.

I didn't drink wine until I met Val. She was quite a connoisseur and always made an occasion of opening a bottle, explaining to me where the grape came from, the climate it preferred. I remember her, working the corkscrew, her fingernails rimmed in soil, sniffing the cork before she poured, swirling the liquid in the glass, holding it up to the light. She was furious when screw caps became popular. Once more, I count my blessings, marvelling at my good fortune to meet a woman who provided me with the kind of attention I needed when she was alive, leaving me the most precious thing, a place to live, when she died. I look around the kitchen, at every scratch on the countertop, every scuff and stain on the floor. These are the marks that Val has made. To see them, to run my fingertips over them, to remember how some of them occurred, is to be close to her. The idea of covering them up, filling them in, ripping them out and throwing them away, is unthinkable.

The wine instantly cheers me up, and while I wait for my dinner to heat through, still thinking of Val, I resolve to check the greenhouse. I haven't looked at the seedlings for a few days because I've been busy at school and distracted over the lotus flower. Although the temperatures have been cold, the afternoon sun can really heat the place up. I need to make sure they don't dry out.

'It's like an intensive care unit in here, sometimes,' Val remarked once, when she was pottering in the greenhouse. 'Trying to keep everything alive when everything outside is trying to do the opposite. Frost. Greenfly. Whitefly. It's a constant battle. And don't get me started on slugs.' Val sometimes came out at night with a torch to lay waste to slugs and snails. I had made fun of her for it until I found myself doing the same after she died. She refused to use chemicals against pests, preferring natural remedies like beer traps and companion planting, but every now and again I would hear a screech of despair as she discovered something had decimated her beloved plants overnight. I grab the torch from the hook by the back door and make my way around to the back of the house.

As I approach the greenhouse, my foot kicks something brittle that skitters along the path. I turn the torch beam on, and the path is littered with shards of glass, winking in the moonlight. A shiver of fear courses through me and I quickly look up to the windows of the cottage, wondering if someone has broken in, but everything is intact. It is only when I face the greenhouse that I see that it is much, much worse. Several panes are broken. The door is wide open, there is glass among the dahlia pots I carefully planted up. The thermostatic fan heater is whirring in vain. A crust of white has settled on the shelves, and it glitters meanly in the light of the torch. The seedlings that had optimistically poked their little heads above the soil are all withered, and below them, on the floor of the greenhouse, are several large stones, lying in the carnage they have made.

Chapter Fifteen

For the first time since Val died, I don't want to get out of bed to swim. I can't bear to face the greenhouse again, but I know I must. I feel as if I have failed Val somehow. I lie in bed, watching the inky-black sky bleed into grey, then blue, thinking about the damage that has been done. The anger that bubbles up inside me slowly thickens, filling me with a dark energy. I get up, flinging the duvet to the side and I call a glazing company. I spend the morning clearing out the greenhouse, making sure every shard of glass is swept up and put in the bin. I throw away the bag of compost that was still open, there are little fragments of glass in there and I cannot pick them all out. I make an inventory of all the seeds and compost I need to replace what has been lost.

When the greenhouse is restored, I dig over the vegetable patch, making it ready for the growing season. The ground is not quite frozen, but it is unforgiving, and requires a level of aggression that suits my mood. The borders are already teeming with early daffodils, their green strappy leaves well clear of the ground. Some of them are showing a slip of yellow, the buds just waiting to break out from their papery spathes. The optimism of them, ushering in the new season, should infect me, but all I can think about as I throw the blade of the spade into the cold, stubborn earth, is Maggie, and what went wrong between us.

Engineers say triangles are the strongest of shapes, because three corners are more stable than four. But in terms of human emotion, trios can be fragile things. I sometimes wondered if Eric chose me because he liked me, or because he thought I'd be compatible with his sister. If that was the reason – that I wouldn't upset their sibling dynamic – it was a mistake we would both pay for, in time.

Watching them together became an addiction for me. I saw them communicate without words: a raised eyebrow, a frown, pursed lips, or a snort. They both knew what the other one was saying, but I was excluded until I learned what every gesture meant. I knew I could never join in, but just to know what they were saying to one another made me feel as if I was part of something bigger than my solitary self.

I discovered that the perfume they wore was CK One, an androgynous scent with a cool advertising campaign. The bottle they shared made its way back and forth from Maggie's room to Eric's. At every opportunity, I would sneak the bottle and spray it on my wrist. I became every cliché I had read about. I was a dog in a manger, a cuckoo in their nest, but neither of them seemed to notice or mind they had an interloper in their company. Until slowly, it dawned on me that I was being watched, that Maggie had been observing me, too, for some time.

'Why do you do that?' she asked me one day.

'What?' I asked.

'When you see me and Eric talking, you mouth the words to yourself. Like you're lip-reading or something. It's really weird.'

'Oh,' I said, feeling caught out. 'I . . . I had no idea I did that.' I could feel my face begin to heat up and I willed it to cool.

When I listened to them talk, it was odd how Maggie's voice had the same quality as Eric's. It was low with a growling, scratchy sound. They could have been mistaken for one another when they spoke quietly together. It was the only similarity they had. Even so, there was a beautiful symmetry that existed between them. If Maggie was told to clean anything or tidy up, Eric would do it for her because she was hopeless at making things neat. Maggie's forte was strategy. Anything that needed building or assembling, something Eric couldn't get his head around, Maggie instinctively knew how to do it. When a flatpack bookshelf arrived at the Bellingham house, Maggie took charge, and the thought that she would make a magnificent army general passed through my mind as Eric and I beavered away under her instructions. It wasn't a coincidence that she captained the hockey team, the netball team, in fact, every team she played in. On the playing field, her position at the top was well deserved, she fought hard to stay there. At home, Eric balanced her out and in turn, Maggie smoothed his flaws. They validated each other's existence. It was a symmetry I was missing in my own life. When I went home at the end of the evening, my parents were often up in a loft, or out on a roof, or in a room that couldn't be entered easily because the floor had been taken up. So I avoided the spaces my parents occupied and consequently led a solitary life in a house that changed around me, shaped by invisible hands.

When Maggie or Eric entered a room, one would make an unconscious beeline for the other, choosing the chair that was closest to their sibling, or standing shoulder to shoulder reading the same book. It was as if they were connected by an invisible thread that could only stretch so far. My feelings for Eric became caught up in the relationship he had with his sister. I wanted him to look at me with the same level of intensity he looked at Maggie, with the same depth of knowledge and understanding. And when he did, finally, begin to listen to me in the same way he listened to his sister, when we began to have conversations that were based on shared memories of an event she wasn't party to, I felt a thrust of pleasure that wasn't entirely innocent. I began to wonder if I was winning him from her. I began to hope I was.

I wasn't proud of how I felt, but I couldn't control my instinct to tunnel into the intimacy they shared and steal it for my own. Like a bookworm that had suddenly found itself in a library, I wanted to devour whatever it was that glued them together and taste it for myself.

Chapter Sixteen

After a weekend of digging over the garden and putting the greenhouse back to rights, I enter school on Monday morning with a fresh resolve. I ignore the nagging voice in my head. The lotus flower can be rationalised. Students often leave things on my desk. There are always little fads and crazes sweeping through the school and I assume that origami was last week's obsession. That flower must have made it onto my desk as a gift, or by mistake. Maybe the cleaner found it on the floor and left it there. The colour is a coincidence. It must be.

The greenhouse is more easily explained. It will have been destroyed by bored or drunken teenagers. My house is easily accessible from the Heath. It's not the first time I've had trespassers in my garden, and it won't be the last. Even so, I feel tender during the day, an uneasy feeling swirling close to the surface. When I stay late at school, I find the light switch before I step into a darkened corridor, and I make sure it is working. I illuminate every space before I enter it. Being haunted by a memory is a very lonely thing. I seek out Lucas more than usual, and he notices.

'Are you stalking me, Eliza? Do I need to alert the safeguarding team?' He is having a crafty cigarette behind the school, in an area near the bins, in the caretaker's territory. I saw him from my window and couldn't resist the warm familiarity of him.

'I think your lungs are more at risk than anything I can do to you,' I reply. 'I can't believe you've started smoking again.'

'I know. I'm pathetic.' He takes a drag and exhales in deep satisfaction.

'Can't you chew gum or something? To wean yourself off?' I waft the smoke away which mingles with the smell of the bins. 'This cannot be preferable to being inside with a cup of coffee. It's freezing out here.'

'Should suit you to a T then,' he says with good humour. 'You love the cold. Like those monkeys. What are they called? Macaques.'

'I thought macaques liked hot springs.'

'They can live in temperatures up to minus twenty degrees. Snow monkeys, they're called. Japan's only primate. They're very good swimmers. And they have red, hairless bottoms. That's possibly two things you have in common.' He grins, crushes his cigarette out and flicks it into an open bin.

I give him my darkest look. 'I always learn something from you, Lucas, thank you for that.'

'My pleasure. Anyway, what brings you to the glamour of the bin store on this dark winter's afternoon?'

I am momentarily caught out, because I haven't come here for anything in particular, but don't want to admit I just need his company. 'I came to tell you I'm taking piano lessons,' I say, thinking quickly. 'With Rosa. She offered.'

'Is this part of your campaign to win over your colleagues?'

'Yes,' I reply.

'One at a time?' He raises his eyebrows.

'Baby steps,' I say.

'Rome wasn't built in a day, I suppose,' he muses. 'It's a start, I guess. Want a lift home?'

When I say yes, Lucas is surprised, because normally I like walking home. But today I want a few more minutes of his easy conversation.

'Why haven't you been crushed by teaching, like everyone else in here? I ask, as I put on my seatbelt. 'You're always so happy, always so good-natured about everything. You never seem ground down by things like the others are.'

'I'm a born teacher,' he says without arrogance as he swings the car around and on to the road. 'I genuinely like teenagers. I think they are complex and funny, and I learn things from them every day. They keep me young.'

'But don't you get sick of it?'

'I get sick of government targets. But I don't get sick of the people in this building.'

'I suppose,' I say, watching the familiar landmarks I usually walk past fly by.

'You know what I mean. I think we're cut from the same cloth,' observes Lucas, as he pulls up on the street outside my house.

'Are we now?' I say with mock sarcasm.

But he looks serious, and he asks me, 'How did you come to it? Teaching? How did it find you?'

My mind is suddenly filled with Val. 'My aunt,' I say, only realising it in this moment. 'When I came to live with her, she spent the rest of her life teaching me to care about things that couldn't care for themselves. I suppose becoming a teacher was the next logical step.'

'We're the same. You were born to teach. You love those kids. And you'd be miserable if you did any other job.'

His words touch me and for a moment I find it hard to say anything in reply. I cannot remember the last time Lucas saw me take a lesson, but it's been a long time since I have been truly understood by anybody. I give him a grateful wave and watch him drive off until his car disappears into the darkness. I shoulder my bag and walk down the narrow driveway to the cottage. The house is a hunched shape against the night sky. I don't usually wish time away, but a part of me wills the spring to hurry up and give me some evening light back.

Not long until the clocks go forward, I think to myself as I approach the front door, scrabbling in my coat pocket for my keys. I am so busy shaking my pockets out, listening out for the tell-tale jangle of metal, I almost trip over it. A box has been left on the doorstep, the top of it comes level with my knee. It isn't a delivery box. The postman hasn't brought it. The cardboard is colourful, painted in candy stripes and it looks expensive. It seems to be some sort of toy. I pick it up, wondering how it could have found its way to me, and then I see what it is. A large doll, her hair neatly parted, in a crisp cotton dress. Her wide brown eyes stare back at me with an unwavering gaze. I am suddenly afraid, aware that this doll knows exactly how she got here but she will never tell. Her lips are shut in glossed perfection. Her dainty ankles are wired into the base of the box, and I see the same wire around her wrists, her neck. The contrast of delicate prettiness and brutal imprisonment unsettles me, and I turn the box over to see if there is a card attached. At the bottom of the box, there is a large white space, a rectangle framed by the tendrils of some kind of vine. At the top of the rectangle is a printed message. *Hi!* It says, *My name is:* and below it, in the white space surrounded by vines, the name *TABITHA* has been scrawled in black felt tip.

Chapter Seventeen

I unlock the door with trembling hands. I should leave the doll on the doorstep, hope that somebody takes her away. I should throw her in the bin. But I can't. Something I cannot resist compels me to bring her in, out of the dark, and put her on my kitchen table, where we can look one another squarely in the eye. I feel the walls close in on me, my childhood pressing down.

My mother once told me she'd suffered a miscarriage before I was born, and that I was the last baby she would ever have. I can't remember how we even got on to the subject, what we were talking about to allow her to share such a personal sorrow. It might have been because I occasionally asked her if I could have a brother or a sister. Then that question turned into asking *why* I didn't have a brother or a sister. From a very early age, I had the sensation that I wanted someone else who was on my side, and that feeling remained as I grew up, an electrical hum in the background I eventually tuned out. Tabitha was my solution to the one thing that was missing in my childhood. My place in my parents' world – forever on the periphery of a job that demanded their time and focus – meant I felt the absence of a sibling keenly. I imagined what it would have been like to have a sister, a constant companion with which to complain about the dust, the noise, the lack of water on a day we wanted to wash our hair, the freezing cold on a winter's morning as our parents installed a new boiler.

When my mother said that word, miscarriage, a word I hadn't really thought about before, I had the image of an old-fashioned horse-drawn carriage, being pulled at a frenetic pace by several horses, nostrils flared, steaming with effort. In my mind's eye, I saw that carriage becoming unhitched, the horses, wild-eyed, galloping off without it, as it lay in the mud, upended. It was a child's attempt to make sense of the words, but as an adult, I can relate to the idea of becoming unhitched, or unhinged from life, by something completely beyond my control.

It was a rare moment of intimacy, that conversation. We didn't often talk about things that mattered, but sometimes she let her guard down and she would tell me something as profound as that. She phrased it in terms of her own grief, as was her right. But what she seemed to miss, what she didn't anticipate, was that it became a loss for me, too. It became a weight I took upon my own shoulders. I could have had a big sister, or a brother. Someone to look up to. Someone to help me navigate life. Company on tap. It was shortly after this conversation that I invented Tabitha, my imaginary friend. It was only later that I understood the connection between her and the conversation I'd had with my mother.

I assumed the desire for a sibling had disappeared with my other childish obsessions. By the time I arrived at Ivydale, I hadn't thought about Tabitha for years. But when I met Maggie, and I saw how she and Eric were with one another, something about the two of them took my childhood desire from whatever slumber it had been in and shook it wide awake.

I told Eric about Tabitha in a moment of confession. The amount of time I spent with him during school and after, it didn't take long for me to open up. I told him about my yearning for a sibling, the fact I would never have one, that I had had to make one up. In the wake of my confession, he must have felt he owed me something back, so he told me something just as personal.

'Sometimes,' Eric said quietly, as we walked back home from school together, 'I wish I didn't have a sister at all.' He looked at me, abashed. 'Don't tell Maggie that, by the way. I don't really mean it. You know that. It's just a feeling I get every now and again.'

Although I had only met Maggie a few times at that point, and, despite the coolness I couldn't seem to get past, I was almost as captivated by her as I was by Eric.

'You never mentioned Maggie when we first met,' I said. 'How come?'

'As soon as I talk about her, people want to meet her. Then it's all about the two of us. People don't see just me anymore. Do you remember me before I introduced you to Maggie?' he asked.

'Yes,' I replied. 'Of course I do.'

'But can you *really* remember what you thought about me, when you looked at me, before?'

I think I loved you as soon as I saw you, I thought to myself. 'I'm not sure what you mean,' I said out loud.

'There's a piece of time,' he said, 'when it's just me. When Maggie comes into the picture, I become someone else. I become half of a whole. And I can never go back to being who I was.'

I reflected on this and couldn't imagine how it was for him. Unlike Eric, I was always the new girl, I could reinvent myself every time I started a new school if I wanted to.

'Sometimes,' he continued, as we passed the cemetery gates, 'I wonder how different I would be, as a person, if she wasn't there. I wonder if I would make different decisions. Maybe it would be easier if she was just my sister. My younger sister.'

'How do you mean?' I asked.

He never replied to this question. It wasn't something that could be easily answered. But now, as I turn the doll around, so her eyes cannot look at mine, I begin to understand the power of Maggie's influence. I begin to doubt my sanity.

I try to imagine how this doll could have innocently found her way to my doorstep. A doll with this particular name. I think back to that conversation I had with Eric on the way home from school, and I imagine Eric telling Maggie about my imaginary friend.

The lotus flower, the greenhouse, and now this, I think, my heart beating like a sick creature in my chest. These objects are innocuous enough, I tell myself, as I draw the curtains and check the back door is locked. All of these things, taken in isolation, would not stir up the emotions that threaten to overrun my composure.

But they are not isolated, says the voice in my head. *They are connected.* And it is the person who is connecting them that makes me afraid.

One event is unremarkable. Two is a coincidence. Three is deliberate.

Maggie has done this.

But why now, when she has spent so long hiding away? I cannot calculate how many hours I have spent looking for her, over the years. It didn't occur to me that she might have been searching for me. A thin trickle of fear pools in my stomach. She knows where I work. She knows where I live. And she's still angry with me, after all these years.

Chapter Eighteen

Iris is sitting at her desk, observing two of her co-workers playing ping pong, badly. When the ball finally gives up and rolls under an enormous purple filing cabinet, Iris clucks in satisfaction. It is only Monday, but already Iris feels irritable, and work-weary. She still can't shake the uneasy feeling she's had since she pulled Eliza out of the water, just over two weeks ago. Now she knows who she is, that she is Val's niece, she thinks about Eliza often, living alone in that cottage, isolated on the Heath.

When Iris was her age, she had nobody in her corner. She hadn't allowed it. She thinks about all the times she refused offers of help, turned down dates, walked home, alone, too worried about repeating the past. It is when she sees people like Eliza, brushing away human contact, that Iris is reminded of the mistakes she made when she was younger. She didn't know Val that well, but she liked her on the occasions they met. She wonders if Val would have wanted someone to help, to be that person in Eliza's corner, after she died. Iris knows she could take on that role quite easily. It seems like Eliza needs it. But whether she wants it is another question.

This morning, Carole mentioned that Eliza hadn't turned up on Saturday, and this set an alarm bell ringing in Iris's head. Eliza swims through sickness and health. What could have prevented her? Iris looks at the time, has a stern word with herself, and turns her computer on. *This is the problem*, she thinks, crossly. Her head is being taken up by someone who doesn't want her help. It's a recent development, this tendency to brood over unsolvable problems. This desire to keep circling back. She wonders if old age is making her less resilient. She hopes not.

The phone on her desk rings. She picks it up, grateful for the distraction.

'Iris, I have a call for you,' says the receptionist, in hushed tones.

'Yes, who?' says Iris, impatiently. The new receptionist is too earnest for Iris's taste.

'Nicola Riley? She says you left a message for her last week? About her husband, Jason?' Even the way the sentence is phrased as a set of questions drives Iris mad. She takes a deep breath and remembers the conversation with Jason Riley. She has left messages for Nicola but has not received any indication she wanted to talk. Until now.

'Put her through,' says Iris, waking up her computer and bringing up Jason's file.

'Hello?' Nicola's voice is flat. 'Is that Iris? I'm returning your call.' Iris's heart sinks. Sometimes she can just tell when things aren't going to go well.

'Hello, Nicola. Yes, it's Iris. You got my message?'

'Yes. But it was half term. I was away with the kids. Otherwise I would have called back sooner. And then, when I realised who you were . . . I wasn't sure. I just needed some time to think about it.'

'It's a lot to take in.'

'A year and a half, he's been away.'

'Yes. You reported him missing to us in August 2013.'

'Seems like a lifetime. I can't tell you what we've been through. Me and the kids. I can understand why he might want to leave, get away from me. But not the kids. They didn't deserve that.'

Iris swallows. 'Would you like to try and tell me? So I can understand how it's been for you.'

She lets out a sigh. 'He left debts. I had no idea he'd lost his job. He was still going out of the house each day like normal. That's what I couldn't get over. That he didn't tell me. I had to sell the house. The mortgage was in arrears. I had to sell the car.'

'That must have been very difficult,' says Iris.

'Difficult? It was a nightmare. I hadn't worked since I'd had the kids. Sixteen years of not working and suddenly I had to find a job, be the breadwinner. Nobody wanted to hire me. A middle-aged single mum with no work experience. It was humiliating.' Nicola makes a noise of irritation.

'How are things now?'

'I got the kids through their exams,' Nicola says, a grim note in her voice. 'That was a terrible time. He left a few months before the GCSEs started. I could have killed him. But then . . . I wondered if he was dead already.' Nicola stops, sobs. Just one intake of breath. Then a pause before she asks the next question. 'He's alive, then?'

'Yes,' says Iris. 'I've spoken to him.'

Nicola's words continue in a steady, angry flow, as if she can't keep the memories in. 'I found a job. I retrained on one of these government schemes to get people like me back to work. I used to be good at my job before I had the kids. Turns out I'm still good at it.'

Iris silently notes the pride in her voice.

'I'm about to move into a new house. It's tiny but it's mine. The kids will be leaving soon. Off to college. And then it will just be me. At least . . . that's what I thought. And now this.'

There is a pause in the flurry of words. A lull in the storm. Iris waits.

'I can't believe he called you,' Nicola says. 'After all this time.'

'It happens like that, sometimes,' Iris replies, quietly.

'What does he want?' Nicola asks.

'He's left a message for you. You don't have to receive it.'

'Well, I can hardly put the phone down without hearing it, can I? He's my husband. We've been married twenty-odd years. I know I might sound cold to you, but I think about him, all the time. Not a day goes by.' There is a hitch in her voice that she turns into a cough.

'You don't sound cold. You sound shocked. It *is* a shock. I just wanted you to know that you're under no obligation to hear the message or reply to it. It's your decision.'

'Just tell me what he said,' Nicola says, wearily.

Iris relays the message, word for word.

'Where's he been? Where is he now? What did he sound like?' Nicola asks.

'I don't know,' says Iris. 'He told me he had somewhere safe to stay. That's all I know. He sounded upset when he spoke with me.'

There is a long silence. Iris can hear it stretch out between them.

'Is he ill?' Nicola asks, eventually.

'He didn't say that he was, no,' replies Iris. 'This must feel quite overwhelming.'

'You can say that again.'

'Would you like to pass a message back to him?'

'I don't know what to say. I'm just . . . empty. I can't get my head around it.'

'That's OK. You don't need to say anything right now. You can have a think about it.'

'I'll need to talk with the children. They're at school. They need to make a decision too. Though I know what it will be.'

'Are they coming home soon? Is there somebody who could be with you?'

'I've been by myself for almost two years. I can manage a few hours on my own, thanks.'

'OK. You can call me back if you like. I'm here until ten o'clock tonight if you want someone to talk to.'

Iris puts the phone back on its cradle. Maybe her first impression was wrong. Nicola has been through a lot, but she can hear the pragmatism in her voice. And she has children, who are usually more forgiving, more willing to wipe the slate clean. Iris feels a little prick of emotion and all of a sudden she feels very, very tired. This job takes it out of you: she feels it, a physical toll for every case she works on. She looks at the ping pong table in the relaxation area, the jaunty pink bean bag chairs. Once more, her thoughts turn to retirement.

Chapter Nineteen

I have not slept much. I woke in the middle of the night, knowing that the doll was directly below me on the kitchen table, eyes glassy and perpetually open, with that name scrawled over the box. Eventually I got out of bed, put my coat on, and marched out of the house to put it in the bin on the street. Even then, my doors locked and bolted, knowing it was nowhere near me, I found it hard to get back to sleep. At last, the hour comes when I can walk through the garden, my swimsuit and towel tucked under my arm, and make my way over the slumbering Heath.

The Ladies' Pond will not close until early next year, but they will begin to tear through the ground to the east in a matter of weeks. I feel a ticking clock counting down to the day I will be barred from entry. Now, when I put my head under the water, I see shafts of sunlight striking through the gloom, reminding me time is moving on, whether I want it to or not. Floating fragments of things that have fallen into the water are illuminated as they make their way down to the bottom, their last brush with warmth and light as they fall into perpetual darkness.

The water pulls me into its dark and silky embrace. I pour myself into it, spilling my troubles into its depths. In the summer it envelops me with a welcome cool, accepting me like an old friend, but the warmth it gave out in the autumn has vanished, and now the pond demands respect. To enter is a test, something to be endured and overcome, and I surrender myself willingly. When hypothermia kicks in, the body begins to feel hot. Blood vessels open in a desperate attempt to warm vital organs. For ice climbers, the desire to remove cold weather gear is fatal. For swimmers, the temptation is to keep going.

I never knew that the sensation of hot and cold could be so close. That two things, at either end of a linear scale, could be brought together, like a join in a circle, until one seamlessly touches the other. I feel it now, as the cold curls itself into a fist and lodges in my chest like a smoking coal. I make my way slowly round the enclosed area, mindful Carole is watching me, feeling the underworld on the soles of my feet. The water burns my skin, flays it until it is raw, and I welcome every painful sensation that passes through me, distracting me from the events of the night before. As I feel my body reject, then accept, the temperature, I slip, hypnotised, into an altered state. I lower my head and plunge my face into the abyss. My eyes are blinded by the murk, but my mind can see beyond the dark. It travels through the inky water, through the debris of the deceased. This pond is full of the dead, from the severed leaves that drowned on the surface, to the rotting matter on the floor. I see a movement, lazy and slow, below me. I feel the pull; I cannot resist.

I'm here, I call, as I follow the shape of him. *I'm right here.*

Carole is waiting for me when I leave the changing room. I nod at her as I attempt to pass, but she doesn't give way.

'I just want to remind you to keep the swims shorter in weather like this. I've never had to ban anyone before, but I will if you go beyond the boundary again. The rope is there for a reason.'

'I'm fine, honestly,' I say impatiently. 'I've never had any trouble in or out of the water. I know my own limits.'

'Iris was worried about you. And when you didn't come on Saturday for a swim . . .'

Iris. I knew she was going to be trouble. 'Iris doesn't know me,' I snap. Suddenly I feel as if everybody is watching me. Why can't I be left alone?

'She's been swimming here long before you started, and she knows the water better than anyone. If she's worried, *I* worry.'

'I just want to be left alone, on my own, without interference.'

Carole gives me a look. 'You know, you're not the first woman to swim here to get away from something.'

'What's that supposed to mean?'

'Women come here, thinking if they can withstand a few minutes in cold water, they can overcome anything. But it doesn't work like that.'

'I have no idea what you're . . .'

'Coming here, day after day. I see women change. But not you. You've been the same since the day I first saw you. You must have been, what? In your twenties when you first showed up here? Ten years ago at least. And you're still the same.'

Suddenly, I think that Carole sees something I have been very careful to hide, and I struggle to compose my voice. 'You don't know me. We barely speak. I don't talk to anyone here for exactly this reason. I don't need your stupid psychobabble. I don't need you to look out for me, either. I can do that myself.'

But Carole is unperturbed by my outburst. 'It's the women, not the pond,' she continues, calmly. 'People come here thinking the pond will heal them. But it doesn't. It's the women.'

I make a move. 'Look. I need to go. I have things to do.'

Carole touches me lightly on the shoulder and her touch feels like a burn. I look at my shoulder, sure she has done something to it. But there is nothing to see.

'Iris asked me to look out for you, and this is my way of doing it. Before you die of hypothermia, you should know this. Many women come here to avoid something, and that's understandable, plenty of us do that. But this pond will swallow you up if you let it. You've seen it, haven't you?' she asks, looking at me once more with an intensity that I can't fend off.

'What do you mean?' I reply, a small finger of fear tracing down my spine.

'There are two sides to this place, and you can't have one without the other. You've seen a heron fly over your head and tear a duckling from the water. You've seen the water snakes, three feet long some of them. There are things in here that most people don't want to know about. But you're different. You go looking for it.'

She sees me, it's true, but she cannot know what I'm looking for. It's impossible for anyone to know but me.

Carole continues, 'This place is beautiful because of all the ugly things in it. You can't appreciate one without the other. But you have to look beyond the dark towards the light.'

I can barely keep my voice under control. 'You are making me late for work.'

Carole steps aside. 'It takes courage to face the things you want to avoid. The pond won't give you courage, but the women in it will. If you stop putting yourself at the centre of everything, you get a different perspective on life.' She shrugs. 'Just saying.'

I storm off, shaking with anger. I think of Iris, less than three weeks ago, telling me off for swimming beyond the boundary. Since then, bad things have happened. Everything seems to be unravelling around me. To my horror, I feel myself well up and tears blur the frozen path in front of me. I wipe my face with the heel of my hand and begin to walk towards the road. I should go home and call in sick today. But I can't shake the sensation that my house is being watched. All I want to do is walk and walk. Fumbling in my pocket, I pull out a crumpled piece of tissue and immediately drop it on the pavement. As I crouch to pick it up, I see a figure on the other side of the road. Her back is towards me, but I would recognise that back anywhere, the dark hair tumbling down in unbrushed curls. She turns slightly, looking up the hill, as if she is uncertain where to go. She pulls out a phone and frowns at it. I stay where I am, shrinking in the gutter, paralysed by her presence. I take in her every detail, remembering it all with a clarity that hurts: the curve of her cheek, the fringe she could never straighten out, the vertical crease dividing her full bottom lip. It all has a sickening familiarity.

'Maggie.' The word barely makes its way out. Her name is a stone in my mouth. It has been so long since I said it out loud. I am on all fours now, unable to move. She begins to walk up the hill, away from me, oblivious to my agony, and I don't know whether to call out to her or keep quiet. I rise, wobbly, torn between fear and anger, hating myself for being such a coward.

A looming impression of movement to my right is followed by the roar of an elderly engine. I only have a moment to understand what is happening as the rear end of a car bears down upon me at a pace I can't match. Slow to stand, I inhale a lungful of exhaust fumes as the chrome and red of a vintage MG ploughs into my body like a fist through dough.

The pain is immediate and unforgiving. It flares deep within my leg, like an explosion within a rock face. I have a fractured second to understand what that cracking sound means before it splinters and snakes its way through my right side. The force of the impact lifts me up, like a leaf in the wind, and I hit the car with my shoulder before landing, finally, on the road. The tissue is still there. It lies half a metre away from my bleeding nose, in mockery.

'Hello? Can you hear me?' A woman crouches over me, her voice rising in panic. She touches my head and I roll my eyes towards her. She cries out my name as I fall into darkness.

Chapter Twenty

The last time I saw Maggie, almost a year to the day we were first introduced, I had already been told the worst of it. My parents had forbidden me to go over to the house, but I couldn't keep away. As soon as my father had finished speaking, I tore out of my room and ran all the way through the village, despite the punishing heat, wanting Maggie to deny the words I couldn't bring myself to repeat. But when she opened the door, her face a mask, I knew the story my father had told me must be true, and that everything I had come to take for granted had gone.

As I ran through the village, my lungs on fire, I couldn't believe people were carrying on with their day when my whole life had caved in. The post office was still open. There were kids on bicycles sucking on ice pops outside, carelessly throwing their wrappers onto the street. Everyone was acting as if nothing had happened. My head felt swollen with words as I ran, my heart bursting. But when I rang the bell and Maggie opened the door, those words deserted me. I thought she would take me into her arms and tell me everything would be alright. I was wrong.

'Maggie,' I panted, pleading with her, wanting her to feel the same as me. I had no idea what else to say. She stood there, looking at me, silent. It was the last time I called her by her name. My face was swollen with tears. I was sweaty from the run. I knew how I must have looked.

'Don't,' she whispered, shaking her head. She was poised, her hair brushed back with a precision I wasn't used to seeing. She wore a pressed cotton dress, and her feet were bare. It was as if she was held together by something that could tear at any moment. She seemed to know it would only be a matter of time before she tumbled into the territory I already occupied.

I was past caring. I hiccupped with distress, unable to talk in sentences. I had lost the ability to say words, I could only sound them out, as if I were a child. 'P . . . p . . . pl . . . lease.'

She stifled a sob, made a swift recovery, drawing herself up like a puppet on a string. 'I don't ever want to see you again. Ever. Don't call here. Don't phone. It's over.' She broke her gaze and shut the door. I remained there on the step for a few moments, trying to take it all in. I had passed through that door scores of times. I knew every inch of the porch I was standing in. I had waited in it on rainy days, I had shrugged off coats, boots, scarves, shaken out umbrellas there and left them in the emerald glazed pot. I had helped decorate it with fake cobwebs and pumpkins on Halloween and strung up fairy lights at Christmas. I couldn't believe I would never be allowed back.

I had no choice, but to return to my own home that day, a place I had never felt a part of. My parents loved me, they made sure I knew that, but I wasn't a part of their world, not in the way I had become a part of the Bellingham family. The Bellinghams had absorbed me into their house like a third child. And I had repaid them all with the worst kind of betrayal. But Maggie . . . Maggie must have known, deep down, I hadn't meant it to end like this.

Time would tell, I thought to myself. Soon, she would see sense and forgive me. She had to. But the hours grew into days. The days grew into weeks. When her birthday approached, I agonised how

I should mark it. To ignore it would extend the silence I so badly wanted to end. If I bought a lavish gift, it would make me seem desperate. I decided to gather all the photographs I had of us together and put them into an album. She would see, then, what she had been missing. She would understand we could get over this, that we were stronger together. That our friendship was worth rescuing. That we couldn't live like this anymore.

I walked over to the house, remembering the last time I had made the journey on that terrible day. The heatwave had passed. A fist of cool air was already squeezing out the summer warmth. As I approached the post office, I remembered her birthday card. I had left it on my bed in my haste to leave. I swerved across the road, hoping the cards they had to sell wouldn't be too tacky, hoping I could beg a pen and replicate the words that had taken me so long to compose. But when I open the door and entered the shop, the chatter died down. Everybody turned to me. The queue of customers and the staff at the counter stopped, as if a gong had been struck. For a blissful moment of ignorance, I thought I had imagined it, that it was just the squeak of the door that had silenced the noise. But the chatter didn't start up again, it muted to whispers. There was an air of embarrassment that hovered in the room, a stink nobody wanted to acknowledge, and I knew their embarrassment was for me. I shrank out of the shop without a card and ran the rest of the way, my face burning with humiliation.

I approached the porch and rang the bell with my elbow, my hands held out in front of me, the photo album carefully wrapped with a fat blue ribbon tied around its middle. The door was opened by a stranger. He introduced himself as Maggie's uncle. He looked worn out.

'Is Maggie there?' I said, hoping he wouldn't know she had barred me from the house. I adopted the face of a friend who might be welcomed, not the face of someone who deserved to be shunned.

He paused, and a look of pity crossed his face. The scene at the post office fresh in my mind, I imagined the birthday gathering behind him in the kitchen, everybody listening into our conversation in embarrassment, wishing I would go.

'I have a birthday present for her.' I pushed it at him, my face reddening again, trying not to lose my composure, so the book was nearer to him than me. So he couldn't refuse it.

'We were just about to call you,' he said, an uncertain look on his face. 'We don't know where Maggie is. Her parents . . .' He looked briefly behind him, towards the sitting room door, which was shut. 'They're beside themselves. She disappeared this morning. Left a note on the kitchen table saying she didn't want to be found.'

He took Maggie's gift from me, the jaunty bow a mockery of my childish optimism and, once more, I was sent away from that house with all the things I wanted to say, unsaid.

When the police came to question me about her disappearance, I didn't tell them what had gone on between us. I simply said I had no idea where she might be; that I was stunned and upset and wanted her to come back. It was nothing, nothing but the truth.

Chapter
Twenty-One

When it becomes clear she cannot accompany Eliza to the hospital in the ambulance, Iris is left on the pavement, shocked and shaken. The street is eerily quiet, as if it is digesting the drama it has just witnessed. The onlookers who assured the ambulance staff it wasn't Iris's fault have gone. The medics have told her she cannot come with them, she isn't next of kin. Nobody has called the police, although she expects a car to come screaming around the corner any minute to cart her away in handcuffs. She was distracted this morning. She was thinking about Nicola and Jason Riley, the meeting she is in the process of setting up between them. She knows there is only one chance of reuniting this family, that if the meeting goes badly, Nicola will walk away. But if it goes well . . . Iris wants a happy ending. She wants Jason's face on her wall. She can't shake the feeling that he might be her last.

Iris looks at the pavement and knows she wasn't focusing properly when she reversed into that space. This road is usually so quiet in the winter, and the car has terrible visibility out of the rear window, especially when it fogs up. Iris gets back into the MG, her hands trembling, and carefully tucks herself into the space Eliza was occupying. She sits there for a few moments, wondering what to do; eventually she pulls herself together and does what she usually does when she is feeling out of sorts. She grabs her swim bag and heads to the pond.

Iris began coming here not long after she arrived in London. It was free back then. She could shower, even though the water wasn't heated. She could sleep in the meadow, undisturbed. It was the only place she felt truly soothed. London was supposed to be temporary, she assumed her feelings would pass. She had only come here because she didn't know anyone and needed some space. Which was odd, because Devon had acres of space. It was just the wrong sort. Everybody knew one another in Devon. She felt like a prisoner. London provided her with the kind of space she needed. The anonymity of a city that didn't recognise her when she walked its streets. It was liberating.

Iris still thinks of herself as two separate people: Constance, the person she left behind in Devon, and Iris, the person she has become. Iris is capable, forthright. That other woman . . . she tries not to think about Constance. There was something broken inside her, something that couldn't be fixed. Even now, she finds it hard to feel sorry for her, though all the training sessions with the charity said she must always extend the hand of sympathy in any situation.

When she started swimming here, what really surprised her was how the women accepted her in a way she could not accept herself. They didn't look at her critically, even when she was naked. She was one of them, part of a family that felt special, secret; a club where it didn't matter who you were or what you did. All that mattered was the fact you had come. She had started swimming in the summer when the water held the heat and the days eked out a honeyed warmth that lingered in the earth. She told herself she would stop when the winter came, but none of the regulars did. She told herself she would keep showing up until she didn't want to anymore. But she always wanted to, the feeling didn't leave her. The days turned

101

cooler and eventually froze. Still, she did not stop. She wondered if she was punishing herself, making herself get into freezing water every day, but the buzz that came afterwards, a flooding of warmth and wellbeing, told her otherwise.

Iris slips past the sign that keeps the men out. She walks down the narrow path, the bare branches of the oak trees arching over her head. She glances to her right and sees the meadow is silvered with frost. At the end of the path where the pond lies, the surface is punctured by points of light where the water ripples with movement. Several heads, covered in knitted hats, are sedately making their way around the enclosed area of the water. Once again, Iris feels the familiar tug of belonging.

Carole greets her with a wave. 'You have a face as long as a horse,' she says, shooing a couple of coots out of the lifeguards' room.

'You're not going to believe this,' Iris says. 'I've just gone and knocked down that woman, Eliza.'

'You hit her?' says Carole, incredulous. 'She must've really overstepped the mark.'

'Not with my fist, I'm not a philistine.' Iris says, impatiently. 'With my car. I was just pulling in to park and she was crouched in the road. I could have killed her. I'm so stupid.'

'You're not stupid, Iris. Don't call yourself that.'

Iris feels a rush of gratitude for Carole.

'Is she OK?' Carole asks.

'I hope so. The paramedics said she would be fine. There's nothing I can do right now. They told me to phone the hospital in a couple of hours. I can go and see her as soon as they'll let me.'

'Was she unconscious?'

'No. But what if something terrible happened? She could have internal bleeding.' Iris's mind races ahead to several doomsday scenarios, all of them leaving Eliza dead.

'She's in good hands. She's being looked after, and she's as fit as a fiddle. There must be bad karma going around for her today because I had a row with her this morning as she was leaving.'

'You're kidding?'

'I'm not,' says Carole brusquely. 'I'm sick of her swimming under the boundary rope. I don't think she even realises she does it. I had a word with her when she got out.'

'We are a pair, aren't we? Can't keep our beaks out.'

'It's for her own safety,' Carole says, unapologetic.

Iris sighs. 'Well, I have some serious making up to do. I'll go and see her this afternoon. Go and apologise.'

'I'll come too if you want. I can see if anyone is around to take my afternoon shift?'

'Thanks, but no. I better do this on my own. No sense dragging you down with me,' Iris says, grimly.

Carole gives her a smile. 'Don't look so stricken, Iris. It was an accident. Go and have a swim. Everything is always better after a dip.'

'You speak the truth, Carole.'

'I always do.'

Iris climbs down the ladder and, as is her custom, she enters the water backwards and slides herself away, forcing her breath out, her face lifted to the sky. Her guilt about the accident is eased in the cold. The pond cradles her body, and she stretches her arms wide, feeling a stray leaf or two run through her fingers as she pushes herself around the enclosed area, mindful she needs to keep moving. Her breath forms translucent clouds that puff out and disappear into the thin air. For a moment she wonders how much breath has been absorbed into the pond from all the women who swim in it.

Sometimes she hears women singing as they swim. Most hum a quiet tune, but she has heard opera being belted out before now. A few times a year, Carole shouts across the water and informs the swimmers of a significant birthday, if it's one of the regulars. As the birthday girl descends the ladder, everyone sings. Iris thinks about all the musical notes that have been sung in this space, the loud and the quiet, how they have fallen through the air like raindrops, disappearing below the surface, tumbling to the bottom of the pond, reorganising themselves into their own, secret songs beneath her.

By nature, Iris is a sceptic, but here, in the water, she is different. She is a believer. The women who swim here come for different reasons. Many of them come to be healed. She has seen women swim their way through illness, trauma and loss. She has seen the way the water repairs them. Iris knows the pond is filled with tears, and hers are here among them, cried in desperation and self-pity when she was younger and still tender. Now, Iris comes here to think. Knots that seem impossible to unravel on land, suddenly loosen themselves in the pond. Paths that are blocked become navigable. As she swims, she thinks about Eliza, how she has come into her life and how she is now causing Iris her own, unique problems. She still hasn't been able to shake off her first exchange with Eliza. She has felt distracted, unsettled, her mind too much in the past. And now this. Iris prays she hasn't hurt her badly. She'll have to make it up to her whatever happens.

Iris progresses through the water with a steady rhythm, and the rhythm soothes her like a heartbeat. She leaves the pond feeling better, as she knew she would, and later that day, she makes her way to the hospital, wondering what the repercussions will be.

Chapter
Twenty-Two

I surface from unconsciousness, and I fall straight back into sleep like a fragment rising to the shallows, only to slip once more into a dark oblivion. I'm aware of people talking loudly around me, and my inability to answer. Time passes. I don't care. I can't speak, but the voice in my head has commenced a ceaseless, tumbling chatter. I have no control over my thoughts. They seesaw, unconstrained by logic or time. My memory is a room full of boxes that have tipped and shaken themselves loose. The box marked *Do Not Touch* has split, spewing its contents all over the floor.

Look at it, the voice in my head cries. *Look at what you've done.*

I think about Eric and Maggie often, every day. But I do not think about the things that destroyed us. Now, I have no choice. They are played before me in crisp detail.

By the spring of 1995, something had changed between Maggie and me. I no longer caught her looking at me, as if she could read my thoughts. The hard centre that I couldn't seem to break open began to yield. Maybe she realised I wasn't going any-where. Maybe she decided I wasn't a threat, that I wanted to be her friend as much as I wanted Eric. We had all received offers from the universities and colleges we had applied to. Maggie had already gained entry into an elite sports school, where she would continue to come home at the end of each day bearing the marks of hockey sticks and her opponents' fingernails on her skin. Eric and I had applied to study as near to her as possible. My offer grades for an English degree were achievable. But Eric would have to work hard to gain a place on the music course he had applied to, it was so competitive. When he began to bury himself in revision, distracted with schoolwork and worried about his grades, Maggie transferred her attention to me. Torn between the two of them, I sided, for once, with Maggie. There had been no indication from Eric that he felt the same way I did. My feelings for him ricocheted between ardour and frustration. I had exams to prepare for, too. I had to knuckle down at some point. I just didn't want to do it quite yet. Not when Maggie had finally let me in. When Eric left us for the peace of his bedroom, Maggie turned her focus from her brother and considered me instead.

I became Maggie's plaything. I was happy to have my toe-nails painted black, enthusiastic about flattening her curls on the Bellinghams' ironing board. She even allowed me to try on her clothes. When Maggie saw she could exert her influence over me and that I was willing for her to do it, we fell, like puzzle pieces, into a harmonious pattern and the prickliness I felt from her, disappeared. She became the sister I wanted so desperately, and I filled the gap that Eric's absence left.

One afternoon, when we should have been revising, she produced a large sachet of henna, a foul-smelling khaki powder, which smelled even worse when it was mixed with water into a mud-like consistency. She took the lion's share for herself and slathered it onto her curls. Because my hair was so short, I only needed a little bit. Eric had taken one look at us, our heads covered with muck, and muttered something about not wanting to be disturbed. As we waited for the henna to do its worst, Maggie started talking about my eighteenth birthday, which was happening in a few weeks. She pronounced I was a Gemini, which was an auspicious sign to be because it was symbolised by the twins, Castor and Pollux. This was a good omen, according to her.

'Gemini's an air sign, too,' she continued, trying to push a few stray strands of hair under the plastic cap we were required to wear while we waited for the dye to work. I had used some clingfilm pilfered from the Bellingham kitchen and looked as if I had sustained some kind of terrible head injury.

'What does that mean?' I asked, watching her miss the strands entirely and smear dye over her neck instead.

She put on a mysterious face. 'It means you bring the winds of change with you.' With her hair piled up onto her head, covered in a plastic turban, she looked like a deranged sultan.

I giggled.

Maggie continued, on a roll, 'It's quite an intellectual sign, actually. You're good with language, and ideas . . .' She counted off my talents with her fingers, which were already stained bright red. 'And you're compatible with our star sign, which is Leo. So that's a relief.'

I tried to control my laughter. 'Are you serious?'

'Deadly. If you put the wrong star signs together it can be a disaster. If you were born a couple of weeks earlier, your star sign would have been Taurus.' Her eyebrows raised in alarm and her plastic cap crinkled loudly.

'I have no idea what you're talking about,' I said, amused.

'Taurus and Leo are both fixed signs, which only means one thing,' she said, her eyes rolling with impatience.

'What?'

'Stubbornness. There'd be no compromise in the friendship. Taurus can be picky, and Leo hates to be criticised, so . . .' She shrugged her shoulders as if I could guess the rest. 'Leos are natural leaders. That's why I'm so good at sport. We don't like losing. We have to win at all costs.'

'You're totally sucked into it all, aren't you?'

Maggie ignored me. 'Gemini is mutable, which means you're flexible. So you act as a buffer between me and Eric. There's no way I would have let him introduce us if you were a fixed sign, like Taurus or Scorpio.'

I liked the idea that I played a mystic role in their relationship. I didn't believe any of the zodiac stuff Maggie seemed so interested in, but I knew I would have been disappointed if my birth date had been inauspicious.

When the time came to rinse off the henna, Maggie went first. She took the plastic cap off and, leaning over the bathtub, rinsed the red out of her hair. When she finished, the bathroom looked like a murder scene, but when she dried her hair with a towel and held up her curls to the light, they remained resolutely brown.

'What a waste of time!' she moaned. 'OK, you next.' She unwrapped my head like a slap-dash nurse and rinsed my hair clean. When I was allowed to look in the mirror, my hair had changed to a dazzling, fiery red, which would stain every towel in my parents' house for weeks to come.

'I look like a human matchstick,' I said, unimpressed at my reflection.

'Who would have thought it? You look brilliant,' Maggie insisted, looking crestfallen.

Chapter
Twenty-Three

My birthday was usually a day like any other. I was in a different school almost every year and because it always landed during term time, I went to school, told nobody, came home, and had a nice meal somewhere with my parents. This didn't happen in 1995. It was a Friday when I finally turned eighteen, and my hair colour was still defiantly red. We had just begun our exams and were in sore need of a distraction. I went to school and followed Eric home, as I always did. For once, Maggie was waiting for us.

'Happy birthday!' she sang as we opened the door. 'I didn't have an exam this afternoon, so I came home early and made you something.'

She pulled me into the kitchen, not giving me a chance to take off my shoes or put down my bag and, with a flourish, revealed a birthday cake on the table. It was lopsided. She hadn't made enough icing to cover the sponge, it was thinning in patches and the birthday message on the top started off confidently and ended up with all the letters struggling for space at the bottom. It read: *Happy 18th Birthday Eliza! Our third twin!*

For a second, I thought I might cry. 'I love it,' I said, meaning every word. It was the most thoughtful thing anyone had done for me in a long time.

'Mum and Dad said we could have a fire in the garden. We can roast marshmallows and sausages.' She jumped up and down, clapping her hands like an excited toddler. 'Come on.'

Eric built the fire. We cooked sausages, badly, and ate them in floury buns. We sat on old striped deckchairs, faded with the sun of many summers, wrapping ourselves in sleeping bags when it grew cold. Maggie stole a few cans of cider from her father's stash, and we drank as the flames danced and then settled to embers, watching the stars come out, one by one. The fact that our summer was about to begin filled me with a rush of happiness I had not experienced for years. If I could freeze a moment in time, it would have been that evening with Maggie and Eric, our heads tilted to the heavens, talking about what we would do together after the exams had finished.

'I need a wee,' Maggie finally announced, throwing her empty can into the fire. She struggled to get out of the deckchair and giggled. We were all feeling the effects of the cider. Eric and I watched her zigzag down the lawn and into the house.

'I almost forgot,' he said and he, too, struggled to get out of his deckchair. 'I bought you something.' He fished in his pocket and pulled out a little box. It was covered in silver paper, neatly turned at the edges.

I put down my can of cider, my heart beating with the strangeness of it all and unwrapped it. It was a silver pendant on a silver chain. It swung in my hands in front of the firelight like a hypnotist's pendulum. I caught the pendant and examined it. It was detailed and beautifully crafted.

'It's the twins, Castor and Pollux. Because you're a Gemini.'

It was heavy. The twins stood out in relief, their zodiac sign beneath their feet. I looked up at him, certain Maggie had had nothing to do with this gift. She would have been bursting to show it to me. 'It's lovely,' I whispered, and all the feelings I had squashed down over the past few months suddenly resurfaced with an intensity that made it hard to speak.

'Here, let me put it on.' He knelt down, gently took the pendant from me and undid the clasp. Then he motioned for me to unwrap the sleeping bag from my shoulders and he leaned in towards me and fastened the chain around my neck. But before he stood back up again, he caught the pendant in his fingers and looked at it, as if he was studying it for the first time. Then he looked right into my eyes, still holding the pendant, and kissed me softly on my mouth. 'Happy birthday, Eliza,' he murmured.

For a moment, it seemed the most natural thing in the world, to be kissed by one of your best friends on your birthday. But then, the realisation of what was happening overtook everything. The feeling of his mouth on mine stayed with me. I felt gloriously drunk, not from the cider, but from something else, something I had never tasted before. A reckless sensation snaked its way through me, the feeling of standing on a precipice, convinced I could fly. But as he drew away, I saw something in his face and the line we had crossed suddenly materialised. Before we could talk about it, Maggie returned with more cans of cider.

'What are you two . . . oh what's that?' She looked at the torn silver paper on the grass in front of me.

Eric took a can from her and threw the paper onto the fire. 'I bought Eliza a birthday present.' He paused. 'From the two of us,' he added.

'Can I see?' she asked, a smile on her face that didn't reach her eyes.

'Sure.' I held up the pendant and she leaned into me, a mirror of Eric only moments before.

'It's beautiful. Where did you get that from?' She turned to him and straightened up. Suddenly I felt as if I wasn't there anymore, that I had vanished, and they were having a conversation only between themselves.

'I went into London last week, when you were out with Mum.'

'You should tell me how much it cost so I can give you half,' she said, a brittle note in her voice. 'It can't have been cheap.'

'It's fine. My treat.'

The conversation between them ended, and suddenly I was back in their company again. But something permanent had changed. I worried Maggie had seen us kissing from the kitchen window. Our profiles would have been visible with the firelight behind us. I worried that Eric regretted what he had done; unsure, in the cold and sober light of day, if I had misinterpreted his desire. But I didn't regret any of it. I could still smell him on me, days later, that citrus scent mixed with woodsmoke. I treasured that memory, and I held it to myself like a warm spark when the light went out of my life, several weeks later.

Chapter
Twenty-Four

I open my eyes, long enough to understand I'm in a hospital ward. As I lie here, drifting in and out of sleep, I can sense the noise of my surroundings: the electric pulse of a monitor, steady and soporific, the soft murmur of voices, the squeak of wheels against a rubber floor. And making its way through these noises, snaking into my consciousness, is a smell I recognise. It is out of place, a discordant note: a grassy, earthy scent, and beneath this, the bonfire stench of smoke and wood. It is a strange thing, to be afraid, and to be unable to act upon your fear. I am aware of a rising sense of panic, a notion that Maggie has been here, leaning over me as I slept, whispering into my ear. I worry that she followed me here and has been watching me as I lie, pinned to the mattress, unable to move. I wonder what she wants. Amongst the jumble of frightened thoughts, my mind detaches itself. It floats past the closed curtains of the bay beside me, past the nurses' station at the end of the ward, out of the building, stained and scarred by years of London's polluted air. My thoughts race through the freezing winter sky and they cross time and space, flying like migrating birds towards a hot August day, in 1995.

When our exams finished in June, the sun began to shine in earnest, like a reward. But by August the temperature in our village soared beyond the twenties and well into the thirties. Nobody could remember the last time it rained. All I thought about was water. I wanted to be showered with it, I wanted to float in it. I wanted to drink it, freeze it, and eat it. School was officially over. I would never again have to enter a classroom as an interloper. My house was almost finished, too. My parents were already prospecting for the next place to work on. Even though I could have invited Maggie and Eric to my place, the habit of living at the Bellinghams had hardened and set. Every morning, I woke up, and went over there, often for breakfast. Maggie had taken to leaving me a key under the dark green pot in the porch so I could let myself in. Eventually, the twins would wake and come downstairs, dumb with sleep, while I was impatient to begin the day.

It was during these mornings, around their kitchen table, that we discussed what to do with the acres of time we had on our hands until results day at the end of August. None of us could drive. The heatwave did not make London, less than an hour away by train, very attractive. Nobody had any money to spend anyway.

'We should have a project,' I said. 'We should work on something over the summer.'

'What, like your parents you mean? My room could do with a paint,' Eric mused.

'We are not going to provide free labour to decorate your room, Eric,' Maggie replied, tartly.

'No, not like that,' I said, an idea forming in my head.

My place as Eric and Maggie's friend was undeniable, but I would always be second best because I wasn't their sibling, and this thought stayed with me no matter how hard I tried to ignore it. I may have looked more like Eric than Maggie did, but I knew looks were deceiving. They had a shared past that spanned almost eighteen years. I was desperate to find a way to forge a history that included me.

Things between the three of us had been a little strained since my birthday. Nobody had dared mention the kiss Eric and I had shared, but the centre of Maggie had hardened once more, and I felt the rejection as a force, subtly pushing me away. I began to regret that kiss, because by now I was as much under Maggie's thrall as I was Eric's.

'Let's do a ritual,' I said, thinking hard. 'A ceremony. To bind us together.'

'What sort of ceremony?' Maggie looked suspicious.

'Well, I'm not sure,' I said, trying to figure it out, 'maybe we could complete a set of trials or something over the summer . . .'

'Like Jason and the Argonauts!' interrupted Eric, who was a fan of Greek mythology.

'Or we could find some buried treasure,' said Maggie, animated.

'That might be difficult to arrange,' I countered. 'But we could set tasks for one another to complete . . . puzzles.'

'Dares,' Maggie said, warming to the idea.

'Yes,' Eric said, sounding enthusiastic. 'We have to complete a set of dares.'

'You can't say no.' Maggie banged the table. 'It's not allowed. You have to try.'

'They should be difficult and dangerous . . .' Eric added.

' . . . but achievable,' I concluded. 'A summer of dares.'

'A summer of dares!' squealed Maggie, delighted, performing a drum roll with her fists on the table.

'We have to have rules,' I said. 'So it's fair.'

Eric thought about it. 'You can refuse a dare. One dare only. If it's too dangerous or scary or whatever.'

'Sounds good to me,' I said. I was too busy feeling pleased with myself for thinking up the idea to notice the mean look in Maggie's eye. I thought she had, perhaps, forgiven me for wanting to be close with her brother, but in Maggie's mind, there was only room for one favourite, one person at the centre of everyone's world.

She took to the summer of dares with a verve that unsettled me, but I wanted to make up for whatever wrong I had done. I let her pierce the top of my ear with a needle and ice cube. The brilliant red she had dyed my hair was fading, so she replaced the colour with a raven black. When she dared herself to tattoo me with Indian ink, I didn't point out that the risk was on me, that it would be my arm that was marked for life. I wanted to burrow into both of their lives in an indelible way, and what better way than to carry a symbol representing the three of us, forever on my skin? I suggested the three dots, three corners of a triangle, marked with equal weight. But when I washed the blood and ink away and inspected what Maggie had done, one dot seemed a little bigger.

Eric had easier dares. Downing a foul mix of alcohol from the Bellingham drinks cabinet, stealing sweets from the local shop. I can't remember if we ever came up with something for Maggie. She moved too quickly for Eric and me, too slippery for either of us to catch.

My dyed hair, the three-dot tattoo, and a dull metal ring at the tip of my ear. Years later, when I began to pull apart the pieces of our relationship and assemble them together with an adult eye, I wondered if Maggie was trying to make me into something Eric didn't recognise, or if she was simply branding me as her own.

Chapter
Twenty-Five

Iris enters the ward and there is a moment when she doesn't recognise anyone in there. People look different when they are laid out, vulnerable, battered and bruised. Iris has a vision of walking right past Eliza, or being told she has already died of some awful complication. When she finally sees the only woman on the ward with a buzz cut, she rushes over in relief. But still, Iris is shocked by what she sees. Eliza's leg is in plaster that goes over her knee, her shoulder is strapped up, one side of her face is grazed, and bruises are already beginning to develop.

'Eliza,' she whispers, the guilt snatching away her voice. She's not sure if Eliza is asleep or awake.

Her eyelids open, slowly, and yet again there is a sightless look about her, something that tells Iris she isn't here. That could be the drugs, she assumes, she must be on some kind of pain medication.

'Mmm,' Eliza replies.

'I'm so sorry. I had no idea it was this bad.'

'Can you pass me some water please? I can't lift the jug. I'm so thirsty.'

Iris sees how helpless she is and springs to her aid. 'I can see you've broken your leg. *I've* broken your leg. Your shoulder . . .' Iris wonders what else she has done. She could have killed her.

'Broken leg. Shoulder isn't broken, just bruised. I'll be fine in a few weeks.' Eliza sips the water.

'I feel terrible about this,' says Iris.

'Don't. It wasn't your fault. I dropped something and was scrabbling around. I should have been looking at the road.' A shadow of something crosses Eliza's face. Pain? A bad thought? Iris can't tell.

'Can I do anything to help? I'd like to do something to make you feel better, and me feel better in turn, I suppose.'

'Could you call the school I work in? Lucas, the deputy head, would be the best person to speak to.'

'Oh, are you a teacher?'

'Yes.'

Iris waits for more information and receives none. 'Right. Give me the details and I'll do that as soon as I leave.'

Eliza dictates the name and number of the school, and, in the jumble of her guilty thoughts, this interests Iris. Most people don't know the numbers of anybody these days, they're all stored in a mobile phone. But Eliza doesn't even seem to have one. Otherwise, she would have made the call herself.

'Is there anyone else I can call? A friend? Family?'

Eliza shakes her head.

'Your parents, perhaps?' This last question, masquerading as concern, is in fact a test to see if she can get a feel for Eliza's life.

'No. That's OK. My parents live abroad. We don't speak very often. There's no point bothering them with this.'

'Are you sure?'

'Just call Lucas. That's all. If you don't mind, I'm tired.' Eliza closes her eyes, begins to drift off, and once again Iris is struck by how young and vulnerable she looks, even though, if Carole is right, she must be in her late thirties.

'Sure,' Iris says. 'But . . .'

'What?'

'If you don't have anyone else you want me to call, apart from your work, I'm assuming there isn't anyone at home. Waiting to hear from you?'

'Correct.'

'Then how are you going to cope when you get home?'

Eliza keeps her eyes closed. 'I'll find a way.'

'With the best will in the world, if you can't walk or carry anything, how are you going to shop, cook, eat? Wash?'

There is a space of time when Eliza considers this. 'They won't let me out of here until I can look after myself. I'll be fine.'

'I wouldn't be too sure about that. This is the National Health Service. They need the beds. Plenty of patients get turfed out before they're ready to look after themselves. They can't afford to mollycoddle us anymore.'

'Look. I'm tired. I can't think about this right now.'

'I'll help, is all I'm saying,' Iris persists. 'I can look in on you, do your shopping for you. Otherwise, yes, maybe you're right, they might keep you in here until they think you can fend for yourself, but I can't imagine you'd prefer this over your own place.'

Eliza mulls this over. 'Yeah, maybe you're right.'

'Shall I start by bringing you some spare clothes? Something to sleep in? How long are they keeping you in here?'

'I don't know. A day or two perhaps?'

'That sounds a bit optimistic. Your shoulder needs to be able to take the weight of a crutch, I imagine. Hang on.' Iris waylays a passing doctor and has a forthright discussion. She doesn't mean to give the impression she is Eliza's mother, but they look so alike it is an easy mistake to make. 'Right,' Iris says, returning to Eliza's bedside. 'You're going to be here for at least two weeks.'

'Two weeks?' Eliza's voice is weak and full of disbelief.

'More if you can't put weight on that leg or use your shoulder with the crutch. You'll need toiletries, underwear, something comfortable to walk around in when they get you walking.'

'I hadn't thought about any of that,' she says, misery etching her voice. 'And my seedlings, in the greenhouse, they'll need watering.'

'Lucky I'm here then. I can do the thinking for you while you get better.'

'I don't know.'

'You'll be doing me a favour. Help me make it up to you. If they think you have support at home, they'll let you out earlier.'

Eliza sighs. 'OK. My bag should be in the locker next to the bed. My house keys should be in there. The key for the greenhouse is in the door.' Eliza gives Iris her address, and even though Iris already knows where she lives, she doesn't say anything. Iris looks in the locker, retrieves Eliza's bag and pulls out the house keys.

'Your swimsuit and towel are in here, still wet through. I'll take them with me and hang them out.'

'Thanks,' Eliza says, in a weary voice.

'Do you need me to bring anything else? A phone charger?' she asks with an innocent air.

'No. I don't have a mobile phone.'

Iris silently congratulates herself on guessing this was the case. People with mobile phones don't memorise numbers. They don't need to. 'OK,' Iris concludes. 'I'll come back this evening with your stuff. Can you wait until then?'

'Yes. One more thing,' says Eliza quietly. She looks up, and Iris sees fear cross her face, like a shadow. It's brief, but it's there.

'What?'

'Has anybody . . . else been here?' Eliza looks vulnerable. Pinched and pale.

'Like who?' Several scenarios go through Iris's head. An abusive boyfriend, perhaps. The uneasy feeling she has had since she met Eliza resurfaces. Something is not right here.

'A woman. My age. Dark curly hair. Long, dark curly hair.'

'I don't think anyone has. I didn't see anyone as I came in. Are you expecting someone?'

'No, I just thought . . . never mind.' Suddenly, Eliza's face changes. She shakes her head as if she's trying to get a bad thought out and she relaxes back into her pillow.

'Do you want me to ask one of the nursing staff?' Iris looks around briefly for anyone she can stop and talk to, but there is nobody around who looks idle enough. She turns back to Eliza, but Eliza is already dozing.

Iris sits by her bed and looks at her bruised and sleeping face. Eliza is different when she is at rest. Less troubled, but not entirely relaxed. *There is a barrier to be broken there*, Iris thinks to herself, *a wall to come down*. She thinks back to her own life, in her twenties, and the walls she built around herself. How the pond, and the women who swam in it, made them fall away. Well, maybe not all of them. There are still a couple of things she doesn't discuss with Carole. Carole might be shocked. But nothing shocks Iris anymore.

As Iris makes her way home from the hospital, she wonders, half seriously, if the pond has conspired for them to meet. Carole has always maintained that the pond has its own form of magic and Iris didn't believe her until she experienced it for herself. There is, after all, a long tradition of water being revered for its healing properties.

Carole once explained to her the importance of the ecosystem that keeps the pond alive, from the enormous swan mussels filtering water at the bottom, to the boatmen skimming across the surface, keeping the algae at bay. Iris had never thought of the pond being a living thing before, but after Carole explained the delicate balance that had to be struck in order for life to thrive, Iris began to think of the pond having its own personality, its own agenda. She began to speculate if the women who swam there were also part of the pond's ecosystem, a small but vital component of something much bigger and more important. Now, as she walks through the dark streets to where her car is parked, she wonders that, if one of the women in that ecosystem was weak, and another was able to lend her strength, the pond might contrive somehow to bring the two together.

Chapter
Twenty-Six

I hear Iris's footsteps retreat from the ward, and I allow myself to be submerged once more into the ambient sounds of the hospital. I hear the chatter of other visitors wash over me, the plastic crackle of bags as gifts are unloaded and treats are shared out. I hear whispered goodbyes, promises to come back, kisses landing on papery cheeks. I want to stay here, cocooned in cheerful murmurs, but as the ward empties out, and the last threads of conversation fray and snap to silence, my mind struggles to stay in the present and travels, once more, to the past. My memory swoops towards the Bellingham house on a hot August day in 1995. It flies through an open window above a tall, sturdy tree bursting with leaf, into Eric's bedroom and a rare afternoon when we were left alone together.

Maggie was out, shopping for shoes with Mrs Bellingham. I savoured the idea of being alone with Eric and when I realised we would have several hours without his sister, I devised a plan that would allow us to spend the day, without many clothes on, in a confined space. The Ivydale pool house. Ivydale was behind us both, but I hadn't forgotten his remark about the key usually being in the door. I had tried to persuade him and Maggie to go there at the beginning of the holiday, several times, but it had never come to fruition. There was always something else to do. Now I had Eric alone, I figured I could wear him down. His resolve was so much more pliable than Maggie's, and recently I wondered – *did I imagine it?* – if his attention was taken up more with me than her.

'Nah,' he said, when I asked him. 'I don't feel like it. It's boiling and I can't be bothered walking all the way there.'

'We can take the bikes,' I pressed. 'We'll be cool on the bikes.'

We argued for most of the morning, but Eric was unusually stubborn, and my wish, that I was uppermost in his thoughts, dwindled. I so wanted to summon up the magic that made him want to kiss me on my birthday, but today, he seemed irritable. The day had hardly begun and already he had soured the mood.

'Is this because Maggie's not here?' I asked, nettled. 'Do you think she'll be upset if we go without her or something?'

He hesitated, looking sheepish. 'Yeah. She doesn't like being left out.'

It was a waste of time, arguing against him. We both knew it was best not to provoke Maggie. So we spent the day in his room, listening to CDs and reading magazines. I sat in my customary place on the rug, my back against his bed. He lay above me on top of his duvet. Despite the window being open, the room was like an oven, but I didn't care. I could feel his breath on my head as he leaned down to speak, I could smell his scent, that familiar citrus turning to bergamot in the late afternoon heat. We were almost a year into our friendship, and apart from the time I had told him about Tabitha, he hadn't said much about being a twin. It was only now that I asked him all the questions I had originally wanted to ask him about being a half of a whole.

'What's it like? Having Maggie for a twin?'

He thought about it. 'She can be a bit . . . suffocating some-times, I guess.'

I was intrigued. 'Suffocating, how?' I asked.

'She knows everything about me. She tells me what I need before I actually know myself. Is that normal?' He laughed.

'Don't you have any secrets from one another?' I assumed Maggie would have plenty of secrets from Eric, but that he wouldn't be extended the same courtesy.

'Uh, maybe,' he said, after a pause.

'What?' I said, holding my breath, hoping against hope it would be all about me.

He shifted uncomfortably. 'Don't tell her. But I keep a diary. It's the only thing about me she doesn't know.'

'What kind of things do you write about?'

'Never you mind.' He put on a silly, deep voice. 'My innermost feelings.'

'Do you hide it from her?' I asked.

'Course I do. She'd have it in a second if she knew. Maggie doesn't like secrets.'

'Where?' It was a test, that question. To see if he trusted me more than he trusted her. 'Where do you hide it?'

'None of your business,' he said, amused.

I was looking up at him during this conversation, and when he said that his eyes flicked involuntarily to the corner of the mattress. Later, when he got up to change the CD, I could see a gap between the mattress and the base where something had been shoved. I reached my fingers into the gap and, sure enough, I felt the spine of a book. I pulled my fingers out. I had no intention of reading his diary. It was enough that I knew he wrote one when Maggie didn't. It was enough for me to know where it was hidden.

Maggie arrived shortly after in a bad mood. Mrs Bellingham had made her buy a pair of canvas shoes in a colour Maggie didn't approve of. Always eager to look the part, to play a role, she had wanted white; she had a vision in her head of tennis and croquet. Mrs Bellingham had guessed, rightly, they would be ruined in an instant on Maggie's feet, and she had bought them in navy instead. Maggie flopped on Eric's bed, shoving him over to make room for herself so she could complain in comfort. I moved away from them to an armchair in the corner of the room. I felt sensitive about sitting on the floor when they were both above me. Maggie moaned about her afternoon for a bit and when she didn't elicit enough sympathy from either of us, she changed the subject.

'So anyway, what have you been up to all day without me?'

'I tried to persuade Eric to swim in the pool house at Ivydale,' I said. 'But he didn't want to go without you.'

Maggie shot Eric a look that I couldn't quite decipher. 'Really,' she said, rolling her eyes. 'I wouldn't have minded if you'd gone without me.'

I didn't believe her. Judging by Eric's face, he didn't believe her either.

'Maybe that could be your dare, Eric?' Maggie said. 'You could break into the pool house and have a swim.'

'I want to swim too. Don't you?' I asked, trying to keep the desperation out of my voice, feeling my idea being wrestled away from me. 'We should all go together.'

'Yeah, why not?' Maggie countered. 'A group dare.'

'The caretaker'll recognise me and Eliza,' Eric said. 'It's alright for you. He won't know who you are.'

'You've already left the school,' said Maggie with an exasperated note in her voice. 'What could he do? He can't throw us in jail.'

I nodded in agreement. Once more, I felt the seesaw of affection tip away from Eric towards Maggie and I think she felt this too. She gave me a big, beaming smile that bathed me in her special brand of light.

'We'll do it tomorrow,' Maggie concluded. With that, she gathered her shopping bags and left the room.

All the good humour that had passed between me and Eric minutes before, evaporated from the room and instead of feeling pleased I had got my own way, I left, frustrated. There seemed to be some kind of obscure law in the Bellingham house that I would never be able to maintain the goodwill of both twins at the same time. If I favoured one, something between myself and the other suffered as a consequence. It was as if our friendship was made up of a finite substance that moved from one sibling to another, like sand through an hourglass. But I cheered up when I thought about what tomorrow would bring. We would break into that pool house, and I would swim with Eric. Finally.

Chapter
Twenty-Seven

Iris has always wanted to see inside this little cottage. She knew where Val lived because she was famous, in her own way. A gardener for West Heath House, Val was a fixture on the landscape, kneeling in a flower border, or discussing the health of the many trees with a colleague. She was a fair-weather swimmer at the pond, before the working day began, and Iris sometimes exchanged a couple of words, but their paths didn't cross very often. It must have been devastating to have to give up her job when she became too incapacitated, thinks Iris to herself. She knew from Carole that Val was wedded to the outdoors and constantly on the move.

The Heath-facing rear of the cottage is secluded by a tall, thick hedge, like a castle in a fairy-tale. To gain access to the front door, she decides to approach via the main road where there is a gap in the trees she has never noticed before. The driveway is narrow and overgrown with shrubs. Iris wonders if Eliza has let it run wild on purpose, to deter visitors. Her little car has no trouble getting down, but she worries about having to back all the way out when the time comes. Sure enough, when the drive opens up to the house, there is not enough space for a three-point turn. She sighs, shuts the car door, and reaches for the keys Eliza has given her.

She did not know what she had expected to see, but it wasn't this. The windows, once the colour of clotted cream, have flaked and peeled until several other layers of colour expose themselves like a history lesson. Some of the leaded windows are cracked and smoked with age, the glass is dirty. Several roof tiles have come adrift and cling on by their corners. Others are missing entirely, slipped and smashed on the brickwork below. A wisteria, too large, really, for this small building, has devoured the guttering, the trunk is swollen and twisted with years of unchecked growth. Not yet in leaf and dark with moisture, it looks like a child has scribbled over the house in an attempt to erase its edges. Iris shrugs. It probably looks spectacular in the spring.

The key turns easily in the lock, but she has to shove the door with her shoulder to get it to move, the wood is distorted with damp. It gives way silently once it breaks free and opens onto a small sitting room. The house is as cold inside as it is outside. It's hard to know if that's because the heating hasn't been turned on for the day, or if it's always like that. She detects an unfriendly breeze moving through the room and sees a small window is permanently held open by a knot of wisteria, elbowing its way inside. Iris tries to close it, but the branch won't budge.

As Iris wanders the tiny rooms, she is struck by a contradiction. While the fabric of the house is left to decline, Eliza's limited possessions are displayed in an orderly way. The books on their shelves are in alphabetical order, like a library. In the sitting room, a pile of textbooks, presumably from her school, are stacked in a neat corner on a desk by the window. There is a laptop, closed, on the low coffee table. But there are no personal items, no photographs. Iris frowns at this, drawing comfort from the many pairs of eyes that follow her in her own house. Odd. The pictures on the walls look as if they are inherited from Val, botanical drawings of flowers and ferns, some historical prints concerning the West Heath, when it was privately owned and run as a farm.

Iris goes into the small kitchen and opens the fridge. The shelves are bare, save for a pat of butter, a few stray vegetables, and a pint of organic milk which will be rancid by the time Eliza returns. Iris's own fridge is crammed with bottles of sauces and marinades, barely used, and hard to throw away; things that were bought in moments of optimism, a desire to be adventurous. There are no whims in this fridge, no fancy flavours. Iris pours the milk away and rinses the carton, returning to the sitting room, which does not have a television, she now realises. She looks around in case she has missed it, but no, there is nothing, in fact, apart from the books, that suggests the occupant of this house likes to relax.

Iris makes her way up the narrow staircase, the stair carpet threadbare in the centre of each tread. The bedroom is orderly, the wallpaper shockingly out of style and peeling in places. Iris guesses that interior trends aren't uppermost in Eliza's mind when she closes her eyes for the night. She opens the drawer of the only piece of furniture in the room and pulls out what she thinks might be useful for a hospital patient. She moves to the bathroom and deposits a toothbrush, a face cloth, soap and toothpaste into a toiletry bag. Then, when she is done, she sits on the edge of the bed, the birdsong of the Heath straining through the thin glass windows and imagines for a few moments what it must have been like for an eighteen-year-old to begin a new life here, caring for her aunt.

They must have been close, she thinks. *Very close, for Eliza to have done that.* But Iris doesn't remember talk of a niece, or of one visiting when Val was healthy. If Carole's description of Val is to be believed, she would have had a child out there alongside her wielding a trowel, if one came to visit. Maybe they weren't that close, then. Perhaps there was another reason Eliza came. Maybe she was made to come. There must have been a reason why nursing a dying aunt was preferable to going to college. Because that's what most young women of that age did these days, wasn't it? It was a rite of passage. Something you did as much for the social interaction as for the learning.

As Iris moves through the house, she is more struck by the things that are not there, than the things that are. Where is Eliza's stamp on the place? Where is her taste? In this quiet house, it is the missing items that have the loudest voice.

Chapter
Twenty-Eight

The day I came to London was the day I left my childhood behind. I arrived with two things: a bag of clothes and a Polaroid photograph of the three of us, the only one I hadn't returned to Maggie. My parents had already sold our house. They were planning on moving much further north. They asked if I wanted to go with them, but I'd spent so much time looking forward to living on my own terms, without the threat of upheaval, I couldn't bear the weight of another disappointment. I thought about university. Despite the drama that had eclipsed my life, my grades had come back, and they were good enough for the English degree I had applied for. But none of it meant anything anymore. The idea of beginning a new life of self-indulgent study seemed preposterous. I have no idea how long it took the university concerned to realise I wouldn't be joining them. The details they had for me became obsolete. My parents never left a forwarding address for their buyers. Just in case there were repercussions.

Val's name cropped up like a gift from the gods. She was my mother's sister. There was a fairly big age difference and not much in common between the two of them as far as I could work out. We had stayed with her once. I remembered a camp bed squished at the foot of my parents' small double, listening to my father snore through the night in a tiny cottage on the fringes of some common land. Val's house was preserved in aspic. It hadn't changed since the 1970s. Every detail about it, from the avocado bath suite to the cork flooring in the kitchen, had a sense of history. The garden was well established and melted into the landscape beyond. The windows and doors were perpetually open. The spiders I came across in the bathtub were huge. It was everything the houses I had come to know were not. Val's house had a sense of permanence, a sense of place, something I had only experienced at the Bellinghams'.

I knew Val had been diagnosed with some kind of illness that would eventually finish her off, it had been discussed at length over our dinner table. Although they weren't close, my mother was concerned about her and sometimes there were conversations about what to do with her *when the time came*. There was the usual back and forth about the practicalities of looking after an invalid on a building site. There were ruminations about selling her house and using the funds to move her into care. Neither of these options were debated with any enthusiasm, the default mode seemed to be to wait and see, until that summer threw us all into chaos, and our minds, in turmoil, were collectively sharpened.

It was only a matter of weeks before my parents moved out, and I had choices to make. I chose Val because the idea that somebody really needed my help was like a safety line thrown into the sea of anxiety I now floundered in. Val was expected to last a few years. It was a death sentence for her. For me, it was a stay of execution. I had time to breathe, in a place where nobody knew me. I had already stopped going into our village. I couldn't endure the muttered words and stares. In Val's house, on the edge of a wilderness, in one of the largest cities in the world, I felt I could have anonymity, and with it, some peace.

In the end, it took Val ten years to die, and during that time, she and I had a good life together. When she found it difficult to walk, I pushed her round every corner of the Heath, making sure to tuck a pair of secateurs and gardening gloves into the pocket of her wheelchair so she could instruct me on some pruning the staff had overlooked. She taught me how to take cuttings for the greenhouse. I read gardening magazines to her when she dozed in the afternoon, and I cooked the vegetables she had raised from seed and fed them to her with a spoon. She pointed out the Ladies' Pond as I pushed her past the entrance during her last summer.

'I used to swim there,' she said drily. 'Don't suppose that will happen again.'

I had lost all appetite for swimming. My last contact with water had been the Ivydale pool. But hearing that wistfulness in Val's voice, knowing this was a pond, not a chlorinated pool, it made me get over whatever hurdle I'd put up for myself. I remembered what she had said, and the way she had said it. Val was very good at getting on with things and not complaining, but there was a wistfulness about her words, a gloomy look in her eye, as if she was finally coming to terms with her fate. A small idea wove itself into the fabric of my thoughts and I kept it there, a gift waiting to be unwrapped. I knew she had good days and bad days. I knew she couldn't walk very far. But on a good day, she could get herself in and out of the water with help, couldn't she? I waited, and one autumn afternoon when the water was still warm from the summer, and she had woken from a peaceful night, I wheeled her up the uneven path, an ancient canopy of green arching over our heads. She sat and watched the pond, remembering fond times there, chatting to one of the lifeguards.

'You have strong arms, Val,' I said. 'Stronger than mine.'

'I don't have anything to swim in, Eliza,' she said regretfully.

'I brought something, just in case,' I replied. Although my desire for the water had deserted me, I still had my swimsuit. At this point, I was willing to do anything for Val's happiness. She had lost so much weight we were almost the same size.

There was a hoist, recently installed, and the lifeguards were keen to put it to use. Between the three of us we got her into the water, and she floated like a lotus flower, buoyed up by a life ring looped on either arm. A pair of moorhens glided past her as if she was one of their own. She was thrilled. The sun began to retreat, and the lifeguards closed the pond, but they didn't ask her to leave. They stayed to watch over her, and she got out when she was ready.

Val died a few weeks later, and I comforted myself with the memory of that day. I wasn't a stranger to grief, so when it swept me up and threatened to pull me under, I took myself off to the pond again to remember the happiness we had both found there.

But the strangest thing happened. The more I tried to lose myself amongst the weeds, the more I found pieces of my past, buried in the mud, floating in the gloom, waiting to be discovered.

Chapter
Twenty-Nine

Lucas is sitting on a chair beside my bed. It is dark outside, and my thoughts are blunt. I feel swaddled, as if I am flying through the night in an aeroplane to an unknown destination far away, my emotions close to the surface, my sense of time slipping in and out, unable to anchor itself on anything.

'You'll do anything to avoid coming to my fortieth, won't you?' he says gently.

'What time is it?' I ask.

'Six,' he says. 'Tell me what happened.'

I tell him what I know, leaving out the fact I saw a ghost from twenty years ago, standing on the street as if nothing was wrong. As if she had never met me.

He smiles, although he looks serious. There is a crease between his eyebrows I hadn't noticed before. 'Nice to know you're going to live. You had me worried for a moment.'

'Don't be ridiculous.' I try to wave my hand in an attempt to shoo him away and a dull flame of pain ignites in my shoulder.

'Best not do that,' he says, with sympathy. Then his eye is drawn to my good arm, which is bare, on the blanket in front of him. What's that?' he asks, leaning forwards, looking at the inside of my forearm.

'Nothing,' I say, looking down.

'Is that a . . . *tattoo*?' He squints at it, tilting his head.

'No,' I lie, bending my elbow so the marks are hidden. 'It's probably dirt.'

He gives me a look, full of humour, that tells me he doesn't believe me. 'Best get a wash, then,' he says with a gleam in his eye.

'Thanks for the advice,' I slur, my words unwilling to do their work properly. 'Don't you have someone to go home to?'

'I'm married to the job, Eliza. Just like you. Besides, you're my work wife, aren't you? I could never be unfaithful to you.'

'I didn't mean . . .' I feel my face heat up.

He grins. 'I'm joking. I see hospital has robbed you of your sense of humour.' He scratches his chin in thought. 'Though maybe we needed to work on that before you got flattened by a car.'

I am suddenly filled with gratitude for his funny, unpretentious warmth, and I think of the seedlings before they got smashed up, turning their faces towards the sun. I realise it is his warmth I have been waiting for since visiting hours began.

'What's so funny?' he asks.

'Nothing,' I say, grinning like an idiot. 'I'm really pleased to see you, that's all.' My mouth feels as if it has finally woken up and is now running away with itself. 'It feels so weird, talking to you like this. I know you, but I don't know you. Do you know what I mean? We know one other, don't we? But not really.'

'Are you feeling the pleasant effects of the painkillers they gave you, by any chance?' he says with a smirk.

A small giggle escapes me.

Lucas laughs in delight. 'Eliza, I think you might be high. I should use this time to ask you stuff you would never ordinarily answer.'

'No, don't do that,' I mumble, another laugh escaping me. I am mortified.

'OK, calm down, I promise not to make you say something you might regret. Do you need anything?'

'No, it's fine. I'm just worried about my classes.'

He rolls his eyes. 'Don't worry about that. We can get a supply in.'

'I'll be back in school as soon as I can walk properly.'

He leans forward. 'Eliza, why won't you just take advantage? Rest up, get better.'

'Did you sort everything out with Noah Linzee? About him having some time away from home to get through his exams?'

'Yes. Everything's sorted. Don't worry.'

'He deserves a chance,' I say.

'I know.'

'*I* deserve a chance.'

'Everyone deserves a chance.'

'With the job, I meant.'

'I know what you meant.' At this, he reaches into his bag and pulls out a clear plastic folder with typed pages inside. 'Here's some bedtime reading. It's the job description. It's not set in stone. But I need to you read it with a critical eye, really think if you are prepared to engage fully with the level of communication that's needed.'

'I can do it. I mean it.'

'I don't doubt you mean it. I just doubt you'll be able to do the grown-up stuff. You're the most engaging teacher in the classroom. I can hear you through the wall of the stockroom. I wish some of that could filter into the staffroom, that's all. I appreciate how difficult you find that, though.' He squeezes my arm, softly. His voice is so full of understanding and sympathy, a fat tear rolls down my face.

I think of the staffroom and the feelings it provokes in me. I know it's ridiculous. 'I'm no good. I'm no good at stuff like that.' Suddenly the jovial atmosphere turns into something else, and I begin to cry. 'This is insane,' I sniff. 'I don't know why I'm crying.'

Without looking at what he is doing, he pulls a tissue from a packet in his pocket, and gently hands it to me. 'You're crying because you've had a horrible fright and they've pumped you full of happy pills to take the edge off. And I also think you're crying because you really care about those kids, and you understand why I'm reluctant to recommend you for a job you might find overwhelming.' He shushes me as I attempt to rebut his words. 'I don't think we should discuss it anymore, Eliza. It's the first week of March. Easter is over a month away. By that time your leg and shoulder will be better, and we'll start planning staffing for September. If you read the description and still want to do it, I'll give you my full support, OK? But you need to be honest with yourself about what your skills are, and what you're prepared to work on.'

I nod, miserably, full of embarrassment for being completely unable to control my emotions.

He leans back in his chair and scratches his chin. 'Look, I know things are messy right now, but they will sort themselves out. Do you trust me?'

I shake my head.

Lucas laughs. 'That was a stupid question. Of course you don't. You trust those kids, though, don't you?'

I think about the kids I teach. From eleven-year-olds who enter the school full of trepidation, wanting to reinvent themselves, put distance between the child they left behind, to the seventeen-year-olds who are still vulnerable and clueless, but more grown up in many ways than most of the colleagues I work with. I know that the emotions and opinions each and every one of them carries inside their young bodies are real, raw and unprocessed by the adult world.

I nod, another tear sliding down my face. 'Yes.' I whisper. 'I trust them completely.'

My kids haven't been tainted yet. But it will happen to them all. It's just a matter of time. I see them as sunflowers, growing in a field, optimistically turning towards the light. But I know from bitter experience that their optimism will eventually shrivel and die because there are consequences for everything that we do, no matter how small. The lessons I have learned came after I left the classroom: the more life choices an adult makes, the more consequences they must face. Life will, eventually, hurt them. Until that time, there are a few golden years, under the roof of my classroom, when they are in my care, and I can talk to them about the world in books, in the stories, plays and poetry we read together. We can laugh at the mistakes of others in the safety of my lesson, where everything is made up and reality is suspended, just for an hour.

Chapter Thirty

The ward grows dark and quiet. The night staff begin their shift, and I am afraid to fall asleep. I have been having drug-fuelled dreams: Maggie, on her doorstep, barely able to control herself. Maggie on a street corner, frowning at her phone. Maggie in my greenhouse, a rock in her hand. Sometimes my body jerks me awake, and I swear she has been standing by my bed, watching me sleep. I cannot separate reality from fiction, and I begin to doubt myself. Was it really her I saw, on the corner of the street? Could it have been someone else? I lie in my bed, pinned down by questions I cannot answer, sensing the scent of citrus in the air.

The consequence of that afternoon in 1995 looms so large in my head, I cannot confront it en masse. Little fragments pass by my mind. I catch them and turn them over, one by one, images I cannot make sense of. I see a silver necklace, sliding through water. I see a pair of shoes, upended in a hallway. I see a green glazed pot, tipped on its side, the umbrellas scattered, like matchsticks, on the porch floor.

Sometimes, I wonder when it all started. Did it begin the day I met Eric? Or did it begin when I met Maggie? Did it begin with the summer of dares? Or did it begin when he gave me that necklace? Maybe it began with all of these things falling into step with one another. A collective march on a road to disaster.

I woke up that hot morning in August so full of giddy optimism. I packed up my swimsuit, folded a towel into my bag. An area of low pressure had nudged the jet stream far north of England and it had sat there, stubbornly refusing to shift. The novelty of the heat was beginning to wear off. People complained about their gardens cracking up, the impossibility of sleeping soundly at night. As I walked through the village to the Bellingham house that morning, the temperature was already in the mid-twenties and the day had hardly begun. I saw the post office opening its doors and the paperboys returning with their empty bags, already sweaty from delivering the news. The landlady of the village pub was watering her hanging baskets, defiant in the face of the hosepipe ban; the smell of damp compost and wet pavement intoxicating, thickening the air. It took me seven minutes to walk to the Bellingham house and during that time I imagined the day ahead.

I entered the porch and stooped to retrieve the key from underneath the green glazed pot. I opened the door onto the hallway, still cool in the morning light, and I listened for signs of life while I slipped the key back to its usual spot. Mr and Mrs Bellingham had gone to work, there were no cars in the driveway. I ditched my swim bag in the hallway and did what I always did, I headed into the kitchen for breakfast. But when I opened the door, Maggie and Eric were already sitting at the table, scooping cereal into their mouths like an old married couple. A newspaper lay between them, still folded from the delivery bag. They had been talking in low voices and stopped when I appeared. Whatever discussion they were having dissipated as soon as I came in, but Maggie gave me a wide smile, indicating the bad mood from the afternoon before was behind her.

'Ready for an adventure?' she asked.

'Sure,' I said, feeling the sting of disappointment that it was Maggie leading the charge to the Ivydale pool, and not me.

Eric gathered up his empty cereal bowl and spoon and put them into the sink and spoke with his back to us as he rinsed them through. 'Maggie thinks it's better that she goes into the grounds first, in case the caretaker is around. If he sees her, he won't know who she is. When she gives us the thumbs up, we can go in.'

'Makes sense,' I said. Once we were in, it would be easy to see anyone approaching the pool house, but hard for them to see anyone in it. We would be really unfortunate to be caught if we kept our voices down.

The walk to school was coloured by a nostalgia we had no real right to feel. We had officially left Ivydale only a few weeks before but already we felt distanced from it. We passed the corner where Eric and I would no longer meet, the cemetery gates hot against our hands as we paused in the shade cast by two ancient yews. The air smelled desiccated and was hazy with pollen. We arrived at the school, following the low wall that cordoned the grounds.

'Stay here,' Maggie said as we stopped at the end of the building. 'In fact, sit down or something, you look suspicious hanging around. Keep a low profile.'

Eric mock saluted Maggie as she turned her back. I tried not to giggle. He started humming the chorus of 'Live Forever' and I joined in, singing the words as a whisper so we didn't draw attention to ourselves. Soon, unable to keep quiet for any longer, we dissolved into laughter, unable to maintain the low profile that Maggie wanted. Eventually we sat, side by side, our arms almost touching, our backs to the wall as we watched Maggie's progress, zigzagging from the toilet block, to the music block, to the prefabs, and finally skirting around the edge of the playing field. We didn't have a direct view of the pool house; we lost sight of her when she was halfway there.

'I can't believe we've left it until now to do this. We could have been coming here every day to swim.'

'She hasn't broken in yet,' he said.

'Yeah, but you said it was easy to break in to.'

'I didn't say that,' he replied. 'I've seen a key sticking out of the door if that's what you mean, but it's not always there.'

'Well it's worth a try,' I said. 'Imagine how cool we'll be, swimming around. We won't have to dry ourselves, we can just walk back with wet hair.'

'Yours'll be dry in a second,' he said, bringing up his fingertips to gently brush the top of my head. He did this every now and again, when we were alone, and it always reminded me of the first day we met, when he asked my permission. I glanced at him, wondering if he was remembering that day, too, but he didn't look nostalgic. His face was full of urgency.

'What?' I asked, my heart thumping hard. *Kiss me*, I thought. *Do it now before she gets back.*

But Eric dropped his arm and put his hands in his lap, staring at them. 'Eliza . . .' he began.

Maggie chose that moment to return, defeated. 'I can't get in,' she said. 'The door's locked.'

I fought the urge to scream at her to go away. 'Did you give it a good push?' I asked. 'Most of the locks in this place are ancient. It should be easy to bust. Go back and give it a good shove.' A feeling of desperation scrabbled in my ribcage. It was so hot. We were almost there. I fancied I could smell the chlorine from here. The promise of the Ivydale pool had occupied the periphery of my summer, like an oasis in a desert. I could put up with any amount of heat and sweat if I knew it would all be cancelled out in one, deep dive to the bottom of that swimming pool. I could almost feel my ears go *pop* as I imagined it.

'It's not an old lock,' said Maggie, in a reasonable tone that infuriated me. 'The building's newer than most of the others here,

there's no way we can break in unless we smash the door or something and that'll attract attention.'

Eric shrugged. 'I guess we'll have to do something else today
then.'

'Seriously?' I said. I stood up, looking at them both. 'You're
going to give up, just like that?'

'Well, what can we do? I'm not a magician. I did try,' Maggie
said, the beginning of a sulk edging her voice.

'Let me have a go,' I said, imagining me and Eric, holding
hands under the water so Maggie couldn't see. 'Maybe we can slide
something into the lock? Did you try that?'

'Well, no,' Maggie said. 'But . . .'

'Then it's worth a go.' I grabbed my bag and marched off.
There was no way a locked door was going to stand between me
and that pool.

Eric and Maggie followed, dragging their feet. I scanned the
buildings, eerie in their quiet. There was no sign of the caretaker.
When I finally arrived at the pool house I could see Maggie was
right. We would have to smash the door down to get through it.
The windows that wrapped around the building were narrow and
didn't open. I took a few steps back to survey the building for weak
points, and, to my delight, I saw the edge of an open window in
the flat roof.

'Give me a hoof up, will you?' I said to Eric.

'What?'

'A leg up. I'm going to see if I can get through that window.'

'Seriously?' he said, sounding uncertain.

'Yes,' I said, annoyed at his lacklustre performance. 'Come on.
If I can get in somehow, I can open the door from the inside, or I
can find something to open it with.'

'What if you can't?' he pressed.

145

'I just want a look.' I motioned at him to make a cradle with his hands, and he boosted me up. I used the joint of the guttering to gain some purchase and I pushed my stomach onto the roof. It was scratchy and hot and smelled of tar, but there was a Velux window in the centre, and it was wide open. I walked over to it and knelt down. The wet, warm smell of chlorine rose up to meet me and that smell alone doubled my resolve. I cranked open the window as wide as it could go, and looked in. The gap opened dead centre over the deep end of the pool, and it was wide enough for me to wriggle through. I contemplated the water below me, three metres at least, wondering if I could hang down and jump. Suddenly, I was gripped by a fear that the deep end might not be very deep, that I might fall in and break both my legs. I made a noise of frustration.

Eric shouted up. 'What's going on?'

I came to the edge of the building. Maggie and Eric were looking up, shielding their eyes from the sun, even though they had sunglasses on. 'The window's open,' I said. 'I'm just figuring out how to get in.'

'And what if you can't? You'll be stuck there for god knows how long. It's too dangerous!' Eric shouted up.

'You were the one who wanted the dares to be dangerous. *They should be difficult and dangerous*, you said.'

He shrugged. 'Well, maybe for me, but not for you.'

The annoyance I'd felt earlier now swelled into anger. It was the first time Eric had treated me as less of an equal. I marched back to the window, hot and full of discontent. I would find a way in if it killed me.

And then it came to me.

There was a much better, safer way. My father had something he called 'blank' keys. It was surprising how many people didn't bother leaving the keys behind for their garden shed, or the back door when we moved into a new house. Some of the houses we bought were sold through probate, and the sellers were relatives of the deceased. They often only had a front door key to hand over. Years ago, my father had purchased a set of locksmith's keys, most of which could open simple locks like the one on the pool house door. All we had to do was go back and get them. I went back to the edge of the building, knelt down and relayed this information to the twins. But instead of being happy at the news, they both looked fed up.

'I'm not going all the way home and all the way back here, Eliza,' Maggie huffed, blowing her fringe out of her eyes as she looked up at me. 'I'm boiling. Let's go home. We can do something else.'

'This is your idea, Maggie. I'm making it easy for you. I thought Leos liked to win.'

When I referenced her star sign, she scowled at me. 'Yeah, well. I'm bored of this dare. I'm not doing it. I don't want to spend my summer holiday in your stupid school anyway. This place sucks. That pool isn't even full size.'

'You can't just refuse the dare!' I said, even more desperate to swim, now I had the solution at hand.

'I can,' she replied, still scowling.

I wanted to slap her. But she was right. I was itchy with irritation. As I hung over the edge of the roof, my pendant, threaded on a silver chain, swung out of my T-shirt and eclipsed Maggie's face. I grabbed it and shoved it back under my T-shirt. Then I had another idea.

'Fine,' I said. 'Have it your way. But it's my turn to dare Eric.'

'What?' He looked confused.

I knelt back on my haunches and took off my necklace. I swung it over the edge of the pool house, so it dangled above his head. 'Remember this?' I asked.

'Sure,' he replied, looking uneasy.

'I'm going to drop it through the open window into the middle of the deep end and I dare you to get it back for me by the end of the week. I'll give you my dad's blank key. You should have no trouble getting in and we can all have a swim while you do it.' Without waiting for an answer, I went back, for the final time, to the open window. I dropped my necklace down into the water, where it disappeared without making a noise.

I didn't doubt he would get it. He must have known what it meant to me, that necklace. He helped me down, looking cool as I wiped the sweat off my brow.

'Well then?' I asked. 'Are you going to get my necklace back for me, or are you going to chicken out, like your sister?'

Maggie folded her arms and turned away in annoyance.

He hesitated for a fraction of a second, glancing through the horizontal window to the pool beyond. 'Challenge accepted,' he said. 'Now let's go home.'

Chapter
Thirty-One

Iris emerges from Goodge Street station and zigzags through the back streets that fringe Tottenham Court Road. The pavements are covered with spent cherry blossom, pink for a brief moment, before turning into a grey mush beneath thousands of hurrying feet. She uses her key fob to let herself into the building and climbs the stairs to the first floor. The reception zone has a vibrant red floor and there is a bubble-gum machine in the corner that Iris has never seen anyone use. The receptionist is nowhere to be seen. Iris walks into the blue zone where everybody sits behind a computer screen and asks where the receptionist is.

'Still sick.'

'Still?' Iris asks, incredulous. She has never taken a sick day in her life. 'It's been a week.'

Her colleague shrugs and answers a phone that has been ringing quietly throughout their conversation. Iris walks back into the reception area and sees a pile of post that has not been touched for two days. Iris knows this, because she is the only one to think about the post when the receptionist is absent. Everybody else is wedded to their computer. Emails are composed, case files are updated, phone calls are answered. But nobody thinks about the post.

She takes the pile, fastened with an elastic band, and goes to her desk. Because she has been there the longest, she has snaffled the corner by the window, and she knows there have been rumblings about who will have it when she retires. She sifts through the letters, putting the circulars into the bin. Then she groups the letters that can wait back into the elastic band for the receptionist to deal with. That leaves a couple of handwritten envelopes, the smallest in size, but in Iris's opinion, the best.

She has a special paper knife to open envelopes like these, and she uses it now, a bone-handled silver blade she found in a charity shop. It makes a pleasing sound as it slices into the paper and produces a clean cut just along the fold. With care, Iris pokes her finger and thumb into the envelope and draws out a card. A thank you, and a generous cheque made out to the charity. This is not from any family she has dealt with, so Iris makes a note to find out who the caseworker was, so she can pass it onto them. Even so, she takes a moment to read it, re-read it and absorb some of the happiness that pours off the paper. The second envelope is fatter and looks more interesting. She slices the letter open and clears a space on her desk, when she sees there are several pieces of paper tucked together. Carefully, she draws the contents out.

She can already tell this will be a new case. Most people email the charity, or call. It's unusual to receive a letter but it still happens. Some people don't like to talk, they're too distressed. Some people want to send supporting documentation. Others just prefer to write a letter, often because, like her, they are older. Iris wonders what category the author of this letter falls into. Everything is folded into the largest sheet of paper, which, she can tell, is a long letter. It's not handwritten, though, it's printed out from a computer. So probably not an older person, Iris thinks, her curiosity piqued. She unfolds the sheet to reveal the contents, and before she reads the letter, she is drawn to several photographs of a young woman, all of them photocopied onto a single sheet. The pictures are old, she can tell by the quality.

My goodness, she thinks, looking at the picture of a young woman seated on a sofa, *we had that wallpaper when I was her age.*

And then, the strangest thing happens.

Iris looks more closely at the woman's face, slightly blurred and overcoloured, and she realises she is looking at herself. She remains like that for some time, locked in a stare. Iris looking at Constance, Constance looking at Iris. The sensation is so peculiar, she feels a little sick, like there has been a violation of some sort, but she can't think what. She doesn't remember these photographs. She can't believe it took her so long to recognise herself.

Iris lifts her head and scans the office, wondering if she is the butt of some sick joke, or a misguided folly. Everyone is either working or chatting. There are no muffled giggles and expectant looks. She looks back to the girl in the pictures. That unhappy girl. She wonders why Constance has resurfaced in her life after so long. Iris unfolds the letter to see who has sent it, and it is not an address she recognises. The name though, the second name, is Danvers. Her own, married name, before she jettisoned it out of her life. But the first name means nothing to her. Freja. There was no Freja in her family, she would have remembered that. The unusual spelling. A Nordic name. Wasn't Freja something to do with Odin? Didn't they divide the dead between them? Her mind is a whirl of questions, all squabbling to be answered. Iris forces herself to calm down and begin from the beginning. She reads the letter slowly, so she can understand.

> *Dear Sir/Madam,*
> *I am writing to you as the daughter-in-law of a miss-*
> *ing person, Constance Danvers.*

Her breath leaves her for a moment, and all she can do is will her heart to quieten down. She makes a fist with her hand and presses her ribcage, trying to disperse the pain she can feel. Or is it hope, relief? She cannot tell. Before she can go on, Iris tries to absorb the information contained in that powerful sentence. Her son. Her baby. He has lived out his childhood, survived adolescence, become an adult, formed a romantic attachment, and married. He has done all of these things without her presence, without her help. She can hardly believe it. But why isn't he writing this letter? For a horrible moment she wonders if he has died.

She reads impatiently through the rest of the text, familiar with the circumstances of her own disappearance, familiar with a previous attempt, several decades ago, to reach out and find Constance. Then, at the end of the letter, she reads the reason this woman has decided to get in touch now.

> *My husband finds it hard to discuss his mother. I think this is because he doesn't know if she is alive or dead. The last time any attempt was made to find out, it was more than thirty years ago. Technology has moved on. If Constance is dead, it would bring my family some closure, at least. But if she is alive, it might bring about the beginning of something that I hope will benefit us all.*

Iris reads and re-reads the letter. She wants to steady herself with a strong coffee, but she doesn't trust her legs to bear her weight. This letter feels almost obscene, her secret self laid out, naked, on the page. And Anthony. She has tried so hard not to think about her baby, not to think about the man he has become. She can hardly say his name out loud, let alone read it. She scours the words once more for details, tries reading between the lines to get a sense of who this woman is and what kind of a marriage she has with her son. And there it is, the thing she had been avoiding, a proprietorial instinct, rising up like a bubbling spring. She knows she must resist it, this sense of ownership, but she is powerless. A jumble of terrible feelings come tumbling towards her: fear, guilt, shame. But through the darkness, there is a small glimmer. A flame that she thought had died out, long ago. Hope. She re-reads the words. *But if she is alive, it might bring about the beginning of something that I hope will benefit us all.*

Does Freja mean herself and Anthony, Iris's son? Or is she including David, Iris's husband, in that? Or does it mean something else, something Iris can hardly think about. Do those two words, *us all*, mean it is more than just the two of then, that she has grandchildren?

In the space of a morning Iris has been found by a family she never knew she had. But not by Anthony, the person she cares about the most. Her son has not written this letter, his wife has. She doesn't blame Anthony for finding it hard to discuss her. She never discusses him, so they are quits on that. But the mother inside her, that secret piece of herself that she has kept hidden from others, she is bruised by this. If Anthony had wanted to find her, he would have done so. And Iris can now acknowledge that it is his letter, his phone call, she has been waiting for, that she has always felt she lost her right to contact him when she walked out. But now, she can finally admit, she would have gone back for him, the second he reached out.

But he hasn't. And his silence says more to Iris than anything his wife can say.

Chapter Thirty-Two

They have allowed Eliza to come home after just two weeks, providing she has help at home. Iris knows Eliza has lied to the hospital staff about the level of support she will receive at home, and Iris has been complicit in the lie because she feels guilty. The guilt she feels about Anthony is wrapped around the guilt she feels about Eliza's accident. Since she received that letter, it's an emotion that colours everything. Keeping busy is what she needs. She can't bring Eliza home from hospital because her car is too low for someone with their leg in plaster, so she uses Eliza's key once more and spends the afternoon filling the fridge with food, changing the bed sheets, and making the house look welcoming. The little garden that surrounds the cottage is awash with daffodils, so Iris picks a few and finds a vase to house them in. She discovers how the heating works and switches it on. When the cottage warms up, the daffodils release their scent and Iris wonders, not for the first time, why Eliza hasn't made an effort to tart the place up.

Iris removes the sheets from the dryer and brings them upstairs to put on the bed. As she smooths the pillows and shakes the duvet straight, she sees something she missed when she came here last. A photograph, one of those old-fashioned Polaroid things. It is behind glass, in a proper frame, propped up on a windowsill behind the dresser. Iris takes the picture and studies it for a minute or two. This is not like the images she has in her own home, even though the shot is cropped to include only their faces. They burst out of the frame, full of life. There are three people in the picture, and Eliza is unmistakably one of them. Her hair hasn't changed at all. There is a likeness between Eliza and the boy she is posing next to. They have the same colouring. But something about the way she is looking at him makes Iris think they aren't siblings, or cousins. The girl to the right of the picture is a mass of dark curls. She has an expressive face, a generous smile, eyes looking defiantly at the camera, like the boy. It is only Eliza who looks away. All three of them can't be more than seventeen, eighteen. Out of all the photographs Eliza could choose to display, it is curious she has picked one from her school days, decades earlier. Iris looks around the room and contemplates the only other items of decoration: a watercolour of West Heath House, a photograph of Val with her parents, a pressed-flower arrangement preserved behind glass. Iris wonders idly if Eliza has lost everything in a house fire. She has heard of that, an entire past burnt away in the space of a day. It would explain why she had kept Val's little keepsakes and not replaced them with her own. She must have arrived here with nothing. Once again, Iris feels the tug of kinship. Eliza's situation doesn't seem that different from her own, thirty years ago: arriving in London with nothing. Since Val's passing though, it is curious Eliza has not felt that very human urge to wipe away what has gone on before and put her own stamp on the place. And then Iris thinks about her own, developing situation. She has no photographs of her flesh and blood either. Who is she to judge?

Iris is the longest-serving employee at the charity. The people who originally took her on and knew her personal circumstances have left. When the charity finally got around to digitising all the paper files, there was one file that Iris didn't hand over. Constance Danvers exists in analogue only, shoved in the bottom of a drawer, bound by elastic, in Iris's desk. Freja's letter has presented a dilemma. It's been almost two weeks since she received it and she still doesn't know what to do. Iris should open a new case file, tap all the details into her computer. But she hasn't, and she is still figuring out why.

Iris hears a commotion outside the window, and she turns to see the clamour of greenery suddenly parting to deliver a hospital van, gamely reversing towards the house. She gives the edge of the duvet once last tug and goes downstairs to meet Eliza.

'I bet you're pleased to be back home,' she says, helping her through the door and into an armchair that looks a little higher and firmer than the sofa. She fetches a stool to rest the plastered leg on.

'That was nice of you.' Eliza nods to the daffodils. 'Val used to bring them in by the bucketload at this time of year. How are things in the greenhouse?'

'Fine,' says Iris. 'Everything looks healthy. It must have been difficult looking after Val by yourself here. She was a sturdy woman as I recall.'

'She was pure muscle,' Eliza says, looking tired. 'All that gardening.'

'How on earth did you manage?'

'I moved the bed downstairs eventually. She didn't go upstairs for the last few months.'

Iris recalls the double beds on the floor above.

'One of the doubles splits into singles,' says Eliza, reading her mind. 'I threw it down the stairs, practically. You can still see the gouge in the wallpaper. It was a nightmare to get back up there when she died.'

'And you were here all by yourself? Doing everything?'

Something that was opening up in Eliza's face as she spoke, now closes. 'I wasn't all by myself. I was with Val.'

'I know, but still. It must have been a lot of work.'

'I loved her,' says Eliza simply.

'Very unusual for such a young girl to give up her life like that.'

A look of annoyance crosses Eliza's face. 'Don't for one minute think I made any sacrifices. Val was very good to put up with me. If anyone was a burden, it was me, not her.'

'I'm sorry, I didn't mean . . .' Iris doesn't quite know what she meant, so the sentence is left to drift. 'I'll make some tea, shall I? Or coffee?'

'Coffee, please. Then I'm sure you have things to be getting on with. This has been very nice of you, but I think I can cope from now on.'

'Well, maybe. But the floor of the cottage is so uneven, are you sure you'll be able to? Maybe I should make up the sofa down here? So you don't have to use the stairs?'

'No. I don't want that. I'll be fine.'

Iris brings the coffee on a tray, and they drink it in silence. She can't help thinking she's put her foot in it somehow, and that Eliza is counting down the minutes until she's gone. She takes the hint, loads the tray, and washes the cups up in the sink, staring out into the garden and beyond it, the Heath. But when she is drying her hands on the threadbare tea towel, something catches her eye. A Christmas card, open on the windowsill, its seasonal greeting and painted reindeer at odds with the month. Most people have thrown away their cards by now, it's almost March. Cards aren't kept unless they're from someone important or contain important information.

She turns her head to the sitting room, checking Eliza is settled, picks up the card, and begins to read.

Dear Eliza,

You know this is my first Christmas since Lorella passed away, so now it is my turn to send the cards. Unlike my wife, I am not going to pussyfoot around you and your feelings. One thing she asked me to do before she died was to continue to write to you in the hope that one day you made contact with Maggie. She never stopped wishing for Maggie's return, and she never stopped hoping you would tell us where she was. She died not knowing what happened to our daughter and I think you know more than you are letting on. Twenty years is a long time and I think you owe me an explanation.

If you don't get in touch with me soon, you can be sure I will be in touch with you.

Maxwell Bellingham

Iris looks at the message once more, commits it to memory. She flips the card over and reads the address and telephone number written there. Eliza has kept this card, despite its nasty tone. She re-reads it once more and tries to understand what it all means. Twenty years ago, a person called Maggie lost contact with her family. Iris's mind travels up a floor to the Polaroid photograph in the bedroom above, the girl with the curly hair. Then she remembers Eliza asking her at the hospital if anybody her age with dark curly hair had come to visit. That Polaroid must have been taken twenty years ago. That girl would be the same age as Eliza now.

Iris stares out of the window, not seeing anything, as the machinery of her imagination begins to tick over. Twenty years ago, she thinks, Eliza came here and left her life behind. Iris isn't in the habit of jumping to conclusions, but she gets the feeling that there are several pieces of Eliza's past waiting to be put back together, and this card is a clue to them all.

Chapter
Thirty-Three

As soon as Iris has gone, I can relax. I can't remember the last time I had company in this cottage, apart from Val, and although Iris means well, I'm not used to having people in my space. I look around the cottage, wondering what has been going on here while I have been absent. Nothing horrible has been pushed through the letterbox. Iris has been watering the seedlings in the greenhouse, and she hasn't mentioned anything untoward. There is nothing that makes me think Maggie has been here. It seems so long ago since I saw her on the street, I wonder if I made her up, if she was part of the drug-induced dreams I have been having.

I make a mental effort to stop dwelling on her and take stock of my surroundings. It's going to be a challenge living here with a leg in plaster. I stand in the middle of the sitting room, noting the seesaw camber of the floor, the narrow, daunting staircase. There is not much floor space to manoeuvre with crutches. I make a mental list of the things I need to gather around me, so I don't make unnecessary trips back and forth. My laptop, a pile of books to read. It takes me a long time to get everything, and I'm exhausted when I'm done. I can't carry much with one arm using a crutch and the other still bruised and sore, so I hang a bag around my neck and load that up instead. I am suddenly grateful that Iris insisted on leaving out some food and drink in the sitting room, so I don't have to go and prepare an evening meal. I look at the phone number written on the Post-it note, stuck onto the telephone. I didn't think I'd want to call her, but now I wonder how many days I can decently wait until I do.

I stare into space for a while, feeling sorry for myself. Then, the room fills with the familiar scent of citrus, and I know it is time to write to Eric and tell him everything.

Dear Eric,

You aren't going to believe this, but I think I saw Maggie, in London. I can't be completely sure because, as I was trying to get a better look, I was knocked over by a car and have spent the last two weeks in hospital. That's why I haven't written to you for a while. I'm back at home now with a broken leg, but I can't shake the feeling that she followed me to the hospital, and she's been watching me while I was sleeping. I know it sounds mad, and maybe it was just the effects of the drugs I was on, but other things have been happening here too, and they can't all be a coincidence, can they? She always had a vindictive streak. I'm frightened. I'm here, alone. If she knows where I live and she's still angry with me, I don't know what she might do next.

I should have told you this before, but I think your dad is very ill. He has asked me to carry on searching for Maggie – he never quite believed me that I didn't know where she was. I think if I manage to find Maggie, confront her, tell her about your dad, it might smooth things over a little bit. I think it

would make me feel better, to do something, instead
of waiting for the next awful thing to happen to me.

I wish I could talk to you instead of writing. I
miss you so much. You always knew what to do. You
always knew what to say.

Love, always,
Eliza

When I finish the letter, I spend a long time looking for any new Maggie/Margaret Bellinghams in London. There are the usual few I keep tabs on. The one in Croydon has qualified as a Pilates teacher, but now she's started posting videos of herself I can't imagine why I thought it might be Maggie in the first place. I search around for anything new, any changes that seem odd, but I find nothing. Then my resolve falters. Maybe I was mistaken. That woman, waiting on the street, could have been anybody. I was upset. I remember, now, Carole telling me off about the boundary rope, I remember the news about the pond closing, Lucas's lack of faith in me.

But the need to know overrides any doubts. Seeing Maggie's double on the street, getting that letter from Maxwell Bellingham, it has set me on a course of action. As soon as my leg is better, I will try and find her, even if it means hiring a private detective like the Bellinghams did. She may have been abroad twenty years ago, but people get homesick, don't they? People come back.

Suddenly, I realise the ache in my bladder that I've been ignoring for the past thirty minutes really needs to be dealt with. I slide the laptop off my knees and onto the coffee table next to my chair, and I reach for my crutch. When I knock it over and it falls to the floor, I don't realise the significance of my mistake until I am tasked with retrieving it. With a struggle, I heave myself out of the chair, my shoulder complaining bitterly at the weight it must bear. The crutch has fallen in a space behind the coffee table, and I realise I don't have the confidence to hop around it. After a few seconds of deliberation, with the use of the sofa, I crash land onto my bottom, my bladder protesting angrily. I bum-shuffle, backwards, like a demented toddler, all the time trying not to panic about how I'm going to get myself onto the toilet with my shoulder on fire, and there comes a point when I'm not sure what hurts the most, the pain in my abdomen or the pain in my shoulder. I reach the crutch, but the effort of hauling my weight up with one arm is too much. I wait for a few minutes to regain some strength, all the time aware of the pressing, painful feeling that won't go away. When I can't stay still any longer I try again, and it becomes clear I need to do better.

Crying with frustration, I shuffle back round to the sofa, dragging the crutch, thinking if I can get myself into a sitting position it will be a step forwards. But the effort required is Herculean. Eventually my bladder decides it can't wait any longer and a warm wet spread of liquid soaks the fabric of my trousers. The humiliation of wetting myself is absolute and the tears of frustration swiftly turn into tears of self-pity. Lying there, on the carpet, my jogging pants soaked and cold, my face caked in tears and snot, I finally pull myself together. I think about what I would tell my kids at school if they were in my situation. I would tell them that crying is helpful, but only up to a point. I would tell them that wallowing in a problem is counterproductive. The focus needs to be on the solution. It is only now that I realise the solution isn't me. I need someone else. I need a friend.

Taking a deep breath to control my tears, I bum-shuffle once more slowly around the coffee table until I reach the phone, which is on a sideboard against the wall. I pull the flex and catch it as it nearly crowns me, thinking Iris is a marvel for leaving her telephone number. I dial the numbers and wait for it to ring. She picks up almost immediately.

'Hello?' she says, and all the resentment I have ever felt towards her for meddling, for asking too many questions, for poking her nose into my business, all of it is swept away when I cry into the receiver, confessing what has happened. I can hear her picking up her car keys before I have even finished speaking.

Chapter
Thirty-Four

Mercifully, the back door is unlocked, so when Iris arrives, I shout for to her to use it and she can hear me through the window. I am still on the floor, still feeling sorry for myself, but my wish for Iris to be here far outweighs my desire for privacy.

'OK, let's sort you out,' she says briskly, looking down at me kindly.

'I'm sorry,' I mumble, embarrassed.

'If this is anyone's fault, it's mine. If I hadn't backed into you . . .'

'Let's not start that again . . .'

'No, you're right. Let's just get you cleaned up. Do you need me to take you to the toilet before we get you sorted?'

'No,' I say sadly.

With some difficulty, Iris gets me vertical and into the kitchen. She pulls down my joggers and underwear in a business-like fashion and throws them into the washing machine. Then she grabs the washing-up bowl from the sink and puts it on the floor, next to the kitchen countertop so I can lean against it.

'Stand in that,' she says. 'Just your good leg, mind. We don't want to get the plaster on your other leg too wet.'

I do as she says, and she gives me a wipe down with warm soapy water, handing me the sponge so I can wash above my knees. Then she wets another, smaller cloth with hot water. 'For your face,' she explains, gently, leaving it on the side. 'Can you manage everything? I'm going to go upstairs and get you some clean clothes. Any preferences?'

'There should be more jogging pants in the dresser,' I say, grateful she is leaving me for a few moments while I wash. The water feels lovely, even though it is dripping all over the floor. I wipe my face, stiff with salt and snot, and I reach for the towel she has left on the countertop, feeling exhausted, and dry myself as best I can.

Iris returns, triumphant. 'Right, let's get these knickers on.' She kneels on the floor and wrestles the knickers over my cast and onto my good leg. Then she does the same with my jogging pants. In the back of my mind I know I should be cringing, but her brisk, gentle manner makes the situation seem less mortifying than it is. I wonder if Iris has been a nurse in the past, and I am embarrassed to realise I know nothing about her, because I've never asked.

'OK, let's get you back into the sitting room,' she says, 'and figure out a better way to help you get around this house.'

'Thanks,' I mumble, relieved to have someone else in charge.

She helps me back into the armchair and disappears into the kitchen.

'Leave everything,' I say, feebly, 'I can clean it all up later.'

'Don't be silly,' she replies. 'I've already used your washing machine once today, I'm a pro.' She has a second sense for what I might want, making tea, delivering biscuits, and arranging cushions without asking questions. I feel myself bending gladly to her considerable will.

When she has put fresh bedding on the sofa – 'no arguments this time, Eliza' – she goes upstairs to find me several changes of clothes, and any toiletries I might need. I hear her talking on her phone as she walks over the creaking floorboards. Eventually, the whirlwind abates, and she flops down into the other armchair with a fresh cup of tea in her hand.

'I'm going to drink this and then I'm going to make you something hot to eat while you have a snooze. You look exhausted.'

'I'm sorry, you've spent the whole day dealing with my problems. I'm probably keeping you from your family.'

'Don't worry. You're not keeping me from anything that can't be put off.'

I want to give her something back to repay the kindness she has shown me. 'Do you have a family?' I say. Asking Iris about herself is the only thing I can do.

There is a brief pause, before Iris replies. 'It's just me.'

'You seem very practised at helping people,' I say. 'Are you a carer?' My mind flits briefly to Val.

Iris puts her head on one side. 'I suppose I am a carer, in a way, now you put it. I look after people at any rate. People in distress. Families, or individuals. No situation too big or too small.' She laughs.

Intrigued, I ask, 'What do you do?'

'I work for a charity that reunites missing people with their families. If they want to be reunited, that is.'

'Really?' My mind immediately turns to Maggie.

'Yes. No two days are the same. You meet all sorts. Keeps me young.'

'How long have you been doing that for?'

Iris lets out a big breath of air. 'Gosh, now. Thirty-five, forty years? A long time.'

'Wow. What exactly do you do?'

'Well, I mainly act as a go-between. Between the families and the missing person. I do some legal work for the charity too. Minor stuff.'

Suddenly the grey-haired woman in front of me appears from a different perspective. I suppose because I always see her in a swim-suit, or naked, I hadn't really imagined what she might turn into when she left the pond.

I try to keep my voice level when I ask the next question. 'Tell me what happens. When someone goes missing,' I say, still thinking of Maggie.

Iris gives me a look, as if she knows this is not a casual question. 'From the missing person's perspective or from the perspective of the family?'

I cannot return her gaze. 'From the family. How do they find the person who's missing, for example?'

Iris's tone is cautious. 'Well, they don't always, and that's the sad fact. Did you know the police receive a call about a missing person once every ninety seconds?' she asks me.

'No. That's a lot of missing people.'

'Well. They aren't always missing of course, some of them turn up within the day. But some people are never reported missing at all. Those are the people I feel sorry for.' Iris smiles thinly. 'The people who aren't missed.'

'It must be rewarding when you find a person though.'

'Well, that depends. Sometimes a missing person contacts us to tell us they don't actually want to be found. That's when it gets complicated. When their family want to find them, but the person who left doesn't want to know.'

I wonder if Iris has a sixth sense for these things, that she can read minds. 'Don't they always want to be left alone?' I say, care-fully. 'I mean, why would they leave in the first place if they wanted to be found?'

'There are plenty of reasons why a person leaves home. Some people genuinely think their families will be better off without

167

them. Some of them are most definitely better off without their families.'

'Oh, I hadn't thought about it like that.'

'Yeah. You have to watch the coercive controllers, they're devious. Like butter wouldn't melt.' Iris gives a dry laugh.

I consider my next question. 'What about the people who do want to be found? How do you find them?'

'Well, we don't actually go out looking for people with a torch and walkie-talkie, you understand. We put their photo onto a poster, and we place the posters in busy areas where lots of people might see it. We do it digitally too, and the posters go onto social media. Very often it's the missing person who calls us themselves.'

'Really?' I ask in surprise, finally looking up at her.

'Yeah. A lot of them are absolutely gobsmacked their families have gone to the effort. They assume everyone's delighted they've left. That's nice when that happens.'

'So, they phone you up, say they've seen the poster, then what? They just go home?'

'No. It's a bit more tricky than you might think. The feeling on either side, the family left behind, and the missing person, they're rarely in sync.' At this, Iris holds her hands out as if she's weighing up oranges. 'You have to level them up so they're both on the same page before they meet. Otherwise it could be a disaster.'

'Like how?'

'Well. Sometimes people go missing for a long time. The family who wanted to find them eventually moves on. But often, the missing person doesn't. They're still the same person, full of regret, self-recrimination, all of those horrible feelings that made them leave in the first place. So, when you find them, they don't fit back into the family anymore. Not in the way they did before.'

'I don't really understand.'

'Well. Here's an example . . .' Iris tells me about a couple she has been dealing with recently, about the disconnect between them that must be smoothed out. She explains she is about to facilitate a meeting between the husband and wife at the charity, in a neutral space, where a counsellor will be in the room with them to help them communicate with one another. 'The emotional adjustment is enormous,' Iris concludes.

'Yeah, I can see that might be tricky.'

'That feeling of inadequacy, that you failed somehow, it never quite leaves you,' Iris says. Her voice drops to a whisper, and she has an odd look on her face. 'Always, in the back of your mind, you're thinking, *They've done fine without me. Why would they want me back?*'

'But how can you know, really know, what they're thinking?' I wonder. 'I can't believe it's the missing person who ends up feeling like that.'

Iris holds up her hand to stop me. She suddenly looks very tired. 'I know this because I've done it myself.'

'What?' I ask, seeing her in a completely different light. For the first time, I don't see the confident, brisk woman who just cleaned me up. I see somebody reduced, a shadow of what they once were.

She shrugs and closes her eyes, tight, as if she's gathering her courage. 'I've been that person. The one that ran away, and those feelings are as close to the surface as they were when I left home forty years ago.'

169

Chapter
Thirty-Five

Iris remembers the day, very clearly, when she saw herself on a lamp-post in King's Cross. She'd been in London for a couple of months, doing some cash-in-hand work that barely covered the room she was renting. She hadn't expected to stay this long. She hadn't really thought anything through. All she knew, was that living here, gave her the kind of space she had not had in her life before.

When she received her first wage, she took it to the supermarket so she could get some food and toiletries. She had been living off handouts and the dregs of what she had brought with her from Devon. But when she was confronted by the acres of shelving, with cash in her pocket, she found out she didn't know what she felt like eating, what brands she wanted to clean herself with. She had been so used to considering others, she'd forgotten what it was, to be selfish.

A mad thought entered her head. She wasn't Constance anymore. She was Iris. Iris could be vegetarian for all she knew. Iris might prefer Guinness over wine. She could buy anything, try anything, she wanted. So she did, within reason. She bought brown bread, something she hadn't been able to do before, because everyone else preferred white. She bought soft cheese instead of hard. She had always put others before herself. Her parents had instilled in her an attitude of subservience. She had spent her youth servicing their needs before escaping to university and making a hash of things. But that was in the past. There was nobody else to put first now. She was the only person in her life. The thought was terrifying, dizzying, and delicious.

She began to think of herself as a new person because it was the only way she could keep going forward. If she stopped for too long to think about the consequences of what she had done, she knew she would run back home and return to exactly what she'd been doing before, which was mad when you thought about it, because she had a nice house and didn't have to go to work every day. Sometimes she didn't understand herself at all, but maybe that's why she needed to get away, she reasoned, to try and understand.

She thought she'd done a good job of shedding her old life, but the shame of what she had done clung to her like a burr. She didn't make friends with anyone at the bar she worked in. She purposely chose somewhere that was perpetually busy, a bar so bustling she was run off her feet and didn't have time for the exchange of intimacies. She had done well to avoid that, so far. Until this. The most shocking intimacy of all: her own face, plastered over King's Cross for all to see.

Suddenly, her old world came crashing into the new. There, unmistakably, was Constance. She remembered that photograph, taken on her twenty-first birthday, a year before things started to go wrong. Two years before she left. She knew full well there weren't any other photographs after that date where she looked that happy. They must have thought it was important she looked that way, rather than find something more up to date. She looked at the text under the photograph, the telephone number and the large letters above her head, proclaiming to all and sundry she was MISSING.

The word felt loaded, wrong. She wasn't missing. She was here. On her way back from work. She looked around, suddenly aware that passers-by might recognise the woman standing next to her photograph and put two and two together. But they didn't. They walked right along, hurrying to get to where they needed to be. Nobody paid the poster any attention, so neither did she. She carried on with her journey home as if she hadn't seen it, but every time she crossed that road, which was twice a day, her own face looked out at her in accusation.

Iris wondered what would happen next. Would she appear on television? The radio? Maybe she had done that already, while she was sleeping rough. She waited, and the poster remained. And then she saw another one, near to the laundrette she worked in during the day. By the time she saw herself near her flat in Archway, she had begun to feel she was being followed by a ghost, but the fact that nobody confronted her brought her some reassurance. Even so, she decided to do something about it. When she cut off her ponytail with a new pair of scissors, she was conscious of a line being crossed, a physical acknowledgement she didn't want to be found, that she wasn't going back.

Over time, her old face became touch points in the geography of her day, and she found this strangely comforting. She kept an eye out for others, but none appeared. And when the face in King's Cross was replaced by something else, she felt a little sad. The weather ruined the poster in Archway, but the one near the launderette, which was under a railway arch, stayed for almost a year, until it, too, succumbed to vandals and vanished under a torrent of marker pen.

When the last poster went, it signalled the beginning of something for Iris. She became very certain that in order to survive, to not go mad, she must put all thoughts of her family out of her head. Every time she pictured her husband, her son, she screwed her eyes shut and pictured something else. When she had done this enough times, it became easier to not think about them, to block everything out. They were better off without her, anyway, and whatever sickness she had. There was something missing inside her. She was a bad seed.

No. She was sure she would never go back, and she knew she would never be found. But the number on the poster had seared itself on her mind, so when she decided to settle and get herself a more permanent job, she called it and offered herself up for work. Her law degree was helpful. Her own status as a missing person was actually an advantage. They even helped her change her name. After almost forty years, she had arranged for scores of missing people to be reunited with their family or to live independently, and Constance became a memory she barely considered, until now.

Since the arrival of Freja's letter, she has found it hard to push away the image of her son, Anthony, and the life he has built without her. Even when it became easy to look people up on the internet, she knew it was a rabbit hole she would have fallen into, a place she would never come back from. Iris has tried so very hard not to think about what she left behind, she knew it would drive her crazy with longing and guilt, so she locked the information away. Just like the file of Constance Danvers, in the bottom of her drawer at work. But now, it is the only thing she can think about. She is tormented by it when she tries to sleep, and when she wakes in the early hours of the morning, it is not her familiar things she sees, but the house she lived in, the baby she held, the husband who left for work every day. People at the charity have begun to comment on how quiet she is, how unlike herself she is behaving. Dealing with Jason and Nicola Riley isn't helping much. She knows Nicola is not going to forgive Jason as quickly as her children will, that things between them have changed. They will never go back to the way they were. Iris knows by leaving her own husband and child she has done a terrible thing and she may never be forgiven for it. It's all very well this Freja woman writing to her, but it is Anthony that matters to Iris, and no matter how many times she reads and re-reads that letter, there is nothing in it to indicate he wants to see her. She has rejected her own son, and in return he has rejected her.

Chapter
Thirty-Six

In the evening after Iris has told me her own, shocking story, I realise I had only looked at Maggie's disappearance from my own perspective. I hadn't thought she might say one thing, do one thing, but think the opposite. I never got a chance to apologise for what I did. Maybe Maggie would have forgiven me if she stuck around. By putting that distance between us, I now see how it becomes harder and harder to go back. She must have imagined everyone getting on with their lives, without her. But how could she think none of us wanted her back?

The next morning, after a night of troubling dreams, I wake up to a ring on the doorbell. I'm groggy from lack of sleep and painkillers. 'Hello?' I croak. 'Iris?'

'No, it's me. Lucas.' A voice booms on the other side of the door. 'Iris sent me. She gave me a key. Can I let myself in?'

Before I can think of a reason to send him away, he lets himself into my house and there he is, larger than life, dressed in mufti, carrying a toolkit. I pull the duvet around me and struggle to sit up.

'What the . . .'

'Stay where you are,' he says. 'I won't be long.'

'What are you doing here?' I ask, baffled and embarrassed.

'I'm fixing a couple of grab rails for you in the bathrooms. Iris said you needed some and I'm pretty handy with the drill.'

I am suddenly gripped by the horror that Iris has told him about my accident yesterday, but he shows no sign of knowing I wet myself. 'Aren't you supposed to be at work?' I ask weakly, but secretly pleased he is here.

'I took the morning off. I decided there were more important things to take care of. By the way, your replacement is a right old taskmaster. I keep being stopped by kids asking when you're coming back. Stay there, I'll get us both a brew. Have you eaten?'

'Lucas, I haven't even woken up yet.' I think to myself how Lucas never takes time off work.

'Great. Then I'll make us both breakfast when I'm done. Nice T-shirt by the way.'

I look down at the T-shirt Iris picked out for me. It was a gift from some students, long since gone, with a huge military-style insignia and the words *Grammar Police* emblazoned over the chest.

Lucas spends the next hour striding back and forth to get stuff from his car, and when he has finished mounting the grab rails, he tidies up and begins to cook breakfast. I start to see him in a new light and the resistance I felt when he opened the door melts away. Suddenly self-conscious, I thank the gods that I elected to sleep in my jogging pants, and they are clean. With less difficulty than I thought, I manoeuvre myself over the side of the sofa and grab my crutch, pulling myself to standing.

'Don't do that,' his voice calls. 'I was going to serve you breakfast in bed.'

'I am not eating breakfast like an invalid while you sit next to me, scraping egg off my chin.' I limp into the kitchen and collapse into a chair at the table.

'But you *are* an invalid,' he counters. 'A very bad-tempered and ungrateful one, but there you go. We can't have everything. This is where you thank me for the work I've done.' He puts the plate down in front of me with a flourish. Scrambled eggs and smoked salmon on toast with orange juice. I suddenly realise I am ravenous.

'Thank you. For everything. For cooking and fixing the grab rail. I mean it. Sorry for being bad-tempered. I hate all of this and . . .'

'And what?'

'And it's very weird having you practically break into my house while I'm half asleep.' I cut a triangle of toast and pile the eggs on top and shove as much into my mouth as I can decently handle.

'Steady on. We don't want you choking to death.'

The flavour that fills my mouth tells me this is a cut above the usual scrambled eggs. 'This is amazing. Where do you learn to cook like this?'

'My brother is a chef. He has a Michelin star actually. He taught me a thing or two.'

'I didn't know you had a brother.'

'You would have met him if you'd come to my party. Which was brilliant, by the way, thanks for asking.'

'Happy birthday. Sorry I missed it.'

'No, you're not.'

'You're an old man now.'

'Forty is the new thirty, so they say,' Lucas sniffs.

'You'll have to take up knitting. Or crochet.'

'Or gardening, perhaps?' he asks, his voice laced with mockery. 'I didn't know you had green fingers. That's a serious-looking greenhouse I see round the back.'

I slump back in my chair, feeling miserable. 'I was supposed to plant all my seedlings out. I've wasted two weeks being in hospital.'

'I can do it for you,' Lucas replies.

'You kill every plant I've ever given you.'

'True,' he concedes. 'But I'm willing to learn.'

177

'No. It's my job. Once I'm a bit more mobile. Talking of jobs, I looked at the job description you gave me in hospital, and I'm in. I definitely want to apply. My application form is in there somewhere.' I wave my fork towards a pile of papers on the kitchen table and his attention slides from my face to my arm.

He leans over, gently grabbing my wrist. I drop the fork and he turns the inside of my arm towards him, like a doctor examining a wound. He brushes the tattoo with the pad of his thumb, midway between my wrist and my elbow.

'Ow,' I squeak. He isn't hurting me, but his touch feels too intimate, so I snatch my arm away and feel my face heat up.

'Sorry,' he says. 'I didn't mean to make it into a big deal. I'm just curious, that's all. I don't think you've ever lied to me before. It feels like new territory, somehow.'

'It's just a stupid tattoo, I had it done years ago.' I sigh. Suddenly, I have lost my appetite. I feel as if Lucas has peeled something away from me, exposing a rawness I don't want him to see.

'Isn't that a gang symbol? Three black dots in triangular form?'

'I have no idea,' I say, pulling the sleeve of my T-shirt down to cover it, without success. 'Is it?'

An expression of fascinated amusement breaks over his face. 'Here's me, thinking you were uncomplicated.'

'Nobody is uncomplicated.'

He raises his eyebrows. 'Some more than others, I see.'

We sit and stare at one another over the table. Me, wary; Lucas, captivated.

'Almost forgot,' he says, breaking the stare first, with the smug grin of a winner. He puts down his cutlery and goes back outside and into his car and returns with a couple of envelopes. 'For you,' he says. 'Get well cards. One from Rosa and one from me. I would have taken mine around the staffroom, but I bought it after school yesterday, so . . .'

I open it, and I'm surprised to feel a twinge of disappointment that his is the only signature. 'Why would anyone else sign a card for me when I never do it myself?' I ask, trying to sound breezy. Gina, one of the drama teachers, is the unofficial organiser who always deals with cards and gifts for any staff member who is seriously sick, or on maternity leave. I know she would have started collecting money as soon as she heard, had it been anyone else. But I never responded to her emails in the past to come and sign a card, and I have never donated money to her collections, because, I can now admit, I am not a team-player, as Lucas puts it. It's hard to explain that my sympathies are always with my colleagues who are hospitalised, or that I'm happy for the ones who come back with a new baby. I just can't open that staffroom door and walk through that room, past all those people, asking for Gina. I have gone past a point of no return. To start going into that staffroom now, to start trying to break into their cosy conversations, it would send my heart rate into overdrive. The sad, solitary signature on this card is all that I deserve.

'Eliza,' Lucas hesitates, as if he's reading my mind. 'You do know we like you, at work, don't you? Your colleagues actually think you're OK. They just . . . they don't know you.'

'I know,' I say. 'I know all of this. And I'm going to try and change that when I come back.'

'Really?' he asks, doubtfully. But his face looks hopeful, and I realise I can't bear to disappoint him.

'Really,' I say. 'I started having piano lessons with Rosa. We get on. I'm going to make an effort. Not just with her.'

He throws his hands up. 'Hallelujah,' he says.

When Lucas leaves, he asks me to make a list of things I need fixing in the house to make life easier. I promise I will think about it. He lets himself out and as I hear his car reversing through the narrow driveway, I get up, slowly, read the card once more. I feel the prick of tears. *This must be the medication,* I think to myself. I haven't cried for years, and here I am, doing it twice in the same week.

I shuffle over to the windowsill to display the cards and notice the Christmas card from Maxwell Bellingham is not where I left it. I retrieve it from the wrong end of the windowsill and read the message inside. It seems like providence that the very person who has recently entered my life is somebody who might understand Maggie more than I do. She could also find her, I suppose. I think once more about what Iris said, about missing people often thinking they are not welcome. A bit like me with my colleagues.

As I look outside into a garden that is flooded with yellow and green, I begin to feel a weight of responsibility pressing down on me. Should I talk to Iris about Maggie? A part of me wants to, but I know if I tell her, Iris will need details, and I am not sure how many I should give away, and how many I should keep to myself. I glance down at my tattoo. Three little dots, equally spaced. One slightly bigger than the others.

Chapter
Thirty-Seven

Iris wears me down. She is like the pond in winter: you think you've found a friend, but if you spend too long in its embrace, you'll never get back to dry land. I am bound to her now, there is a debt in her favour. So when she suggests we begin walking together to build up my strength, I agree. My shoulder has healed nicely and I have mastered the crutch. We often walk slowly around the West Heath. I hadn't realised she knew of Val, and I am pleased to resurrect Val's memory with her. I show Iris the flowerbeds Val designed before she was signed off permanently sick, I show her the silver birch she planted and never saw beyond a sapling, now towering over our heads. Through this time, during our walks, our meals together, over cups of coffee and tea by the fire, Iris works on me, making me pliable like the willow branches at the pond. She softens me and bends me to her will.

Today, on the last day of March, we are sitting on a bench, our backs to West Heath House. The weather has turned, the sunlight is thickening and gaining strength. There is an old magnolia tree in front of us that Val used to love, and I still do. It stands alone, the sweep of grass behind it spooling down the hill to the lake beyond.

It is heavy with elegant white blooms and Iris and I both stare at it, drinking in its beauty.

'This will be gone soon,' I say. 'The flowers will be all over the grass, turning brown in a week or two.'

'Well, aren't you the optimist?' observes Iris, drily.

I ignore her. 'Val used to love it when this magnolia flowered because it meant it was officially spring. Which reminds me. They'll be removing the boundary rope on the pond soon.'

'Actually,' says Iris carefully, 'They removed the boundary on the Ladies' Pond yesterday.'

My heart sinks. I haven't been able to swim for so long. The removal of the boundary rope only happens when the temperature of the water creeps over twelve degrees, allowing us to swim the full length of the pond once more. It signifies the changing of the season, it's a marker in the year. I don't like the idea of not being there when it happens, that I have somehow missed something important. Yet again, I feel tears, close to the surface. Even though I am off my pain medication there seems to be some kind of heightened emotion associated with the accident. My thick layer of resilience has thinned to a translucent, sensitive skin.

Maxwell Bellingham is weighing heavily on my mind. The file he sent has been thrust into a drawer like a guilty conscience. I have lost so much time because of my leg, and I don't know how long he has left. Iris could be my shortcut to finding Maggie before it's too late. So I take the plunge and I ask her.

'Do you think . . . you could find someone for me? A missing person?'

Iris is silent for a moment. 'That depends on a lot of things,' she answers, finally.

'Like what?'

'If they want to be found, for starters.'

'I don't know if they want to be found, but you mentioned something about being a go-between? So you could, perhaps, find out for me?'

'You need to tell me a little bit more about the situation,' Iris says quietly.

'Maggie was someone I knew for just a few months really,' I say, trying to make it sound normal. But the words come out sounding trite, as if she didn't matter to me at all. It feels like a betrayal. 'She left a note saying she didn't want to be found. It was her birthday.' I give Iris a sad smile. 'She got her wish. She never came back. That's the top and bottom of it.'

'It must have been an important friendship, for you to want to find her,' says Iris kindly.

It is impossible to describe the significance of our friendship in a single sentence, impossible to mention the guilt I feel. Impossible to think about the drama that enveloped us. It bound us so tightly, it cut off our lifeblood.

'Actually,' I swallow, trying to get the words out, 'she's the reason you ran me over.'

'Really?' Iris asks, unable to hide her interest.

'Yeah. I thought I saw her on the street. I was so . . . surprised. I didn't hear your car.' Although that woman standing at the foot of the hill, squinting at her phone, looked as if she didn't have a care in the world, I know that would not, could not be true. Not even after twenty years.

'Are you sure it was her?'

'Yes,' I say, my voice flat.

'And how did that make you feel?'

Panicked. Guilty. Frightened. 'I don't know,' I lie. 'It was a shock, I guess.'

'Do you think she might have been looking for you?' asks Iris. 'Is that why you thought she might be in the hospital?'

'How . . . how do you know?'

'You asked me about her. Several times. You probably don't remember. You thought she was visiting you, and you seemed concerned you'd missed her.'

'I was so out of it after the accident, I don't remember that.'

'Eliza,' says Iris gently. 'Are you afraid of her?'

Yes, the voice in my head whispers urgently. 'No,' I reply firmly.

'Would you like to see her again?'

I turn to Iris and look at her, properly. 'Her father wants to find her very much, and he's ill. I'm worried he'll die before it happens.'

'How long has she been missing for?'

I let out a breath. 'Twenty years.'

There is a pause before Iris answers. 'That's a long time.'

'Sometimes it feels like a lifetime, and sometimes it feels like nothing.'

'So . . . you must have been eighteen, too? Or around that age?'

'Yes. There are three months between us.'

Iris shifts in her seat to get a better look at me. 'I'm curious that you are doing this for her father, not for yourself.'

'Well. He wrote to me.'

'The card in your kitchen? The Christmas card?'

'You don't miss much, do you?'

'There's not much to look at on the walls of your house, so things like that stand out. It's a bad habit of mine, looking at other people's cards. Sorry. The tone of that card . . . it wasn't very friendly.'

'Max has a lot to be unhappy about. He already apologised for the card.'

'Was it her decision to go? Or was she forced into it?'

'No. Nothing like that. She decided to leave.'

An image swims by in my memory. Maggie on the doorstep, holding herself together as if she might split open at any moment.

Iris considers something. She drops her gaze and looks at her hands. 'I have to be careful, you see. When I was very new to the job, I once tried to persuade a young man to be reunited with his family. I didn't realise that he was being badly treated. They were careful to hide it from me. It's a mistake I will never make again.'

'It's nothing like that. She had a good relationship with her father.' I pause, embarrassed. 'It's me that's the problem. I just want to find her for him.'

'What happened? If you don't mind me asking.'

'We fell out,' I say, trying not to think about the way things ended between us. 'If there was anyone Maggie wanted to get back in touch with, it wouldn't be me.' I despise myself when I use these insipid words. I cannot tell her I tore that family apart.

'But you want to get in touch with her? That's the question here.'

'I need to find her for Max. I know he wants to see her again, but he's given up.'

Iris asks me a few more questions. And then, 'Maggie is the girl in the Polaroid, isn't she? Upstairs, in your room.'

My mind drifts to the spring of 1995. The Polaroid was taken on my birthday, at the end of May. That week was unseasonably warm, a warning of what was to come. The temperature was a novelty, and we had been out in the garden, lying on the grass, eating cake. I had been gifted the camera by my parents. Mrs Bellingham, on a rare afternoon off, had helped us load the cartridge into the slot to record the day I officially turned into an adult. It was the first image ever taken of the three of us together. I remember Mrs Bellingham had posed us, bunching us together like flowers so our faces filled the frame. It was a good shot.

That afternoon, in the Bellinghams' garden, was a golden one, honeyed with sunshine. But the weather soon turned. Before long, the air around us began to vibrate with warmth. Nobody imagined how the heat would turn from something we welcomed, into an adversary; how the relentless persistence of it would burrow under our skin, driving us all crazy. At night, it became heavy and hard to breathe. By the end of the summer, it felt as if we were all under siege. The moment captured in that image was a moment of innocence. We had no idea that there was a ticking clock, counting down the minutes of our happiness.

Chapter
Thirty-Eight

Although Iris is used to being asked to find a missing person, she resists promising to help Eliza, because this case is more complicated than it seems. Maggie left a note, asking not to be found. There is something Eliza isn't telling her, and she needs some time to consider what to do.

The next morning, Iris swims in the pond before she goes to work. The trees are finally spritting. The mallards are nesting. The yellow water irises are beginning to bloom. Iris feels the optimism of the season course through her as she swims a full lap of the pond, now the boundary rope has gone.

Carole is sitting on a bale of barley straw and is stuffing handfuls into net bags as Iris emerges from the changing room.

'Isn't it a bit early for that?' Iris asks.

'The pond is so unpredictable now, it's best to get a head start. The temperature can shoot up without warning. I've known it reach twenty in March. Global warming,' mutters Carole.

'I thought that was an old wives' tale, barley straw.'

'It changes the acidity of the water as it decomposes. The algae doesn't like it. That's science.'

'If you say so,' replies Iris, amused.

'I do. How's Eliza?'

'Pretty good. Her cast is coming off soon.' It strikes Iris she doesn't have much time left with Eliza. In a couple of weeks there will be no more visits, no need for her help. Maybe that will be a good thing, some time apart. There is a complexity to Eliza she doesn't have the energy to unravel.

'That's gone fast,' remarks Carole.

'Well, she's young and fit.'

'You don't look as pleased as you might.'

'It's not that. She's asked me to find somebody.'

Carole raises her eyebrows, stops stuffing her bag. 'A missing somebody?'

'Yes.'

'Well, that's an unexpected development. Who is it?'

'A friend. From twenty years ago.'

'She's taken her time looking, hasn't she?'

'It's complicated.' Iris relays some of the information to Carole, and as she does so, she realises how little she really knows about Eliza.

'Are you going to do it?' Carole asks, resuming her stuffing. The net bags of straw lie, like supersized sausages around her feet.

'I don't know, actually. Something doesn't feel straightforward.'

Carole narrows her eyes briefly. 'You got into a lot of hot water when you encouraged that boy back into his toxic family, remember?'

'I'm not likely to forget, am I?' Iris replies, annoyed. She had no idea families could be that conniving. She hadn't experienced adults lying like that. She hadn't understood that children would lie to protect the adults who harmed them. Now she knows better. 'I don't think this is the same,' she says. 'But something's off. I offered to refer her to the charity, let someone else deal with it. But Eliza wants me to do it. Quickly.' She explains Maxwell's illness.

'Rather you than me,' says Carole, tying up a bag and tossing it onto the growing pile. 'There's nothing to stop you having a private look, though, is there? See what's what. If you don't like what you see, you can tell Eliza you can't help her.'

'I don't know.'

'Then don't do it.'

'No,' muses Iris. 'Perhaps I won't.'

Later that morning, Iris gets the tube into Goodge Street station and walks south along Tottenham Court Road. It is already busy with taxis and tourists. The shops are beginning to open and there is a lively crackle of activity as she cuts through the back streets and zigzags through the damp air to the office. She has always liked the journey to work. It gets her out of herself, makes her feel as if she is part of something, but today she is bone-tired. The fact she is the oldest person working at the charity never used to bother her, but her age is beginning to catch up with her and today, because she hasn't slept so well, she feels every year of her six decades as she makes her way to work.

By the time she swipes her key fob to open the door, her mood has lifted. As Iris checks her emails, she reads that the meeting between Jason and Nicola Riley has been successful. They plan to meet again, with the children, and if that goes well, they will arrange for Jason to visit the family home. As Iris reads the report, she feels hopeful for the Rileys. The buzz she feels from a successful reunion hasn't waned over the years. If anything, it has increased. Iris sits back in her chair and stares out of the window. Perhaps she is being unreasonable. Maybe she should help Eliza. Maxwell Bellingham is ill, and time is running out. She remembers the suggestion Carole gave her at the pond. She could take a look, do some rudimentary searches and see if Maggie's name has cropped up in the system.

The address on the Christmas card from Maxwell Bellingham was a village not far from London. Iris knows parents are reluctant to move house when a child goes missing, even after twenty years. It's more than likely the police referred the Bellinghams to them, all those years ago, and their records are kept meticulously, stretching beyond 1995.

She opens the database and types in the year. Then she types in the words *Bellingham, M* and begins scrolling down a long list of names.

Chapter
Thirty-Nine

Since I came home from hospital, over two weeks ago, I haven't heard from Maggie. I still dream about her, and sometimes I wake in the middle of the night, certain I can hear the splintering of glass, the sound of footsteps running up the drive. On April first, I waited all day for something nasty to happen. But the panic in my chest, my lack of appetite, was all for nothing. Perhaps that was the joke, that I am the fool.

Maggie is an itch I will always want to scratch, the monster under my bed. She is a splinter in my thoughts, and I can't pull her out. I told Iris it was all for Max, but I am beginning to wonder if I need to find Maggie too, to make sure she is not a ghost. To save my sanity. Restless and depressed, unable to swim, I think of ways to distract myself until finally, in the late afternoon, I decide to go to work.

In two more weeks, it will be Easter break. My cast will be off, and I can return to my classes. I could use this time to plan my lessons for the summer term. I could also see if Lucas is around and talk about that job. Anything to get out of the house. I pick up my crutch and my bag and hail a taxi on the main road.

The main entrance to the school lies at the top of a long set of wide stone steps. I have never thought about the difficulty of climbing these stairs until now, when I have a crutch and a bag and a broken leg. The main doors to the school are already shut, but I know there will be a side door that is left open for staff who want to work late. It is around the back of the building, where aimless children won't see it and saunter in. Sure enough, when I finally reach it and press my weight against the cold metal frame, it swings open, and I find myself, as I knew I would, in the music block. Practise Room B is only a few steps away. I tell myself I need a rest. The stairs have taken it out of me. But really, I am drawn to the piano, the memory of my few lessons with Rosa still firm in my mind. Now I have the room to myself I can practise what Rosa has taught me in the luxury of solitude.

I sit at the piano, my plastered leg at an awkward angle, and touch the varnished lid. The cool, smooth curve of it familiar under my fingers. It opens, noiselessly, and I feel pleased someone has remembered to put the red cloth back over the keys. I fold the cloth carefully and put it to one side. I spread my fingers over the ivory, and I begin to play the first few notes of 'Für Elise'. It goes well, for a few seconds, and I imagine myself playing with grace and confidence, until I stumble, forgetting what Rosa did next. My fingers falter as they struggle to remember, and I start from the beginning, like the amateur I am, playing the notes I know well, hoping this time I will miraculously know what comes next, until frustration gets the better of me and I finally have to stop.

Rosa taught me how Eric tried to teach me, by following the shape of her hands. I still can't read music. To learn it first was a stumbling block that would have delayed my prize. But now, I wonder if I should try. The Easter break this year is just over two weeks. I could come here every day and learn a little more.

Looking around me, I see the cabinet that houses the music scores, and I wiggle my leg to a better position, heaving myself off the stool. But when I reach the cabinet, it is locked and my enthusiasm wanes. After a few seconds of indecision, I decide to try and find someone who could help me. There must be someone with a key.

I hobble back to the piano to retrieve my bag, leaning down next to the stool where I left it. And then, I see a curious thing. A hinge on the seat. It is the same kind of stool the Bellinghams had, where they kept their music scores. I wonder if it is my lucky day as I open the stool, like the lid on a chest, and there, in front of me, is a pile of sheet music, yellow with age. I heave it out, close the stool and sit down on it, throwing my crutch to the floor in my haste to see if my luck holds out, hoping a simple version of 'Für Elise' is among the papers. Near the top is a slim volume and my heart jumps when I see the title: *Selected Beethoven Favourites For The Pianoforte*.

Too impatient to look at the contents, I flick through the book from back to front, scanning the titles until, finally, the book falls open at a page that has been looked at again and again, a page that has been folded back on itself, many years ago. I read the title. Not 'Für Elise', but an arrangement of letters defaced by a blunt pencil on an autumn afternoon. My name is there, recorded in carbon, as legible as if he had written it yesterday. *For Eliza*.

My hands tremble as I trace the name with my fingers, too shocked to comprehend. I hold my breath as the passage of time compresses to nothing, and I remember Eric doing this to please me. The world stops as I hear that particular sound of lead on paper, the soft scratching noise as he altered the letters. The smell of citrus fills the room, and I feel sick with knowledge.

If this is Eric's music, this must be his stool. This must be Eric's piano.

I wonder if some kind of witchcraft has pulled me here, to a room I have rarely entered before now. Since it arrived in the school I have found it hard to keep away from this piano. I assumed it was the memories it provoked. Now, I wonder if it is something more. With the score in my hand, I grab my crutch and limp around the school until I find Lucas in his office.

'You're keen,' he says, looking pleased to see me.

'The piano in the music block,' I interrupt, my heart hammering, 'how did it get here?'

Lucas sits back in his chair looking confused. 'I think they just wheeled it through the door.'

A noise of exasperation escapes me. 'No. I didn't mean that. It was donated, apparently. Who donated it?'

Lucas looks blank, shakes his head.

'Come on, you must know.'

'Someone in the music department should know. What's all this about? You look . . . odd.'

'Is there anyone still here? From music? I couldn't find anyone in the music block.'

'I saw Rosa earlier, she might still be in the staffroom.'

'Thanks.' I make to leave, and Lucas stops me.

'Job interviews for the pastoral role are to be held in two weeks. We have some strong candidates from outside of the school, but I have let it be known that my preference is you. Don't let me down.'

'Great,' I manage to mumble before I leave. I can't even think about it now, my head is full of questions.

'You don't sound very pleased.'

'I am, really. I am.'

'I'm counting on you,' he calls after me. 'Eliza?'

I don't answer, I'm too focused on getting to the staffroom at pace without falling over. I barrel into the door and the room is blessedly empty, apart from a handful of my colleagues standing around in the small kitchenette. Rosa is with them.

'Rosa,' I call, out of breath, and hot with effort.

'Eliza,' she replies, looking delighted. 'When does the cast come off?'

'Who donated the piano in Practise Room B?' I ask.

She blinks once or twice, looks up at the ceiling. 'I can't remember the name. They sent a piano mover to the music department a few weeks ago. I think whoever donated it just emailed to arrange everything and sent it over. Why?'

'Can you dig out that email? The one from the donor?'

'It's not dodgy, is it?' Rosa asks, uneasy. 'Are we going to have to return it?'

'No, nothing like that. I just need to know who donated it.'

There is a silence when everyone in the group, now fully invested in our conversation, waits for my reasons why. Before, I would have ignored them and pressed Rosa for an answer, but now I decide to throw them a bone. 'I, uh, recognise the piano and it might be a friend I haven't seen for a while, that's all.' I try to laugh. 'It's a crazy coincidence if it is.'

Rosa scrolls through her phone, looking for the email. 'Oh, here it is. That's weird. It's not actually signed by anyone. And the email address is corporate. I mean, it's a company name, I think, not a person.' She hands the phone to me. The email address, Info@lepetitchien, means nothing.

'Seriously?' I say. 'This is all you have?' I cannot keep the impatience out of my voice.

'Um, hang on,' Rosa scrolls through the email exchange between the music department and the donor. 'The head of music asked them to whom we should attribute the donation, and the sender replied that the piano was gifted by . . . hang on . . . here we are . . . Eric Bellingham.'

Rosa has not even finished talking before I instruct her to forward me the email. 'Are you OK?' she asks. 'You look funny.'

I stumble out of the staffroom, unable to trust myself to say any more. As soon as the door is closed behind me, I stand in the empty corridor, the music score still in my hand, unable to move.

Is this some kind of joke? I think to myself. *A game?*

And then I remember a conversation I had with Maggie when I first met her. We had been in her room. Eric was having a piano lesson. I could hear the notes of the music infusing their way through the air of the house, like scent. I hadn't known Maggie very long. We were still trying to find our way around one another. There was an edge to her I desperately wanted to soften. I remember walking around her room, admiring all the sports certificates she had won. High jump, first place. One hundred metres, first place. There was a hockey trophy, a netball trophy, rosettes with ribbons festooned on the walls.

'Is there anything you aren't good at?' I asked.

'No,' she replied, not looking at me. That week, she had come home from a hockey match sporting a black eye. Her face had caught her opponent's ball, preventing it from finding the back of the net. There was a get-well card on her dresser: *To The Lakeside Legend,* it read.

'How come you like sport so much?' I pressed, unable to understand what the draw was. Unable to reconcile the difference between her and her brother. Wanting to understand.

'Because I like to play games,' she answered, in a matter-of-fact voice. Then she looked at me, square on, her left eye swollen shut. 'I like to win.'

Chapter Forty

When I get home, I open my laptop and go straight to the email that Rosa has forwarded to me. There is no name at the bottom, and it is only when I read the sign off, I see the email address isn't gobbledegook at all, it is a French restaurant in Highgate Village, Le Petit Chien. I google the restaurant and realise I know it. I walk past it sometimes, and there is, indeed, a little dog that lies on a red velvet cushion in the window, watching the people of Highgate walk past with a disdainful look in its eye. There is a photograph of the proprietor on the website, a busty woman with a shade of lipstick that is too loud and doesn't suit her. But no photograph of Maggie. Even so, she must be there.

'No time like the present,' I mutter to myself, hailing another taxi and giving the address. As the car closes the gap between my place of comfort and a sea of uncertainty, I start panicking about what will happen when I get there. If the piano was donated by Maggie, and the lotus flower was left by her, it means she has been roaming the school corridors, tormenting me. Why hasn't she confronted me? Why leave me cryptic messages buried in objects? Objects, she knows, that hold a certain kind of darkness for me.

When the taxi pulls up, and I am no further deciding what I will say to her, I get out, pay, and see that the restaurant is not open. A flood of relief courses through me. I don't have to confront

Maggie today. I wonder if it is too late to catch the departing taxi, slide back into it and instruct the driver to take me home. But as I am turning to flag it down, I see a woman emerge from the shadows of the restaurant. She picks her way around the tables, which are already covered in linen and cutlery. When she moves towards me through a patch of sunlight, the monochrome turns to colour and I see her hair is not brown, it is blonde. Her shape is too curvy, her height is too short. She is the proprietor, the woman from the website. She advances towards me, a large bunch of keys in her hand, the little dog trotting at her heels. As she opens the door out on to the street, the dog leaps up onto the broad wooden sill, taking up its customary position in the window.

'We aren't open for lunch,' she says to me, as she fastens the door open with a metal hook. 'Evenings only today. I'm only opening up for deliveries.' Her voice has a pleasant lilt to it, a precision of pronunciation native speakers don't trouble themselves over.

For a second I hesitate how to ask. Pretend I know that Maggie works here, or ask if she does?

'I was wondering if Maggie was here.' I say, aiming for something in between. It seems extraordinary to discuss Maggie with a stranger like this, to say her name as if she is flesh and blood, not a ghost.

'Maggie?' The woman stops, turns to me, curious. 'You know Maggie?'

'We go way back,' I say, faking nonchalance, my heart jumping in my chest.

She straightens up, puts the keys in the pocket of an apron that is tied around her waist. 'Then you give her a message for me, huh? Seeing as she was supposed to finish the week with me.'

A splinter of disappointment lodges in my stomach. 'I was actually hoping—'

'You can tell her the money she took from me was not owed to her and I would like it back. She should have finished her shifts.'

'Oh,' I say.

'You can tell her that?' she insists, narrowing her eyes, taking in my cast and crutch. A look of suspicion crosses her face.

'No,' I reply, 'I don't actually know where she is. I was looking for her. We lost touch. I thought she worked here.'

'She did. Past tense. I fired her for being rude to the customers. But I would have taken her back if she hadn't stolen from me. She spoke French like a native.'

'Do you know where she lives?'

She considers me for a moment, folds her arms on her pillowy stomach. 'So you don't know her that well, then?'

'We lost touch,' I admit.

'How am I supposed to know you're not a bad person? She owes me money. She might owe you something more, huh? She stole from me, but I like her. She has spirit. I don't want her to come to any harm.'

'No. It's nothing like that. I think she's been trying to get in touch with me, that's all. So I thought I'd try and find her. We lost touch.'

'Yes, you said that already. I find it strange that if she wanted to get in touch with you, she would have left this as the only address. You don't have her number?'

'No. I don't.'

'Then why do you expect me to give it to you?'

'It's complicated.'

'Hah.' She lets out a large laugh. '*Maggie* is complicated.' She shoos me away from the doorway. 'Go away. I'm not going to help you. If Maggie wanted to see you, she would find a way. I think it's possible she does not want to be found. By either of us.'

Chapter
Forty-One

The phone rings, a rare occurrence, and the noise wakes me up. It is late afternoon, and I haven't been sleeping well. I swing my good leg off the sofa and reach over to answer it, silently thanking Iris once more for insisting I sleep down here where everything is close.

'Eliza, it's me.' Iris says.

'Weird. I was just thinking about you.'

'Can I come over? I have some news.'

'What sort of news?' I ask, wondering what Maggie has done now. I am developing a healthy paranoia where she is concerned. I have started drawing my curtains at night, looking over my shoulder when I leave the house, certain I am being followed.

'I'd rather talk to you face to face, if you don't mind,' Iris replies.

My heart sinks, knowing the news won't be good. 'Sure. Come over.'

We decide to walk to a bench on the West Meadow, a grassy area fringed with trees. There are wood anemones and bluebells covering the damp floor of the forest, and the cow parsley is beginning to push up through the tall grass. We find a bench, damp, but dry enough, overlooking a vast area of grass, ringed by trees and scrub. Several dogs are entertaining one another, racing around in circles and tumbling together on the ground.

'I always fancied a dog,' says Iris, watching them play.

'Why don't you then?'

'I don't have the lifestyle. Maybe when I retire. I might need a companion, I suppose.'

'You never married?' I ask.

Iris gives me a look I can't fathom. 'I don't think I'm the marrying type,' she says. 'Anyway, I came here to talk about you. I have some information.'

'Have you found her?'

'No.'

I put my head in my hands, my elbows on my knees. Maggie feels like a sound I can't quite locate, a movement out of the corner of my eye. It's only been a few days and already I'm sick of trying to find her. 'You better tell me,' I say.

'OK. So, I looked on our database for missing persons in 1995 that matched Maggie's description and name, though missing people don't always want to be called by their family name so it can get a bit complicated—'

'Just tell me, Iris.'

'Maggie was registered missing in October 1995 with us. Her name is still on our database.'

Suddenly a piece of her has been pinned down, like a butterfly under glass.

'Go on,' I say.

'Her father, Maxwell Bellingham, was the contact name. Maggie was reported missing in August 1995, but because of the note she left, the police were satisfied she meant to leave home. They didn't pursue the case because Maggie had clearly waited until her eighteenth birthday to leave. There wasn't really anything they could do. You can't make an adult go home.'

'I know this.' I remember very clearly being interviewed by the police at my house and they were obviously just going through the motions for the sake of the Bellinghams.

'Anyway, every January we send out an email to ask if the family wants to be kept on our database and if there are any updates we should know about. Plenty of missing people go home, but because everyone is so wrapped up in their return, they don't bother to update us.'

'OK,' I say, hoping to speed her along.

'We sent one to Maxwell Bellingham's email account at the beginning of the year.'

'And?' I prompt, when Iris doesn't finish. Suddenly her face changes. No longer full of anticipation, she looks troubled. She leans over and squeezes my knee. 'I'm so sorry to tell you, but Maxwell Bellingham is dead.'

I think about the file he sent, still sitting in my drawer like a guilty secret. He must have died shortly after posting it. I feel terrible that I didn't take his letter more seriously, that the very fact he had passed the file on to me should have sent alarm bells ringing, telling me he only had weeks, not months, left.

Yet again, the voice in my head hisses, *you have failed the Bellingham family*.

'His wife died last year. Is that right?'

I sigh. 'Yes, she did. Lorella.'

'It sometimes happens like that. One partner dies and the other follows shortly after. Were they very devoted?'

'I think so.'

'But because of Maggie's disappearance, they were probably more so, I imagine. It can happen like that. The loss of a child often pushes people apart and, equally often, it brings them together.'

I'm not listening to her. 'Poor Max. Did you find out how he died? What his illness was?'

'No. We just got an email from his account saying he had died, and we were to close the case. I double-checked it wasn't someone fooling around. There was a report in the local paper online. It's him alright. Same village. I remembered the address from the Christmas card.'

It is the end of something. The closing of a door on a part of my life I have spent years remembering and trying to forget. 'Well,' I say, a part of me relieved it has been taken out of my hands. 'I guess that's that then. There's no point trying to find Maggie for him. I'm too late.' But I still feel the weight of guilt. If I hadn't broken my leg, I might have been quicker to help.

'Eliza,' says Iris gently, 'I think you should still try to find Maggie. For your own sake. I can see how much it troubles you to talk about her.'

'Maggie left twenty years ago,' I say. 'The last person she wants to see is me, knocking on her door.' What I don't tell her is Maggie may well have found me already, and clearly doesn't want a reconciliation.

'Why? What could you possibly have done wrong at your young age?'

And there it is. Lodged in my throat like a dybbuk waiting to be purged. An old confession, never spoken, but thought about, constantly, every day.

'I killed her brother, Iris. There will never be a reconciliation between us. She left to get away from me.'

Chapter
Forty-Two

I have spent many hours in the last twenty years trying not to think about the details of that afternoon. I wasn't there when it happened. Nobody was. But I bear the responsibility.

I was out with my parents that day. They had seen a house, miles away, and we had set off early to inspect it. Although I wasn't consulted on the renovations they did, there was a pretence I had some say in which house we lived in next. I think it must have been the guilt of subjecting me to months of noise and dust, only to take me away when it was over, thrusting me into another building project. Eric and Maggie knew I would be gone for the whole day. We had arranged to meet the next morning.

The traffic was light, we arrived early. The estate agent was obliging, they wanted a sale. Not many people were willing to take on such a project. We had a look, I passed comment, and all day I thought about missing out on time with Eric and Maggie. I loved my parents, but the process of separation had begun many years ago. In the skill of independence, they had schooled me well. Plans to stop off at a beach somewhere on the way home were made solely for my benefit. I knew they wanted to get back to make a start on their financial position for the auction. I had no desire to lengthen our journey home, we had no air conditioning in the car and the breeze that blew into my face was as hot as the breath of an oven. In a few weeks' time, we would all be off to university, and that would spell the end of a chapter in our lives. Time was running out to shore up my bond with the two people I loved best in the world.

When my parents asked me where I wanted to break the journey, I told them I wanted to go straight back. They dropped me off on a street near to the Bellinghams and I walked the short distance, anticipating Eric and Maggie's reaction at my early return. There was a cut-through on the Bellinghams' street, not far from their house. As I walked down the road, my stomach buzzing with pleasurable expectation, I saw a flash of russet emerge from the leafy tunnel, and I recognised Maggie instantly in a dress that used to be red until she washed it with some jeans that bled indigo, depressing the brightness into something more sombre. I called her name, but she didn't hear me, she was too far away. She crossed the road, disappeared down her driveway and into the house.

I sped up and followed her, arriving only half a minute behind. The porch was like a furnace, trapping the heat of the afternoon. I rang the doorbell and hoped Maggie would be quick before I melted. But she didn't come. I rang the bell again, and again. Irritated and sweaty, I remembered the key and looked down to the green glazed planter, which had been tipped to one side, scattering the umbrellas into the corner of the porch. Frowning, I tried to remember if I'd done this the last time I'd used the key, and then I came to the conclusion that Maggie must have used it to let herself in. I rang the bell once more, and when there was no answer, I opened the letterbox and peered through. In the hallway, I could see Maggie's new canvas shoes she had kicked up a fuss about, lying haphazard on the stone flags, a trail of sweaty footprints leading to the foot of the stairs.

'Maggie?' I shouted through the letterbox. 'It's me, Eliza.'

There was no answer.

By this time, I was so hot, I had to leave. It was clear I was unwanted, and I put it down to one of Maggie's moods. I trudged back home, disappointed, under a sweltering sky. I let myself in through the back door of our house and used the telephone to ring the Bellinghams' number. It was an act of defiance really. She must have known it was me, but I let it ring and ring, imagining the noise in the Bellingham house reaching through the empty rooms, following the path of the bell, wondering what the twins were doing without me. Defeated, I climbed the stairs to the top of the house where I stayed for the rest of the day in my room, lying on my bed, resenting the time dragging by.

I often wonder about those few hours I wasted, willing the next morning to come. I could have done a few nice, innocent things that afternoon before my life turned to ashes. Instead, I stared at the ceiling and cursed my boredom.

I heard my father's footsteps on the stairs, his soft knock on the door. He entered my room, stammering an apology. He knew what he had to tell me would break me apart.

'Something terrible has happened,' he began, as he sat on the bed, his hand patting my knee, attempting to offer comfort for something I had yet to know.

I knew he meant the Bellinghams. They were my world. My mind flew to Maggie, not answering the door. I felt my body wind itself tight, like a spring and I moved my knee away from his reach.

'It's Eric,' he continued. 'He died this afternoon.'

'What?' It was such preposterous news I didn't believe him. I almost laughed. Eric was the most alive person I knew.

'He was found, by the school caretaker. In the pool house at Ivydale.'

Still, my stubborn brain refused to understand. I imagined him being caught by the caretaker, one leg out of his shorts, the rest of his clothes discarded on the tiled floor.

'What was he doing?' I asked stupidly.

'He must have been swimming. He must have . . . got himself into trouble somehow. He drowned. Darling, I'm so sorry.'

I didn't need to hear anymore. Now I had the right image in my head, it would be the same one that would stay with me for the rest of my life. I pushed past my father. 'I need to see Maggie,' I mumbled, clinging to the time, only moments before, when Eric was alive in my mind, not dead in a swimming pool. I would only have a few moments, I knew, before it would all sink in. I wanted to hold on to the disbelief for as long as I could.

'You mustn't, Eliza. They won't want anyone over there. They've had a terrible shock.'

'I'm not *anyone*!' I shouted at him through a veil of tears, angry that he didn't include me in their grief. I took the stairs two at a time, and ran all the way through the village, my lungs bursting with pain. For every breath I drew in, I thought about the breath that Eric must have fought for, and for every breath I let out, a part of me died too.

Maggie was my last friend in the whole world. As I reached the gate of the Bellingham house, a small, nagging voice in my head warned me she would blame me, that this was all my fault, but I silenced it, convinced I could repair whatever I had broken. I had to. There was no other way I could go on. But as soon as she opened the door in that pressed cotton dress, her hair brushed and parted, she didn't look or talk like the Maggie I knew. She had been over-taken by an imposter. It was only when I was well into adulthood that I realised her altered appearance must have been the beginning of an unbearable transition from a half to a whole.

Two weeks later, she was gone. It was worse than being alone. It was as if the friendship I had had for the past year had been a dream, and I had woken up to the nightmare I would live in for the rest of my life.

When my mother suggested I write to Eric, to help manage my feelings, I dismissed her suggestion. But the idea persisted. I put pen to paper, and the words I wrote to him brought me comfort.

Chapter
Forty-Three

Of all the things that Iris expected Eliza to say, it wasn't that. She listens to the story. The summer of dares, the pool house at Ivydale, the rivalry for Eric's affections. She hears how a girl asked a boy to dive for a necklace, like a scene from a fairy tale. She hears how Eric chose to return to the pool, alone. How he was found, hours later, face down in the water, by the caretaker of the school.

Eliza is crying now. Iris lets her. She sits and listens.

'I just don't understand how it happened,' Eliza says, her voice choking. 'He was strong. The pool wasn't that big. Maggie left before I could talk to her about it. I've had all these questions, for all of these years, and nobody to answer them.'

'Oh, Eliza,' soothes Iris. 'What a mess.'

'After it happened, I missed him so much, Iris,' Eliza sobs. 'I looked for him, everywhere. Sometimes I caught a glimpse of him in the street, and I would follow complete strangers until I couldn't keep up the fantasy anymore. And then one day, when I was swimming in the pond, I saw him, under the water. Just a flash. I see his face sometimes. If I hold my breath for long enough, I can see his face.'

Iris sighs and takes her hand. 'So that's what straying beyond the boundary rope was all about.' She listens to it all, and her distress increases, not just because Eliza is turning herself inside out with misery as she remembers the details, but because Iris can see she will have to do something extraordinary to right this wrong. Iris has heard all sorts of stories, even worse than this dreadful tale. She knows it will take courage for Eliza to do what must be done. And to have courage, one must be inspired to acquire it.

'I want to tell you something,' she says to Eliza when she's finished crying, and Iris has comforted her. 'Something I've never told anybody else. And I'm only telling you because I want you to know how important it is to make things right between you and Maggie before it's too late.'

'I can't, Iris, I just can't,' says Eliza, her face ugly with tears. 'I had a chance to make things better when Max was alive. But now there's no point.' Iris knows how she feels. She knows how wretched guilt can make you. She will have to show Eliza it's not a good look to wear for the rest of her life.

'You asked me if I was married earlier. I'm afraid I wasn't very honest with my reply,' she begins. 'I was married once, many years ago. I was a different person then. I lived quite a sheltered life. I grew up on a dairy farm in Devon. Spent most of my childhood helping my parents.'

'That sounds idyllic.' Eliza sniffs.

'Well, it wasn't. I didn't like farm work. Early hours, no time off. It's relentless. Cows need milking whether it's Christmas day or not.'

'Oh. I see.'

'I was quite a bright child, I did well at school. When it came to university, I decided to study law, probably because it was the complete opposite of what I was used to. Lots of sitting and reading, always being indoors. Not like farm work. My parents were unhappy about that, but they agreed if I studied at the nearest university, and helped at home during the holidays and weekends, I could go. So I did.'

Iris pauses, remembering that slice of time where everything seemed to be filled with optimism. 'I had mapped out my life for myself. I was going to get my law degree, leave Devon, and start life properly. But then I met a boy.'

'Oh,' Eliza says, a note of understanding in her voice.

'I hadn't really met many boys. There were the odd Young Farmers' socials, that sort of thing, but I didn't fit into the farming crowd, so I never had anything in common with them. David was my first boyfriend.'

'Was he at university too?'

'Yes. He was a student. Anyway. I was swept up by everything. If I'm honest, I saw him as my ticket out of there. If I had a husband, it would be easier to leave the farm. It wouldn't just be me against my parents, you see, I would have somebody else backing me up. But it didn't really work out like that.'

'What happened?'

'Well, as soon as I got my degree, we decided to get married. I was delighted, my parents less so. They could see they were going to lose me. And then I found myself pregnant.'

Eliza doesn't reply.

'So there I was, hastily married, expecting my first child. All my plans to become a barrister out of the window. There was no way my parents could get involved in childcare, they were too busy. And they were annoyed with me anyway for going against family tradition. David's parents lived miles away. By this time, we'd moved to the Midlands, David had a job. I was stuck in a village with a baby while David worked long hours. I didn't know anyone, and as I saw him begin his career, I saw mine take a nosedive. It created a lot of resentment.'

Iris is trying to recount the story in an impartial way. She doesn't mention the constant sensation of being trapped, unable to breathe. The hours she spent weeping, alone, in a house she didn't like, in a place where she was a stranger. The unsatisfying conversations with university friends who were brimming with anecdotes about their new jobs. That she began to feel worthless and depressed.

David worked late. She came to understand they had nothing in common, only this little life they had recklessly brought into the world. Iris remembers, but doesn't mention, the mounting feelings of desperation as she tried, and failed, to bond with her son. She doesn't mention a recurring fantasy of being knocked over by a bus so she could just spend a few quiet days in a hospital bed being looked after by somebody else. Overnight, it seemed, she had turned from an attractive, intelligent woman with thoughts of her own into a worthless mess. She couldn't think of anything interesting to say. She couldn't drive. She couldn't do anything apart from stew in her own despair. When she tried to breastfeed her baby, she couldn't escape the parallel between her own situation and that of the cows on her parents' farm. David couldn't understand. She was a woman, wasn't she built to do this? Shouldn't it come naturally? Her family and friends were the same. She should be happy, she was told repeatedly, why wasn't she happy? There were plenty of women who couldn't have children. She was blessed.

She hadn't planned anything consciously, she was only aware of a persistent, desperate desire to step out of her life, just for a few days. Even now, she can't help thinking if certain things hadn't been aligned, it wouldn't have happened.

It was a Friday morning when one of the cows kicked her mother. The weekend ahead was a bank holiday. When her father rang for help, David was already looking forward to spending time with his son, who was now an energy-sapping toddler. He was a good father, David. He didn't insist he accompany Iris to Devon. He could cope for a couple days with his boy; he was more than equal to the task. She knew he didn't mean it, but the way he said it irked her, as if it was going to be an easy few days for him, a break from his demanding work. She left one house, filled with resentment, only to enter another in exactly the same state. As she batch-cooked for her parents and changed her mother's dressings, Iris couldn't remember the last time she hadn't spent the day looking after someone else. When her father asked her when she had to go home, instead of saying *Monday morning*, which is what she had arranged with David, the word *Sunday* popped out of her mouth. Her father had no idea it was a bank holiday. Every day was a workday for him.

She said goodbye to her parents on Sunday morning, after labelling all the meals she had cooked and stacking them in the freezer. Even when she arrived at the train station she hadn't formed a plan. All she knew was that she couldn't stay in Devon anymore, and she didn't want to go back home. She remembers very clearly looking up at the departures board and seeing a train for London, and the deliberate decision she made to get on it.

'What were you thinking, when you did that?' Eliza asks. 'Did you know you weren't going back?'

'That's the thing,' says Iris. 'I hadn't planned it. In my head I was going to London for the day, and I didn't think much beyond that. But when I arrived, I started walking and I found I couldn't stop. Every step I took, I felt lighter. One day turned into another. And the further I walked away from the train station, the more impossible it was to turn back. I felt I was watching myself. Half of me couldn't believe what I was doing, the other half was thrilled.'

Iris slumps. The shame of leaving her husband and son never went away. 'People are more understanding when a father leaves the family home, but if a mother does it . . .' She doesn't finish the sentence. 'You're the first person I've told.'

'How long ago was this?'

'Over forty years.'

'So what happened when you got back in touch with your husband?'

Iris clears her throat. 'Well,' she begins slowly, 'that's not something I ever did.'

There are a few moments when Eliza processes the information. 'You mean, you never went back? You never told anyone where you were?'

'That's right.' Iris talks into her hands, which are clasped together in her lap.

'Not even your parents?'

'No.'

'You didn't write a letter? Or give anyone a call to say you were OK?'

'No.'

'Why?' Eliza sounds baffled. She doesn't understand.

Iris tries to explain. 'Because I knew if I did, I would go back to the life I had just left, and the idea of that was unbearable. I don't expect you to understand . . .'

There is a pause, and Iris sees the expression on Eliza's face harden.

'I understand that you want me to do something you never did yourself, Iris.'

'My situation is completely different.'

'Was your husband a coercive controller? Were you in danger?'

'No, of course not.'

'Then I cannot comprehend why you think it's OK for you to sever all contact with your loved ones, while spending the rest of your life making others do the exact opposite.'

The outrage in Eliza's voice pierces Iris. She can feel the conversation cartwheeling out of her hands. 'No, you misunderstand. I could never go back. I would have died.'

'But you could have let your family know you hadn't died, that you were alive and well. All that worry they must have felt, all the time spent thinking about what you were doing, where you were on your birthday, on Christmas Day, all those little anniversaries you shared with others. Your son's birthday, for god's sake. The devastation you must have caused!'

'They were all better off without me. Trust me, Eliza, they were. I was wrong from the start.'

'That's not your decision to make though, is it?' says Eliza roughly. 'You don't get to decide how others feel about your disappearance. *I'm* the one on the other side of this. I know how it feels to be left. When someone does that to you, they inflict a wound that never heals. There is no resolution. There's a reason people would rather know if somebody were dead than not know anything at all. It's called closure.'

'This is exactly why I think you should contact Maggie. Exactly why. Don't you see . . .?'

But Eliza is developing her own train of thought and it is ploughing through all of Iris's good intentions. 'You are such a hypocrite, Iris, you know that? Telling me to do something you know I find very painful to think about, and all this time you haven't got the guts to do it yourself. Why should I take your advice?'

Finally, Iris plucks up the courage to face Eliza, to really look her in the eyes. 'Because it's too late for me, you see. My son has grown up. My parents are probably dead. Maybe my husband is too. I've lost them all. But it's not too late for you. There's still time.'

Chapter
Forty-Four

Cutting off a full leg cast is a brutal business. The blade whines through the carapace sending dust into the air. In the weeks I have worn it, the plaster has changed from a virgin white to a dirty, knowing grey. If there was ever anything that felt like a new beginning, it is this. I feel as if I am being cracked from a chrysalis.

When it is prised off, a ripe, feral smell rises up to greet me. My leg is a mess. I have shed a whole skin during my convalescence, and it has had nowhere to go. The urge to slough it off is strong, but the new skin feels tender, and my nerves are jangling with newfound sensation. My muscles have atrophied, and my leg looks withered and strange. I'm given a sheet of exercises to do, and I am assured it will fill out and the sensitivity will pass. I try and listen to the advice like a good patient, but it is all I can do to stop myself from sprinting out of the door. Like a prisoner on release day, I cannot wait to put the hospital behind me and begin my new life.

A few days ago, I would have called Iris to ask that we mark the occasion with a swim together, but I've told her I don't want to see her for a while. I cannot separate out the feelings she has stirred up in me. I imagine myself like the pond, the dirty muck at the bottom floating to the top after a particularly bad storm. I need time for things to settle. I get a taxi home. The lightness of my leg, the ease with which I can get into a car, it should all please me, but I don't feel pleased. I feel used. The more I go over the conversation I had with Iris, the more I feel she has deceived me. The fact she sees no irony in her own situation beggars belief.

By the time I get home I am too tired to swim. I so wanted the occasion to be filled with something other than how it was before. My first swim should be a new start, filled with optimism. I can't do it now, Iris has ruined everything. Unable to shake off the need to talk to someone, I pick up the phone and call Lucas. It is the last week of the spring term and I hope he will be in his office, eating lunch, as he usually is.

'Eliza!' His voice is full of warmth, and a rush of gratitude for his uncomplicated friendship courses through me.

'My cast came off today. I wanted to let you know.'

'Congratulations. I have the schedule for the job interviews. I was just about to email it to you.'

'Why don't I come in? We can talk about it.'

'Sure. This afternoon at kicking-out time?'

The idea of going back to school, being somewhere familiar where the day has structure, and the kids are welcoming, is the tonic I need. I use the couple of hours to rest up, eat some lunch and order a taxi to take me there. I decide the next time I come here I will walk, like I used to. That it won't be long before everything returns to normal. I don't have to see Iris anymore, I don't have to listen to her advice. I can carry on as before, as if nothing ever happened. By the time I climb out of the cab, my spirits are lifted and the swarm of kids leaving the school, excited to see me again, raises them further. A crowd of teenagers gathers around me, asking when I'm coming back, cursing the supply teacher they have been allocated because they are too strict. *This is where I belong,* I think to myself.

In a matter of minutes, the students thin out, until there are only a few stragglers left. Just as I prepare to pull myself up the concrete steps that lead to the entrance, I see a boy, a teenager, not in school uniform, waiting near the corner of the building, above my eyeline. There is something about him, something familiar, and I am trying to place him in my classes when he turns towards me, looking up the street.

It is Eric. I know it is.

I grab the rail of the steps to stop myself from falling, my eyes never leaving the boy's face. He doesn't notice me, he is looking at his watch. I feel winded, sick, and for a second, I look at my own hands for confirmation I am not going mad. The boy is the double of Eric. A little younger, perhaps, but the same. A noise escapes me, and as I cover my mouth with my hand, I lose the strength in my legs and slump down on the stairs, momentarily losing sight of him. But now I cannot get up. I feel too dizzy and faint. A few students stop and ask me if I need help. I shake my head and wave them away.

'Eliza, are you OK?' Lucas comes racing down the steps. 'I saw you from the window.'

Still feeling sick, I clutch onto him and look beyond his shoulder, but the rake of the steps obscures my view. 'Can you help me up?' I ask, weakly.

He pulls me to stand, and I scan the path that surrounds the school building. The boy is gone.

Lucas is filled with concern. 'This was a terrible idea. I should have made you stay at home.'

The loss of Eric pulses through me like a headache. I know it can't be him. He's not a teenager anymore. He's not even alive. But a part of me is so desperate to see him again, I wonder if I've done this, if I have manifested him somehow because I have been talking about him with Iris.

Lucas gets me up the steps and into his office. He makes me a strong, sweet coffee and forces me to drink it. 'Your colour's coming back,' he observes, pleased with himself. 'Do you feel better? Have a biscuit.'

I feel embarrassed. How could I possibly have mistaken a boy hanging around the school, for Eric? It's ludicrous. 'I don't know what happened,' I say, unable to look at him. 'I just . . . felt weird for a second.'

And then a terrible, outrageous thought begins to unravel in my mind. *Has Maggie done this?* Has she found a boy that looks like Eric, and somehow planted him there, to torment me? Like the lotus flower, and the piano? My thoughts skitter forwards to my return to school, a place she must know I will be every day, unable to escape. I imagine my career being derailed by her, I imagine her going to the head and telling her what I did twenty years ago. Would I be able to continue in my job? Is that what Maggie wants – for me to lose everything, as I have made her lose everything? I imagine her, turning up at my job interview and sabotaging everything, humiliating me in front of my colleagues. I will not be able to withstand the whispers, the sad nods and stares of disbelief. Not again. And Lucas, he would never forgive me, my only friend. I can't stop myself imagining this trail of destruction that weaves its way through my mind.

'Look,' says Lucas, 'we can talk about the job on the phone. You don't look well at all.'

'There is no job for me,' I say, the slow dawn of realisation breaking over me. 'I came to tell you I couldn't do it. I've thought about it and you're right. I'm not up to it. Not at the moment anyway.'

'But I have you down on the interview sheet. I've recommended you.'

I cannot look at him. 'I should have told you earlier, I'm sorry.'

219

'You're damn right you should have told me earlier. I've spent the last few weeks laying the groundwork for you.'

'I didn't ask you to do that.'

'Yes, you did. You virtually begged me for that job. After I said I didn't think you could handle it.'

'Well, you were right. I can't. Can you call me a cab? I need to go home now.'

Lucas does as I ask. He is silent as I leave his office and so am I, unable to explain how I really feel.

As I sink back into the seat of the car, I feel exhausted. It's a physical feeling, pressing upon me, but also there is something else. I am so tired of second-guessing Maggie, wondering where she is and what she is doing. I have lost that job because of her, I have possibly lost the friendship of the only adult I care about at work. But I have the Easter holiday. I have a full two weeks to track her down and find out what she's playing at.

Chapter
Forty-Five

The dam works are well under way. Heavy machinery has been moved on to the Heath and they are draining half of the boating lake to the east. The whole landscape is already scarred with orange plastic fencing, cordoning off the areas where they will dig, barring the way for walkers. I don't know what I'll do when they start on the Ladies' Pond next year. I'm trying not to think about it.

The journey to the pond is slow. My leg feels tender and bruised. I have been following the physio exercises religiously, but they don't prepare me for the walk. I feel exposed without the reassuring presence of my crutch. I stop, several times, holding onto the black railings that form the boundary of the West Heath estate. By the time I reach the gate to the Ladies' Pond, I am sweating, even though the air is cold, and the sun is barely risen.

Carole isn't there, the two lifeguards on duty are talking to one another as I approach the ladder, one of them gives me an absent wave. Before I climb down, I notice the changes that have taken place over the last few weeks. Everything is in leaf now, the bones of the trees now clothed in green and there is a wall of vegetation shielding the perimeter. The boundary rope has been put away for the winter, and the mallards are sitting on their eggs.

April is a tipping point for some when it comes to the pond. The Easter holiday marks a point in the calendar when the fair-weather swimmers begin to think about coming back. I feel as if a door is closing behind me, that something is coming to an end. These are the last few weeks I will have this place to myself before the water becomes more welcoming and I have to share it with strangers.

The skin of the pond is pewter, reflecting the low, thin sun. I inhale the mineral scent of it as I gingerly climb down the ladder. My body isn't used to the temperature, and though it would normally feel like a warm bath at this time of the year, because I haven't been going regularly, it feels like sandpaper across my chest. As soon as I am swallowed by the water, and my breathing is steady, my body remembers the sensation of being held. The pain in my leg eases as the weight of it is cradled, the burden taken away. I swim slowly around, testing out its flexibility. I lie on my back, stretching all of my limbs as far as I can, allowing the water to hold me up like a starfish, keeping an ear out for Iris's voice. The morning sun warms my face and I close my eyes for a moment as I listen to the sounds of the birds begin their business of the day. But their optimism isn't enough to distract me from the voice in my head, nagging me under the waterline. I swim to the end of the pond, past the weeping willow, far from the watchful eyes of the lifeguards. I take a breath, I dip my head and I kick down into the gloom.

There is an ancient river that snakes its way below the surface of the pond, and I feel it now, an icy tendon that forms the hidden structure of the water. I move around, avoiding its reach, until I find a warmer spot to focus my mind. But every time I put my head below the water, I am conscious I am missing the trickle of women descending the ladder. I make myself turn away, hold my breath, and concentrate, searching for the sweet spot between awareness and oblivion in the darkness, but I am not permitted entry. Something has changed. Instead, my attention is continually drawn to the ladder, observing who is entering the water and who is exiting. Every time I see a body that resembles hers, a small stab of pain nudges me, but none of them are Iris.

As I dry myself in the changing room, my eye is trained on the door. I leave the pond and walk slowly back home, telling myself I should be pleased I have avoided another confrontation. But I know, deep down, I am not.

The lack of focus I felt in the pond bleeds into the day. I open the laptop and search for Maggie, scrolling through the lives of her virtual namesakes, all the women I have come to know. Then, a thought uncurls and stretches itself out. Somebody sent Iris that email informing her that Max was dead. Somebody has inherited that house. And now I understand why that piano has been donated to the school. Maggie has returned to sort out Max's affairs. I wonder how many other things from our shared past will worm their way into my life, how many nasty surprises I will find when I come home from work. London isn't far away from that house. She could be here and back in a day. And then I have another thought. Maggie didn't want to stay in that village any more than I did. Why would she want to live in that house, without Eric? In my browser, I type in the Bellingham address, and the words *For Sale*.

The house is there, beautifully photographed on the estate agent's website. I scroll through the pictures of the rooms on the ground floor, spaces I am so familiar with they could be my own. There is the porch with the Virginia creeper, bare branched, waiting to break its sleep. Over every image the words *Under Offer* are stamped at forty-five degrees. I don't have long, then, before Maggie moves on.

I climb the stairs, pack a bag, and prepare myself for the journey home.

Chapter
Forty-Six

The walk from the train station is shorter than I remember, and although my leg is stiff, it doesn't give me much trouble. When I was seventeen, the journey seemed interminable. Now it is a leisurely twenty-minute stroll. Twenty minutes moving forwards, twenty years going back, until I am on the street where the Bellingham house lies. The name of the road is still there in black and white, on the corner by the post box. The font looks old fashioned somehow, and the wooden posts that hold up the sign are fractured with age. I walk along the pavement, keeping an eye out for the cut-through, wondering if it has been swallowed up by greenery, but halfway down, I see it, a new signpost sunk into the pavement indicating where the passage ends. I remember a flash of russet, streaking out of here like a fox from its earth and as I take each step, the years roll back until I am standing at the end of the Bellinghams' driveway, seventeen once more and full of insecurity. I remember the countless times I stood here, waiting to enter their world. I never took their friendship for granted. I think a part of me knew it wouldn't last.

There is a large removal van obscuring the front door, and I imagine Maggie, standing in the hallway, directing everybody with her gravelly voice. I wait at the gate, feeling sick with nerves, until I take my courage in both hands and walk around the lorry to the porch. I expect to see a hive of activity, but there is nobody there, though the door is flung open, despite the chill in the air. I pause, listening for Maggie, alert for her voice, but there are only the distant murmurs of men, coming from the garden. I follow the sound around the side of the house and can see several men sitting at a wrought-iron garden table, eating sandwiches, cans of energy drinks scattering the floor of the patio. Some have their feet up, smoking, one is reading the paper, another scrolling through his phone. I retreat, unable to resist the opportunity for a snoop around while they are preoccupied.

The porch is as I remember it to be, the front door the same colour, but the emerald-green planter is gone, the wellingtons tidied away. The hallway is also empty, and I wonder if this happened after Maggie left, after Lorella died. Or was it preserved by Maxwell, just as it used to be? Is it only now, that four lives have been unsentimentally swept aside and put into boxes? Once more, I pause, listening for her voice, waiting to hear her shout instructions to the men outside. But no sound breaks the birdsong. The doors to the kitchen, living room and dining room are all flung open. There are boxes on the flagstones, some of them built and taped, some of them still flat-packed, stacked against the wall like a giant pack of cards, waiting to bank the history of the house. The kitchen table is the same one I braced my arm against, watching Maggie heat a needle on the gas ring as Eric unboxed a new bottle of Indian ink. The butler sink with the crack in the corner, the taps, crusted with limescale, are the same taps I turned to rinse the ink off, watching the blue-black wash away to leave three indelible dots on my skin.

I walk into the dining room and the place has been cleared, but there are ghosts here too, reminding me of how things used to be. The wallpaper has retained a vibrancy where the Welsh dresser once stood. There is a thick patch of dust below it, where the vacuum couldn't reach. Marks on the wallpaper, imprints on the floor, all of them reminders of lives once lived. There are four deep dents in the carpet at the end of the room, where the piano once stood. I crouch down and push my fingers into these hollows, not knowing why I need to do this. There is a scuffed and flattened area where the piano stool was dragged back and forth over the years, and I can still feel the excited hum that zipped through me when I sat next to Eric and watched him play.

I turn to the foot of the stairs, remembering how my hands would grip the handrail, as I take the steps two at a time, and I wonder if there are still traces of my fingerprints stored in the surface of the wood. As I reach the landing, my heart beats thickly in my throat. This floor hasn't been touched. It is all as it was, a faithful reproduction of my memory. The stair runner is the same, a little more threadbare in the centre. There is the bathroom, where my hair was coloured red, the hair dye chasing around the plughole like blood. There is the mirror where I watched Maggie pierce my ear, her tongue poking out in furious concentration.

There were no photographs on the estate agent's website of Eric and Maggie's rooms. When I open the door to Eric's room, time rewinds and my composure wavers. It has not changed, not one bit. The bright-blue bedspread, the shelving full of CDs, the decision to keep it as it was troubles and touches me. There is a bookshelf full of music scores; tunes he learned to play by heart, in between the pages, waiting to be released. A collection of old birds' nests, fossils and bones gather together on the deep windowsill, as if he had just left them momentarily. I imagine Lorella coming in here to dust, picking up each item and laying it down again, exactly as it was. I imagine her coming in here to weep. I see Max closing the door quietly, unwilling to confront the loss.

The tree at the window has grown tall and unwieldy, obscuring some of the light. I remember how we loved to hang out of this window, hold our breath and make the leap into its branches. I wander around the room, touching his things like a thief, and sit on the bed, remembering lazy afternoons, his dizzying scent, his discarded, balled-up socks. The room is not covered in cobwebs and dirty with age, it has been cared for, preserved. It might be the room of a teenage boy today, and this makes me feel like a teenage girl. I cannot help it, I lean into the pillow, hoping to inhale citrus and woodsmoke. There is nothing there, but twenty years of emptiness. I look over the edge of the bed to the floor. The rug is familiar, the same one I always sat on. I lower myself onto it, like I used to do, my back to the bed.

My mind drifts to one of the rare times we spent an afternoon together, without Maggie, listening to music, talking about nothing, and flicking through magazines. I remember him telling me about writing a diary, and the involuntary dart of his eyes towards the mattress. I kneel, running my fingers between the mattress and the base. But I feel nothing, only the edges of the cotton sheet, elasticated in the corners. I lift the mattress away from the base, wondering if it has been pushed further in, hidden from prying eyes, but there is nothing there.

I keep a diary. It's the only thing about me she doesn't know.

But Maggie knows everything, I think to myself. She is always one step ahead of me. She always was.

Chapter
Forty-Seven

I leave Eric's room, hearing the men return to the ground floor. They remain below, packing the boxes in the kitchen. Nobody comes upstairs. Maggie's bedroom is at the end of the corridor, and with the same trepidation I felt at Eric's door, I turn the handle and push.

It, too, is the same. The room has been faithfully preserved, though I don't remember it being as tidy as this. A very old bottle of CK One, the straw-coloured liquid turned to amber, stands on the dresser. I open it and inhale the spoiled scent, made rotten by the passage of time. Maggie's walls are covered in posters. A picture of Kurt Cobain has pride of place above her bed. Jim Morrison is not far away, with James Dean and Marilyn Monroe. I look at the other celebrities on her walls and realise that most of them died young, and I wonder if that is something Maggie deliberately did, collecting souls in her bedroom, people who wouldn't change and wouldn't disappoint her. I never felt comfortable in this room, always aware I was playing some kind of game only Maggie knew the rules to. There was always a sense of chaos in here, and it remains, the details of her life thrown carelessly over the surfaces. Her rosettes, the ribbons a little dusty and bleached by light, pinned haphazardly to a cork board. Among the sports trophies and school certificates I see handwritten poems, clippings from magazines, and dried flowers stuck to her mirror with Blu Tack that has hardened to stone.

A gauzy headscarf is draped over the lamp at her bedside table, and I recall Mrs Bellingham telling her not to do that, that it would set the house on fire. My throat swells with regret as I imagine Lorella putting the fabric back, a last concession to the daughter who would not come home to turn on the light.

Maggie's shelves are stuffed with novels and children's picture books she refused to throw away. It is hard to imagine somebody so sentimental, someone so attached to material things, that she would want to leave all of this behind. The childishness of this room, the room of an inexperienced girl, makes me feel less afraid of her now.

Then, I see it. The fat spine of a book, a blue ribbon tied around the middle. I pull it out gently, extracting the photo album I put together for her for her eighteenth birthday. I withdraw it from the shelf, sit down on the floral bedspread and untie the bow. It doesn't look as if it has been opened. The bow looks pristine. The only crease marks in the satin are those made by twenty years of being squashed between the 1994 *Guinness Book of World Records* and a *Bunty for Girls* annual, 1979.

I open the photo album and the pages squeak, the translucent film protecting the past complaining at being prised away from itself. There we all are, documented in vivid colour for only a matter of weeks, although it feels as if my whole life is laid bare before me. We all look so happy. How could we know that happiness was finite? That it would slip through our fingers like water? I don't get past the first couple of pages, it's too painful, so I fold the book in my arms, and look around the room once more, the last few moments I will ever have in this house. I wipe my eyes with the sleeve of my coat and get up. When my hand reaches for the door, my fingertips touch several sets of beads and pendants looped over the handle. A small part of me wants to select one and take it with me, a keepsake of a friendship that never ran its course. A small part of me wants revenge for the things she has broken, the way she makes me feel.

Why not? says the voice in my head. *Take what you want. It's what Maggie would do.*

The necklaces are thrown over the handle in no particular order, and several have become entangled and twisted with the others. My fingers trace the different textures of plastic, coral, wood, and glass, cool and smooth against my skin. But then something shiny catches my eye, a flash of silver so shocking I drop the photo album on the floor. With both hands free, I kneel on the carpet and scour through the collection, certain I have made a mistake, wondering what it was I actually saw. When I pull it out, I know it can't be anything other than my own necklace, the twins, Castor and Pollux standing on their zodiac sign of Gemini. I remember the chain in my mouth, the metallic links knocking against my teeth, slipping over my tongue. There is no mistake. It is the same.

With clumsy fingers, I take the necklace and when I put it over my head, the familiar length of it, the weight of it, throws up more questions than answers. How did it find its way here? For a few moments, I torture myself with the thought that Eric died holding it in his hand. Then, I wonder if the caretaker found it at the bottom of the pool and returned it to the Bellinghams, thinking it belonged to Eric. Either way, Lorella must have put it here with the other necklaces, unwilling to refuse it in case it belonged to the child she had lost.

Before I can unpick the scenarios that are forming in my head, the door swings open and one of the removal men comes in, almost tripping over me as I kneel on the floor.

'Sorry!' He holds his hands up. 'The boss said there wouldn't be anyone here today. I would have knocked otherwise.'

He must think I am Maggie. 'It's OK,' I say, as breezily as I can muster, getting to my feet. 'I was just about to leave. I forgot something.' I hold up the photo album, glad my hands have something do to, and clutch it to my chest. 'Help yourself.'

'I can start on the other bedrooms if you prefer?'

'No, it's fine,' I say, desperate to get out. 'I have to get off now, anyway.'

'OK, if you're sure,' he says, looking beyond me to the room, calculating what needs to be done.

'Go for it,' I reply. I push past him and walk as casually as I can down the stairs. But he shouts down to me as I reach the bottom.

'By the way, would you prefer the paperwork to be posted, or do you want to take it now? It's right there.' He points to a large cardboard box at my elbow that has been taped and labelled. On top rests a half-empty bottle of Lucozade and a clipboard with papers in pink, yellow, and white.

'Just post everything,' I say quickly, without thinking. He nods and disappears, leaving me alone in the hallway, heart beating like a bird. And I am just about to leave when I glance at the papers and see the address of the person who is selling this house.

Chapter
Forty-Eight

Iris is standing in her hallway, surveying the wall of faces. When others pick up the phone and call their family for advice, Iris does this instead. She looks at her success stories, looks them all in the eye and they comfort her, as they always do, despite the uncertainty she is feeling. Iris has always been aware there is one face missing from the wall, and that is her own. She knows she has failed in that regard. Nobody at work has ever suggested she contacts her own family. Missing people who call the charity are supposed to make the first move, and if they don't, if they just want a chat with the person on the other end of the phone, then that's fine.

Except she knows what it's like now, for those that are left behind. She didn't need Eliza to spell it out, exactly, Iris has had enough experience to understand how the abandoned feel. That's why she never got in touch with David. She knew what he would be going through. She knew she didn't want to go back. There was no reconciling the two, in her mind. What was the point in getting in touch to say she didn't want contact anymore? Except, now, she wonders if she's been mistaken all these years, that she's skated too easily over the feelings of others. That, perhaps, she has not taken them seriously enough. The disappearance of Maggie has stained

Eliza's life. Iris wonders how her own family have had their lives tainted by her departure.

Iris has not allowed herself to think about the baby. Her son. But now she does, as she stares at all the young men pinned onto her wall. She wonders what he looks like now, what kind of a man he grew up to be. She knows David will have done a good job raising him. A better job than she could have done, but she also acknowledges the stigma they must have had to face: a wifeless husband and a motherless son. She thought the shame was hers alone to bear. But now, she understands, they must have had their fair share, too. The realisation brings a fresh wave of remorse.

It's a funny thing, feeling ashamed for something that hasn't happened to you. She didn't have a husband that hit her. She didn't live with poverty. She didn't have issues with drugs. She wasn't suicidal or psychotic. The lack of drama in her own story makes her feel more unworthy than the people she meets who ended up like her. Most of the cases she'd met through the charity, they had a story that made you shudder. They had proper reasons for leaving, not the paltry excuse she had. She didn't tell anyone she had a child, because she knew what the response would have been. The nods of understanding would have slowed and stilled, when people found out she'd abandoned a child. It's one thing to abandon a husband, quite another to leave your own baby. Even Eliza has turned on her.

Iris is about to grab her swim bag and head to the pond when the phone rings.

'Hi, it's Lucas. Is that Iris?'

'Yes, it's me.' Iris is surprised because she thought her relationship with Lucas ended when Eliza's cast came off.

'I'm wondering if you've seen Eliza recently?'

Iris thinks back to the uncomfortable conversation they had last week. 'No,' she says, 'I haven't.'

'Oh. I'm a bit concerned. She came to school a few days ago and . . . well . . . didn't seem herself. Now she's not answering the phone. Usually, she returns my calls.'

'I'll go,' says Iris, grabbing her keys. 'I was planning on going for a swim anyway. I'll park in her driveway.'

'Not you as well? I can't understand the attraction myself.'

'Don't knock it till you've tried it.'

'That's what Eliza says.'

Iris is reversing down Eliza's driveway in less than fifteen minutes. She rings the bell, looks through the windows and walks around the house. There is no sign of her. The bedding on the sofa has been packed away. Iris makes another trip around to the back of the house and tries the door, which is locked. She glances down to her keyring, to the copy of Eliza's door key she had made. Just in case. In case she fell again, or something worse. She meant to give it back, but they'd parted on bad terms. It's been on her keyring ever since. She turns the key in the front door, calling Eliza's name.

The house has a motionless quality about it, Iris senses there is no one there. She walks through to the kitchen, touches the kettle to see if it is warm, something she saw on a police drama once. She goes upstairs. The bed is made. Eliza's swimsuit hangs over the bathtub. Iris touches it and it is dry.

She's allowed not to be at home, Iris thinks, *it's almost Easter after all.* She makes her way back down the stairs, and when she is halfway down, she notices Eliza's laptop on the little table by the window. It is open, the screen is black, but when she hits the return button, the screen lights up. When she sees the website of the estate agent, the address of the house she has been looking at, she understands where Eliza has gone. Iris imagines her taking the train to the village where Maxwell Bellingham lived. Now she knows the full story, Iris appreciates how difficult that journey must have been to make. And although Iris told Eliza she doesn't agree with her, that she isn't in any way responsible for Eric's death, she knows her words meant nothing to Eliza when she said them, and that there is a very real possibility that Maggie still holds her responsible, and her arrival will be unwelcome.

Iris leaves her car at the house and walks to the pond, filled with doubt. Eliza's disappearance should make Iris feel happy. But as she squeezes through the back gate of the house and into the wood that skirts the West Heath, she is filled with apprehension. She has the sensation she is standing, alone, on a cliff and Eliza has already jumped into the water below. The letter she received from Freja is still unanswered. Her family will be expecting a response.

Carole is leaving as Iris arrives. 'I'm off duty now. I'm on early this week.'

'Have you seen Eliza this morning?'

'No. What's up? You don't look like your usual chirpy self.'

'I had an uncomfortable conversation with her.'

'A row?'

'Not exactly. But close. I think I've been a bit too . . .'

'Pushy?'

Iris lets out a sigh.

'Oh, Iris, what's the matter? I was only joking. Don't look so sad.'

Iris bites her lip, to stop it from trembling. 'Do you have to get home right away?'

'No, come on, let's walk. But not near the earthworks, there's diggers everywhere you look. I can't bear to see what they're doing. Let's go up through the South Meadow.'

They set off at a brisk pace, and because they are both looking at the ground as they walk, Iris tells Carole everything, including her own uncomfortable history. 'Eliza was right, you know,' Iris says, when she has finished, 'I am a hypocrite. I've told her to do something I won't do myself. I feel wretched about it.'

'You don't usually get affected like this. What's so different between this missing person and the last one?' Carole asks.

'I think Eliza reminds me of myself, a little bit. And I don't usually hear the story in such detail from the person who was left behind. Being with her these past few weeks seems to have brought everything up to the surface. I'm usually so good at putting what I did in a box.' Then Iris decides to tell Carole everything. She is not kind to herself when she relays the story. She admits to her friend how wretched she feels.

Carole is a comfort, a tonic, a balm. She is all the things that Iris needs. 'Iris,' she says, 'maybe it's time to take your own advice and unpack that box. It's obviously causing you grief.'

Iris finally turns to her friend, ashamed. 'I abandoned my own boy, Carole. What must he think of me?'

Carole squeezes her elbow. 'You'll never find out if you don't ask him now, will you?'

Chapter
Forty-Nine

I should be heading home, but I am reluctant to leave the village. There is a bicycle propped up against the side of the removal van. On impulse, I take it, and cycle out of the driveway and down the cut-through, to where I used to live. The village has grown. The post office and grocer have been joined by a cafe, a takeaway and a hairdresser. Some of the fields have been developed for housing, there are modern estates eating up the farmland. My own house has also changed. It has been extended, again, there is a dormer in the roof and the garage has been converted into living space. I think about the amount of work my own parents did on this property and wonder if it is destined to be the subject of dissatisfaction for every generation that owns it. I get back on the bike and aim it to the only other building I want to see.

The journey to Ivydale is embedded in me. As I cycle down the quiet streets, I am reminded of all the times I walked this way with Eric at my shoulder. What I have completely forgotten, something that brings me up short when I reach it, is the high, stone wall of the cemetery. We passed that wall every morning on our way to school, and every afternoon on our way back. We didn't consider what lay behind it, it figured so little in our imagination.

The cemetery was something unthinkable at our age, a place we would not have to be acquainted with until we were old, but now I remember that Eric is there, behind that wall. When the thought lodges in my head, I cannot shift it.

I make the necessary detour and seek out the gate, hopping off the bike and wheeling it beside me when I find it, searching for the place where the newer headstones lie, the plot of earth I remember standing next to as an eighteen-year-old, sweating and miserable. It takes longer than I imagined, the names of the dead are transient under my gaze as I seek out the one that matters most. I abandon the bicycle and walk between the headstones. The air is cool and damp, the ground between the graves is springy underfoot. Birdsong ricochets back and forth above my head in the oak trees; the squirrels pause, briefly, to see who the intruder is, before leaping between the headstones, digging their own holes in the ground, searching for treasures. For a place that houses the dead, the place is bursting with life.

Finally, there it is, a sleek black stone, glossy with polish. I am reminded of the piano, and I look for his reflection in the surface. I lean over, absorbing the letters of his name. But, this time, there is only my own reflection staring darkly back.

The funeral was quiet, and afterwards, nobody felt like chatting. Even the adults stood in their own bubbles of misery, unable to communicate with one another. During the service, barely anybody sang, apart from a man who might have been Eric's uncle. He belted out the hymns loudly and beautifully with a Welsh lilt, carrying the whole congregation with the strength of his voice. I remember my view of the back of Maggie's head, bowed, next to her mother's. It never lifted and turned, no matter how much I willed her to look at me. Max stood upright, a fixed stare straight ahead and I don't think he made eye contact with anyone for the whole afternoon. The cool of the church provided short respite from the temperature outside, and when we emerged to walk the distance to the graveside, the sun meted out its own punishment as I stood, brutalised by the heat, at the edge of the freshly dug earth.

I never got to see Eric's headstone, I left before it could be set. Now, I pause by the words, detailing his dates with my fingertips, tracing how much he will be missed. The earth has levelled, and grass has grown, softening the edges where the ground was split. There are no flowers, but there is a piece of folded-up paper that has been wedged into a crack at the base of the headstone. With a shaking hand, I gently tease it out and open it up. It's a Rosetti poem, not the full seven verses. Whoever has written this has selected certain stanzas. The paper is fresh, untouched by the weather. It hasn't been here long.

> *The door was shut. I looked between*
> *Its iron bars; and saw it lie,*
> *My garden, mine, beneath the sky,*
> *Pied with all flowers bedewed and green:*
>
> *From bough to bough the song-birds crossed,*
> *From flower to flower the moths and bees;*
> *With all its nests and stately trees*
> *It had been mine, and it was lost.*
>
> *So now I sit here quite alone*
> *Blinded with tears; nor grieve for that,*
> *For nought is left worth looking at*
> *Since my delightful land is gone.*

I am familiar with the words because I use them, occasionally, to teach my students about metaphor. The poem is not about a garden, it is about exile and loss. I can tell Maggie has written it

down and left it here because it suits her taste for drama. I also recognise her handwriting. She always wrote her *Fs* backwards, like a
continental *7*. The familiarity of those letters, formed by her hand,
it's like looking at breadcrumbs, and I try to decipher the path she
means me to take. I look over my shoulder, to see if she is there,
standing under one of the oak trees, watching me.

Chapter Fifty

Ivydale looks like an old friend who's opted for plastic surgery. Even though I was only there for ten months, the contours of it are as familiar as my own face, but there have been some new additions that jar and disappoint. The front looks the same, apart from a new weatherproof noticeboard, the name of the headmaster in copperplate font.

The building is silent because of the Easter holiday, but the part of me that never grew up is still afraid of being spotted by the caretaker. I hop over the low wall, remembering the time I sat there with Eric, waiting for Maggie to break into the pool house, remembering the moment when he touched my hair and looked troubled, as if he had some kind of premonition this place would be his downfall. I duck round to the back of the building, noting that the prefabs have gone, and a new science wing has been built with little regard to the original architecture. I peer through the windows and see smart new lab tables, polished and waiting for students to spill and scratch their way through GCSE Chemistry. When I notice a window, carelessly ajar, I am seventeen again and sorely tempted to break in and wander the halls. But instead, I walk the length of the building, peering into the windows, seeing snatched glimpses of my past. The outbuilding that housed the draughty girls' toilet has been demolished in favour of a set of allotment plots, alive with promise. There is my old classroom, the noticeboard stripped bare, ready for the term ahead. The canvas is pockmarked, ghosts of staples and drawing pins scattering the surface like forgotten casualties in battle.

I hold my breath when I round the corner and find myself confronted by the music block. I don't have to think which practise room was his. It is here, at the end, where the afternoon sun slanted through the window, illuminating the dust motes that fell between us. The armchair has gone, but the piano looks the same. Like flies in amber, all is preserved, slightly distorted and glossed by time. It's as if he's about to step into the room, walk over to the stool with those easy, graceful strides and sit down. I can see his fingers, elegant and long, opening the lid. They settle on the ivory and there's a moment of stillness when he draws his breath and begins to play.

The scent of mown grass tells me the caretaker has been busy, the lawn is clipped and the lines on the sports pitch have been newly painted. There is some warmth in the air now, and I slide my sandals off and touch the same soil I played hockey on, cold and shivering, waiting for the ball to come my way. The same roots I trampled are still nurturing the grass I feel now, brushing the soles of my bare feet, their clipped blades giving off the moist scent of spring. I look around. Ivydale has not altered much, but the changes I have seen are enough for me to know that this is a different place now, and I have been swallowed, forgotten, into its past. It is Eric's memory that endures. His death in the pool house will have turned into legend, embellished by generations of students who neither knew him nor cared.

I scan the field and a stab of anxiety catches my breath as I see the building is still there. It is smaller than I remember, but a certain, familiar, quality of light emanates from the narrow windows. I had thought it might have been demolished, after what happened, but it appears it's still being used. I stand on my tiptoes and look through the window. The pool is flat and dark, and there is that familiar movement, a ripple under the skin of the water, the twitch of a muscle, inviting me in. Whenever I swim, I feel Eric at the edges of my consciousness, but I wonder if this particular pool is too close for comfort. As I hesitate, wondering what to do, I acknowledge a moment of truth. It is the whole reason I came here. To turn back now would be to deny myself an intimacy I will never have the opportunity to experience again.

I try the door and it is locked. But there is a large flat stone near my feet, and something compels me to nudge it. It moves away to reveal the key, and I enter the building and shut the door behind me. A hush fills the room. I am aware of a transition, a movement into a place between past and present. I am aware of him, standing in this spot, staring at the water, searching for my necklace. I see him diving in, kicking down to reach it.

And then, my imagination falters.

The guilt, the weight of it, crushes any further thought. So I walk towards the water, I crouch down, and break the surface with my hand. A ripple sends itself out, little messages to the furthest reaches of the pool. The skylight directly above pours sunlight onto the surface, and it traces the ripples with silver.

The temperature is cool, the heating is off. I turn the key to lock the door and remove my clothes. The water is clinically clean, the smell of it completely at odds with what I am used to, but the embrace is familiar, welcoming, and the urge to disappear into it, is still strong. After a few strokes, I lower my head under the surface and swim to the bottom, letting all my breath out so I sink to the floor. The pool lights are off, and the dark of the deep end is suffused with a cool blue grey. I wait for him, looking through the gloom of the water, hearing my heartbeat in my ears.

I know he will come.

Sure enough, there is a shape in the water, and, after a moment, I see the detail in his face. He swims towards me and stops, suspended, looking amused.

You finally made it, he seems to say. *You finally got your wish.*

What happened? I ask him. *What happened in here? How could you possibly die?*

I could reach out and touch him if he just swam a little nearer. But something tells me if I move, he will go.

I'm sorry, I say silently, hoping the words will travel through the water and reach him.

He gives his head a little shake. Then he reaches for me, and I can feel his fingertips touching my hair. That same sensation of being blessed.

Chapter
Fifty-One

Although Iris knows any of her colleagues will do a commendable job as a go-between, she would rather use a stranger, someone less close to home. Calling Freja, writing to her, is not something Iris feels she is ready to do. She needs to know if Anthony wants to talk to her first, and instead of finding that out from his wife, who seems to have her own agenda, Iris needs a neutral party to do the work. She has already done some rudimentary research, she couldn't help herself. Her parents are dead, she knows this now. It's the people who bought their farm that might prove useful.

Iris types the name of her parents' farm into a search engine. She waits for her sluggish internet to process the words, her pulse jumping thickly. As the images and the farm website appear before her eyes, she is not prepared for the level of fascination and desire for detail she feels. Points of familiarity are blurred and overlayed by the new. What she sees before her is at once intimate and completely unknown. The farmhouse looks the same, but the farm itself has grown exponentially. It is now a modern operation. No longer just milk producers, the farm now makes its own cheese and yoghurt. One of their cheeses has won an award, she notes, and they are thinking of going into ice cream. There is a family history page, and sure enough it is a short story. Iris learns that the couple who run the farm now are ex hedge-fund investors, who grew tired of making money in the City and decided to fulfil a long-term dream. When the farm came up for sale, they swapped their Savile Row suits for overalls, and made a success out of a failing operation.

A failing operation. Those words hurt Iris, even from a distance. She knows how much work her parents put into their livelihood. Years of their sacrifice, difficult decisions and penury are swept away in a short, smug sentence. But the smugness will suit her purpose. Smug people like to feel important, and she has a job for the wife, who Iris thinks will be more sympathetic than the husband. Men care less about other people's tragedy, Iris has learned. The well of empathy is deeper in women.

She calls the number on the webpage and leaves a message. Sure enough, that evening, she receives a phone call from a perfectly pleasant woman whom she identifies as the wife in the pictures she has seen online.

Iris introduces herself as a contact from the charity. 'I'll try to be brief,' she says in a sunny voice. 'I know how busy you must be.'

'Well, it all sounds very intriguing, I must say.'

Iris smiles to herself. This woman is already eager to help. 'Well, it's unusual, for this length of time to elapse. But it's not unheard of,' Iris replies. 'We've been contacted recently. A missing person would like us to try and put her back in touch with her family. She gave us your address. She grew up there with her parents.'

'The previous owners both died before we bought the farm. We bought it from the people who inherited it. So I'm not sure how I can help.'

Iris closes her eyes briefly. 'Yes,' she says as evenly as possible, 'I think she assumed this would be the case. It's the family who sold the farm to you she is anxious to make contact with.'

'I can barely remember their name.'

Iris holds her breath while she resists the urge to shout it down the phone. She knows there was no other family on her parents' side, that they would have passed everything onto David and her child, in the hope that their grandson might grow up to be a farmer. 'Well, I have the name here,' Iris says evenly. 'I'm looking for a David Danvers. Does that ring a bell?'

'Not really. Hang on a minute, I made a file. It's probably still here in the office. I never throw paperwork away.'

Iris offers a silent prayer for the well organised and waits while the woman roots through her filing cabinet.

'Yes. Here. Not David Danvers though, the person who inherited the farm was called Tony. Tony Danvers.'

Anthony. To hear his name spoken out loud sends a shiver down her spine. Of course. He wouldn't stay a baby for ever. She can hardly believe he has inherited and sold a farm in her absence, let alone grown up into a man and married a woman called Freja.

'Yes,' Iris clears her throat. 'That's the son of David Danvers. Is there a phone number for him on the documentation?'

'Well, yes, but . . .' There is a change of tone in the woman's voice. 'I shouldn't just give out his number, it feels a bit . . .'

'Oh, I don't expect you to do that,' says Iris smoothly. 'I'm going to give you a number and a message, if you wouldn't mind? He doesn't have to contact me if he doesn't want to. That will be part of the message.'

'Um, I suppose so.'

'It's important you speak to Anthony in person and just give the message, word for word. Do you think you could do that?'

That was almost a week ago, and every time the phone rings Iris jumps out of her skin. She vacillates between wishing she hadn't contacted the farm and hoping Anthony will call. She has no idea what it is she wants to say. She is hoping the right words will come if she is given the chance to speak to him. One thing she knows: an apology is long overdue. She passes the photographs in the hallway, all of them her happy endings, and she wonders if she will be able to put her own image up there before long.

The weather has warmed up. The Easter weekend has meant Iris has been able to spend three days working in the garden, uninterrupted. She has been to the garden centre and treated herself to a tray of bedding plants that will see her through to the end of the season. When she comes into her house to wash her hands and clean the plastic plant pots, she forgets, momentarily, about the phone call she is waiting for, she is so absorbed in the moment. Iris is drying her hands when the phone rings, and before she can think about it, she picks it up and answers, a muscle memory she is too slow to stop.

'Hello?' she says, absently.

'Constance? Constance Danvers?' a voice asks.

Iris drops the tea towel on the floor and holds the phone to her ear with both hands.

'Yes,' she whispers, knowing her plan has failed.

'This is Freja. Freja Danvers.'

The woman's voice has a Nordic lilt. It has a hypnotic quality that Iris likes. 'I take it Anthony didn't want to talk to me, then,' Iris says.

'It's not quite like that. He is angry with me for contacting you.'

'I'm so sorry. I assumed you'd discussed it.'

'I have discussed it with him, but I don't think he realised I would act so quickly. It doesn't matter. Now we can talk together.'

'Yes, I suppose. But I was hoping to speak to Anthony directly.'

'You want to be in touch with him, then?'

Iris has thought very, very hard about this. 'Yes,' she says. 'I really do.'

'Then I think we should meet. Just the two of us. To start things off.'

Chapter
Fifty-Two

The day is bright and when Iris enters the pub after a long drive, she is momentarily blinded because it is much darker inside. She stands in the entrance, blinking, waiting for her eyes to adjust to the gloom. It's an old building, the walls are thick, and the windows are tiny. There is a yeasty, beery smell she likes, and she can smell something cheesy wafting through from the kitchen. Normally it would make her feel hungry, but today she feels sick. She pulls a bright, printed scarf around her shoulders, feeling self-conscious. She has dressed carefully for this occasion. She has spent a long time standing in front of the only large mirror in the house, making sure she strikes the right note. Not too jaunty, for the meeting is serious. Not too sombre because the subject of the meeting is positive. She hopes Freja is as kind as her voice. She hopes she doesn't leave the pub worse off.

A tall, slim woman rises from a table in the corner and calls her by her old name. Iris will explain her name isn't Constance any more at some point. But maybe not today.

'Freja.' Iris smiles, nods, as she sits opposite this woman who has married her son. This woman who knows more about him than her. Freja is beautiful. A long curtain of white-blonde hair has been swept back into a business-like twist at the nape of her neck. She is dressed in expensive-looking clothing: a pale, tailored suit jacket over a pristine white T-shirt and a thin golden chain around her wrist, with some kind of emblem Iris can't decipher. Iris is absurdly pleased that her son must be appealing enough to attract the attention of a woman like this. She wishes she had asked Freja to bring a photograph of him.

As Iris sips her tonic water, she touches her hair, arranges her scarf, and waits for the elephant in the room to be addressed. She has already told Freja the journey was fine, that the weather finally looks as if it means to be spring. That soon they won't be needing their coats.

'Tell me why you came,' says Freja, her cool grey eyes looking at Iris.

'Because you asked me to,' says Iris, ruffled.

Freja laces her fingers together in a graceful manner. 'I mean, what do you hope will happen? I would like to get an idea of how you feel about Anthony and how you see the future if he decides to meet you. I don't want to set something in motion that might hurt him.'

Iris is taken aback at Freja's candour but likes her even more because of it. 'Shall I just tell you everything? From the very beginning?' Iris asks.

'You feel comfortable saying these things in front of me?'

'I don't feel comfortable talking about the past with anyone, but I can see you have Anthony's best interests at heart. He must want to know.'

Freja gestures elegantly with her fingers. 'Then please begin.'

Freja listens, her cool gaze resting lightly on Iris as she speaks. She does not interrupt, and Iris is grateful. She does not comment or pass judgement, only nods when Iris finishes, and touches the emblem that is tethered to her wrist. Iris realises with a thumping heart the emblem is an oval with the impression of a child's finger-print at the centre.

'I have one more thing to tell you,' Iris says.

Freja nods.

'I have spent almost forty years working for a charity that reunites missing people with their families. It was because of David's first attempt to find me that I discovered the charity. The letter you sent landed on my desk.'

Even Freja's calm exterior is momentarily thrown. 'That's extraordinary.'

'Yes. Is David . . .'

'He is well.'

'Does he know we are meeting?'

'No. He doesn't speak about you. I think this is why Anthony doesn't speak about you. He has learned it from his father.'

'And now?'

'Now we begin to speak together, just me and Anthony. David only needs to know if Anthony wants to take things further. There is no point upsetting him.'

'Did he ever remarry?'

'No.'

Iris doesn't know why, but she feels guilty about this. 'So what now?' she asks. 'Do you think Anthony will . . . want to take things further?'

'I don't know. I will explain your story to him.' Freja hesitates. Iris senses a discomfort. She sees Freja's fingers catch the thin gold chain and find the emblem. 'I have also experienced what you went through. It is hard, even now, for me to talk about having postnatal depression. Impossible to imagine not being able to bond with my own child. I cannot conceive what you went through forty years ago. Society wasn't built to understand it. Thankfully, things are changing.'

Iris is lost for words.

Freja tilts her head in curiosity. 'You didn't know that's what you had? It sounds to me like you had it bad.'

Iris is dumbfounded. 'I never thought about it. I . . . I just assumed I wasn't cut out for motherhood.'

'Some people, even the wisest people, are blind to their own situation,' Freja says gently. 'I have found that motherhood is something we must learn. Like yoga. Something to be practised every day. We cannot master it. We can only continue to practise.'

Freja smiles at Iris and excuses herself, promising to be in touch as soon as she has found a good time to talk to Anthony. Whatever his decision, Freja says, she will tell Iris the news personally, good or bad.

Iris does not leave the pub straightaway, she can't. There is no strength left in her legs. It is not just the kindness that Freja has shown her, the understanding of her mistakes. It is the singular, magical fact that Freja is a mother. And that Anthony must be a father; that she is a grandmother to a child she desperately wants to meet. Iris is filled with the delicious hope a second chance brings. She likes Freja, very much. She wants to meet her son and her grandchild. But edging that hope is a kind of despair. Iris has tasted something today she never knew she wanted, or needed, and that taste, she knows, is something she will never be able to get out of her head.

Chapter
Fifty-Three

I return in disarray, the enduring image of Eric, swimming towards me, etched on my brain. It is dark when I get off the train and I feel a chill wind, whipping itself up into something spiteful, pushing me along to the bus station. I sink into a seat on the top deck after a few minutes' wait, leaning against the window, my head banging uselessly on the glass as it records every bump and pothole that lines the journey home. The rain begins to fall. It gathers strength and obscures my view, forging twisted rivulets, writhing with purpose, racing across the glass and onto the tarmac below. The journey does nothing to calm my misery, and, as I get off at my stop, a wash of relief breaks over me, knowing I will be home soon, alone with my thoughts, away from the noise of others. I walk along the main road, the rain easing off and the gap in the trees where the passage to the house lies is like a pair of open arms, welcoming me back.

Except, when I arrive at the end of the driveway, there is Lucas's car, and the lights are on in my house.

I stop, dropping my bag on the gravel, wondering how he got in. I pat my coat pockets and sure enough, I feel the comforting rattle of my house keys. I'm sure I locked the doors. I see him through the open curtains, the lights on in my living room. His cheery wave means he is not here because I have had a house fire, or the cottage has been burgled. He is here because he thought it was alright to let himself into my empty house without asking me first.

As I walk towards the front door, I wonder how I have got to this stage in so short a time. A few weeks ago, I had a private life. Now, it seems, my personal space is public property. The feeling of coming home, to my safe place, where I can think about the events of the day in peace, is shattered in an instant as a hot ball of fury wells up inside me. To Lucas and Iris, I am not a grown up, I'm a child who must be looked after, whose best interests must be catered for whether I ask for help or not.

You allowed this to happen, nags the voice in my head. *You encouraged it.*

But now it will stop.

I shoulder my bag once more and stride around his car. I don't need to unlock the front door, he is opening it now for me, like an eager footman. His smile, innocent, willing, pleased to see me, does nothing to soothe my anger as I push past him into the living room, dropping my bag onto the floor.

'What are you doing here?' I ask him loudly, wiping the last of the rain from my forehead.

He is disarmed. All the goodwill that was filling the room vanishes in an instant.

'I couldn't get hold of you,' he says, 'I was worried. I tried calling, you didn't pick up. After our last conversation . . .'

I hold up my hand to stop him. 'And is this what you do if your friends don't return your calls? You break into their house and prowl around like some kind of cat burglar?'

He looks astonished. 'No . . . no. Iris gave me the key.'

'Iris doesn't have a key. I took it back.'

He looks sheepish. 'I think she may have had one cut. When you had the cast on.'

'She did *what?*' I am filled with rage. 'She has no business making a copy of my key, let alone giving it to you. How dare you? How dare both of you? I'm not a child, Lucas. I'm allowed to go away, I'm allowed to ignore my own phone. This isn't some kind of assisted living. It's my *home.*'

Lucas suddenly deflates. He looks around, blinking, as if he has just woken up and realised where he is. He runs his hands through his hair, and not even this act of contrition helps him. 'I'm sorry. I didn't realise you didn't know about the key. Now you put it like that . . . I . . . I just thought I was being helpful.'

'There is a line between being helpful and . . . this.' I gesture to him, standing in my space. 'You just crossed it.'

He shakes his head. 'I don't know what I was thinking. I'll get my coat and leave you to it.'

'Yes, you will,' I reply, smartly.

Then he stops, struck by a thought. 'I left you some food in the fridge. Shepherd's pie. It's vegetarian. I know you don't like . . .'

I try and contain my anger in the face of his kindness. 'Lucas, just leave. I don't need meals delivering. I'm not infirm. I'm capable of cooking for myself.'

'I know, I just—'

'What do you see when you look at me, Lucas?' I demand.

He stares at me, a worried look on his face, as if I'm asking him a trick question.

'Am I sick?' I twirl around, demonstrating the strength of my healing leg.

'No,' he says quietly.

'Am I incapable in any way?' I ask.

'No.'

'Then, what?'

He looks as if he is about to say something, but then he closes his mouth.

'I need my . . .' He looks beyond my shoulder, pointing to his coat. There is a moment when we both dance around one other, unwilling to touch, when he leans past me to retrieve it from the sofa, so close I can smell the fresh scent of him. He struggles to put his coat on as he walks over to the front door, and there is an awkward moment when he finally gets his arm through the sleeve and neither of us can think of anything to say.

I hold out my hand. He looks confused when it suddenly dawns on him what I want him to do. Embarrassed, he pats down his trouser pockets until he finds what he is looking for and drops the shiny new key into my open palm, mumbling another apology.

As he opens the door and steps out into the darkness, I call out after him. 'Don't phone me. Don't visit here unless you're invited. And if you happen to speak to Iris, you can tell her the same. I'm sick of being treated like an invalid. I'm better. There is nothing wrong with me anymore. I'm fine.'

Lucas looks at me through the darkness, slightly afraid. For a moment, I see myself through his eyes, knowing that none of my words ring true.

Chapter
Fifty-Four

Despite my anger, I open the fridge and sniff the shepherd's pie. Layers of creamy mash, crisped to perfection. I touch the dish and it hasn't cooled down. Sitting at the kitchen table, I take a fork to it and eat it straight out of the bowl, trying not to think about the scene I have just caused.

With a full stomach, I fall into bed and experience a rare unbroken sleep that leaves me refreshed and full of energy the next morning. Putting Lucas out of my mind, I prowl around my house, a piece of toast in my mouth, unable to settle down properly at the table to eat it. I haven't showered yet, and my skin still smells of the pool water at Ivydale, a faint chemical scent.

A strange kind of clarity has settled since yesterday. All the landmarks I felt were important to see in the village, they have lost their significance, now. Everything has changed in my twenty-year absence. The world has kept turning, and people have moved on. Perhaps it's time I did the same. Hiding in Val's cottage, worrying about ghosts, rejecting a job I know I would be good at, is no way to carry on. I look at the house I have lived in for the last two decades and begin to see it for what it is. Shabby and unloved. I had thought I was preserving Val's memory by not altering it, but she would have been horrified to see how the house has declined under my care. Pushing these thoughts to the back of my mind, I go and get an A to Z from the bookshelf, determined to act.

The address I think Maggie is living at is uncomfortably close to where I live. I touch the necklace, the weight of it a comfort under my T-shirt. When I have gulped down the last of my coffee, I throw some clothes on, feeling jittery, and leave before I can change my mind. I hail a bus and ride the few stops to Archway, imagining the distance between us getting narrower and narrower, the years rolling back to when we were kids. I rehearse what I am going to say to her, and everything feels flat and trivial. Then I realise I don't need to say much, I just want to listen to her side of the story. All of my questions can be answered over time.

The flat is on a rundown, treeless street. There is rubbish blowing around the pavement and graffiti on the walls of a low-rise building on the corner. The street sign has been neatly and cleverly altered into a swearword and I wonder if one of my kids has done this, because the area is in the catchment of my school, and I cannot help feeling an amused respect. Eventually, I find the building. It used to be a nice old Victorian house, but judging by the other, newer, buildings on this street, it was one of the few that survived the bombs in the Second World War, and now it looks like an anomaly amongst the brutalist concrete architecture that springs up around it, stained with pollution. There are three bells on the front doorframe and two of them have names on. One of them doesn't. I press the bell with no name, and it peals, far away in the basement of the house. The urge to run rises up in me like nausea and I battle to keep it down. I am just about to ring the bell again when I hear the sound of a bolt being pulled back, a door open, and then slam close. I hear footsteps slowly tread the stairs and then, in the hallway, I see a shadow, its owner obscured by the stippled glass in the door.

When the door opens, my first thought is: *it's not Maggie.* My second thought is: *it's Eric.*

He can't be more than sixteen. He's the image of Eric as I remember him. I can't tell if he's the same boy I saw at my school, or if I have conjured him up and he's a figment of my imagination. I sniff the air between us, hoping to catch something familiar, afraid of what it might mean if I do. I wonder if ghosts carry the scent of their human form.

'What's your name?' I ask, a note of hysteria in my voice.

'Seriously? You just rang the bell. I was asleep.' He even sounds like Eric, the emphasis he has on certain words, but his accent is not southern English, it sounds European and hard to place.

'Who are you?' I ask, unable to put into words what I'm feeling.

An angry look crosses his face. 'Who am I? Who are *you*? I'm sick of you people.' He takes a step towards me, and I shrink back, afraid he is going to hit me. Then his hand reaches around the doorframe for the bell, and he rips it off with a force that is older than his years. 'Now get lost and find somebody else to bother.' He slams the door and I hear his footsteps echoing down the stairs, the door to his flat shutting hard, the tremor of it reaching the glass in the door before me, rattling it gently.

Unable to process what just happened, I decide to try and speak to him again, but realise I can't ring the bell anymore to summon him. All that is left is a sticky white glue pad where the bell used to be. I stand there for a few minutes, unsure what to do. I ring the other two bells, hoping they will let me in so I can knock on his door. But nobody answers.

Eventually, I turn back, wondering if I'm having some kind of breakdown. When the sun goes down and I'm too troubled to sleep, I have an idea. If I can't find the answers myself, the pond may be able to help me.

Chapter
Fifty-Five

The Ladies' Pond closes in the evening, there is a padlocked chain wrapped around the metal gate. But the gate only reaches to chest height. It's not hard to climb over. I haven't done it much, because I go so early, I usually have the place to myself, but in the summer months, I have been known to sneak in at night to reclaim the space and swim in the silence that's so hard to find. I am not alone in doing this. Carole told me once, that boys and men sometimes break in, curious to see what the Ladies' Pond is like, answering a primitive urge to mark the territory of others with their own, invisible scent. The Mixed Pond and the Men's Pond are easy to see from the paths that criss-cross the Heath. The Ladies' Pond is private, cloaked in greenery that's hard to penetrate. That's why it's easy to swim, undisturbed, once the gate has been negotiated.

The path to the water, a smudge of grey, disappears into obsidian as the canopy closes over my head. Eventually, I see a glimmer at the end of it, so I keep my eyes fixed on that and pray I don't fall over. When I reach the concrete platform, the darkness falls away, and I can see the body of water I am so familiar with revealed in a different, more mysterious light. The birds are silent, their heads tucked beneath their wings and a wraith of mist hangs, suspended over the water, like an enchantment. A shadow leaks across the meadow and disappears with the speed and grace of a fox.

Without hurrying, I remove each layer of clothing and fold my garments neatly, leaving them on the lifeguard's chair near the ladder. I descend the steps slowly, my feet disappearing into the layer of mist before they touch the water. When my head reaches the surface, it occupies the space between the water and vaporous grey, and it feels as if I have entered a new, inky dimension that could be high in the clouds. Taking care not to splash, or make any noise, I move gently away, pushing a lip of silver ahead of me, watching it splinter into threads before they scatter once more into a flat, black mirror. When I reach the end, where the willow branches fall, I tread water and offer a silent prayer to the pond.

Please, I ask it, *give me some answers.*

I take a deep breath and close my eyes, lowering my face into the void. Then I kick, hard, sending my body down to the past. At first, I see nothing, not even my own hands as they move through the water, keeping me under. I peer through the pitch-dark but then, as the cold begins to penetrate my skin, a glimmer of light pulls my focus, and it develops into colour.

A blur of russet against the green of a privet hedge. Blue canvas shoes on the grey of the pavement, slapping hard and fast. The red-brick wall of the Bellingham house, the black of their wrought-iron gate, still swinging. The enamelled green of the upturned planter as my hands reach down to find the key. I can feel my fingers touch the cool silver of the letterbox, feel the metal give way as it opens wide, wide enough for my face to fill. I can see the grey stone flags of the hallway, the brown oak panels burnished by the sun. And there are those canvas shoes, discarded in a heap. She had wanted white shoes, but was made to have these, a practical colour for Maggie, who cannot be trusted to keep anything clean. And sure enough, Maggie wore them carelessly over the summer, allowing them to become coated with a thick layer of dust from the dry streets. Here they lie, upended near the foot of the stairs.

But the shoes are no longer dusty, they have taken on the same deep blue they had when they were new. And the shadow that they cast is not static. It is moving, creeping across the flagstones with a life of its own. My eyes follow the passage of Maggie's bare feet to the stairs, recorded in sweat. But they do not disappear, shrinking under the relentless heat in the air, they remain stubbornly wet, the soles of her feet faithfully reproduced in water.

In fact, now I look closely, everything is wet.

The shoes are dripping, there are dark smudges on the stone, from the foot of the stairs, right to the door. I take a step back and look down at my own feet. I have sandals on, the day is hot, uncomfortably warm, the heatwave has yet to break. But the journey that Maggie has taken, from the porch to the hallway, to the foot of the stairs, it has been marked out as if she has been caught in the rain.

I burst through the surface of the pond, gasping for air, blinded by the water. Then I swim hard and fast back to the ladder, choking and coughing, on the cusp of understanding what I have just seen. I haul myself out and pull my clothes on, the fabric tugging and sticking to my skin. Raking the water through my hair with my fingers, I allow myself a moment when I cover my face, afraid of what it means. Then I grab my coat, march down the path, and get myself home as safely as possible.

I have always been reluctant to reconnect with Maggie because she told me she did not want to see me. I have always been afraid of what she thought of me, but now, I wonder if she was the one who was afraid. The pond is a lens through which I can see more clearly. I have no doubt the images I saw under the surface are true, because they are my own memories, made sharper.

I have left the light on in the house and it guides me home, a beacon of safety, through the long shadows of the Heath. I go in through the back, and unlock the door, and my kitchen looks so pedestrian it fills me with relief. I collapse at the table, my head in my hands, running over the images I saw in the pond, piecing them all together.

Slowly, I become aware I am not alone. I think of the fox in the meadow, but this shadow is bigger. It rises smoothly from the sofa in the living room and turns to me.

'I see you didn't follow in your parents' footsteps,' the shadow says as it steps into the light. 'This place is a dump.'

She comes towards me, a hostile look on her face, every inch of her as I remember her to be before Eric died. For a moment, I wonder if I am imagining her, if my late-night swim has delivered me into a different dimension and I am still there, under the surface of the water, conjuring up an alternative life.

'Maggie?' I ask, wanting confirmation, needing her to say it out loud.

'The very same,' she replies, in a voice that sounds exactly like Eric's.

Chapter
Fifty-Six

We stand apart in the kitchen, no more than a few feet between us, but the gap feels cavernous. Now I look more closely, her hair is greying at the temples, and she has some lines on her forehead, enduring ripples of the emotions she was never good at hiding. She looks tanned, slightly weather-beaten, the whites of her eyes and her teeth seem to stand out. I try and catch the grassy scent of her, the one I remember, but it remains stubbornly out of reach. I study her face as if it were a painting, trying to ascertain how genuine it is, how much of the detail is as I remember it to be. I used to be able to tell what she was thinking, she was such an open book. But now, there is something guarded about her, a wariness I don't remember, and I wonder what has happened in the time she has been away to make this expression a permanent part of her physical landscape.

'How did you get in here?' I say, not able to articulate the questions I have waited so long to ask.

'I broke in. I'm good at breaking things. As you probably know.'

'So it was you who did that to my greenhouse. And the doll on my doorstep?'

'You seemed to be living a perfect life. Nice house. Nice job. I had an urge to ruin it.'

'Appearances can be deceptive.'

'Really?' Maggie folds her arms. 'Shall I tell you about the dingy flat I live in? The crappy waitressing job I just got fired from?'

'Maggie, I've been looking for you for . . . for a very long time.'

'Well, you didn't do a good job of finding me, did you? And you were supposed to be the clever one. Must try harder, Eliza.'

An uneasy prickle of fear traces itself down my spine. 'Maggie, what do you want from me?'

She gives me a hard look, and then suddenly looks defeated. 'Do you know what? I don't actually know. I just . . .' Her voice trails off, as if she's lost energy. 'I came back because Dad died, and then I couldn't help myself. I wanted to see how you'd coped. Quite easily, by the looks of things,' she says, a brittle note in her voice.

'I was devastated when you left. I tried to say sorry. I would have done anything for you.'

'That's not the case now though, is it?'

'What do you mean?'

'Well you've clearly moved on. Reinvented yourself.'

I shake my head. 'I haven't, Maggie. I really haven't. I think about you and Eric every day. Every single day.'

'Good.'

I cannot believe the person I have spent so long looking for is sitting opposite me in my kitchen. 'I'm so sorry about your dad.'

'I'm not.' She folds her arms, defensive.

'Maggie . . .'

'Don't. If it wasn't for you, we'd all be fine. Eric would be alive. My parents would probably still be alive. We were fine before you turned up. Until Eric brought you home.'

I have an urge to please Maggie, I want to seek out her warmth. 'Why did you go?' I persist, 'Without saying anything to me? Why did you leave me behind?' The question seems so childish, but I feel like a child with a desperate need to know. A wet tear escapes me and drops onto the kitchen table.

'That's a very long story,' she says without emotion.

'Then tell it to me,' I beg. 'I've waited this long.'

'Do you have anything to drink?' she asks, looking around.

'I'll put the kettle on,' I reply.

'Anything stronger?' she asks.

I know what she wants, and I want it too. She wants the sharp edges of this moment to be blurred and softened. But the voice in my head tells me if it's clarity I want, it must come with pain.

'No,' I lie. 'Just tea or coffee.'

Maggie sighs. 'Coffee, then. Black. No sugar.'

We sit opposite one another as if we are adversaries in a game. And when we have been silent for long enough, warming our hands on our mugs, Maggie chooses her moment and begins to speak.

'Eric talked about you for a long time before he brought you home. He told me everything about you from the first day you arrived at Ivydale, and he was chosen to show you around. I could tell he liked you straight away, that he wanted to be your friend. He found it difficult making friends at school, after we were separated.'

'I never understood why he didn't have more friends.'

Maggie shrugs. 'When we were growing up, I was the dominant one. Dad made me that way, I suppose. It started off with a joke – I was born first, the bigger baby, but when we got older, I was more outgoing, and Eric was more introverted. Dad was disappointed. He was forever trying to get Eric into sport. He'd been sporty himself at school, the house was full of his old rugby trophies. Anyway, Eric wasn't having any of it.' She looks at me. 'He was strong, in his own way, Dad just couldn't see it. I became a kind of intermediary between them. I wanted to consolidate my position as favourite with Dad, but I wanted to be favourite with

Eric, too, so I worked hard at pleasing them both. I protected Eric from most of Dad's disappointment by doing the things he had wanted Eric to do.'

I remember Maggie, coming home with cuts and bruises on her legs from hours on the hockey pitch. Bringing back armfuls of trophies and medals.

'I loved the idea of being the leader, and Eric was so happy to follow me, we fell into a pattern we couldn't get out of. Before he went to Ivydale, I was the only person Eric wanted to be with. He found it hard to fit in without me. Boys found him a bit . . .' Maggie doesn't finish the thought. 'You know how open he was, he was just so . . . nice.' She takes a sip of coffee and winces.

Even after all these years, I find it hard to hear him spoken of this way, in the past tense.

Maggie continues. 'He didn't like football or have any interest in dating. He never really developed that macho stuff most boys are in to, and the boys seemed to sense that, like Dad did. They liked him well enough but kept their distance from him. When Eric started Ivydale without me, he said he lost a part of himself. Until he met you.'

'He told me your relationship was stronger when you were split up,' I say.

'I told him that. It was a way of keeping him close, even when he was away from me.'

I remember the conversation I had with Iris, and I wonder if children are capable of coercive control.

Maggie shakes her head as if I have spoken my thoughts out loud. 'He did make some friends, in the beginning, and he brought them home for me to meet, but I was such a bitch to them he stopped doing it. I didn't really want him having any friends that were more important to him than me.'

'Why did you agree to meet me, then?'

'By the time he met you, I'd grown up a bit. He also told me what you looked like, and I figured you weren't one of those simpering girls who occasionally attached themselves to him. I was very protective of Eric. I felt so responsible for him. It did him more harm than good. Our parents shouldn't have allowed us to be the way we were.'

'How do you mean?'

'When we were little, they were developing their business. Having twins must have been a godsend and a curse for them. They got two kids for the price of one, but it must have been exhausting, so when I began to take care of Eric, they encouraged it. I became his babysitter. We didn't need anyone else, and they were probably happy not to have to arrange playdates or whatever they were called back then. We were living in a vacuum. And that's not sustainable. When you showed up, I think he saw something in you. He hadn't met anyone else like you before. I think he might have thought about you as . . .' Maggie trials off.

'As what?'

She looks at her fingernails. 'As a means of escaping me.'

'But he loved you.'

'That's a very complicated word, Eliza.' Maggie's voice is low. 'I loved him too, but I wanted him all to myself. I didn't want him to have anyone else that would knock me off this pedestal I'd spent my whole life building. You must have felt that, when we first met.'

I think back to that first meeting in the Bellingham kitchen, the note of heartbreak in her voice. The coolness that radiated from her. 'Maybe. But you did a fairly decent job of hiding it. Most of the time.'

Maggie looks up at me. 'The day he brought you home, I made a promise to myself. I wasn't going to interfere in Eric's friendships anymore. We were supposed to be going to university the next year, I knew splitting up was inevitable, that I'd done a terrible thing making him so reliant on me, so I made a decision to encourage your friendship. I told myself I wouldn't stand in his way, that I'd let him go.' Maggie wipes her nose with the end of her sleeve. 'I tried, Eliza, I really did. I tried to welcome you like the friend he wanted you to be. I tried to be happy he'd found someone else who understood him. But when I saw how you were together, how different Eric was becoming. He was so much more confident when you were around. I just . . .' She stops, covers her face with her hands.

I lean over and squeeze her arm.

Maggie moves her arm out of my reach. 'I just couldn't separate out my feelings. I couldn't find a way through the jealousy. I couldn't be happy for him. I couldn't be happy for myself. And I blamed you for it. I blamed you both.'

Chapter
Fifty-Seven

I don't usually feel the cold, I'm so used to it, but I am still damp from my night-time swim, and the coffee hasn't warmed me up, it's just made me feel nervous. I scratch around the cupboard for some herbal tea and, while Maggie makes us both a cup, I light the fire in the sitting room and find a thicker jumper. We both sit down and watch the flames catch. I have so many questions I want to ask her, but she is jittery too, unable to settle. I wonder for how long I will have her attention before she bolts into the night and leaves me again.

'Do you remember the birthday cake you made for me?' I ask, hoping to anchor her to our past.

She allows herself a wry smile. 'I wasn't much of a baker.'

'It was the best birthday cake I've ever had. I mean it. I knew it wasn't easy for you, sharing me with Eric, but you were good at hiding it.' I touch the pendant at the base of my throat. The necklace I stole from her room, *my* necklace, lies hot against my skin, under my jumper. It is only a matter of time before I have to mention it; I wonder if it will close down the conversation, so I lead her, gently, to the place I want her to be.

'The last time we sat and watched a fire together was on that night, on my birthday,' I begin.

'I wanted that night to be so perfect,' she said. 'And then when I saw you together, it ruined everything.'

'So you did see us. I never said anything to him to make him do that.' I remember the kiss, I still think about it sometimes, and I still wonder what he meant by it. Did he mean it to be the beginning of something between us, or was it the natural conclusion of a birthday wish?

'I often wondered if that was the way things were going. I saw you looking at him sometimes. I hated you for looking at him like that.'

'I'm sorry.'

Maggie continues as if I'm not in the room. 'I suppose, towards the end, I couldn't work out whose attention I wanted the most; yours or Eric's. Eric found you first, but I think we could have had something special too.'

'Yes,' I whisper. 'Yes, we did.'

'You're a teacher, aren't you?' she says. 'An English teacher?'

'How did you find that out?'

She waves her fingers in the air, dismissively, to fend off my questions. Then she nods to herself. 'See? I told you, didn't I? Intellectual, good with words. Gemini traits. Horoscopes and star signs, they were my thing, not Eric's. He never would have thought about giving you that necklace if it hadn't been for me.'

I wish I could reach over to her, but she is sitting too far away. 'I know,' I say. 'I know that.'

'It was stuff like that, that really upset me. Those little acts of defiance. I would have been so happy to go into London and get you a birthday present with him. We could have made a day of it together. By that time, we were hardly doing anything just the two of us . . . but to wait until I was out of the way. To just go and do it without even asking, it felt like a slap in the face. He didn't even tell me he'd bought it for you. He didn't even show it to me.'

'I'm sure he didn't mean—'

Maggie raises her voice, cutting me off. 'You don't understand, Eliza. It's not like being rejected by a friend, you know. When your own twin doesn't need you anymore, it's different. When I heard you both in his room that day, talking, when you thought I wasn't there . . . it was such a betrayal.'

I frown, trying to recall what she means. 'What day?' I can't think of many times we were away from Maggie, and it was just the two of us. And then it slowly comes back to me. 'The day you bought the shoes,' I remember.

'I thought I'd climb the tree and surprise Eric. I knew he'd be in his room. The window was open, and he was fussy about shutting it if he wasn't in there. He hated the idea of anything flying in or his precious magazines being blown around. Anyway, I shinned up the tree and heard you both talking, so I stopped and listened in.'

'Oh.'

'I had no idea he kept a diary. It was like . . . another slap in the face. He used to tell me everything. You remember how open he was. We had no secrets from one another. Well,' she says bitterly, 'I didn't think we did.'

'I didn't know about him writing a diary, either, if that makes a difference.'

'But he chose to tell you, not me. And he told you he didn't ever want me to know. He called me . . .' Maggie looks away, into the corner of the room. 'He said I was suffocating.'

'He didn't mean it, Maggie, come on.'

She turns to me, angry. 'Yes, he did. And he was right. That's what's so awful about everything. He was right about me. I *was* suffocating.'

'Maggie, please . . .'

'And then I made up that stupid dare. I think that was the point where it all began to go wrong.' She shakes her head. 'We could have had such a great summer together. We could all be sitting here right now, laughing. Instead . . .'

For a moment, I cannot tell if she is angry with me, or angry with herself.

'Maggie,' I say, 'none of this is your fault. It's mine. I thought up the whole thing with the dares. Eric died because of me. That's my burden to bear, not yours.'

Suddenly, an expression of great clarity crosses her face and for a moment, she looks quite different, older. 'I thought you were supposed to be the clever one. You've not been listening to anything I've said, tonight,' she says in that husky voice. 'Have you?'

And then I remember the vision I had in the pond tonight. A pair of shoes in the Bellingham hallway. Questions I need answers to. Uncomfortable thoughts swimming through my head.

'I have been listening,' I say, slowly. 'But I don't think I understand what you're saying.'

'I thought you knew,' she says, her head on one side. 'I thought you understood.'

I feel as if I'm navigating a map that's both familiar and very new to me. Nothing feels as it should, yet I think I know where we are both heading.

'I thought you understood why I had to leave?' she presses.

'You left to get away from the awful thing I'd done. To punish me.' I pause. 'But then, sometimes, I wondered if you were trying to protect me. I waited for your parents to find out it was me who'd dared Eric to go to the pool to get my necklace. But they never did. They never found out it was my fault. I thought perhaps it was some way of acknowledging our friendship. Not to blame everything on me. But you couldn't keep lying for me, so you left.'

'Yes, you're right,' she says, sitting back in the chair, unable to hold herself up anymore. 'I couldn't maintain the lie. But not to hide the awful thing you'd done. I left to hide the awful thing *I* had done.'

Chapter
Fifty-Eight

'It wasn't a spur-of-the-moment decision, leaving,' Maggie says to me. 'I planned it all. I knew that nobody could make me go back home after I turned eighteen, and there was no way I was going to celebrate a birthday without Eric, so I took my passport, packed a bag, and left that morning before anybody was awake.'

'Your parents . . . I saw your uncle. He said they were devastated.'

'It was the only thing I could do. I couldn't stay.'

'Where did you go?'

'I hitched into London. Got a coach from Victoria station. I was in Paris by the afternoon.'

'France.' I try to imagine Maggie living the life of a Parisian. 'Why France?'

'Why not? I could speak a bit of French. I got a job waitressing and eventually started teaching English as a foreign language. I travelled around a lot, mainly in French-speaking countries. I couldn't settle. I thought about you. What you were doing. I assumed you'd gone to uni. Forgotten all about me.'

'You've been away all this time? You never came back?'

'There was no reason to come back.'

'Did you even know about your mum getting ill?'

'I kept tabs on them, as best I could. You know how they were, always so busy. In 2002, their company set up a website, and they used it to document events they'd been part of. There were plenty of pictures of them, so I could see how they were. When they finally retired, they joined Facebook. But they didn't set their privacy properly, so I was able to see what they were up to easily enough.'

I think about the amount of times I have tried to find Maggie on Facebook, when she was doing exactly the same thing, trying to keep tabs on her parents. They probably didn't use any privacy settings for just such a possibility, hoping their estranged daughter could see them, even if they couldn't see her. 'Why didn't you come home when she was ill?' I ask.

'I told you. I couldn't. I couldn't face them. It was better this way.'

I shake my head in confusion. 'So why are you here now?'

'Because they're dead. And you're the only one who knows what happened.' She gives a short, dry laugh. 'It turns out that no matter how angry I am with you for ruining my life, I still want to talk to you about everything that went wrong. All the time I was away, I couldn't think about Eric and what happened that summer. But since I came back to wind up their estate and sell the house, I can't stop thinking about anything else. It's been driving me mad.'

'Maggie, I left as soon as you did. I've been living here in London since you went. I really *don't* know what happened. You wouldn't talk to me, remember?'

She looks puzzled. 'But you followed me that day. I saw you. I ran into the house, and you tried to get in. You rang the bell.'

Footprints on the flagstones, shoes on the floor. A narrow view through a letterbox that never made sense. I feel like strangling her because she's being so obtuse, and I so badly want to understand. 'Just tell me exactly what happened, Maggie. From the beginning.'

The fire has caught, and the flames send out shadows into the room, flickering on the walls, but when Maggie begins to speak, everything slows down as if the whole house is holding its breath. She talks in a low voice, with a faraway look on her face, as if she is reciting a dream.

'You were away that day, you'd told us you wouldn't be back until the next morning. You'd gone to see a house with your parents. I hadn't had Eric to myself for so long. I wanted to make a day of it, just the two of us. And he did too. He said he had an idea, and it was going to be a surprise. So I did what I had never done before. I let him take the lead. I didn't ask any questions and I let him plan everything.'

Maggie tucks her feet underneath her on the armchair and leans towards the fire as if she, too, is feeling the chill in the air. 'He packed a picnic,' she remembers. 'He shooed me out of the kitchen. It was so nice. It felt like it used to feel when it was just the two of us. Then we left the house, and he started walking. I followed him. As we walked, we talked about him going away to university when he got his results; how we would work out seeing each other if we ended up on the opposite sides of the country. He told me he would come and visit me, that we would take it in turns, that it would be OK.

'I didn't really pay any attention to where we were going, I was just so happy to be with him. Until we stopped outside Ivydale. You'd dared him to get the necklace a few days before and he'd decided to come and spend our day together doing something to please you.'

Maggie swallows and carries on staring into the fire. Her face is lit up with an orange glow, but her skin looks waxy and ethereal, like a ghost. She regains her composure. 'I was so angry with him. I felt like he'd taken me for an idiot. All along, he hadn't wanted to spend the day with me, he wanted to do something for you. We had a big row outside the school. I can't believe nobody saw or heard us, maybe they did, who knows? Anyway, he persuaded me to go to the pool house with him. I didn't have a choice, really. That's what I was so angry about; if he'd just asked me, explained what he wanted. But he didn't. He made me think our day out together was all about us, when in fact it was all about you.'

I frown. 'Why didn't you just wait for Eric to get the necklace and then you could have gone and done something else together? You could have done both. I'd already given him the blank key. It wouldn't have taken him long.'

When she finally turns to look at me, Maggie has an expression on her face I can't understand. 'We didn't need your dad's blank key. I already had the key from last time. I took it out of the door and put it in my pocket so we couldn't get in. And then you pulled that stunt on the roof, dropping that stupid necklace through the window. Unbelievable. I could have slapped you.'

A crease of confusion folds itself into me.

'Eric couldn't swim,' Maggie says without emotion. 'He didn't want to go into the pool house. He made me swear not to tell you. It was the most shameful thing for him, not to be able to swim. He was terrified of water.'

Chapter
Fifty-Nine

I am too stunned to speak, so Maggie continues in the same, dull voice. 'Dad's idea of swimming lessons was to throw his children into the local pool. Sink or swim. When he did it to me, it worked. I got on with it. Kept myself afloat. With Eric, it was different. He sank under the water and the lifeguard pulled him out. There was a scene with my dad. It was awful. Eric refused to go again. So Mum tried to teach him. I tried when I was older. But that experience with Dad, it scarred him. He began to have nightmares about it. I don't know,' Maggie shakes her head, 'it sort of annoyed Dad that he was so affected by it. I think Dad felt very guilty at what he had caused, but he could never apologise. He was pretty old school like that. Eric would wake up in the night screaming his head off. I think it was more than nightmares, actually. What are they called?'

'Night terrors,' I answer, in a whisper.

'Yeah. Night terrors. It drove us all mad, for a while. Eric would scream the house down in the middle of the night, and when we went in to him, we couldn't wake him up. His eyes would be wide open, he'd be sitting up in bed. But when we talked to him, pleaded for him to wake up, when we tried to tell him it was just a bad dream, he couldn't snap out of it. He stopped having baths. He would only have a shower. Mum and I wanted Dad to stop making a big deal of everything, but Dad wouldn't let it go. *If he learned to swim, he wouldn't be afraid.* That's what he said. But every time he threatened Eric with another lesson, Eric got worse and worse.

'I guess we assumed he'd learn when he was older, but there's a kind of window for learning how to swim. If you can't do it when you're a kid, it sort of passes you by. Everyone forgets about how important it is. We never went on the kind of holiday that involved swimming. My parents were great walkers and skiers; we often got dragged up and down mountains. We never went to the sea or splashed in a pool. When you become a teenager, all any adult cares about is passing exams. Besides, you can't go to swimming lessons with five-year-olds when you're that age. It's humiliating.'

'Why didn't he tell me?' I whisper, the flames blurring through my tears. Eric was such an open person. I couldn't believe he kept the door shut to the darkest part of himself.

'He was embarrassed,' Maggie replies simply. 'Dad made sure of that. He made him feel ashamed.'

'I wouldn't have minded.'

'I know. But I think your obsession with breaking into the pool house made him think differently. It made him want to learn. Early in the summer, he mentioned that I should try teaching him again, but I knew he wanted to do it for you, so I refused to help, because I was jealous and unreasonable.'

I try and unpick the events in my head. 'So, why did you dare him to go swimming?'

'Like I said, I was jealous and unreasonable.' Maggie shifts in the chair. 'We both knew he couldn't do it, I wanted him to be humiliated. I wanted that precious bond you were developing to break. But after you went home that afternoon, he begged me to change my mind and cancel the dare. I was too much of a bitch to cancel everything, but I did feel sorry for him so I made a plan for him to fail so he could save face. I didn't want him to hate me. When I went to the pool house, I pocketed the key and pretended I couldn't find it. I assumed we would all go home and forget about it. And then Eric would be in my debt.'

I remember sitting with him by the wall, while we waited for her. I remember him turning to me, as if he was about to say something. A confession. And then Maggie came back. I groan as I remember that afternoon. 'I ruined your plan.'

Maggie looks grim. 'Yup. When you threw your necklace through the window, I assumed he would tell you, eventually. I knew he wouldn't go in and get it himself. But when he packed a picnic for us both, he packed my swimsuit, too. And a towel. I couldn't get over that. How sly that was.'

'He wanted you to get it for him.'

'Yes, he did. At first, I refused to go with him. But he said he was going to try and do it without me. I couldn't believe he was being so stupid. It was right in the deep end, right in the middle. There was no way he could dive down and get it. I was angry with him for being determined. It was so unlike him. I could usually talk him around to my way of thinking, but that summer, something had come over him and he just wouldn't toe the line anymore.'

Maggie shoots me a look and says, 'I thought to myself: *He must really like her to want to do this. Maybe he likes her more than me.*' Then, she looks away again and continues her story. 'Sure enough, there's your necklace, just where you dropped it. He looked around for something to get it with. There was a long pole with a kind of hook, for rescuing kids, I guess. He tried getting it with that, but the chain was too fine, and the pole was too thick. He begged me to get it for him. And the more he begged, the more I hated him.

'Eventually, he threw the pole into the water and took his clothes off. He had his swimming shorts on. Mum had bought him a pair for the summer in the hope it would encourage him to learn before he went away to uni. Even then, when his clothes were in a pile on the floor, I refused to believe he was actually going to get in. Turns out I was right.' Maggie bites her lip, brings her fingers to the blood. 'He couldn't. He just couldn't do it. He got angry too, then. We were both standing on the side of the pool, yelling at one another, and I remember he reached for me, just to touch my arm, to make a point. I think . . . I think just then, he was trying to reason with me. Trying to change the tone by saying we could do whatever I wanted to do after this if I would just get the necklace for him. It was how I would have spoken to him, like an adult to a child. He said the whole day would be mine. But I resented the role reversal. I pushed him off me. Hard. I just wanted to get his hand off me, but I was so angry. He staggered back and fell in.'

'Oh my god.' I put my hand to my mouth. I am with her in the pool house, and I can see with utter clarity how this must have happened.

I hold my breath, not wanting to hear any more, but at the same time burning with the need to know.

'I jumped straight in after him, Eliza. I promise I did.'

I nod, seeing it all play out in front of my eyes.

'But he was so big, and so frightened. He couldn't see the side, he couldn't see anything. He just . . . flailed about, he was so disorientated. We were both screaming. The acoustics of the room . . . There was water everywhere. I tried to calm him down, but he grabbed onto me and pushed me under, trying to get out. I thought I was going to die. I had that dress on, the rusty-coloured dress. And my shoes. They weighed me down. Every time I got to the surface to breathe, he grabbed hold of me and pushed me under again, anything to keep his own head above water. He lost his grip and I managed to swim away from him. But I was so exhausted and frightened, I climbed out. The pole had floated away from him. I pulled it out of the water, and I tried to use the hook, but

281

I just couldn't do it. He seemed completely unaware what I was trying to do. Like he didn't know how to help himself. Eventually, he stopped moving. So I made myself get back into the water. But I was so afraid if I put my arms around him, he'd wake up or something and push me under again, so I grabbed him by his foot and pulled him to the side of the pool. I didn't have the strength to pull him out, though. The sides were too high. I tried everything. I got the pole again. I got the hook around him, but I couldn't pull him out. He was so heavy.'

Maggie is stony-faced as she carries on speaking in her deadpan voice. 'And then I became really frightened. For myself. I convinced myself I'd go to jail for what I'd done. Because however you look at it, I pushed him in. So I got back into the water once more, and I dived down, into the deep end to get your necklace so there wouldn't be any questions about who it belonged to and why it was there.'

She turns to me now, her voice almost a whisper. 'I want you to know that despite all the bad feelings I had towards you that day, I thought about you. I didn't want you to be involved. I left his clothes on the side, put the pole back where he'd found it. It was hot in there, the window in the roof was open. I knew the water on the side of the pool would dry up quickly, and when he was found there would be no trace of me. I took the bag with the picnic in and threw it into a hedge. When I ran home, I thought about what I was going to say to Mum and Dad, and I knew I'd never be able to lie about what happened. Not for the rest of their lives, anyway.'

'I can't imagine . . . to know this and not be able to share it. I'm so sorry.'

She looks away, back into the fire. 'Don't feel sorry for me. You're lucky you can cry about it. I haven't been able to cry for a very long time. When Eric drowned, a part of me drowned with him, and I will never, ever get that back.'

'But your parents . . . they knew he couldn't swim, surely? They must have told the police that. They must have wondered why he was there by himself.'

'Yes, my parents were the only other people in the world who knew he couldn't swim. And they were too ashamed to tell the police they'd neglected to teach him. Besides, I'm not even sure the police thought to ask them. Everyone just assumes everyone else can swim. Especially if you find a teenager who's broken into the school pool house in their swimming trunks. Why would a non-swimmer do that?'

'Didn't your parents wonder why you weren't there with him?'

'Yes, of course. They asked me. But I told them I got my period that morning. I always get really bad cramps on the first day or two. They were used to me spending the day in bed looking awful. So, when they came to look for me, to tell me what had happened to Eric, there I was in bed, looking terrible, with my dress in the washing machine. I always took care of that sort of thing myself. It wasn't unusual.

'I told them the truth, that Eric had been thinking about learning to swim, that he'd asked me to teach him, and I'd refused. I told them we'd argued about it. It helped me, that. To feel conscience-stricken in front of them. I needed to make it look bad because I couldn't keep the guilt in. It poured out of me. My mother tried to comfort me, but I wouldn't let her.'

'But it wasn't your fault he couldn't swim.'

'Well, that was the other side of it. If Eric had been able to swim, none of this would have happened. Because Dad had made him so afraid of the water, Mum ended up not speaking to him for days, so I blamed myself for that, too. I couldn't stand it, the bad feeling in the house. I couldn't stand to see them both, every day, dealing with the fallout of what I had done. I knew that the truth would have killed them, so I figured it was better for me to leave, because I couldn't have kept it in. I would have told them, eventually.'

'Maggie, I don't know what to say.'

She looks at me, defiant. 'At least they still loved me. At least they thought of me with fondness over the years. Now they're both dead, it's safe to come back. You're the only one who knows the truth, and I don't care anymore who else knows. All I wanted was for them to never find out what I did to Eric, and I achieved that. At least I did that for them.'

Chapter Sixty

I'm familiar with the burden of shouldering guilt. I've done it for twenty years. The weight of it wraps itself around you, like weeds in water, dragging you down and muffling life. When Maggie has finished, I have a distinct sensation of weightlessness, of a surface being broken, my lungs filling with light and air. But the light is edged with darkness. For years I thought everything was my fault, how that could have been so easily erased by Maggie.

'I can't believe you kept this a secret all this time.' I try and swallow my resentment but the voice in my head demands I kick her out of the house. She let me believe it was all my fault for so many years, and she could have stopped that with a sentence. 'Why didn't you write to me?' I ask. 'Why didn't you let me know why you'd gone? You could have saved me so much heartache.'

'Because you were part of the problem, Eliza. You set everything in motion and I couldn't forgive you for that. Besides, I couldn't risk you telling somebody and it getting back to my parents. It was the one thing I could do for them, let them believe I was a good girl.'

'You could have kept in touch from a distance. You could have sent them a card,' I argue.

'Maybe I should have. But I thought in the long run it was easier to make a clean break. I didn't want them hanging over the post box every Christmas and birthday. I wanted them to get on with their lives. And that feeling became stronger when I became a parent myself. I knew if I ever let slip I'd had a baby, it would have been torture for them to have a grandson and not know him.'

Now I remember the boy at the flat, pulling the bell off the doorframe and shouting at me. 'I think I met your son.'

'Cameron. Yes, he told me about your visit. I stupidly rented a flat that used to belong to a dealer, and we get all the local druggies ringing on the bell wanting a fix. As soon as the house sale goes through, I'm moving to a nicer area.'

'How did he know it was me?'

'He didn't. I put two and two together. When the removal company phoned me to confirm everything had been packed, they mentioned your visit to the house. They assumed you were me, having a last look around. I knew it must have been you. I guessed it was only a matter of time before you found me. It was you, wasn't it, at the old house?'

'Yes,' I answer. 'I found the necklace in your bedroom. I took it back.' I pull it out from beneath my jumper, unfasten the clasp and let it dangle between us. But Maggie moves away from me and averts her eyes.

'I don't want to look at it again,' she murmurs.

I tuck it back under my jumper. An image surfaces in my mind of her diving under her brother's body to fetch it, to protect me and I feel sympathy for her, leaking into the pool of resentment that wells up inside me.

'Weeks ago,' I say, 'I saw someone I thought was you. You were standing on a street at the edge of the Heath, looking at your phone.'

She shrugs. 'Probably. I've been trying to find a school for Cameron and somewhere more permanent to live once the sale goes through.'

'So you're going to stay?' I don't know how I feel about that, having Maggie in my neighbourhood.

She sighs. 'Cameron needs some structure in his life. He's not a kid anymore. And now I have enough money to settle down, London seems as good a place as any to do it.'

'So it *was* him I saw at my school.'

'Yes. I did some digging around when we arrived and saw you were an English teacher there. You're on the school website, it was so easy to track you down. I couldn't resist finding out what kind of a life you'd built without me and Eric. And when I saw how comfortably you lived, I wanted to mess it up a little bit.'

'The piano. The lotus flower.'

'Well, I needed to find a home for the piano, anyway. I don't want it. At first, I thought it might make a good peace offering, but when I found out where you lived, and I saw the nice life you'd made for yourself, I just wanted to remind you who I was. Who we both were. So I left the lotus flower on your desk . . . I couldn't help myself.'

'How did you find out where I lived?'

'I overheard one of the teachers talking about your broken leg. She mentioned how hard it must be to get around, living in your cottage on the Heath and it didn't take me long to figure out where she meant.'

'Have you told Cameron? What happened to Eric?'

'Not yet, but I will. He's old enough now to understand.'

'Where is he now, is he by himself?' I look at my watch and it is getting late.

'Oh, playing some kind of computer game. He's used to being alone, unfortunately. But I think it might be time he put some roots down, makes some friends.'

'What about his father?' I ask.

She waves her fingers again, in that dismissive way, warding off any more questions.

'So it's just the two of you?'

'Yeah. Just the two of us. He's my second chance.'

I look at Maggie carefully, and although she says she hasn't cried in years, she blinks too fast when she says this, and hides her face behind the sleeve of her jacket.

I have to ask her. 'He looks . . .'

'Just like Eric, I know. Do you think it's creepy? The way he looks?'

'No, not creepy.'

'I haven't been able to talk to anyone about the resemblance because nobody knows anything about my past. You're the only one left.'

And then I feel it. A common thread, dangling in front of us, waiting to be woven into something we can both cling on to. A shared history. Memories. All the things that take time to form, they bind us together, these experiences, they make us stronger. They help us forgive one another. But I can't forgive Maggie in an evening, and I don't think she can forgive me. Not tonight, anyway.

Chapter
Sixty-One

I dream about Eric that night. I am with him in the pool house, and when he falls into the water, I fall with him. There is no shouting or screaming, nothing like the scene Maggie described. In fact, Maggie is not there. It's just Eric and me. We sink to the floor of the pool and there is only the quiet movement of the water around us, rocking us both into a drowsy state, a soporific rhythm that surrounds us like a slow and steady heartbeat. I take his face in my hands, every contour and imperfection as clear as they ever were, and I do not let him look away. I hold his gaze and tell him there is nothing to fear. We look at one another for a long time. When the light begins to leave him, I bring his face towards mine and I kiss him, and it is like a conversation we always meant to have but never had the courage to voice.

I don't wake with the choking feeling of a nightmare. Strangely, I am comforted by what I have seen. I spend the morning, still in a dream state, unable to put aside the vision in my head. It might be the conversation I had with Maggie yesterday, the feeling of lightness that came over me from her confession, the knowledge I am not entirely to blame. I don't know. I look out of the window onto the back garden, and notice the daffodils are fading now, to be replaced by bluebells, pushing their way through the ground.

Without giving myself the chance to change my mind, I grab my swim things and head to the pond, hoping that Iris will be there.

I recognise her dress when I enter the changing room. It lies there, on the bench, like a reproach. My resolve falters, and I am just about to make a sharp exit when she comes into the changing room, pulling her swim cap off and shaking it out. There is a shadow edged by a brown line, staining her neck, tracing the curve of her chin and jaw; dirt that has transferred from the pond surface onto her skin. She looks as if she has a beard, badly painted on, and the effect is comical and out of place.

'Don't go anywhere. I mean it. I need to talk to you,' she says, diving into the shower for a quick rinse. She doesn't bother drying herself for long, she just slings the tunic over her head, wraps a thick cardigan around her body and grabs her bag. 'Let's go and sit in the meadow, it's warm enough this morning.'

We sit, side by side. The meadow is a gentle slope to the water. There is a view through the trees to the pond beyond, which is now filling up with women. The sunlight feels good against my skin.

'I'm sorry about the key,' Iris begins, 'I meant to tell you and then I meant to give it back but the last time we met things didn't go so well . . .'

'What were you thinking, giving Lucas a key to my home? My home, Iris, not some public space.'

'Temporary insanity. I don't know what I was thinking, well I do. I wasn't thinking at all. The last time we saw each other, it set me off on a tangent. It's taken a while to get myself back on track. I really am sorry about the keys. I should have asked your permission.'

'Iris,' I say, suddenly feeling contrite in the face of such a gracious apology. 'You told me something very personal the last time we saw each other and I'm afraid I was harsh on you.'

'Ah, but you were right, as it happens. I am a hypocrite.'

'It's your business, not mine.'

'I could say the same to you. I shouldn't have interfered.'

'I followed your advice. I found Maggie. Well, she found me.'

I tell her about going back to the village and about finding Maggie in my house. I don't tell her about Maggie's confession.

'Are you going to see one another again?' she asks.

'I think we have to. I'm going to meet her son.'

'That's funny. I'm going to meet my son tomorrow,' Iris says quietly. 'That's why I've been a bit . . . discombobulated recently.'

I turn to her, incredulous. 'Iris. That's . . . that's huge.'

'I know. I can't believe I'm actually going to meet him. I can't believe he wants to meet me. It's incredible. Wonderful. Terrifying.'

Her voice is shaking, and I put an arm around her shoulder. 'I thought you didn't want to make contact?' I ask, gently.

'I thought I didn't, too.' Iris tells me about the letter she received from Freja. 'I think, deep down, I have always wanted to do it, I just needed a little encouragement.'

'Have you spoken to your husband?'

'No. Just my son, Anthony. David, my husband, was very hurt. I did a terrible thing to both of them. But Anthony is ready to talk about it and, understandably, David is not. Not yet, anyway.'

'Where are you meeting him?'

'In London. He's a clinical psychologist. Can you believe it? He's here for some kind of conference and I'm meeting him for a drink. I'm so nervous. What if he hates me? What if he doesn't understand?'

'If he's a clinical psychologist I'm sure he'll be a very good listener.'

'Yes! That's what I thought. It's odd, isn't it, that we both went into a caring profession, though I think what I did to him might have been a factor.'

'Well, you can ask him yourself, can't you?'

'I haven't told you the best thing, though.'

'What?' I ask.

'I have a grandchild.'

'Woah,' I exclaim.

'I'm trying not to get ahead of myself, but he wouldn't have told me that, would he, if he didn't want me to know about her, to be involved?'

'So she's a little girl?'

'Yes. She's six.'

'What's her name?'

'Summer. It's a ridiculous name, I know. His wife is a yoga teacher. But I bit my tongue and stopped myself from pointing out to him, that Summer was the name of a season, not the name of a child.' She lets out a snort. 'Do you know? I think I'm turning over a new leaf. It felt good not to interfere. I just said, *how lovely*, and moved the conversation on. It felt quite liberating.'

I stifle a laugh at the idea of Iris being diplomatic. 'Well, I guess you can completely reinvent yourself, can't you? You can be whoever you want to be. You've been given a clean slate.'

'I don't think it's going to be that easy. I have a lot of apologising to do. A lot of explaining. He's very close to his father. For obvious reasons.'

'But he's agreed to meet. And that can only be a good thing.'

'Like you and Maggie.'

'Yes. Like me and Maggie.'

'Tell me, is everything forgotten between you? Has she given *you* a clean slate?'

I can see she wants me to give her only positive news, so she can feel optimistic about her own situation. 'It isn't as simple as that,' I say. 'But there aren't many people who know me as well as she does.' I find it hard to articulate the importance I place on history. The fact she has been in my life for so long, our relationship deserves to be preserved. Even after the mess we made of our lives, something remains between us, an invisible force, drawing us together.

Chapter
Sixty-Two

Before I leave the cottage, I run upstairs to retrieve the photo album I made for Maggie's eighteenth birthday. A peace offering. The ribbon looks a little flattened, and the spine of the book has faded over the years where it stuck out of Maggie's bookshelf at the Bellingham house and caught the sun in the afternoon light. Inside it is pristine. I can still remember the desperation with which I stuck those pictures down at jaunty angles, trying to pretend everything would soon be OK between us. When I arrive at Maggie's flat, the doorbell has been put back. I press it and hear the familiar clunk of the door in the basement, footsteps on the concrete staircase.

'Hi,' I say, shyly, feeling weird.

'Hey,' she replies. She doesn't hug me. It's too early for that. 'Welcome to our hovel.' She waves her arm and motions for me to go through.

The flat is dark and depressing. The air feels cold and there is a lingering smell of damp, even though the walls have been recently painted and it looks perfectly clean.

As if she is reading my mind, Maggie says 'It's all I could afford when we came back. We'll be out of here soon.'

'It's fine,' I lie.

'It's really not,' she replies in an amused voice, ushering me onto a tired-looking sofa. 'Cam! Eliza's here,' she calls. 'Leave the screen and come and say hello.'

I turn to the only door I can see that is closed. It slowly opens and a boy, Eric's doppelgänger, emerges. 'Hey,' he waves, a self-conscious teenage wave, echoing his mother's greeting.

'Hi there.' I put my hand out and he shakes it firmly. I cannot help staring at him. He is so similar to Eric, but the more I look, the more I can see there are differences too.

'Sorry about the bell. I wasn't sure who you were,' he says awkwardly.

'I must have given you a shock. You gave *me* a shock, you see.'

'Yeah, Mum told me.'

'I brought you both something,' I say to him. 'Well, actually, I made it for your mum, many years ago, but she left before I could give it to her.'

We all sit, in a line, on the sofa. I am in the middle, but I pass the album to Maggie so she can untie the ribbon and read the childish message I have written in colourful felt tip pen on the first page of the book.

'For Maggie,' she reads out loud, *'Happy 18th Birthday. Love, always, Eliza XXX.'*

'Did you know about this?' I ask. 'I brought it round to your house, but I was too late. Your parents must have put it in your room.'

She shakes her head. 'No, I didn't know. And I must have missed it when I came back to the house. We look so happy,' she says, sadly.

We look through the photo album together and when we do, something interesting happens. The more we talk to Cameron about the three teenagers in the book, the less tragic everything seems. As we describe the friendship we forged, the stupid things we did together, I begin to see the summer of 1995 through a different, less melancholy lens.

Cameron is keen to get to know me. I suppose I am the first person in his life who could be called family, other than his mother. I tell him about the school I teach at, and he replies shyly he has already asked Maggie to register his name there. I don't stay for long. My time with Maggie feels tender and vulnerable. But we agree to keep meeting like this, because neither of us wants the alternative. Before I go, she gives me an object wrapped in newspaper. It is tattered, and old-looking. 'I think you should have this.'

'What is it?' I ask.

'It's Eric's diary.'

'Oh.' Suddenly the package takes on a weight I'm not sure I can carry.

'I was going to take it and confront him with it after I heard what he said through the window. But I never got the opportunity because we were always together over the summer. And then . . .' We both allow the end of the sentence to peter out. 'Anyway, I decided to take it with me when I left in case there was anything in it about the dares. I didn't want to go to the trouble of disappearing, only to have him confess all when they got hold of his diary. So I stole it.'

'Have you read it?' I ask.

She looks at me and gives me a look that is hard to read. 'I started. But I stopped. There were things in there I didn't want to know.'

'Why are you giving it to me, then?'

She pauses as she thinks about her answer. 'Because it might be a comfort to you.'

'I'm not sure I should read his diary, Maggie. It's private.'

'Well, I don't want it. It's yours. Take it home. Burn it. Keep it. I don't care. I don't want to see it again.'

I walk briskly, the evening is chilly, but I soon warm up as I zigzag through the streets and back onto the Heath. I push through my gate and wander through the garden, noting new nubs of green, pulsing their way through the soil. I crouch down and touch the earth. It is getting warmer every day, just like the water in the pond.

I pour myself a drink and settle into the sofa, putting the package onto the coffee table in front of me, unwrapping it slowly. When I uncover the diary, I take a deep breath before I open it.

I imagine Maggie, listening in to our conversation, waiting until the right moment to steal it and confront Eric with it, only to be forced into taking it with her on the morning she left. As I read through Eric's words, I can see why Maggie didn't want to keep it. It must have been painful for her, but it is a panacea for me. Maggie's words come back to me: *Burn it. Keep it. I don't care.* I wonder why she kept it, all these years. And then I wonder if she kept it for me, if she knew it might one day become a peace offering.

As the hours tick by, I wallow in Eric's thoughts, and I begin to understand that the distance he kept between us was an attempt to retain our intimacy. He was so afraid of spoiling our friendship by confessing how he really felt. I read how he agonised over choosing a birthday gift for me that meant something. How he wanted to reflect his feelings without alerting Maggie to them. He spent the last few months seesawing between wanting me and wanting to remain loyal to his sister. His anguish rolls off the page. Then he writes about the pool house. His terror of the water, his desire to swim with me, the guilt he was betraying Maggie.

I can hardly bear to read the last entry. The optimism that he could retrieve the necklace and finally, in a quiet moment, fasten it around my neck once more, and tell me how he felt.

Chapter
Sixty-Three

Iris has woken feeling guilty and aimless. She's not down for a shift today, but as she cleans her teeth and picks out what to wear, a part of her wonders if a few hours sorting through some paperwork at the charity might take her mind off things. The meeting with Anthony, her son, went as well as could be expected, considering the circumstances, but their conversation was cautious and full of things unsaid. They both danced around the main topic, the reason they were there together, walking along the canal that flowed through King's Cross. She did manage to get an apology in, though. The first of many, she thinks grimly. She will never stop apologising for the mothering he has missed. He doesn't need it now, of course, he has a family of his own. She is superfluous to his life now. It is a privilege he has afforded her, to allow her to re-enter it at this late stage.

Iris has never been a patient person. She can see that one day, things might be easy between them. But she wants the easiness to happen now, not this wary, cautious politeness. Time will heal, she knows this, but it can't come soon enough. *It's funny*, she thinks, as she makes the bed, *how we spend our lives wishing time to slow down, speed up, loop back and forth. We are never happy with things ticking along as they are.* The only place she feels time unspooling at the pace it should, is in the pond.

The phone rings. Iris hopes it isn't a cold caller, but somebody she knows who wants to have a conversation about something distracting. When she hears Eliza's voice, it is like having a little prayer answered.

'Oh, am I glad it's you,' she says warmly. 'I'm feeling out of sorts today.'

'Did everything go OK with Anthony?'

She sighs. 'It will, I think, eventually. Nothing's going to change miraculously overnight. And I don't think I'll ever be on David's Christmas card list. How did it go with Maggie and Cameron?'

'Pretty good. I've invited them over for dinner next week.'

Iris is surprised, and a little hurt. She has never been invited over for dinner at Eliza's house. 'I didn't think you did that sort of thing.'

'No. I don't. I don't know what came over me. I just said it without realising, and now—'

'Do you want me to help?'

'Yes please.'

The relief in Eliza's voice is a balm to Iris's mood. 'I'm a pretty good cook,' says Iris. 'I can give you some ideas for an easy dinner.'

'Oh, not with that. I can cook a meal. Nothing too fancy. And I'd love you to come as well, did I mention that? I'd like you to meet them. I need an ally. Things are still a bit awkward.'

The day is turning out well, after all. 'Well, that sounds lovely. I accept your invitation.'

'But it's not the cooking I need help with.'

'Then what?'

'I've been thinking about the house. It's . . . not really ready for visitors.'

'Ah.'

'I thought I was doing the right thing, leaving it just as Val had left it, but it's . . .'

'In dire need of some TLC?'

'Yes. I want to tart the whole place up, eventually, but just the sitting room for now. If I can give it a lick of paint before they come, hang some new curtains or something, it'll look like I actually care.'

'When is this meal, exactly?' Iris asks.

'Next week. I have a few days' holiday left and then a weekend. I think I can manage it before I start work.'

'You'd manage it faster with Lucas, too. Have you called him?'

Eliza hesitates. 'I can't ask him,' she says quietly.

'Why ever not?'

'I was so awful to him last time I saw him. I don't think he's going to forgive me any time soon.'

'He doesn't strike me as the type to bear a grudge.'

'He's not. He's the kindest person I know, and I've trampled over his trust in so many ways . . .'

'I can't believe that. What have you done?'

'I'm too embarrassed to tell you.'

'You know I don't care about embarrassment.'

Eliza tells her about the job application, the argument they had in her cottage. 'I-I don't think I told you this, but my greenhouse was vandalised at the beginning of the year and all the seedlings I was growing just perished. Every time I think about Lucas, all I see are those seedlings, shrivelled up. We had something that was light-hearted and nice. I betrayed his trust, and I was so ungrateful for his help. I don't think I deserve his friendship.'

Iris snorts. 'The last time I looked inside that greenhouse, your seedlings were thriving.'

'They're different ones. I planted everything out again.'

'So do the same with Lucas. Start again.'

Eliza groans. 'I don't know.'

'Friendship takes practise, and perseverance.' Iris thinks of Freja's words in the pub concerning motherhood, and not for the first time she thinks how wise that woman is. 'You should invite him for dinner too, by way of an apology. We can dilute your embarrassment. No big deal.'

'Maybe.'

'Definitely, I think. With all three of us on the job, we'll have that room painted in no time.' And then she adds, not quite under her breath, 'I bet you Lucas would love to help too. That man was born in a DIY shop.'

'Stop it,' Eliza scolds.

Iris laughs. 'Just stating the obvious.'

'Alright, fine,' Eliza grumbles. 'I'll give him a call.'

The drive to the store is fun. Iris is feeling bold and puts the roof down, it is just getting warm enough, if they both wear a scarf. Iris cuts through the traffic smoothly, nipping in and out of the lanes of cars, making it to the retail park in double quick time.

'This place is insane,' Eliza says, squinting at all the paint charts. 'I don't know where to start.'

'Well, I do, thankfully. You're looking at masonry paint there, Eliza, which is not what you want. We need interior paint.'

They round a corner and enter a long aisle devoted to interiors. 'Well, look at that,' Iris says, trying to keep the laughter out of her voice. 'What a coincidence.'

'Lucas . . .' Eliza says, looking shy.

Lucas, startled, drops a paintbrush he has been examining onto the floor. He stoops to pick it up, looking wary. 'You said you needed some help. So here I am. I'd like to make up for breaking into your house.'

'Lessons have been learned,' asserts Iris. 'Water under the bridge. We will only interfere when we are invited. Like now.'

Lucas nods, clearly finding it hard to tear his eyes away from the colourful aisles. 'Are we talking gloss or eggshell?'

'Both, most definitely,' Iris concludes. 'Rollers and paint-brushes too.'

Lucas counts on his fingers. 'You'll need some masking tape, for cutting in. Some sugar soap for preparing the surfaces. And some dust sheets.'

'Oh yes,' muses Iris, 'I'd forgotten about dust sheets.'

'Do you even need me?' asks Eliza, exasperated. But Iris can tell she is secretly pleased. There is a small smile in her voice.

'Just your approval, and your bank card,' says Iris smoothly. 'Now, am I right in thinking that your living room is north facing? You'll need a colour to counteract the colder light. Something warm and cheerful, but not too sudden, if you know what I mean. And we may as well look for kitchen paint too, we might be able to do both rooms if we get a move on.'

Iris leads Eliza around the huge store, pointing out things they might need, colours that might work. Eliza pushes a trolley behind them both, nodding her agreement, or vetoing their suggestions. When they can't fit everything into Iris's tiny car, Lucas agrees to take most of the paint in his and make a start straightaway. Whether Eliza phoned Lucas just to please her, Iris will never know, but Eliza's lack of resistance is noticeable, her brittleness all but gone.

Chapter
Sixty-Four

I have read and re-read Eric's diary. The grief I felt for all three of us has had an effect on me. Life is fragile, and everybody deserves a second chance. Even me.

Lucas is already in his office when I poke my head around the door. I could have picked up the phone, but I know school is already open for teachers who want a quiet day to prepare before the students arrive tomorrow.

'Hello,' he says. 'Finished painting?'

'Almost finished. The house looks much better, thanks to you and Iris.' I take my jacket off and I plop down on the chair opposite him, putting my elbows on his desk.

'Well it would,' Lucas says thoughtfully. 'That was several decades of paint I scraped off those window frames.'

'I can't believe it took me so long to do it. I'm very resistant to stuff like that. Was, I should say.'

The kitchen walls are now an acid yellow, the colour of the water irises that flower in the spring. The sitting room is a beautiful duck-egg blue. Upstairs, in the bedrooms and bathroom, there will be shades of green. Without realising it, I am clothing my house in the colours of the pond.

'You could start on the greenhouse next. It's wrought iron. Just needs stripping back and repainting. The glass is still in good condition.'

'Mmm,' I agree, deciding not to tell him that half the panes have been replaced recently.

'Ready to get back into the fray?'

'I can't wait to start. I'm even planning on coming to the next staff social.'

'Good,' Lucas says, though not with the enthusiasm I had expected.

'How about you?' I ask, frowning. 'Is everything OK?'

Lucas looks apprehensive. 'I haven't told anybody else this yet, so keep it under your hat, but I'm leaving.'

His words cut me, physical pain. 'What? Why?'

He shrugs. 'I can't work here anymore.'

'But . . . Lucas . . . I thought we'd sorted everything out? You know how sorry I am about . . . I just said I was going to come to the next social . . .'

He waves his arms as if shooing me away. 'Yes, yes. I know all of that. It's not that.'

'Then what?' My brain scrambles to figure out what my life here will look like with a Lucas-shaped hole in it. I can't believe he is telling me this when I've finally decided to turn over a new leaf.

He opens his palm and reaches out for me, and I give him both hands. Very gently, he unbuttons the cuff of my sleeve and rolls up the cotton to expose the three black dots on the surface of my skin. It is just like that morning in my kitchen when he made me breakfast. He brushes the pad of his thumb over the tattoo and this time, I don't move my arm away. I can't.

'I thought, for a very long time,' he begins, 'that we clicked so well because everything I knew about you was up on the surface. That you were easy to read, easy to understand. I suppose it's because I didn't bother to do any digging that I didn't realise you were hiding so much. My fault.'

'Lucas, I . . .'

'Shh,' he says quietly, still brushing his thumb across my arm. 'Then, when I realised there was a lot more to you than meets the eye, I found I wanted to know what it was. And when you didn't want to talk to me about it, it compromised our friendship, I think.'

I shake my head. 'It didn't. It hasn't. Lucas—'

'It compromised our friendship, because I stopped wanting to be your friend.'

'What?' I feel tears sting my eyes. I can't believe this is what it has come to. That he is being so cruel.

'I can't keep working here, seeing you every day, wanting to get to know you more, and knowing it won't happen.' He takes a deep breath and lets it out. 'I think the day I came to visit you in hospital, and I thought for a small moment that you could have died, it triggered something. An idea of what life without Eliza would be like. And I was more miserable about that than I thought was decent. I have tried to put those feelings to the back of my mind, but I can't.'

The penny, finally, drops.

'Honestly?' Lucas continues, looking at the tattoo. 'I always valued your friendship, Eliza. I did. We were the best of colleagues. Inside these walls, you are my rock. The one person I can count on to be there. But now I want to be able to count on you outside these walls. And I don't think you feel the same, do you?' It is only then that he raises his head and looks at me.

I am so shocked I can't find the words to respond. 'Where are you going to go?' I ask, and I hate myself for sidestepping the real question, because it's too big for me to answer.

He lets go of my arm and slowly rolls my shirtsleeve down, buttons the cuff. 'There's the chance of a headship and I'm going to take it, in another school.'

'In London?' I ask, hardly daring to think where else it might be.

'Yes. Not far from here.'

I am flooded with relief, and I put my head in my hands, feeling sick.

'I'm sorry I dumped this on you. I don't have any other friends in here I'm close enough to tell.' He gives a rueful laugh.

'Join the club,' I reply, raising my head and looking at him square in the eyes. Then the tears that threatened, begin to spill. 'I don't want you to go, Lucas,' I sniff. 'I know it's selfish to ask. But I've only just got my life on track. If you left me, it would be like starting over again.'

'I'm not leaving you. I'm leaving the school.'

'You just said you don't want to be friends anymore.'

'I do. But not like before. I have a hard job trying not to think about you all day long. It's very time-consuming and exhausting. Not to mention unprofessional.'

'I think about you, too,' I say, my voice small and full of misery. 'You are the one person who keeps me sane. I don't want to lose you.'

'Then you need to decide what happens next. I've told you what I want.'

'I don't know how to do that. It's a miracle I even became friends with you. I keep trying to tell you, I'm rubbish at relationships.'

'All I'm asking is that you let me in. Tell me something meaningful about yourself. Something I don't know. Show me that hinterland I got a glimpse of.'

I touch the tattoo under my shirtsleeve. Three indelible dots. I realise, now, that Lucas is already inside me. He has crept under my skin in the same way the Indian ink has remained in me all these

305

years. He has Eric's uncomplicated good humour. He has Maggie's energy and sense of fun. Iris said that friendship takes practise and perseverance. I suppose relationships do, too.

I take a deep breath and I roll up my sleeve once more. I lay my bare arm on the desk between us, and I point to the marks on my skin. And then I begin to tell him about the summer I made friends with two of the most important people in my life, and the terrible events that tore us apart.

Chapter
Sixty-Five

Iris struggles to open her front door, because an enormous white cake box is balanced, precariously, in the crook of her left arm. Most of the cake has been eaten, so the weight is now unevenly distributed in a box that is too big, making her wish she had just put the whole thing down on the step before trying to get into her house. With a sigh, she does just that, and this time, when she turns the key, it glides effortlessly through the mechanism and the door swings inwards in welcome. She takes her key out of the lock, pockets it and stoops to retrieve the cake. When the box is safely on the kitchen table, she returns to the car and retrieves another box, this time made of brown cardboard containing her belongings. When the car is locked and her front door shut, she slumps at the kitchen table, the brown box on the floor beside her, and she feels herself succumbing to post party blues.

It has been an emotional afternoon. She didn't want any fuss, but she's been at the charity for so long they told her it didn't feel right, not giving her a proper send-off. She has spent most of her life trying to reunite people, and Iris is bad at saying goodbye. All the families who called her during her career, distraught, not understanding why their loved one didn't at least leave a note, Iris always nodded in sympathy, but, not so deep down, she understood the need to slip away without making a fuss about it. Saying goodbye, it makes everything official. It's a commitment to not coming back. If you slip away when nobody's looking, there's always a chance you can slip right back in again and pretend you never left.

Iris looks through the brown box, her eyes resting on each item before she moves on to the next: a pot plant in dire need of watering. A collection of colourful pens she liked to use for different families, to differentiate which case she was making notes about. An insulated coffee mug. A cardigan for when the heating in the office was on the blink and her bone-handled silver paper knife. Iris cannot believe this paltry collection signifies forty years of service, and now she has said her official goodbyes, she wonders how much she is going to miss it, and what she will do instead.

Her thoughts turn to her own family – a word she has begun to use, tentatively, first trying it out on Carole and Eliza, before dishing it out more liberally to others. Last year, after Freja phoned her, something was put into motion. Iris thinks of it as a complex machine with many delicate parts, one relying on the cooperation of the next in order for things to move along smoothly. After a few short meetings with Anthony, a walk, a drink, they progressed to having a meal together. Iris has explained as best she can what went through her head when she was younger, and to Anthony's credit, he has listened to her side of the story before explaining how it was to grow up without her, not knowing if she was dead or alive.

'I went through a period when I very much hoped you were alive,' he said. 'And then I went through a period when I thought it was best you were dead.'

Iris digested this, and it was like swallowing splinters. 'And what do you think now?' she asked him.

He had looked at her then, without judgement or rancour. 'I don't wish you were dead,' he'd replied. 'No. Not anymore. I'm glad we are back in touch.'

Since then, she has been introduced to Anthony's daughter, Summer, who has just had her seventh birthday. Although Iris wasn't invited to the party – David was there – she was allowed to send a gift and a card. She has met her granddaughter several times and is shocked by the ferocity of emotion she has for her, this little girl she didn't know existed. Her relationship with Summer is the least-complicated thing in her life. It is a simple, pure exchange of feeling, untainted by her past, because her granddaughter is only ever concerned with the future.

Iris has refrained from using Anthony as a go-between. She knows she needs to mend fences with David, and he would resent her involving their son. But it is a tricky situation. Anthony told her David was unwilling to see her, but over the months, she has felt a softening, a change in the pauses between Anthony's words when he talks about him, and she wonders if David is beginning to yield.

She loved David once, and he loved her. That should be enough motivation to repair what she broke, but without seeing him, without talking to him, it's a difficult task. As she sits at her kitchen table, the remains of her working life in a box at her feet, she suddenly remembers what Eliza used to do. Iris finds some paper, picks out one of her pens, and begins to write. In her letter to David, she tries to explain herself. She apologises, unreservedly and congratulates him on rearing their son without her, turning a sad little boy into a successful, caring man. Before she changes her mind, she walks to the end of the road to where the post box lies and thrusts it through the slot, sealing her fate.

When she returns, the wall of faces greets her in the hallway. She takes a few moments to go through them all, remembering all of their names, reliving their stories. And then, without thinking too much about it, she removes them, one by one, wrapping each one in newspaper before putting them in several neat piles on the floor. When she is done, only one picture remains. It is a studio portrait of Anthony, Freja, and Summer. A Christmas gift from the family. Her family. It is only a photograph, but she knows it is an olive branch from her son, a gesture of acceptance.

Iris looks at the empty space, the long wall in her hallway. She will fill this wall again, but, this time, with pictures of her own family. New stories, new memories, until every square inch is covered once more.

Chapter
Sixty-Six

The Ladies' Pond reopened yesterday. I have hardly noticed the year go by. It's strange how quickly time passes when there are things to do.

Without Lucas to look out for me at work, I have had to look out for myself, and it hasn't been as hard as I thought. I'm six months into my new role, and already I feel I am part of something important, something bigger than me and my own concerns. I am good at navigating the vulnerabilities of my students, but I am still learning how to ingratiate myself with my colleagues. Thankfully, Rosa has laid much of the groundwork. The piano lessons have brought about a friendship between us, and that has paved a way for me through the staffroom.

I finally learned to play 'Für Elise'. Now, on a good day, I make only a few mistakes, and when I do, I feel Eric at my shoulder, an amused look on his face, a shadow in the varnish of the wood. It doesn't happen often, though, he seems to have stopped wanting me to find him, so I have decided to stop looking.

The sign is the same: *WOMEN ONLY. MEN NOT ALLOWED BEYOND THIS POINT.* I open the gate and close it behind me, looping the rope around the post to keep it shut. They cut back the trees that line the path to ease the building installation, but the path itself is not much altered. The ground is damp underfoot, the cool air dappled in a lemon-soaked light. The changes are not as drastic as I'd imagined. But change has certainly occurred.

The familiar green building has been replaced and the concrete platform is a little bigger, a little cleaner, and when the pond opens out before me, the water looks different somehow. It is the same body of water I have always been drawn to, the memory of it consoling me, nearly killing me, has not dimmed. But it seems less like an adversary, now, more like a friend. I look at it, a layer of mist rising up from the surface, giving the saturated air an eerie quality, stifling sound. There are already spiderwebs tucked into the roof of the new lifeguard's room. They are sketched out, heavy with dew, and the absence of a breeze gives them a brittle beauty.

'Long time no see,' Carole calls from inside her new home. 'Welcome back.' She comes out, grinning. 'What do you think?'

'It's very smart. I think I like it. What about you?'

'I'm just happy we got our pond back. I couldn't care less what the building looks like, as long as I can come here every day.'

'How was it yesterday, at the opening?'

Carole rolls her eyes. 'It got quite raucous towards the evening. Somebody smuggled in a wine box, but I turned a blind eye. Everybody was in such high spirits. I didn't want to be a party pooper. You should have come. It was fun.'

'Was Iris there?'

'She was. With bells on. Literally.'

'Is she still annoyed at having her request for a diving board turned down?' I ask.

'I think she's forgotten all about that now she's busy with her granddaughter. I thought she might be with you this morning?' Carole looks up the path behind me.

'I wanted to be by myself today. For my first time back.'

Carole nods. 'In that case, I'll leave you to it.'

Carole disappears back into her new home, and I turn once more to admire the surface of the pond. It is the colour of oxidised bronze, a murky green made metallic by the morning light. The sun has brought out the damp smell of vegetation, the season is readying itself for the battle of summer, new shoots fighting their way through the straggle of spring greenery to grab their share of light.

There is an air of Scandinavian simplicity to the new changing rooms. Black on the outside, unpainted within, the scent of freshly milled wood still lingers in the fabric of the walls. I pass through the door into a room with no roof, and glance up to a sky that is charged with blue. I notice the familiar stack of plastic washing-up bowls is still there, next to the sink, waiting to be filled with lukewarm water to soothe frozen feet when the weather turns. I remove my clothes slowly, enjoying the anticipation of what is to come. *Nothing has changed*, says the voice in my head. *But everything is different.*

The chalkboard tells me the temperature of the water is fourteen degrees. As I approach the ladder, the metal rungs coiled in fresh rope, I take a run towards the edge, leaping as high as I can. For a moment, I am suspended in the air, weightless, between the water and the sky. I see the life rings floating ahead of me. I see the world above me, teeming with promise. Striking out to the far reaches of the pond, I am giddy with the pleasure of being reunited with an old friend. I reach the curtain of willow branches dipping into the water, still drawn to the same, hidden place, and a memory surfaces, like a tadpole wriggling free of its spawn. I see myself, sullen and unsmiling with Carole, who tells me off for swimming beyond the boundary.

People come here thinking the pond will heal them. But it doesn't. It's the women.

At the time, those words made me shake with anger, but now, I can see she was right. I tread water, feeling its cool embrace, knowing the pond remembers me, sensing its welcome.

I haven't removed the pendant from my neck since last year. I thought it would become a talisman, a connection to Eric, but instead it is a fault line between the past and the future. The division is as thin as this chain, but it is there. For Maggie, it is a symbol of everything that went wrong between us all. I catch her looking at it sometimes, and when she does, the conversation falters, her eyes flick away from me. I can feel her thoughts descending to a darker place. Besides, my life is with Lucas now.

I take a breath, duck under and kick down.

The water is murky brown, still sulking from the building works. I keep my eyes open as I remove the pendant from my neck. Caught between two choices, to please the living or the dead, I choose the living. I let the pendant fall through the water, feeling no regret. It will always be here, waiting for me. A smudge of light beyond the darkness.

AUTHOR'S NOTE

The Heath and the Ladies' Pond in *Where Water Lies* are never actually named, but some of you may recognise descriptions of Kenwood Ladies' Pond in Hampstead Heath, London. Although I have occasionally taken some artistic licence for the purpose of storytelling, I have tried to remain faithful to the place, and, in doing so, I read many interesting books and blogs when I was researching. Of particular interest to me were the following: Ruth Corney's *Kenwood Ladies' Pond*, a photographic record of the pond between 2000–2020 and Sarah Saunders' *Goodbye Hut*, a touching photographic tribute to the old green building before it was replaced in 2016. Both books are hard (but not impossible) to get hold of. *At The Pond: Swimming at the Hampstead Ladies' Pond*, published by Daunt Books, is still very much in print, and is a fascinating collection of essays celebrating the pond, written by women who swim there regularly.

For those of you interested in the history of the pond, Ann Griswold wrote *The Kenwood Ladies' Bathing Pond*, which covers the history from 1925–1998, including some of its flora and fauna. Annabel Bird wrote a month-by-month account of her experience as a year-round swimmer, in her blog *Bleak House* and I found the Hampstead Heath Ponds Project blog, written by jenniferwood2015, a well of information about the dam works, which were carried out on Hampstead Heath in 2015–2016.

There are not many films made about the ponds because they are private places, and access is rarely granted. *Church of Pond* is a lovely short documentary of winter swimming in the Ladies' Pond, filmed in the winter of 2014/15 by Shula Hawes. *The Ponds*, a feature-length documentary directed by Patrick McLennan and Samuel Smith was released in January 2019 by Curzon and documents both the Men's and Ladies' Pond swimmers over the course of a year.

The Ladies' Pond is a protected area. When you visit, there are rules that must be followed, including no photography and mobile phone use. This is one of the reasons swimming there is so special. If you decide to visit, please respect these rules and consider becoming a member, or making a donation to the Kenwood Ladies' Pond Association who work throughout the year to protect this special place.

To those of you with a keen eye for detail, Valentine's Day in 2015 didn't fall on a Friday, as it does in this novel, and Easter was much earlier that year. I have changed these key dates to suit my own narrative.

Lastly, some of you may detect a familiarity between Iris's place of work and that of the charity, Missing People. In 2014, BBC Radio 4 aired a radio drama called *Ambiguous Loss*, written by Michael Butt and directed by Toby Swift. Made with the assistance of Missing People, it tells the story of a family, waiting for the return of their loved one. This three-part drama is well worth a listen and inspired some of my writing.

ACKNOWLEDGEMENTS

Reader, I am going to thank you first. Thank you for buying this book, thank you for reviewing this book. I had no idea reviews were so important until my debut, *The Vanishing Tide*, was published in 2022. I spend a lot of time reading through all your kind reviews, and I see how those reviews spur on others to take a chance on a new author. You have my eternal gratitude for investing in me.

I continue to be amazed at the number of professionals it takes to transform a novel from an idea into a physical, audible, digital book. I would like to thank my agents, Becky Ritchie and Oli Munson, for their wise advice, and support. I feel very lucky to have two editors, Victoria Oundjian and Sophie Wilson, who pinpoint the heart of my writing and always make it better. Thank you to all the people who work hard behind the scenes, from the designer, Emma Rogers, who did a beautiful job on the cover to Nicole and her team at APub; the blurb writers, the copyeditors, cold readers and proofreaders who spend hours looking at every full stop, semi-colon, and comma. Thank you all.

I talked to many women who swim at Kenwood Ladies' Pond, and I would like to acknowledge their help: Mary Powell and Pauline Latchem, Caroline White, Penny Borrow, and lifeguard Nicola Hurley spent time reading and answering my questions. Thank you.

Thanks to a fine group of women, The Great Tits, who took me under their wings and saw me through my first winter in the pond, in particular: Fiona Fraser-Allen, Suzy Barber, Serena Cross, Debbie Cummings, Nathalie Davis, Susan Feldman, Sarah Holmes, Kate Leftly, Lisa Waite, and Anna Wise. Special thanks go to the extraordinary Rosie Ruddock, Sian Hurst, and Elizabeth Walton for your enduring friendship, encouragement, and support.

Writerly friends who are a great source of inspiration and help, thanks go to Fran Littlewood, Brenda Eisenberg, my Curtis Brown buddies, and members of the North London Writers' Group who have warmly welcomed me into their fold. Nicola Fox, Frank Tallis, and Emma Tait, thanks for your wisdom and encouragement.

To my mother, Gill, who continues to help me every day, in every way, bottomless thank-yous forever. Milly and Ruby, my greatest creations, I treasure your endless humour, intelligence, and kindness. I'm so proud of you both. May you continue to shine.

This book is dedicated to Satish, the yin to my yang, who wasn't a reader of books until he took out an Audible subscription so he could listen to mine. I am, finally, without words.

READING GROUP QUESTIONS

1. Eliza believes she keeps herself to herself, but Carole accuses her of putting herself in the centre of things. Who do you think is right?

2. Do you think Maggie was overly controlling, or just being a protective sister to Eric?

3. Do you think Maggie should have explained the full story to Eliza, or do you think she was right to stay silent to protect her own parents?

4. Carole tells Eliza that it's the women who matter, not the pond. Do you agree with Carole, that people are more important than places when it comes to being healed?

5. Throughout the book, Eliza struggles to make a home for herself, and, instead, adopts the homes of others. What do you think defines a home?

6. Do you think Iris was justified in leaving her family to strike out on her own?

7. Iris's job is to act as an impartial go-between. Do you think it is possible for a go-between to be completely impartial, or do they always colour a situation with their own attitudes and beliefs?

8. Do you sympathise with Eliza's desire not to renovate her aunt's house, or do you think she was neglectful in letting the house decline?

9. Eliza forgives Maggie because they have a history together. Do you think different emotional rules apply if you have known someone for longer?

10. Do you think the relationship between siblings is more significant than the relationship between close friends?

Turn the page for an extract from Hilary Tailor's debut novel, THE VANISHING TIDE

PROLOGUE

It is always the same. The sun is setting and there is no sign of her yet. She sits on the sea-wall, back to the lagoon, kicking the heels of her sandals, waiting for Clare. She has developed a quiet patience for her sister's timekeeping, but the baby will be awake soon and she must get back. Her gaze tracks the cockle wagon as it trundles down the long stretch of sand, the men sitting on the edge with their rakes and buckets, their legs dangling and swaying as they laugh and joke. Their voices become faint and begin to recede into the wail of the seagulls and the advancing tide. She squints into the sunset as it suddenly stops: a solitary man leaping from the back, tearing into the water.

This is when the shouting begins.

The wagon becomes alive with men, jumping onto the sand and sprinting through the sea, kicking up foam and stone like so many wild horses. They surround the object of their disquiet. One of them, still a boy, turns and vomits into his hands. She sees them gather a dark shape and heave it clear above the water. It is only when that beautiful hair falls back into the waves like an inky waterfall that she knows Clare isn't coming back.

Chapter One

ISLA, MARCH

Sliding the key into the lock was harder than she thought. Isla had waited almost ten years to enter this house and now she didn't need Astrid's permission, she still felt like an intruder. A salty wind stung her skin as her wrist angled itself against the doorknob, a complicated sleight of hand only three people, now two, could perform to get the key to turn. A click gave way to a groan as the door swung slowly in.

Isla put her rucksack down, hung her coat on the only hook in the hallway and considered her inheritance. The old leather armchair was still there in the sitting room, but the floor was uncluttered by the mess she remembered as a child. It had never been this tidy when she was growing up. The air didn't smell as if it had been sealed up against the world and there were no strands of tobacco scattered across the coffee table; the bowl containing Astrid's Rizlas and her carefully wrapped chunks of resin had gone. It could have been an ordinary room where a normal family might live an unremarkable life. The deception was unsettling. The only thing that looked familiar was an enormous metal shelving system running the length and height of the wall. Hundreds of art books, hurled together and threatening to topple at the lightest touch. She looked at the titles and recalled that several of them had once been aimed at her head, one after another, whizzing by in a blur of colour.

She opened the door into the dining room, quickly averting her eyes from the painting above the fireplace – a habit from childhood she could not shake off. It had always given her the creeps. Maybe she would have liked it more if somebody else had painted it, somebody nicer. It was worth more than the house, she knew that, and the house was worth a fortune. You weren't allowed to build this close to the shoreline any more and the view to the sea was stupendous. Astrid had regularly fended off estate agents who came knocking. The building, more than a hundred years old, needed renovation and was ripe for profit. She never let them down kindly. Upsetting people who wanted something from her was a sport in which Astrid excelled. Now it was Isla wandering through the rooms like a prospective buyer, noting the jobs that needed to be done, the cracks that had to be filled. It wasn't too bad. The white weatherboard on the beach side was peeling, but the skeleton of the house had endured. She would enjoy doing something with her hands while her mind considered what to do with the absence. Loving Astrid had been a burdensome task. London was too far from here to make social calls, especially when you knew you weren't welcome. Although Astrid seemed to tolerate a phone conversation once every couple of months, it was always Isla who made the call. Astrid had never courted anyone's company but her own.

The house felt unnaturally cold. A damp breath of wind snaked around her neck, stirring the curtain drawn against the window, making her shudder. Spring came late this far north, and she cursed herself for leaving her warmest jumper behind. She had spent almost two decades of her youth here and on the few occasions she'd returned, it was always in the futile hope that the weather would be as warm as the capital. She'd forgotten how the cold crawled into your bones and squatted there till summer. Isla peered back into the hallway to see if she had left the door open. It was shut.

The last time she'd visited, she had brought wine and flowers. It had been a significant birthday for Astrid; Isla had felt there should be some acknowledgement, even though Astrid had not remembered Isla's birthday for years. Astrid had given her a curt nod of appreciation when she'd handed the flowers over. There were only eighteen years between them. They should have been more like friends. But, just as before, she'd found herself cold and alone for the weekend while Astrid painted in the studio. Isla had used the time to brood. She was past forty and still with no family of her own. She didn't want to be here. Astrid didn't want her here. No wonder she couldn't hold down a relationship – she had never been shown how to care for anyone else. Astrid was all she had, all she would ever have. Isla was suddenly floored by the understanding that this would never change. She had lost her opportunity to make her own family; she'd been too busy moping over the mess she'd left behind in this house.

Two days later, when she saw the flowers lying on the kitchen countertop, wilting in their cellophane, something inside her snapped. This would be the last time. If Astrid wanted her company, she would have to ask for it. The request never came, and when the time stretched between them it had been more a relief than a heartbreak. As Isla looked around the place, remembering that weekend, it struck her that Astrid had always been incapable of nurturing the living, and she had passed this affliction on. It was probably the only thing they had in common.

A faint chemical scent she couldn't put her finger on drew her to the foot of the stairs. There was a large circular stain on the oatmeal carpet, pale grey in colour – not what she'd imagined. She crouched down and touched it, conscious of being close to something very profound. It was dry and crisp and when she drew her hand back, a fine white powder coated her fingertips. She wondered who had taken the trouble to do this. It must have been hard to clean.

She stood. Using the stairs would be difficult without thinking about Astrid's last moments, but even so, as she stepped over the stain, a small seed of excitement began to grow in the pit of her stomach. Maybe the information Astrid refused to provide when she was alive could be prised from this house now she was dead. Astrid had always delivered the truth like an unwanted meal. It didn't matter if it was unpalatable to the recipient; you were to eat it all without complaint. If Astrid had wanted to tell Isla about the circumstances surrounding her Aunt Clare's death, no doubt she would have taken delight in frightening her with the gory details. But to refuse to talk about it at all – well, that was something else. The story of Isla's father had been repeated like a folk song through-out her youth: *He was a waste of space, he didn't care, he's gone, gone, gone.* Astrid could have used his death to curry sympathy, but she didn't. It was the women who mattered in this family. Men added a layer of complication. It was a lesson Isla was still trying to unlearn.

As she reached out to steady herself, she noticed the finial at the end of the balustrade. The tip was missing, broken off by Astrid's fall. Isla touched her own head and winced at the thought. She had felt fine about coming alone, staying here by herself. It hadn't crossed her mind to book into the only hotel in the village, but when she started to walk up the stairs she felt a resistance, the flex of a muscle, willing her to go back down. Halfway up she paused, unsure what to think. Astrid was gone. Isla would never again bear the brunt of her disapproval. But the house was charged with friction. She could feel it gathering round her like mist rising up from the sea.

She said out loud, 'This is my house now.' The words sank through the air like stones through water and before she finished saying them, she knew it wasn't true.

ABOUT THE AUTHOR

Photo © 2021 Rob Rowland

When she's not writing fiction, Hilary Tailor runs a design consultancy, specialising in colour and trend forecasting. She has worked with adidas and Puma and sits on the Pantone View colour committee. Hilary was raised on the Wirral Peninsula and graduated from the Royal College of Art. Her debut novel, *The Vanishing Tide*, was published in 2022 and has thousands of five-star reviews. *Where Water Lies* is her second novel.

Follow the Author on Amazon

If you enjoyed this book, follow Hilary Tailor on Amazon to be notified when the author releases a new book!
To do this, please follow these instructions:

Desktop:

1) Search for the author's name on Amazon or in the Amazon App.

2) Click on the author's name to arrive on their Amazon page.

3) Click the 'Follow' button.

Mobile and Tablet:

1) Search for the author's name on Amazon or in the Amazon App.

2) Click on one of the author's books.

3) Click on the author's name to arrive on their Amazon page.

4) Click the 'Follow' button.

Kindle eReader and Kindle App:

If you enjoyed this book on a Kindle eReader or in the Kindle App, you will find the author 'Follow' button after the last page.